PARIS SECRETS

Author's updated edition printed 2018
Previously published as The Paris Secrets Trilogy.

This paperback edition published by Swell Cat Press, LLC.

For questions and comments about the quality of this book, or review inquiries, please contact: toastfaery@gmail.com

Find the author online at: michelerenae.com
facebook.com/michelerenaex
pinterest.com/michelerenaeX/
twitter.com/MicheleRenaeX

Window

Part 1

One

When life gives you windows, you peer through them.

But do you ever really see what's on the other side of the glass? What mysteries go unsolved because of a dismissive glance? What adventures await? What secrets lie beyond the glass?

Do you think I think too much?

I do.

But today I looked through the window. Really looked.

A new neighbor was moving in across the street from my building. He presented a delicious mystery. And if he had any secrets, I wanted to learn them.

It was about time this neighborhood, generously peopled with geriatrics, received an infusion of young and sexy. And from what I could see below as I stood before my third-floor living room window, the new blood was both.

My building sat at an angle to the opposite building with the backs of both jutting up close to one another. The street that arrowed between the two buildings started as a narrow dead end at the back only accessible with bicycles, and from there it widened out and parted into two streets at the corner where stoplights ushered the elder residents to and fro on their daily lives. Similar to a Haussmann wedge.

The first two floors on the opposite building were businesses and offices. The third floor was residential. I'd watched the previous across-the-street resident move out last week and had waved to the elderly woman from my bedroom when I'd seen her directing the moving men to carry out boxes labeled Dishes, Sewing, and Pantry.

The reason my heart had begun to pitter and patter now, was the tall, lean man with the swishy brown hair who hefted a box from the back of the moving van. Currently on a break from work, I watched him haul in a couple of loads. A sword stuck out from the top of the box he carried, one of those long, thin blades with the little red button on the end of it. A rapier, or epée.

Fencing equipment? He looked like the type who worked out, because even from the distance I stood, the flex of his biceps revealed by the gray tee shirt he wore was formative. *En guarde*! All for one and—oh, look at that sexy smile. Mm… I'd swoon for that musketeer.

I confess I have a thing for musketeers. I'm pretty sure I was born into the wrong century. Musketeers wore the cool tunics emblazoned with the silver cross and fleur de lis, plumed beaver hat, and suede bucket-top boots that folded down at the knee. Add in the sword, the adventure of fighting for a king, perhaps a dashing duel against the cardinal's men, and don't forget a night spent surrounded by candlelight servicing his lady's every need… Sigh.

Beneath the uniform must be hard muscle and an equal iron will to serve. In all ways in which service was possible. I wanted my musketeer kneeling before me, his head between my legs, his tongue dashing slow and lingering traces along my achy, wet clit. Dip in the tip of that hot tongue and tickle my insides, then lash it along my folds, teasing at the sensitive nerves that hugged either side of my opening.

I'd tug up my long skirts. Shallow breaths would heave up my bosom against the tight corset in anticipation of him hitting that perfect spot. The swollen, tender, slick spot that, when touched just so and with the right amount of pressure, would release my voice…

A deliciously erotic tingle at the juncture of my thighs drew me up from the daydream with a gasp and a sigh. As if I'd had a little orgasm. Close, but not quite.

Clove and cinnamon cloyed about my nose, luring me back to reality. I sipped the tea I'd been holding while captured by reverie. Tepid. How long had I been standing before the window?

Long enough to daydream my way into a lusty liaison with an imaginary hero.

My mind had a tendency to wander, and to fantasize. Sometimes to my detriment. Yes, I was the girl who missed her train because her thoughts were somewhere else, like lying across a bed, skirts pulled up to my tits, while a gorgeous musketeer dined on my moist, quivering pussy.

As I tilted a hip against the living room window, I wondered if the new guy was a local settling into different digs, or if he'd traveled from another town or even country to make his home here in Paris.

I'd arrived in Paris two years earlier, a transplant from the Midwest. Good ole Iowa. Go, Cyclones! Okay, so I wasn't into sports, but in Iowa it had either been cheering for the local teams or farming. Corn didn't do it for me. Nor had the marriage proposal that had come the day after I'd caught my boyfriend in bed with my ex-best friend.

I mean, had he seriously thought an offer to marry him would erase the sight of his head buried between my friend's legs? The guy hadn't been thinking straight. Or perhaps he'd been thinking with that other head, the smaller one that had never completely satisfied me.

I was determined to never put myself in such a sorry relationship again. The days following that breakup had served up some amazing luck, for which I would be forever grateful.

My girlfriend Melanie, longtime penpal and Skype buddy since the eighth grade, had heard about a research position at her local library—local for her being Paris. Knowing my love for words and pouring over books, she'd given my name to the HR department. Melanie knew everyone. Everyone who mattered, that is. I didn't get the job, but that had directed me to a lead from a Parisian author who had needed an American to vet her fiction set in the Midwest. Score!

So, thanks to a small trust fund my mother had left for me, I'd packed up my few belongings, flipped off the ex-best friend, and moved to the city of love.

I'd moved to get away from my recent past. I'd moved because I'd wanted a new beginning.

I moved for adventure. I crossed the ocean for discovery. I moved for the pastries and the baguettes. I arrived on foreign soil for the sexy Frenchmen and the Eiffel Tower.

I moved to Paris for the thrill of it, to utterly defy that inner part of me that whispered 'You can't do this on your own. You don't even speak French!'.

I'd come to Paris because I'd secured a job, which had paid well enough to survive, and had garnered more leads with authors all across the country, and other countries, including the good ole US.

My client list consisted of mostly novelists who required detailed information on anything from how to poison a person without leaving a trace, to baking crepes at mountain level, or scuba diving procedures in the Venetian canal. I even did vampires—could a person survive on blood alone?—and werewolves—what were the effects of shapeshifting on a tattoo?

The beauty of being a research assistant was that it could be done online and through email. I didn't need to live in Paris, but I could.

But if I'm to be completely honest—and fess up to that introverted voice who likes to hide when the doorbell rings, or walk away from groups gathered at parties, and yes, who even ignores phone calls because making small talk is so difficult—I had moved to Paris to have sex.

No, not to find love or even romance. Been there, done that. Plan to be more cautious from here on out. The idea of finding myself a Frenchman to take as a lover appealed in no small way. (Yes, I get the irony. Introvert seeks hot love affair with gorgeous man who speaks a language she doesn't even understand. Sure, that'll happen.)

It's my fantasy. Allow me the indulgence.

I'd stepped onto French soil with a list of qualifications required for my French lover. He must be ruggedly attractive, but not necessarily handsome. I admired the Gascon profile, all awkward angles, thick brows, and bold nose. If he could be a musketeer all the better; of course I understood the job of wielding a musket and protecting the king was not a popular one nowadays. And I preferred he not speak English too well. French should be his principal language. (That added to his mysterious appeal.)

I, of course, spoke little French, save a few words such as *merci* and *tres bien*. *Je voudrais* meant I would like, which came in handy when shopping for macarons. (A weekly must, trust me.) If I managed to combine one or more French words in a makeshift sentence I was quite proud of myself. I'd learned enough to get by over the years.

This imaginary, and slightly rough yet handsome Frenchman (who may have been a musketeer in a past life) will simply want to fuck me. Again and again. We will while away the days between the sheets, speaking with our bodies, bonding with our touches, learning one another's secrets, and performing every sexual position we can imagine. We'll probably make up a few new positions, too.

There you have it. My quest for a Frenchman.

I've been here for two years and haven't snagged a Gascon yet. I've dated a handful of guys. One was British, two were American, and the others were Italian. Not that I'm complaining. My sex life was good. Not turnstile busy, but I didn't want that.

I didn't hook up with any of them for more than a few weeks. The word boyfriend always got caught at the back of throat. It was so teenager. I preferred lovers. Men who moved in and out of my bed, at my discretion, and who never clung or demanded more than I wanted. I saw the Brit once a month. We were both clear that it was a hookup, and that worked for us.

I didn't have time for a relationship. Or maybe it was that I didn't have the personal constitution for it any more. I had never been able to care for a pet. I had a pet hamster when I was ten who got out of his plastic cage and crawled into the bathtub, ate the soap, then died a long and tragic death under my bed.

What made me believe I could take care of a man?

So while I waited for my fantasy man to come knocking, I was thankful for reality. I had an apartment I could afford, thanks to a job that satisfied.

In addition to the research work, which occupied around thirty hours a week, give or take depending on my client list, I also held a part-time job at a little map shop in the fifth. One or two days a week as sales clerk, and sometimes a few hours on the weekend helping the shop owner (another Brit) organize his stock.

Yep, I had a pretty sweet gig. And did I mention I live in Paris?

Letting the white sheer fall back into place before the window, I tilted back the rest of the cold cinnamon tea, then settled behind my desk and considered sorting a research list.

I leaned back in the chair and pulled aside the curtain once again. The moving van was no longer parked before the curb.

"Wonder if he's French?"

The musketeer who had been supping between my thighs, stretched up his hand and grazed my nipple. The bud hardened between his fingers, swelling under his pinching touch. "*Vous appartenez à moi*," he said in French that I understood perfectly to mean *you belong to me.*

"Mm... I wouldn't mind being yours."

I shook my head and laughed at my straying thoughts. A list of European holidays awaited completion on the computer screen. This work was not going to get done while I daydreamed about the sexy new neighbor.

I'd reserve that for later tonight as I soaked in a hot tub.

ΔΔΔ

I'd closed the map shop around seven-thirty, early for Paris. Most shops stayed open until eight. The tourist traps in the fifth—where the shop was located—often stayed open well past ten p.m. Thankfully, Parisian shops didn't open until ten a.m., which was awesome for my need to sleep in. This city had been invented for layabeds such as myself.

On the way home from work, I stopped by a small, four-aisle food market a few blocks away from my building. Most days I took the Métro to and from work, but the walk along the Seine was a pleasant forty-five minute stroll, and I didn't have many groceries to carry.

Taking advantage of the beautiful autumn evening, I lingered along the river. I watched the *bateaux mouches*—cattlecar riverboats stuffed to the gills with tourists gawking and pointing at the ancient monuments—cruise by. The air smelled both as sweet as the nearby crepe stands and as sour as the dank river. I loved it all.

Once home, I set the mesh grocery bag on the kitchen counter, and filled a glass of water from the sink. In the kitchen, a table and two chairs sat beneath the only window in the place that actually opened.

The entire apartment was painted white, with minimal furnishings. I found the idea of picking out colors and figuring out my decorating style intimidating. Gray furniture. White walls. A vase or pillow here and there added a splash of blue. It didn't get easier than that. Besides, I wasn't sure what went with stacks of books, and notes and file folders scattered everywhere.

I did have a desk in the living room for my office, but that designated space tended to bleed into the living area, on the floor before the floor-to-ceiling windows, onto the kitchen table, and even around the corner and into the bedroom where more stacks of books lined the walls.

I could use a secretary.

What I needed were book shelves. I'd write that on my shopping list (if I could find it).

An open archway led into the bedroom that tempted strongly with a comfy, king-size bed. The white iron frame had been a welcome prize the former owner had left behind. I'd ordered one of those cozy air beds that came in a box, put it together myself, and *voila*! Mounded with a fluffy white comforter and crisp white sheets, it was my favorite place to land. But it was only nine. Too early to hit the sack.

I could crack open the book on string theory that I didn't want to tackle—research job—but then reminded myself that it was Friday. I never worked on weekends, and the weekend officially began at six p.m. Friday evening (or noon if that's the way I wanted to play it). Working freelance, a girl had to set rules and boundaries. Otherwise, I could so wear the queen of procrastination crown.

Tonight I looked forward to sinking my brain into a novel instead of the usual non-fiction. But first, I hadn't peed all day.

Sitting on the toilet, I let my eyes wander along the line of clear subway tiles that cut a center dash around the room, otherwise completely tiled in white. I mused on the utter clean whiteness of the apartment. I, who surrounded myself with vibrant clothing and insensible shoes, had to admit I liked the starkness. It felt new and clean. Vast. Promising. Not much a girl could hide from here.

I smirked. What was I thinking? I had nothing to hide from. I was an open book. Granted, a sequestered book that didn't like to have her pages bent at the corners, and who would most certainly protest should someone crack my spine, but still.

Okay, so I wasn't as open as I liked to believe. Yet somewhere within my squishy depths lived a tiny vixen who would step out and have a good time if invited.

The apartment reminded me of one of those chic love nests the smart, business-savvy heroine in a romance novel would own. She collected numerous lovers, none who ever came to her home. They always ended up making love in the back seats of cars, or in the alleyway outside the Louvre, or in the dew-tipped grass of a garden courtyard enclosed within ancient buildings.

I could be such a heroine. I was that heroine. On the inside.

I sighed. Okay, so mostly I was that heroine.

I stripped off my clothes for a shower. French showers are not a treat. I like to soap up and linger under the stream, but the French apparently haven't discovered that attaching the showerhead to the wall frees up both hands. I'd spotted the perfect showerhead in a nearby hardware store months earlier, but wasn't so skilled that I thought I could install it without creating a permanent leak. So, once again, I struggled with the ungainly steel hose as I shampooed one-handed. Despite the awkwardness it felt refreshing after a long day standing on my feet.

Still didn't stop me from yawning.

After drying off, I strolled out of the bathroom, bold in my nudity. Curtains hung before the windows; sheers in see-through white, with heavy white draperies hanging to each side. I kept the left side drape pulled because the window stretched halfway behind the bed. The right drape I pulled aside during the day to let in light but kept the sheer pulled.

My bedroom was positioned at the back of the building, so our bedroom windows were separated by fifteen feet of air space across the narrow dead end. The across-the-street neighbor had usually kept her heavy-backed bedroom curtains closed. I didn't blame her. With the lights on, I could see all the way into that apartments' connecting bathroom.

I'd once stood on the street below and looked up, wondering if passing cyclists might get a glimpse of me standing *en deshabille* in my bedroom with the lights on. Thankfully, no deal; it was just too high up, and the angle from the street didn't work. Whew! I tended to walk around naked after a shower, and hopped into bed sans jammies.

Like I said, the former resident across the street had kept her curtains closed all the time, so I had never feared flashing anyone.

It had been two weeks since the new guy had moved in and I'd only caught sun-blurred details as I'd noted him moving through his living room. His bedroom curtains hadn't yet been pulled back.

I could feel my body wanting to fall toward the bed before I even decided that sleep was what I wanted. No comforter tonight. September was proving much warmer than usual. Though the leaves on the trees had started to brighten in color, I lamented the fact that the building was not outfitted with central air, and that my window unit in the kitchen had gone kaput during a particularly steamy July.

Gliding my hands over my belly awakened my flesh to a prickling awareness. I was comfortable with my body, and touching it. But for some reason, standing naked— In Paris! Before the window only covered by sheers! —felt naughty. Decadent.

I loved that word: decadent. Unrestrained self-gratification. Indulgence. And here I was, engaging in decadence. And yet, my kneeling musketeer was strangely absent. Oh, to grip him by the hair and pull his face closer to sup between my legs.

I glanced to the bed. The romance novel I'd tossed near the pillow beckoned. I ordered them from Amazon because the bookstores here did not carry a sufficient selection of romance in English. Rarely did I drift off to sleep without reading for at least half an hour. Non-fiction during the week. Escape novels on the weekend.

Opening to the bookmarked page, I wandered toward the big, gray velvet easy chair before the window—a match to the tufted chaise in the living room—and paused before the chair as a sentence held me riveted.

I wanted to find out if Lucette would realize that Chance was two-timing her with the secretary who wore the tight pencil skirts, and who always left the top three buttons on her blouse undone. I also wanted to snuggle into the velvet chair and lose myself in the story before going to bed, but the chair was overflowing with discarded clothing, tossed shoes, and a stack of hardcovers that awaited sorting into various research stacks.

Navigating a turn, I strode before the window. Lucette wasn't so stupid that she didn't notice Chance was taking more care with his looks lately. Hell, the guy had started manscaping, and he was wearing that new cologne.

Mmm, I loved a spicy smelling man. I could fall to my knees at the mercy of Old Spice.

So? I'm easy.

But seriously, Lucette needed to notice Blaise. Now there was a fine man. The gardener had landscaped her yard to bloom throughout the year in varying stages of colors, and he always brought her fresh chocolate eclairs on Monday mornings when he arrived to weed and tend her garden.

I'd like a man to tend my garden. And I wasn't thinking about turning over dirt or plucking off dead blossoms.

Movement out of the corner of my eye caught my attention. I paused, the opened book falling against my naked breasts. A three-inch opening beckoned between the pulled sheers. I peered out the floor-to-ceiling window and across the narrow alleyway.

The neighbor's curtains were pulled to the sides. The window opposite mine revealed the interior of a bedroom thanks to a lamp on the short dresser next to the bed.

Suddenly I remembered I was naked. I threw an arm across my chest cupping one breast, and scooted my hips backward, bending my knees and pressing my legs together while I angled the book over my pussy. I leaned forward, maintaining my sight on the bedroom across the street.

I spied the neighbor strolling around his bed, his attention also focused on a book. A fencing manual? Possible. I'd seen him practicing a few days ago in the other room. The position of the buildings didn't allow a good view. Either he'd been stabbing a sword at something or he'd killed an intruder.

Sexy Fencer Guy wasn't wearing much of anything, save underwear. Oh, baby. I'll take a musketeer in skivvies any day.

Fortunately, we both had windows sans wrought iron railings across the lower halves. Rare in Paris, but it did provide a full-length, unhampered view.

He hadn't noticed that he had an audience as he stood there before the end of his bed, the thick book held with both hands, and his head bowed intently over the words. I did like a man who read. Hands-down, it beat burping the alphabet as a means to impress the girl.

Boxer briefs hugged a nice, tight ass and the tops of well-muscled thighs. On my list of preferred underwear types for males, boxer briefs came in at numbers three, two, and one. They snugged the male form, yet landed lower on the thigh, like boxer shorts. His were gray, and they conformed to his hips and ass and...unfortunately, he stood at an angle that didn't reveal the front package to me.

Biting my lip, I savored the sight. What fortune, to catch a glimpse of a half-naked man out my window and have him look like some kind of Adonis. I mean, how often did that happen? Most women were lucky to spy a slouchy, middle-aged divorcee who stood in his tighty-whities, scratching his crumb-riddled belly waiting for someone to notice him.

"Welcome to the neighborhood, Mr. Sexy," I declared.

My neighbor was long, lean and ripped. Muscles strapped his back like skin-colored armor. Biceps curved with power and strength. He stood straight, his shoulders tilted back. From the side, the ripples defining his abs and chest resembled steps a girl—like me—would gladly skip up.

Fencing did all that? I had never thought the sport good for much more than the thighs and calves. I'd tried it one summer in high school. Strenuous on the legs. And the padded vest and required mesh mask had been smelly and smothering.

He probably owned his suit and fencing sword. I'm sure it smelled like him. Spicy? I could hope.

Suddenly he lifted his head, and as if remembering something he'd forgotten—he turned and looked right at me.

Two

Frantic, I almost dropped my book, but in a miracle save, I tossed it onto the bed and tugged the sheers closed.

"Really?" I argued with my beating heart. "Is that the way you're going to let this one go down?"

The man was a god. I'd seen him in his skivvies. He'd seen me spying on him. Naked. Hell. I grabbed the yellow silk robe from the end of the bed and tugged it on. Embroidered across the breast was a little black bee. Save the bees, save the world!

Yeah, I was into that. *Tres serieux.*

Holding the two sheer curtains together with one hand to each, I stood there, vacillating my options. If I didn't open the curtains, it would be over. But not really, because I'd always worry about seeing him on the street and having to explain that stupid moment when he'd caught me naked and spying on him.

I was not a pervert.

At least, I didn't think I qualified for pervert status. It had been a quick look. And it wasn't as though he'd been trying to hide behind curtains. He'd been standing there before the window, waiting to be seen.

Maybe *he* was the pervert? Did it work that way? I was out of my league on pervert knowledge. Hadn't had the displeasure of researching that for any of my clients.

"Get it over with." I tugged the curtain aside, and managed a silly little wave and said, "Hi" even though I knew he couldn't hear me.

His smile was nice, reaching his eyes. He waved back, and didn't seem to notice his lacking attire. He wore dark rimmed glasses and his loose hair was thick and waved over his ears. It looked as though he might sweep his fingers through it to make it go back, otherwise it probably fell over his face and into his eyes in an unruly challenge.

He pointed to me, than tapped his book.

"Uh. Oh!" Grabbing the romance novel, I pressed the cover to the window so he could see that it was indeed one of *those* books with a man and woman embracing on the cover. Didn't embarrass me. Romance readers had the best sex lives, don't you know?

Then I pointed to him and my book.

He pressed the cover of his book to the window. *Advanced PHP*, and...I couldn't read the tiny subtitle. Computer stuff I couldn't begin to understand. Beauty and brains, eh?

He pointed to me, and gave me the thumbs up sign. Stabbing his book with a finger, he then made the gesture of a gun shooting his brains out.

"Romance always wins," I said to myself. "But I'll take a sexy computer geek in his underwear any day."

Thankful he couldn't hear my lusty thoughts, I shrugged and performed the silly wave again. Standing in my robe, communicating with the man across the street? This was already more exciting than half the dates I'd been on lately.

He put his hands to his tilted head to indicate sleep, then made the thumbs up gesture.

"Have a good night," I deciphered. I performed the same gesture. "You too. Good night."

I plopped onto the bed, stomach-first, and bent up my legs. Elated and grinning like the cat that had eaten the canary, I searched for the last sentence I'd read. I was aware that I'd left the sheers open, and from his perspective across the street, he could probably see my bare legs bent upward, my feet bobbling as I read. I didn't move them out of view.

Hell, I wanted to dive off the bed, push my nose up against the window, and drink him in like a fizzy glass of champagne. But I wasn't so bold. My fantasies could prove even more interesting.

I resumed reading. And suddenly Blaise the gardener looked a lot like Mr. Sexy with the computer textbook.

Two nights later, I filled a glass of water from the kitchen tap and wandered back into the bedroom where the green LED from the clock lasered a blurry line across the wall beside the bed. 2:30 a.m. A sigh was appropriate.

I was having a bout of insomnia, thanks, I think, to my inability to let things go. I'd just handed in some disturbing research to a thriller novelist. He'd needed to know how to remove the skin from a human being, and then how to take out the bones while maintaining the integrity and form of the body.

I hadn't thought it possible, and I certainly hadn't thought that I would find the information anywhere online. Turns out there was a booming industry for the bones taken from corpses to be resold for marrow transplants. The thieves would remove the bones from the body and replace them with PVC pipes so the family wouldn't be the wiser during an open-casket funeral.

I decided to refuse requests for such macabre research from now on. I loved researching thrillers. The weaponry, police procedure, and martial arts and fighting skills were interesting to me. But serial killers? I'd had enough.

Stubbing my toe on a hardcover, I clicked on the nightlight to make it easier to spot the killer tome. A volume on Henri XIII. I set it aside on the top of a stack, knowing I'd need to finish it soon and hand in my notes.

It was either bone removal keeping me awake, or the chemicals in the book glue at the library—where I had spent the afternoon pouring over plates from a pristine version of Diderot's Encyclopedia—were infesting my brain and slowly deteriorating it.

I preferred the glue version. Such a tragic way to die, and the tombstone could read: Glue sniffers unite!

Before clicking off the nightlight, I noticed the light from across the street. Mr. Sexy was up too?

I pulled aside the sheer and attempted to engage x-ray vision to see through his curtains. The way the night muted the window I couldn't see well, though if the curtain were open his light would reveal the interior of his bedroom as if it were a diorama lit up at a museum.

When the curtains suddenly parted, I panicked and almost slammed the sheers shut, yet made the save by raising my glass in a silent toast.

"Just your friendly peeping Jane," I muttered. "Can't sleep?" I wondered.

The man held up a glass of milk and rubbed his eyes in the universal signal of sleeplessness.

I lifted my glass in another toast, and he matched it. We drank our respective libations. If a girl could get drunk off water, it was going to happen when the view was so tantalizing.

He leaned a shoulder against the window, brazenly unselfconscious of the fact that he stood in only his boxer briefs—that emphasized his package nicely. Or maybe he was aware and wanted me to take a good long look.

I did. And I wished it was my birthday. Or Christmas. This Catholic chick would even settle for Hanukah at this point. Right now any reason to open a package was good by me. As I assessed the abundant gift displayed behind glass and cotton, it hardened noticeably, forming a nice firm bulge that angled toward his hip. It must serve a good handful for him.

I sucked in my lower lip.

Call it lack of sleep. Call it needing to get laid more often than the once every month or so rotation I'd been on lately. Call it...fascinated by his soft, sexy smile that twinkled in his eyes, and that extremely enticing, hard, huge package.

He winked at me.

My heartbeats stopped for a full ten seconds. Count out ten seconds. That is one hell of a long time. His sexy wink stole away my breath and threatened to keep it from me. His regard glided over my heart, stunning it still with a powerful beguilement spell.

Smirking, I resumed breathing. Arousal tended to make me breathe faster. My heartbeats kicked back into gear, though a little faster and lighter now, like butterflies beating the airstream that encircled the universe.

Touching the empty water glass to my lips, I dipped a lash flutter at him. I wasn't an expert in flirtation, but I'd read books, and had actually researched different forms of kissing for a romance novelist. I pointed at him, and gave him the thumbs up sign.

He lowered his head in an embarrassed shrug. A few dark curls spilled over his ear, and he brushed them back. Could the man be any cuter?

Setting his glass of milk on a marble-topped dresser across from the end of his bed, he then put his forearm to the window and propped his palm against a temple. His gaze sought mine and I let him have the connection. Or was it my soul he'd connected to? Could souls flutter?

No, wait. I was getting ahead of myself. It was just a look shared between two people who stood, scantily clad, in their respective windows. No soul mating going on here, folks. Move along. No pictures allowed behind this line.

What he did next was to be my undoing. I just wouldn't know it for months to come. He pointed to me, holding the gesture for a few seconds...then, he made a motion of slipping the robe from my shoulder.

Eyebrow lifting, I defied him with a tilt of my head. My slightly-longer-than-shoulder-length hair spilled off one shoulder. Cheeky of him. Very forward. I wasn't that kind of girl.

But right now I needed to be that kind of girl more than I needed to breathe.

He shrugged and splayed his palms in a 'what can I say?' gesture.

And for some reason, maybe lack of sleep, or glue-induced insanity, I tapped into the vixen I knew existed somewhere inside me. That part of me who pranced before the mirror on tiptoes when I tried on a new dress or a sexy pair of panties. The seductress who pursed her lips at the reflection in the mirror, yet who shuddered at the idea of actually doing such a thing before a real, live, breathing male.

Oh, tiny vixen. It's your time to shine. Or at least turn up the dimmer switch to the next level of brightness.

I slipped the yellow silk robe from my shoulder. Taking particular notice of the slide of fabric over my skin, I focused on that instead of the man watching me. Swift, light, as if a brush of a lover's hand, it sent a shiver down my arm and perked the hairs over goose flesh. The silk draped above my breast, the little embroidered bee crushed within the folds.

As I shifted my shoulders back, allowing the other sleeve to drop down, the robe spilled even further, both sleeves landing at the crooks of my elbows. My nipples tightened, much less from the fabric, and more from anticipation. Or was it fear? The tremble in my chest gave me away. But I was determined, so I continued.

I didn't feel compelled to cup my hands before my breasts, so the lightweight fabric splayed open, shifting across my skin in delicious tingles, and inspiring a heavy inhale of courage on my part.

The man's smile deepened, and he nodded at the sight of my exposed breasts. His thumbs up sign didn't seem lecherous so much as a quiet thank you. Because there I stood, in the middle of the night, exposing myself to a complete stranger who I hardly knew. Hell, I didn't know him at all.

Wait. The other night's window wave and book sharing counted as a first meeting, right? Sure, we were old friends.

Struggling with the weirdness of my newly-emerged exhibitionism and the need to wrap the silk back across my breasts and flee for safety under the comforter, I exhaled slowly and breathed in through my nose. Aware that the action lifted my breasts, I noticed that he was even more acutely tuned in.

Too much. Too fast. What the hell are you doing?

Right. Enough with playing the wanton for the night. I pulled up the robe, kissed the palm of my hand and blew him a kiss. Then I shuffled into bed and switched off the lamp.

Snuggling into the sheets, my head crushing into the pillow, I closed my eyes. A smile curled my mouth. I'd never done anything so brazen before. Ever. It was completely out of character.

My introvert's crown had just tilted. And the vixen within giggled.

I wondered if he was still standing there, waiting for my return? Dare I look?

I pulled up the comforter to my nose.

"Tomorrow night," I whispered. "It'll be his turn to reveal something to me."

Three

I fantasize about shoes, a lot. Or are such dreams simply a natural trait indicative of the female species?

After working at the map shop, I beelined toward the shoe store in the sixth arrondissement that had been calling my name for weeks.

Christian Louboutin called every woman's name. It was an elite little shop that boasted a doorman who only let in so many shoppers at a time. On any given day it was normal to see a line outside the storefront windows, and in that line, women pushing and cursing one another for better positioning closer to the door. Seriously.

Ever since those black, ribbon-tied, fuck-me pumps had made their appearance in the front window, I had not been able to stop thinking about them. I wanted to slide my feet into those pretties, and wearing nothing more than those and a smile, prance before a sexy stranger and watch his eyes follow my every move.

Did I have a sexy stranger in mind? After last night I did. I'd done it. I'd actually flashed a stranger my naked breasts. And I'd stood there some time, allowing him a good long look. How crazy was that?

Every time I thought about the flashing incident I stood taller. Oh yeah, I was no wallflower. I could seduce a man *like that.*

Maybe in an alternate universe.

Ah hell. Baby steps, right?

Back to the mission.

Something about the perfect shoe worked magic to a woman's heart—to her very soul. High-heels, stilettos, and precarious skyscraper-stripper-heeled shoes made us stand taller, jutted our breasts, and emphasized our asses by the tilt of our hips.

But we didn't need to walk in them (and who could endure that torture for long?). Just slipping on a gorgeous pump, lying across the bed, our arms stretched out above our heads as we gazed upon the pretty shoes capping our feet, changed our religion.

Shoes were sexual toys. And we women did not need a man to help us operate those devices.

The narrow sidewalk before the shop was clear of women jostling for line position, so I pressed a palm to the window, eyeing my prey. Smooth black leather, wrapped about the heel with black velvet ribbons that crossed over the top of the foot, around the back of the ankle, and then tied into a pretty bow that said 'tug me, if you dare'.

It wasn't my birthday (much as I had wished for just that the other night). I hadn't even achieved a great accomplishment at work or otherwise. I was simply answering an age-old call to nourish my soul.

It occurred to me that the male sales clerk on the other side of the glass was watching me. I sucked in the corner of my lower lip. Dressed in a black suit, his hair shaved to a shadow on his scalp, he personified smug. Dare I flash him some nipple as I had my handsome neighbor last night? Ha!

He smiled at me, dashing away the smug with a hint of warm welcome, and gestured I come inside.

I stood there for a few seconds, ruminating over our silent exchange. There's something oddly intimate about communicating through glass and at a short distance. The only thing between the two of you was a thin sheet of ultra-heated limestone and sand. Clear enough to reveal everything we wanted to present on our complicated surfaces. And yet, what lay hidden within could never be seen through that glass. Maybe?

Rolling my eyes at my sudden plunge into window philosophy, I opened the door and strolled in, knowing my credit card was going to scream bloody murder and not giving a care.

Thanks to research, I knew how to hide a body.

ΛΛΛ

I made it home as the setting sun blazed orange across the Seine. The river was always alive with lights from the boats and the reflections from the grand buildings and landmarks edging its shores. The occasional bonfire down by the waters tended to hook my wondering brain. Had they been started by the homeless, or by a bunch of ruffians? Perhaps one had been set ablaze for a glamorous evening roasting marshmallows down by the smelly old river?

My apartment did not face in the direction of the river, and even though the Eiffel Tower was less than a five-minute walk away, I had no view to speak of.

Unless you considered washboard abs a view, which I would gladly take over the Iron Lady any day.

The phone in my front pocket jingled as I rushed into the bedroom to abandon the shoes on the unmade bed. Answering the phone, I tugged out the elastic binder from my hair. My temples relaxed, as did my shoulders. I generally wore a ponytail when working at the map shop. Simple, no-nonsense, business style.

I slipped out of my well-worn, red kitten heels (I'd only been a little embarrassed to walk into Louboutin in the poor things) and unzipped my pencil skirt, letting it hang at my hips.

It was Richard, from work. I hadn't run into him today since I'd worked half a shift for Rachel, and Richard tended to come in over supper hours. The owner of the shop was a middle-aged Brit who had never married. Richard traveled the world searching out the maps he sold in the cozy little shop that sat kitty-corner to the Nôtre Dame cathedral. I imagined that he was an Indiana Jones adventurer, because he certainly boasted some biceps under the sweaters he wore and was always darkly tanned. Not ugly, though he had no girlfriend that I was aware of. I didn't think he was gay either, but who knew?

"Tomorrow?"

I shoved the piled clothing on the big velvet chair aside and managed to plop one thigh onto it as I leaned back over the strewn mess. Strained relaxation at its best. I popped open my blouse buttons and undid the front snap on my bra. Ah, freedom.

"Of course I can open the shop for you tomorrow, Richard. You know I'm almost always available to fill in." Yet I never wanted to work full-time out of the home; I was too satisfied being my own boss.

Rachel, the pretty French ingénue who had married last year, and who worked full time in the shop, had gone into labor this afternoon two hours after we'd switched shifts. (Must have been at the moment I'd slashed my credit card at Louboutin. Its plastic scream had likely drowned out Rachel's cry of alarm.)

"Don't worry about a thing, Richard. I'll be there by nine-thirty to open by ten."

I hung up, and before I could get too comfy, my feet tingled expectantly. The shoe box on the bed looked absolutely miffed that I'd tossed it aside, as if a leaf of lettuce that always got picked off the sandwich before eating.

"Sorry."

I retrieved the beige box and this time, transferred the piled clothes from the chair to the floor, before settling into the soft, velvet hug and carefully, lovingly, unboxing the prize. As some geeks did with their Apple computer products—the unboxing process was ritual (I'd seen the photos online)—I did with my shoes. Though I refrained from taking pictures.

The lid was a nice weight, and designed to glide off the box with the slightest *schush* of welcome, as if the innards had been hermetically sealed, pristine, and in wait of the first stroke of a woman's glossy red fingernails.

Setting aside the cover, I pulled open the white tissue paper and ran my fingers (sans red gloss; I only polished my toes) over the inner sportscar-red fabric bag. It was soft and embossed in black with the Louboutin logo. It spoke of luxury, and a big credit card bill next month.

Yeah, so, a girl should never put a price on satisfaction.

A smaller drawstring red bag included extra heels. Yay!

Carefully untying the bound bag ties, I trailed each ribbon out to either side of my lap. I worked the fabric ruched about the ribbon straight until the bag emitted the shoes. They slid out like a dream. I set the box aside on the floor and smoothed out the bag on my lap before placing the shoes on it.

Hey, we all have our quirks. I know some of you do this with a box of chocolates, carefully perusing the chart to ensure you don't pick that awful orange cream. Or what about those phones that come with the factory-placed plastic shield to protect the glass? Don't deny you keep that plastic on to preserve the factory seal.

The shoes sat upright, facing me, the bows at the heels plumping out from their forced containment. I stroked the black leather and the velvet ankle ribbons.

"Mine, all mine."

I hadn't bought myself a gift since the thin silver toe ring—that I always wear—last Christmas. A girl should be more generous to herself.

I leaned forward to sniff the leather. Smelled like...leather. And glue.

Screw the ritual. I needed to feel these babies against my skin. Sure, I'd tried them on in the store. So the whole first-wear hermetic seal thing was total bubkiss. But the fantasy was still running in high gear. My heartbeats had already raced me to the bottom of the grand staircase where the makeshift princess waited for the prince—make that a musketeer—to place the shoe on her foot. And then they would ride off to his castle and live—

Seriously? I'm sure that castle had like fourteen toilets. And who do you think got stuck cleaning them?

I intended to select my Prince Charming with great care and get a tour of his house before saying 'yes' to anything, and that included scrubbing toilets.

I tucked my toes into a shoe, slowly sliding my foot in until the platform conformed to my arch and my heel snugged against the curved leather. The fit was not cozy like bedroom slippers. High heels were not designed to be comfortable.

I laced up the ribbon, which wrapped about my ankle once then tied it in a bow at the back of my calf. If there was a body part I could be proud of it was my feet. They were size seven, had high arches (made for high heels, don't you know) and the toes were straight and perfectly graduated from big to small, no odd middle toe sticking out longer than the rest. I only polished my toes, never my fingernails. And always a chili red that matched the finish of a Smart Car I'd once owned.

Sliding my fingers along the smooth gloss of the red spike heel and sole, I couldn't help a lingering moan, sort of a milk chocolate melting on the tongue combined with the first imminent waves of orgasm moan. Yeah, it was that good.

I bent and slid my other foot into the remaining shoe, gliding a finger along the leather—I think the sides were called the shank—and brushing the edge of my foot where the arch showed a sliver of space between the shoe and skin. Soft there. I loved having my feet touched. Not ticklish at all. I could make a serious argument for the soles of my feet being an erogenous zone.

The second ribbon bound about my ankle, I leaned forward, pressing my chest to my lap, palms to the hardwood floor, and admired my prizes. The supple leather basked in the glow of the bedroom lamp.

A tilt of my foot and the light flashed regally on the red soles. Louis XIV had started the red-soled fashion trend back in the seventeenth century while occupying the court of Versailles. Thank you, Louis. I feel like a queen.

Leaning back in the chair I lifted my feet. All hail, the Louboutins! I didn't intend to take them off. Ever. I'd sleep in them tonight. I swear.

I noticed movement outside the window. The sheer was pulled aside and I'd forgotten my lighted bedroom served as a stage. Leaning forward and placing my feet on the floor in what I deemed was a sexy pose, I remembered my open blouse and—I didn't pull it closed. The bra was open, but the cups hadn't slid off my breasts yet, so I wasn't revealing anything he hadn't already seen.

He stood there, an arm to the window, other hand cocked casually at the hip of his snug fitting jeans. (Yes, to any man who didn't subscribe to the slouchy jean fad!) Yet for as snug as they were, they also sat low on his hips, exposing those gorgeous Adonis arches, muscles that veed down toward his delicious package and compelled me to stare.

I gave a sheepish wave, wondering how long he'd watched my silly shoe ritual.

His thumbs up both relaxed my worry and heated my neck with a blush. He pointed toward my feet.

Yes, they are my goddess gear. Bow down before them and worship the red heels—and me—if you dare.

Wow. One incident of flashing a stranger had pushed all of my sliders up to ten. Someone must have slapped a piece of duct tape over my inhibition button. I think it was because of the privacy we shared. Despite the two of us standing before windows, we were three stories up, and no one from street level could see either one of us unless we stood right up against the glass.

Enclosed within my dollhouse stage, I was safe to explore the vixen's fantasies.

Standing, I walked before the window, not so much displaying the shoes to him—he was a guy; they could care less about shoes—as testing the feel of them. I walked a few paces, head down to keep the shoes in sight. The ribbons tickled the backs of my ankles. A shiver tracing from toe to thigh and up higher tightened my nipples.

Turning, I walked toward the chair, ensuring the fit and making sure the torture level wasn't unbearable. I bet I could wear these puppies for half an hour, tops, before begging for mercy. Forget about walking any farther than my apartment down to the sidewalk to catch a cab; I'd never make it to the Métro stop three blocks away. And trust me, Louboutins and band-aids lashed across my heels were a fashion faux pas I did not want to commit.

I paused, and assumed a high fashion pose, one foot crossed before the other and toe angled outward; one that would emphasize the shoes for all the viewers. (Hey, it's my fantasy. And again, don't tell me you haven't done this before the mirror hundreds of times.) And then, a side view for him. Bending forward slightly and lifting one leg in a pinup, *oh you've startled me,* position. I did all but the fingers to the mouth mock gasping. Didn't want to push it.

Oh hell, why not?

Fingers going to my mouth, I feigned a surprised, 'oh, you caught me slightly undressed swooning over my shoes' expression.

Results were hearty laughter from across the street. I wished I could hear the sound of it. I imagined the tenor was deep, full from the chest, and that it came easily, not forced. Did he speak English? Or was he all French? Was he even French? He could be British, or maybe a displaced American like me.

Please let him be French. He'd seemed to understand me the few times I'd spoken to him through the glass, and the textbook he had been reading was titled in English, so I was falling on the 'knows English well' side of things.

Now he crossed his arms and leaned a shoulder against the window to watch my show. His hair was tousled this evening, and I decided that was his look. Sexy messy with a finger comb now and then, and yet, it looked as if a stylist had worked on it forever. It must smell freshly showered with a hint of spicy shampoo lingering in the wet strands. Mmm...

Standing upright and matching his gaze, I wondered what came next. I'd done the runway walk and the pinup bend. While such blatant posing should make me feel foolish and shameful, I hadn't touched embarrassment. It felt natural standing there, my blouse open and my skirt unzipped, ready to slide over my hips with a shimmy.

It was the shoes. Had to be the magical power of the shoes.

He lifted his shirt, revealing abs so hard and taut they could blow out a truck tire. I licked my lips. He laughed again, and pointed at me.

I tugged apart both sides of my shirt in question.

He nodded, and mouthed something I couldn't understand. With a shrug, he then spoke an unmistakable, "Please."

Or at least, I'd interpreted it as please. Maybe he'd initially said *s'il vous plait*? He could have said anything. No, he'd asked permission. He'd begged for me to remove my shirt. Kind of, sort of, maybe? Yeah, I was going with begging.

Turning away, more to hide my sudden blush than anything, I didn't vacillate over his request too long. My back to him, I shrugged my shirt down to my elbows. Remarkably, the bra stayed in place. Attribute that little miracle to underwires and a perfect fit La Perla black lace pushup.

Dropping my arms at my sides, the blouse glided down to my wrists. A shake of my hands and a swing of an arm swept it onto the velvet chair beside me. The black lace bra clung to my almost-C cups as I turned slowly toward him. (I was closer to a B-cup, but when a girl wavers between two cups, she always rounds up. And that is gospel.)

He kissed his fingertips and blew the morsel to me. The intangible kiss permeated the glass between us and scurried beneath my skin as if some kind of injected heat. A man's silent approval of what he saw before him. I didn't even worry about the nudge of muffintop that had blossomed thanks to the many macarons I was forced to consume every time I passed a patisserie. Yes, forced. If I didn't eat them, the pretty pastel treats would sit under glass all day and grow hard, crunchy, and unpalatable. Who could live with such a horror?

He tugged at the waistband of his jeans, then pointed to me. Skirt off, too, eh?

Again, I didn't think beyond what the flirtatious, wanting, giggling vixen inside me desired. This was fun and daring, and I knew I wasn't going any farther than shirt and skirt until he gave a little on his side as well. Besides, we were separated by two sheets of glass and fifteen feet of air space. We stood in completely different buildings.

It could never be completely safe—I might run into him on the street some day and then, whoops! But I cautioned myself from thinking that far ahead.

The skirt dropped to the floor, puddling about my Louboutins. I stepped out of the white pinstripes on gray rayon and kicked it aside. Twisting, I stood before the window in my matching black lace set and beribboned high heels. A shiver scurried from my neck down my arms and through my stomach ending at my mons where it swirled expectantly. There's something so sexy about wearing shoes while in lingerie. It was unusual for me, so it felt forbidden. It was even more daring, to me, than walking around naked after a shower.

The man touched his fingertips to his mouth and blew me an approving kiss. I would dream about that intangible kiss tonight. While I wore the shoes.

I dragged the chair closer to the window and sat, knees together and feet spread. An adjustment to one of the ribbon bows. Perfect. Leaning forward, I pointed to him.

He stabbed a thumb toward his chest and perked his brows in question.

"Yes, you." I nodded. "You gotta give if you want to get, Mr. Sexy."

That should probably be *Monsieur* Sexy? What was the French word for sexy? I think it might simply be sexy. I'd have to look it up later.

Splaying his hands out, he momentarily considered the request, or rather, made dramatic show of considering it, then nodded that *yes,* indeed, he must comply. It was a teasing compliance. He had a sense of humor, and that rocketed his appeal exponentially.

He unzipped his jeans. I'd already seen him in his skivvies, so the unveiling would be nothing new, but the slowness with which he eased the snug denim down his thighs and to his knees almost undid me. His thigh muscles were toned from fencing, and they flexed as he bent to shove the jeans past his knees.

I bit my lip, catching my chin in palm, and experienced a moment where I thought I might start drooling.

When he stood in black boxer briefs he straightened and splayed his hands out in a *look at me* gesture. *Does this please you? I am a sexy Frenchman who has just dropped trou. Only for you, my pretty mignon.*

Was it weird that my mental version of his voice had sounded like Pepe le Pew? Oh yeah.

He flexed a biceps. Nice muscles, and so cute with the way he tried to macho it up. A nervous reaction, I thought, not so much showing off, as attempting to make light of the sexually charged, yet anxious, moment.

He lifted a bare foot and pointed to it as he shook his head sadly.

"Poor guy. No shoe that you own could compete with these pretties."

I leaned back and lifted a foot to admire what was more distracting than the man in the underwear. Almost. Red-soled shoes or the hard body across the street?

Absolutely no question.

Turning on the chair and leaning my elbow onto the arm I tugged out the waistband of my underwear, let it snap back into place, and pointed to him.

He thumbed the waistband of his boxer briefs and toyed at tugging them down, which revealed a peek of hair as dark as that on his head.

I nodded and put on my best pout. I added hands pressed together in prayer for good measure. Please can I have some more, sir?

I don't think I'd ever seen a sweeter, yet devilish grin. A shadow of a mustache darkened his upper lip, emphasizing his slightly crooked grin. His eyebrow arched on the same side as his smile lifted.

Running a palm down his abs—yes, slowly, so I could imagine the hard, hot plane of strapped muscle as if it were beneath my own palm, breathing, tensing, growing hotter—he stroked the hand over his boxers, and even though the fabric was black, I could see the thickness beneath reacting to his touch.

He gripped the package. I was reminded of that Transporter movie—*Rule number three: never open the package.*

Bedamned rule number three. I wanted to tear open the package and look, touch, and lick, and enjoy.

He sucked in a corner of his lower lip. The man was turned on by his own touch. Or was it me watching him touch himself that did it for him?

A combination of both, I decided. Because hell, my nipples were hard as diamonds, poking against the black lace bra. I recognized pain, and realized that I was biting my lip. I released it without a flinch. I didn't want him to see my profound reaction. But then...I decided my reactions were the only part about this that mattered. We couldn't touch one another. We were denied sound, smell, and taste. This slightly dangerous liaison was all about sight and imagination.

I waggled my finger and tapped the air down, down, down.

And his boxers slid slowly down to reveal the thick thatch of dark hairs and the head of his cock. Then the enticing bulge disappeared. He'd tugged the boxers back up and waggled a chiding finger at me.

God, I loved that easy smile.

Forgetting that I wasn't normally so sexually forward, I pressed my palms together in another *please* gesture.

He shrugged, and then dropped trou in a swift slide from thigh to ankle.

"Fuck."

I mean, seriously, there was nothing else I could say.

He stood there boldly, eyes glued to mine, noting every reaction, every minute movement as I leaned forward and pressed the cool glass with my fingertips. A poor replacement for what I wanted to get my hands on.

He was hard and ready to go. So rigid and firm that his cock stood at attention, pointing toward his abs. The head of him was a deep magenta and thick like a summer-sweet plum. His testicles hung heavy behind and below the gorgeous rod, and I almost made a squeezing motion with my hands. Almost.

Thumbs up for him. Oh why not, *two* thumbs up.

He smiled and shook his head, bowing it as he might have blushed. But he didn't reach to protectively cup his equipment. I adored his confidence. How often did a woman get to watch such a sight? And to direct it?

Louboutins and a hard cock? I was one spoiled girl.

“Mercy.”

The owner of the upright cock pointed to me. My turn.

But just the underwear? I stood and fingered the strap of my bra, then my waistband.

Both, he mouthed. I understood that request perfectly. It seemed fair enough, since he was naked. And he'd already seen my breasts last night so no problem going there again.

I toed out a foot and tilted my head in question.

He shook his head adamantly. Keep the shoes on, was the message.

I hadn't a stripper bone in my body, but the idea of getting naked for a nameless man whom I may never speak to rubbed all the erogenous zones in my body. Hard. At least, I hoped to never speak to him if we were going through with this. How embarrassing would it be to meet over the fresh fruit in the supermarket? Hey, nice cock—er, bananas you've got there.

Commit, I told myself. And have fun with it, my inner vixen chimed. I'd deal with the fruity situation if and when it ever occurred.

Right.

Turning around to give him my back, I glanced over a shoulder and winked at him. I slipped down a bra strap. Just because I didn't have stripper moves didn't mean I hadn't seen them in movies. A shimmy of my arm dropped the strap lower and I glided it down and off my hand.

Sight of his cock standing at attention made me smile, and I almost giggled. Oh hell, why not? I burst into giggles, catching a palm over my mouth. A dip of my head to look around and through the window received a wink from him.

Silly girl, giggles made me feel even sexier. And he was enabling me. Scandalous. Absolutely brazen.

Good boy.

Shrugging off the other strap, I let the lacy black slip of almost-nothing fall to the floor where I caught it on a toe of my shoe and lifted it to display for him. With a flip of my foot I sent it off to land near the end of the bed.

I cupped my almost-Cs, which were high and perky. I was proud of them, and loved to have a man touch and lick them. I actually couldn't get off without a lot of breast stimulation. It was as if my nipples had a direct get-off line to my pussy. No sucking, no coming.

I lamented the missed sensation of touch from Monsieur Sexy, but as I turned to face him, I caught him with an open mouth, gliding his tongue along his teeth. The look in his eyes, part pained want and another part soft desire, served me well enough.

Nipples hard against my palms, I bent forward, teasing him with a peek—but not yet.

I turned away again, and now I slipped my fingers down each side of my panties. He nodded encouragingly, and as the black lace slid down my ass and thighs, I bent, drawing them to my ankles and then carefully stepping out of them, giving him a view of my backside. While down, I glanced around my hair and there was that appreciative open-mouthed gape again.

Too cute.

I stood and turned, displaying my high breasts and neatly shaved crotch (no particular design; I just liked trimming the shrubbery). His regard swept over my skin and I felt that intangible look tingle at my breasts and lower. Mmm, my stomach was soft and my mons warm. Yes, I was already wet.

This vixen was getting her naughty on.

He gripped his cock. I cupped my breasts, thumbing the nipples. And as he nodded, I watched him stroke his rod.

We were doing this. Mutually pleasuring ourselves before a window, while all around us in the neighborhood below, life went on. People strolled the sidewalks on a late-night walk or in search of Fluffy gone rogue. Lost tourists prayed they'd find the nearest Métro stop. Cars rolled quietly over the cobbled streets.

Could anyone see us? Not from the street. There were no other apartments on the third floor on our sides of the buildings. Someone on the roof might get a good view, but no one ever went up there. At least not that I'd ever noticed.

He pointed to me and then moved his hand down from his chest to his crotch and made a rubbing motion. I understood what he wanted me to do, and glided my fingers down my stomach, panting in daring anticipation.

Daring to do this. Daring to meet his challenge. Daring to take what I desired without concern for whether or not it was right or wrong. I wanted to do this...

I could do this.

I...

Bon courage? I shook my head, indicating that tiny niggle that wouldn't allow me to make the leap.

I kissed my palm and blew him the reluctant send-off. He reciprocated, but not without a disappointed shrug of his shoulders.

I know, I know! So close and yet unable to grasp the prize.

With a wave goodnight, I pulled the sheers closed and scampered into the bathroom. My heels clicked on the tiles, echoing my daring foray into exhibitionism.

Four

Staring at my reflection I winked at the brunette. I had begun something exciting and daring with a stranger. I wanted it to continue. But it had rushed into extreme territory tonight.

"Not that extreme," I muttered, retrieving the toothbrush from inside the medicine cabinet and adding a dollop of Elgydium toothpaste to it (clove flavored). I started to brush.

Right, because extreme would be getting together with a stranger too quickly and having sex. Like on the first date.

All right, all right, I had to confess to one—no, two—one night stands. I wasn't proud of them. And yet, I wasn't ashamed of them either. I'd been safe, using condoms, and sometimes I needed it when I needed it, and that didn't imply that I had to start dating, go to the guy's family reunion with him, start dreaming about matching bedroom sets, or ponder the many uses for rhubarb in baked goods.

Guys had no-strings sex all the time. Why should women be stigmatized for wanting the same thing? I certainly wasn't going to wear the guilt crown about it.

I wasn't about to feel guilty about my window affair, either. But I had the right to refuse when things didn't feel right, as did he. No matter how much I'd wanted to keep going tonight, I had to listen to that inner voice that reminded me that I am the quiet introvert who would be appalled to witness such a scene from the streets below.

Appalled at first, but then, I'd probably grin and walk on.

There was something about sex, the act of undressing together, of learning each other's bodies—well that was it, wasn't it? We hadn't gone the route of undressing one another and trailing our fingers over skin to read subtle curves and muscles. What we'd shared was pseudo-foreplay. There wasn't anything wrong with that. In fact, it might be an interesting get-to-know you process, instead of the standard fingers over skin scenario.

I spit and rinsed and stared hard at myself in the mirror. Really?

Fine. I missed the skin contact.

Oh, man, I wanted to wrap my fingers about his cock. Feel its hardness, the heat of it, the utter strength of it. Cup my palm over the head and—I wondered if he was circumcised? He'd been hard so it was difficult to tell. I'd never seen an uncircumcised penis up close and friendly-like. My love for knowledge, and the desire to learn and explore things I was unfamiliar with, wanted him to be uncut.

But did it matter? I'd chickened out tonight.

I clicked off the bathroom light and wandered out to the bed in my pretty high heels. No, I hadn't been a chicken. I was being smart. I'd already stepped out of my box and had toed the comfort zone line.

Perhaps tomorrow tonight, I'd stick a red-soled toe across that line. I wanted to do that. It wasn't the safe distance we had between us, or the daring eroticism of the imaginary boundary that excited me about this liaison so much. It was simply new and fun and not ordinary.

Spreading my arms wide, I did a back-first full-body plant onto the fluffy comforter on top of my bed. I lifted my legs to stare at the Louboutins, pretty black enticements caressing my feet.

Intangible kisses moved along my legs, traveling toward my ankles until his fingers touched the black ribbons and tugged, gently, yet insistently.

Mmm, my sleep would be laced with delicious dreams tonight.

ÅÅÅ

"I'm ticklish," I whispered in my dreams.

A kiss pressed to my anklebone, Monsieur Sexy paused and looked up at me. Eyes of an indiscernible color dove into mine. I exhaled to counteract the sudden increase in my adrenaline. He knelt before me, my foot in his hand, the black ribbons spilling over his wrist. He wore nothing. I wore a black lace bra and panties.

And the shoes.

"Relax," he said in a deep voice that worked like a shot of whiskey to my nerves. Of course it was in French, too. And my dream-self understood every single word of it. "I want to worship you."

I settled back on the tufted gray velvet chaise, hands dropping to my sides. The perfect spot for reading, the chaise was curved so my body melted into it. I *became* the chaise when I laid on it.

His tongue dashed out to lick my ankle near the ribbon. The soft *schush* of velvet across my skin was punctuated by my breaths that had grown more shallow and quicker.

The ribbon struggled for hold as the tug at the knot beckoned. He'd snatched an end with his teeth and as he sat back on his heels, he pulled the ribbon free to its full length. The straps slithered from my skin as if a silk robe slipping away.

His cock jutted upright, a proud column. I could reach for it, but, no, I wanted to linger in this seduction. Receive what he wanted to give. I sighed, closed my eyes. I needed his touch, this foray into the forbidden with the man behind the glass.

Ribbon still in his teeth, he growled and playfully tugged at it. I popped open an eyelid and chided him with a waggling finger. "Bad puppy."

He dropped the ribbon and pouted. Then he lunged to my foot and kissed me where the ribbons had left a slight impression around my ankle. Slowly, tenderly, he kissed and licked, then drew his tongue down the side of my foot along the shoe's shank. And there, he touched my exposed arch. The zing of sensation made me spasm in my gut and my foot jerked—but his hand slapped over the top of it, holding me firmly.

His eyes admonished while his tongue lashed out in a teasing lick along his lip.

I breathed rapidly. He looked hungry. I couldn't wait for the devouring.

His tongue slid along my arch and my back curved in tandem. The exquisite torture curled my fingers at my sides and into the velvet chaise's decadent nap. I moaned. His other hand loosened the back of the shoe from my heel, and his fingers glided firmly over the base of it.

I reached for his head, but he was too far away. I wanted to run my fingers through his glossy hair, grip it hard, and tug.

It was when he kissed the side of my heel, then bit gently into the meat of it that I sucked in a gasp and moaned as the sensation fluttered up my leg and to my groin. Every nip, every lash of his tongue, the firm pressure of his kisses, effectively imitated the flutter in my rapidly moistening pussy.

I slid a hand down my stomach and pressed against my clit.

"Good girl," he whispered. A tongue lash to the underside of my arch lifted my hips and I dove my fingers between my folds. "So pretty."

He slipped the shoe from my foot and admired it a moment, then tossed it over his shoulder.

I couldn't manage a protest to his careless regard for my prized possession, because his tongue now traced the inner side of my foot and ventured toward my toes. I paralleled his motions with strokes across my clit.

A lash of hot wetness strode between my largest toe and the next where the thin silver ring coiled. He made a point of his tongue and speared the delicate curve at the base between the two toes.

"Oh, *mon Dieu*," I moaned. And I'm not even French! "*Oui.*" The word drawled out in a plead for him to never stop, never stop, never...

He tickled and traced between all my toes, and then he shifted his body around to the end of the chaise. One hand held my ankle firmly, while the other danced his thumb along the underside of my foot where it was softest, pale from lack of sunlight, and ultra-sensitive.

I writhed on the chaise. My fingers dove into my heat and I wet them to draw out and slick against the swollen labia. No window between us, yet still, I pleasured myself.

Correction: he was pleasuring me in the most exquisite way. I was merely enhancing that touch.

His mouth enveloped my toe. He suckled the tip of it, pressing his tongue against the soft underside and gently impressing his teeth there, and then there, but never for more than a second. It was as if he were at my breast, sucking deep and hard, and...

"Oh, yes, like that," I purred as my nipples tightened with a zing.

As he moved to the next toe, I realized his hands strolled along my skin. One gently stroked the inside of my arch, tracing the curve back and forth softly, while the other glanced over the top of my foot and up my ankle and calf.

And at his mouth my toes were worshipped, teased, and devoured. The littlest toe inspired his comment, "So cute."

Kneeling and straightening, he added a new touch treat to the mix. Rubbing the head of his cock under my foot, he teased the bold, hot head against my sensitive skin. I curled my toes about the molten shaft. Mm, it was soft and suedelike on the outside, yet so incredibly hard overall. He tapped my toes with his rod. The man's moan vibrated across my skin, raising the hairs and coaxing the imminent orgasm up, up, up...

He swore softly as he eased his cock between my foot and his hand.

"Yes," I hissed.

He again slid around the side of the chaise. Moving his tongue down to explore my arch, his hand glided up the inside of my thigh. The moment his fingers plunged into my wet pussy and brushed, perhaps accidentally, across my swollen clit, my body surrendered and my shoulders thrust back.

I cried out.

Bliss won. Laughter spilled from my lips.

And Monsieur Sexy tilted his head aside my knee and winked at me.

ÅÅÅ

Early evenings usually provided a slump in the parade of curious tourists who wandered into the map shop facing the Seine. Fine by me. My mind was free to wander as I absently dusted the map drawers. I'd tucked the Louboutins in my bag and wore them today. Every step I took reminded me of his tongue lazing over my arch. Of his hard cock rubbing against my soles, his hips rocking, his jaw tightening as he pleasured not only me, but himself as well.

My boss called me into the back room. His voice startled me so abruptly from the fantasy I dropped the feather duster behind a wooden file cabinet. I'd figure out a retrieval method later.

As soon as I saw Richard standing there in his button up Mr. Rogers sweater with a twinkle to his blue eyes, I knew he had found something that excited him.

I had too, but window voyeurism, plus a side order of foot fetish, was not something I would bring up in conversation with my boss.

He splayed his hands to sweep over the map he'd carefully laid on the drafting table before him. The aged wood table that was pocked and slashed from years of use was tilted slightly so the map, unattached to the edges with the usual metal clamps, did not slide off.

"Something you found on your recent excursion to Scotland?" I wondered, lingering in the doorway.

The room was small, and though he'd never made a pass at me, and I didn't feel as if he ever would, the closeness always felt odd. Besides, my nipples were hard and my pussy wet after that little foray into remembrance. *Bad puppy.*

"Yes, come take a look and tell me what you see."

He was fond of puzzles and muddling over the prizes he collected during his travels. Sometimes he brought back a rare map, other times they were copies. Most often he returned with dozens of reproductions because they sold for a good price, and quickly.

I approached the drafting table and, keeping my hands behind my back as I'd learned to do so I wouldn't absently touch what could be ancient and delicate paper, I inspected the yellowed map.

"It's Milan," I said.

"Yes, yes. Very good."

I'd never been to Italy but when one works in a map shop recognizing cities merely by shape becomes an unexpected talent.

"What year?" he quizzed.

"Hm..." I studied the key on the lower left corner, which was elaborately framed with baroque curliques and a cupid. (Always the cupid.) I didn't read Italian, so the words were like Greek to me. Make that Italian. I recognized the city name and... "Is this the year?" I pointed to some words that I thought could have been numbers.

"Very good. 1496, actually."

"Ah. Medieval Milan. Nice. Who drew it?"

"That's for you to puzzle out."

"But you already know, right?"

"I have my suspicions. Look at it a while. I'm sure something will catch your eye that will lead you down the same path I've already explored. Tea?"

He turned to the tea service behind him, and I nodded. Richard brewed a killer mint tea spiked with lime. Like a hot little mojito in a cup, I'd once said to him. He hadn't understood the reference, or my thrill, so I'd restrained myself from mentioning that it would have tasted super with a shot of rum.

Lime-tinged mint filled the room as he poured. And I studied the map, blessedly relieved that this fascinating challenge had diverted my lusty thoughts while standing in such a small space with my boss.

Old maps were gorgeous, works of art in and of themselves. Before landing this job I'd never appreciated their beauty. Now, I had begun my own collection, and I was searching for a post-Revolutionary

New Republic Parisian map that featured all of the changed names the city had endured for those years. Nôtre Dame, the Temple of Reason? I had to find that map.

"This symbol looks familiar." I hovered a fingertip over the circular design of intricately woven ribbon. Knotwork, actually. A monogram of sorts rested in the middle. "Where have I seen it before? On another map?"

"Unlikely," he provided. "But that symbol is your key to naming the cartographer who designed this map."

I tugged out my cell phone. "Do you mind if I take a picture of it?"

"Go ahead. Take a shot of the whole map and various parts of it. You know I'm not going to reveal who I think made this until you provide your own guess."

I snapped a few shots, smirking to myself. The man was eccentric, but sweet. Turning around, and shoving my phone back in the front pocket of my skirt, I was handed tea.

"To new discoveries," he pronounced

We toasted with a ting of our glass teacups against one another.

Five

Dinner at Angelina with Melanie was a treat that we indulged in. Because Melanie was uber-busy, always jet-setting the world, our standing date at Angelina became a priority for us. We cancelled meetings for it.

Melanie's job title wasn't exactly clear, but party planner for foreign clients was close enough. She spent half of the year in the States talking up potential clients for her firm, and the other half in Europe schmoozing the clients with alcohol, parties, and weekends spent at Marseilles sunbathing on yachts. Or Greece. Or the Bahamas.

Nice job if you could get it.

Melanie and I were opposites on the scale of introvert to extrovert. She could attract men at a party with a laugh and a flash of her bright green eyes. She had that bold, carefree, Audrey Hepburn laugh that I found myself even worshipping at times. And she was gorgeous, all six feet two inches of her, and miles of red hair that she tended to twist about her fingers while talking. Mercy.

I strived never to refer to my hair as mousey or washed out. It was chestnut, or at least that's the term that made me feel the best about the growing-it-out bob. My blue eyes stood out, distracting from my plain hair. I also liked my mouth. It was perfectly shaped and soft—thanks to the sugar scrubs I used on it once a week. I actually scrubbed my whole body with vanilla sugar all the time. I did like to take care of myself. My mother had taught me that if I didn't love myself first, no one else was going to.

Wise words.

My mother had died at forty-five; much too young. She'd been killed in a car accident. She'd never gotten to see me walk down the aisle (though I'll take her advice and wait until my thirties, thank you very much), nor had she lived to see me move to Paris, fulfilling a lifelong desire to cross the ocean. We'd been close when she was alive, but I can't make any claims to feeling her presence near me in times of need now that she's gone. I am a skeptic about all that woo-woo ghost stuff. But I do take comfort in knowing that her conscience has moved on, blending into the universal conscience, and that someday we would meet again; in another lifetime, as different people, perhaps as friends, lovers, or even next-door neighbors.

"You're trying the white chocolate today?" I asked Melanie as the waitress in her nineteenth century maid's uniform—ankle-length somber black dress, with a ruffled white apron a la Mary Poppins—delivered pots of hot chocolate to the table. One pot offered creamy brown chocolate, the other a strange ochre that didn't appeal to me at all. "What's up with that?"

"The chocolate is to die for." Melanie thanked the waitress with perfect French. "But I'm in the mood for something different," she said, switching seamlessly back to English. "Don't want to get stuck in a rut."

"You could never get stuck in a rut. Ruts see you coming and they run screaming. Mmm..."

I bit into the vanilla macaron that I always ordered to accompany the rich hot chocolate. Both had clearly been made in heaven. By cupids. Wearing ruffled aprons and singing like Mary Poppins.

Have I mentioned my mind tends to wander?

Melanie and I had long ago decided that since Angelina served high quality chocolate, perhaps the sugar content was lower. With that said, we reasoned that we weren't actually consuming as many calories as we thought while drinking the syrup-thick concoction. So we poured more, and then even more into our dainty porcelain teacups.

Uh-huh. A woman's mind can twist any scenario to result in negative calories. Just try us. It's a talent worthy of two thumbs up and three perfect tens.

"So does that mean you've dumped Jacques, or Francois, or whatever his name was?"

"Philippe," she said, licking the demitasse spoon that accompanied the precious little porcelain cup of Chantilly cream. "Yes, it has been a month, darling."

"Heaven forbid you let a man fuck you beyond that one month expiration date."

"They get so tiresome when they start to want to talk."

"Oh, talking is the worst."

I rolled my eyes, but we both laughed. Talking and breathing topped the list on our Favorite Gripes About Men. Lying there late at night listening to a man's allergy-stuffed breathing? Ugg.

"He wanted to discuss plans, and even do things like walk through the park and hold hands." A pout of her lips produced that pained look that always made me laugh. "I mean, who wants to hold hands in the park? It is très boring, cherie. So bourgeoisie. I simply want some hot sex, when I want it, where I want it, and don't stop until I shout for you to stop. Am I right? Oh."

Melanie placed her hand over mine. The pained expression returned. "I'm sorry. I know it's been a while since you've dated."

"Just because I don't date men exclusively doesn't mean I don't hook up."

"Right. Hookups bother me, too."

"I know. No time for the man to actually learn how to please you." I'd never tell her I thought her month-long tête-à-têtes were simply extended hookups.

"It does take a few times for the man to learn what makes we women squirm and moan," she added. "Years to master us."

"True. But sometimes a hookup is what I need and all I want. A quickie to remind me that I'm sexy, that a man desires me, and..." I giggled and dropped the spoon into the thick hot chocolate with a clink. "What am I saying? Melanie, you will not believe what I've begun."

The redhead's green eyes brightened, a scoop of Chantilly cream paused before her lips. And over another macaron and the dregs of our calorie-free (and don't try to convince us otherwise) decadent drinks, I told her about Monsieur Sexy.

After leaving Angelina, we strolled down the Rue du Rivoli and turned onto the elite Rue Royale. I accompanied Melanie to Chanel and watched her ooh and aah over the perfumes. I wasn't a perfume girl. Natural oils were all I wore, because the chemicals in colognes gave me a raging migraine. Melanie had sensed my descent into solemn disinterest as the headache snuck up, and quickly rushed me outside, forgoing her purchase.

The sales clerk called in our wake that he'd have the perfume sent to Melanie's apartment. He had her address and credit card number on file. *Naturellement*. The woman was a shopping diva.

We parted ways at the Place du Concorde in the long shadow of the Luxor Obelisk, and I strolled through the Tuileries for another hour. Paris in September smelled humid and earthy. The warm autumn evening was a boon to my tender senses, and eventually, I was able to recall the sweet taste of hot chocolate as opposed to the evil smell of perfume.

By the time I got home, it was nearing ten p.m. I tossed my purse on the counter and—noticed some action out the living room window. As I've explained, the angles of the buildings didn't allow for more than flashes of movement in the third floor windows, and the distance was too great for detail. But if I tilted my head against the glass, I could see the edges of the main, empty area that I assumed was a living area. A hanging plant partially blocked view of the room. It looked like a man, dressed in white, and he was...

"Fencing."

My heart performed the proverbial pitter-patter. "Oh, my musketeer."

Fencing rated top of the scale as a sexy sport, along with snowboarding (Shaun White, anyone?) and surfing. Ripped abs were a perfectly acceptable reason to watch a sporting event, am I right?

I watched as the fencer moved before the window, obviously in a match with another that I couldn't quite see because the streetlight's glare made only the closet things visible.

The man wore a mesh mask. I imagined the long, sinewy thigh muscles that must stretch as he lunged forward to deliver a thrust. I loved watching duels in movies. Particularly French movies. Subtitles and historical costumes? I am so there. Michael York had played the ultimate D'Artagnan. Yeah, he was an Englishman. Who cared when there were bucket-topped boots, rapiers, and daring escapades involved?

The fencer moved away from the window, and I decided that this particular window felt more voyeuristic than the one in my bedroom because he was going about his life in the other rooms. He'd not invited me to share what he did beyond the bedroom. It seemed like a boundary I should respect.

Pulling the curtains closed, I headed for the shower. Gossip and perfume had worked a number on my tender senses. But I wouldn't have traded the girlfriend date for the world.

And now I had a new mystery to explore. I knew I'd seen that symbol from the Milan map before. I suspected it would come to me in the middle of a dream, popping me up in bed as dreams often did. Or maybe as I rode the Métro, my mind a mile away while my body swayed to the lulling rhythm of the train.

Tugging out my cell phone, I opened the pictures I'd taken of the map and sent them to my printer. Stripping, I headed into the bathroom.

After a steamy shower, I stood outside the tub dripping, and reached for a towel. Monsieur Sexy's image danced into my skull. Actually, he performed a fencing move across my vision, and then poked me gently with the tip of his rapier right...there. Right where the headache lingered, despite the relaxing water.

If I took the night off and didn't open the curtains, would he be upset? Would he even care? It wasn't as though we'd established that every night we'd meet at a certain time before the window to watch each other jack off. Not that either of us had done that.

Though, wouldn't that be cool?

Even if we had, we weren't on a touching basis, let alone a talking status, and I needed the freedom to live my life and do as I pleased. That's why dating generally didn't work for me. It didn't take long for me to feel as though I was in a partnership, and that was just too much pressure for me. Like Melanie, I tended to break off relationships at first sign of clinginess. Call it the burn of the awkward marriage proposal. Call it growing up.

I had always felt that I'd know when the right man came along. The man I'd want to spend all my time with, to lose myself with, to just *be* with.

I managed to brush my teeth while trying to ease the tension in my neck muscles with my free hand. Once I got the headache, even if I took the time to control it, to fight it off by relaxing, it generally stuck around, lingering at the back of my skull or strafing the muscles in my neck, and wouldn't completely be gone until after a good night's rest.

Rapping the toothbrush against the sink edge to spatter off the water, I put it in the medicine cabinet and padded naked into the bedroom. Through the pulled sheers I saw his light across the alley. I didn't see any movement, but I didn't stare. He was probably still fencing.

Sighing, I slid between the sheets and tucked the pillow under my neck so my head was tilted upward; the best position to fight the headache.

"Tomorrow night," I whispered. "I'm all yours. And you'll be mine."

Six

Anticipation can be the strangest thing. All day at work (yes, in my living room seated before the computer) I caught myself staring out the window, but not seeing anything in particular.

Or was it because I was looking out the window for him? I hadn't seen him fencing. If he worked at home, it wasn't near any windows. Though I'd never seen him leave his building in the morning, I didn't know if he worked from home or not.

Not that I rose early enough to catch a businessman leaving for work. Layabed, remember?

I felt great today. Headache averted. Body dosed with my monthly shot of decadent hot chocolate and gossip. And it had been a week since I'd had my period. You know what that means? I was ovulating. I always know when I am because my body and thoughts changed markedly. My breasts get sensitive to the slightest touch, such as pulling off a tee shirt or tugging on a bra. I feel invigorated, and notice that I walk with an extra swing to my hips.

I'd once read that men were more attracted to women when they were ovulating, for that one simple fact: women acted more sexual at that time because it was the one time of the month their bodies were most receptive to pregnancy. Nature performing its finest mating dance.

I didn't need a baby, but I did need to satisfy the sexual itch that had me thinking about Monsieur Sexy's cock behind glass. And his abs. And those ripped Adonis arches that veed down to that gorgeous shaft. And who could forget that sexy smile of his that blew me a kiss every time it graced his gorgeous lips; a kiss I could literally feel every time it soared through the glass.

At one point during the day, I'd summoned the fantasy of him licking my foot and languorously rubbing his cock against the arch. I'd moaned out loud. The noise had stirred me from my voluptuous daydream and I'd abruptly sat up at my desk and looked around. Alone in the room? Of course. Sometimes I forgot that I worked from home instead of in a cubicle.

When the four o'clock bell rang—so to speak—I ended my work day. I billed by the hour, so it didn't matter if I worked an eight-hour stretch or broke it into smaller chunks.

My muscles tended to bind up after a day bent over the keyboard, so I headed out for a walk to stretch and soak up some sun. I wandered over to Les Invalides, the site of an old military school and hospital, but also a nice park. I liked to watch the tourists and guess where they were from based on their foreign chatter. I'm sure I was never right. Dialects were not my thing. And there were so many variations of French alone I could only imagine the countless possibilities with other languages.

Later, I wandered over to the Seine and bought some artificially dyed pink daisies from a stand near the river. The flowers caught my eyes because their color matched the underwear I wore (no, I did not explain that to the seller). I walked away, hugging the flowers to my chest, swinging my hips in a sensual proclamation that let all of single men around me know that I was fertile. I probably broadcast to the married ones as well.

Who was I kidding? Did my hips even advertise? I don't know... Yes, yes they did. Let's leave it at that.

In the blue-and-cream-painted *boulangerie* a block down from my building, I picked up a baguette and some fresh goat cheese that the owner's wife made in small batches and sold for an extravagant price. I loved bruleed goat cheese. The caramelized crispy crust was sweet and surprising with each bite. I paid the inflated price and almost skipped in anticipation on my way down the sidewalk.

Once home I arranged the flowers in a vase and set them on the kitchen table. Then I carefully prepared the cheese under the broiler, watching as the swash of butter and brown sugar I'd painted over the top bubbled and quickly formed a crunchy crust. I poured a glass of red wine and cut a few slices from the baguette. The crust was light and flakey; the crumb chewy and thick. Spread with the warm cheese, absolute heaven. I could survive on bread, wine and cheese. So long as my monthly hot chocolate and gossip date was included in the rations.

Lounging on the tufted velvet chaise in the living room, I kicked up my bare feet and glided the underside of one foot along my shin.

Something so sensual about bare feet. Monsieur Sexy, on his knees, his cock bobbling expectantly, appeared before me.

"Soon," I whispered through a nibble of bread.

He nodded, and wisped away as easily as he had appeared.

I watched the news with the volume on low. I didn't care what was going on in the world around me, because right now the world moved within me, swirling in my core, tingling across my skin. Pleading with me to saunter into the bedroom and pull aside the curtains.

I could wait. (Not really, but it was still light out. I didn't want to seem too eager.)

Smooshing the bread into the last few crumbles of cheese, I savored the bites with a moan. Setting the plate on the floor beside the chaise, I laid my head back, closed my eyes, and ignored whatever the weathergirl du jour had decided tomorrow should be like. I'd be inside working anyway.

I pulled my hair from its chignon and eased my fingers around my temples. A tight knot had formed and strained all day as I'd poured over a book on fly-fishing techniques. (My clients' fictional interests were vast.) The sensation of the muscles relaxing beneath my skin as my fingers moved around the hairline tightened my nipples.

I glided a hand over my breast. It's fascinating how our bodies change and alter with only a thought. The brain is the biggest sex organ in the body.

I'm pretty sure I think too much.

I know I think too much.

I laughed out loud at my overactive thoughts, then collected the plate and goblet. I was in the mood for a hot bath.

ÅÅÅ

Fresh from the tub and smelling like vanilla sugar scrub, I slipped on my silk bee robe, even though I didn't intend to keep it on long. My body hummed in anticipation of what could be revealed with the sweep of a curtain. I'd been thinking about him all day in between thoughts on casting a line and tying flies. My brain was already there, in an embrace, receiving what he wanted to give. Giving back what he wanted to take. My body was ready. And willing.

I saw light across the street. My nipples tightened as I stepped to the shaded window. I pulled aside the curtain. Then I remembered.

I dodged to the bedside and flicked on the lamp. It was dark outside and the glow from the nearest streetlight didn't reach this far, so without the light, he wouldn't be able to see me.

I wandered back before the window, focusing on the slip and slide of silk over my thighs, my stomach and hips, my breasts. My nipples could not get any harder. I likened them to a man's erection—hot, hard, and eager for touch. The steamy bathroom had moistened my scalp and temples, and I perspired sweet vanilla even after I'd dried off. I felt moistness between my breasts. And between my legs.

I caught movement out of the corner of my eye, and turned to find Monsieur Sexy standing in his boxer briefs—deep blue tonight—holding something before his chest. It was a notebook, turned on its side in landscape format. He'd written in bold black letters: Hi.

I waved to him and couldn't prevent a beaming smile. Our first venture into a new form of communication. Yay, for us! Or at least for him.

He pointed to the notebook and grabbed the thick marker that was lying on the end of the bed. He wrote: English, yes? Then pointed to me.

"Yes, English."

I put up a finger for him to wait, then scampered into the kitchen. On the table, a stack of books balanced precariously close to a dead succulent I'd bought at a flower shop near Nôtre Dame. I'd attempted to nurture it, but overwatering had done that baby in but good. The research notebook for my last project sat waiting to be filed in a non-existent file cabinet. I'd only used the first few sheets inside the wire-bound spiral notebook. Perfect.

I sorted through the junk drawer and found a marker consigned to the back. Pulling off the cap, I sniffed it, and the strong solvent coiled into my nostrils.

"Oh, yeah." Call me a dork, but the sniff high was a doosy. My recreational drug of choice. Heh. Not.

I quickly wrote Hi, back on the page, and dashed back into the bedroom.

He read my pithy reply and bowed, accepting the introduction.

Then it occurred to me that I could write an entire book about all the things I'd been thinking of doing with him, but I didn't want to scare him off. Did he even like feet? Better take it slower. Simple and short should be the standard. Especially because I didn't want to stand before the window all night dictating my desires.

I wrote out two short lines, and turned it for him to read.

2 rules. 1: No names.

He nodded, agreeing easily, then put up two fingers and shrugged.

I flipped over the page, and wrote what I felt was the most important rule if these window sexcapades were to work: If we see each other, walk away. No contact beyond windows.

I turned it around and waited as he mouthed the words he read. He scrubbed a hand over his hair, imparting some tension with his pulsing jaw as he made a show of considering my rule.

"No contact," I muttered, and shook my head. "Not yet. I'm not ready for that."

He nodded and gave me a thumbs up. Whew.

I tossed the notebook aside. I didn't want to write. I wanted to show him how I was feeling. But he was writing now, so I stepped to the window and pressed a palm to it. I gazed across the street that could be a thousand mile distance, yet felt as if he were standing only but a breath away.

I wanted to smell him. To feel his body heat so close to mine that we created sparks.

He turned the notebook over and I read: Exquisite. Bold. Gorgeous. He pointed at me.

My heart fluttered and I pressed my palm over it. I hadn't realized I needed that until—just, wow.

I kissed my fingertips and blew the morsel to him. He made a show of catching it and pressing his fingertips to his lips, as if to taste my kiss. Soon, I thought. Or maybe never? I didn't know where these window sessions would lead, and I decided not to worry about the future.

Monsieur Sexy drew his fingers down his chest and abs and hooked them at the waistband of his briefs.

Teasing a fingertip at the corner of my mouth, I walked to the chair and turned it to face the window, then settled into it, relaxing and crossing my legs. The silk robe innocently slid open, revealing legs to my bare crotch, the fabric catching on my hard nipples. A tilt of my shoulders would set it free, exposing me completely to him.

I settled deeper into the chair, my shoulders sliding back. The robe slid open more. I lowered my head, smiling wickedly at him.

"Let the games begin."

He tossed the notebook on his bed and stepped up to the window, pressing both palms to the glass as he studied me sitting in repose. A wanton queen upon her throne. The entire day had coiled me into a lustful, covetous web of agonizing need. I closed my eyes and brushed my hands against my cheeks, over my temples, and through my hair, luxuriating in the feel of the soft strands. The smell of vanilla lingered on my skin and in the steamy air.

When I opened my eyes, he was rubbing a hand over his erection. It looked so thick beneath the clingy briefs that emphasized the ridge on the underside and the plum-like head of it.

I turned in the chair, twisting at the waist, but kept my legs crossed. Catching my chin in a palm, I twirled my free hand, indicating that he should drop trou.

His gaze swept streetward. As nervous about being seen as I had initially been? Silly man. Don't think like that. We were alone, even in a city of millions; highlighted by the glow from our bedside lights, exquisitely framed by our third floor windows, yet safely sheltered from prying eyes by the positioning of the buildings.

His briefs got caught on the head of his cock, and he had to use both hands to pull them down. As he did, he swept one hand over his erection, and used the other to tug them off and toss them aside. He looked to me, tilting his hips forward to display his mighty sword. It bobbed heavily. I imagined it bobbing against my mouth; the salty, musky scent of him becoming embedded in my skin, my eyelashes, my hair.

I licked my lips and nodded. I bet he smelled like spice cologne. I wanted him to. I wanted to nuzzle my face against his cock and smell the rich tones of mingled spice and man. I squeezed my thighs together, mining a twinge of orgasmic promise. I was noticeably wetter than when I'd gotten out of the tub.

Taking his cock in hand, he slid his curled fingers up and down, not establishing a rhythm or going too quickly. He was displaying the goods, letting me take him in. The tension in his ab muscles visibly increased, and he winced and closed his eyes briefly. Already feeling it.

I wondered if a man's orgasm felt like a woman's did? How to ever know? The best of my orgasms were brain bursting, mind shattering, scream-from-my-gut amazing. Men came strong and hard, but so quickly. They collapsed after, and...end of party.

Inhaling through my nose, I leaned forward, my breasts falling upon the padded chair arm. Absently, I swept a hand across my breast and thumbed the nipple. He nodded. *Yes, do that more.*

Sitting boldly upright, I uncrossed my legs and pressed them knee to knee, cupping both breasts as I did. The intensity of his gaze felt more intimate than quiet sex with a lover in the dark. In the dark, I was safe from roaming, judgmental eyes. Here, he saw everything, yet I was emboldened to permit his gaze to take in all that it wished to see.

So inspirited, in fact, that I spread my legs brazenly. The air cooled the insides of my thighs, but only for a moment. Wet and hot, my pussy hummed with anticipation. Each finger tweak of my nipples activated the want in my core and ignited that signal between my legs.

Mmm, I should have been wearing the shoes. Hell, why wasn't I wearing the shoes?

Wait. Don't think like that. I was moving out of the moment. The shoes bedamned. (Sorry, shoes.) I'd wear them some other time.

Back lengthened, and legs propped wide, I pinched both nipples. The pleasure shock sensation stirred up a moan. I wanted him to hear me, and then I was glad he could not. Voice felt too intimate just now.

He stroked his cock faster, and without missing a beat he scooted along the side of the bed to the nightstand. He pulled a small blue bottle from the drawer and drizzled clear lube onto the head of his cock. It looked like sweet liquid sugar spilling onto a rich dessert, and again I licked my lips to show him my appreciation and want.

"I'd lick it for you," I whispered. I wished he could understand me, but I wasn't in the mood for dictation right now.

He slicked his hand over and off the bold column that jut up hard against his belly. It stood up straight, not an angle or kink to it. Proud as its master. And in reward, it was squeezed, slicked, and vigorously rubbed.

Men tended to get brutal when they jacked off. I suppose the main stick had been designed for some rough handling? I began to question my delicate touch whenever I got cock in hand. Perhaps something more firm next time? I'd make a note of it.

His free hand slapped the window and he bent forward, completely focused on the fast drill, skin against lubed skin. Slick, slick, slick. Faster, harder...

I wanted to catch up. I hadn't even begun to explore the folds and dark sweet spots in my pussy. He wouldn't get himself off before me, would he? And if he exploded, then the party was over. At least, that's how it worked with the guys who had been in my bed. Thanks for the thrills, sweetie, now let me go to sleep.

Tonight, this one would not roll over.

I had no control over that.

And yet, perhaps I did.

I waggled an admonishing finger at him, then glided my other hand down from my breast and over my stomach. That got his attention. He didn't stop jacking off, but he did slow his pace measurably. He reached down to squeeze his balls. Closing his eyes, his tight jaw pulsed.

The hairs on my body prickled at the sensation of the light strokes across my belly. Self-love was something I practiced often enough that I knew how my body responded to specific touches. Such intimate knowledge then allowed me to direct my lovers toward the best touch needed to get me off. Therefore, I knew the gentle effleurage was better at increasing my heartbeats and the zinging, swirling want in my core, than, say, a firmer, more intense touch. At least to begin with.

It was all about the anticipation.

Gliding my fingers downward, they skimmed through the trimmed thatch. I closed my eyes, guiding a forefinger between my slick folds. So freaking wet. I spread my legs wider, and eased the finger firmly against my apex. My clit responded. Oh, that touch was nice. 'Bout time you decided to play with me. So I slicked across it again, delicately, not too firm.

Nodding, because the touch was just right, not too hard and not too soft, I remembered that I had an audience. I flashed my eyes open to find him staring at me. His hand did not move on his cock. He looked...mesmerized. And he wasn't focused on my crotch, but rather my face.

I dipped my head into a shy smile because he surprised me with that intense regard.

Then I shook my head, surrendering to a little laugh. My finger had not stopped the soft, teasing strokes. I squeezed a nipple, intensifying the stirrings of release. Tilting my hips forward, I spread my legs wider. I don't think I'd ever sat quite like this when I'd jilled off before. I had to scoot forward to the edge of the chair so my fingers wouldn't jam into the seat with each downstroke.

Monsieur Sexy had switched up his moves. His cock sprang free against his stomach while he pinched his nipple. Pointing to me, he then pinched his fingers before him and dashed his tongue between them.

I arched back my shoulders, feeling his tongue on my nipples, hot and wet. I bent a leg and pressed the heel of my foot on the chair, which moved me forward a bit. Catching my hand against the glass, I quickened my strokes, slicking into my folds to juice up, and then swiped back across my swollen clit. My core swirled. My loins hummed. My hips wanted to rock quickly, but I couldn't in this position. It was a different feeling though, and I liked it.

He flicked his tongue over the top of his little finger, and the sight of it released a moan from deep in my throat. I imagined his tongue at my breast. Taking my hand from the window, I glided the fingers over my tongue, then slicked them over my nipple. Yes!

Feeling the wobbly, loosening stir of orgasm focus between my legs, I increased pace of my strokes and made them firmer. Yes, so close. And he jacked off quickly now, his eyes no longer on me, but unfocused immediately before him. Concentrating, probably as close to orgasm as I was.

His shoulders shuddered. Ab muscles tightened, unreal in their sweaty, glistening appeal. He was so strong, so powerful. His jaw clenched, and suddenly, he opened his mouth and—I switched my gaze lower. He spilled over his hand and a splash of creamy ejaculation spotted the window. Still gripping his cock, he pressed his forehead to the glass.

The sight of his orgasm pushed me over the edge. I pressed my legs together, and my rapid strokes lured up the explosion that shimmered through my thighs, hips, and torso. My hips bucked forward and I cried out a short, blissful sound. "Yes."

Bowing my head and falling back into the chair, I panted through the delicious reward of my efforts. And then I laughed softly. My limbs were loose. I brushed a hand across my face to cover it as the laughter subsided. I dropped my arm along the side of the chair and lay there, spent and blissed out.

Tilting my head, I saw Monsieur Sexy grab the notebook off the bed. He slammed it against the window and I reread the words:
Exquisite. Bold. Gorgeous.

I blew him a kiss and wished him a good night.

He saluted me, and then wandered off into the recesses of his bedroom where it connected to the bathroom. I didn't need to see him. I would close my eyes and dream about him all night.

Seven

I caught him dancing about his bedroom, a towel hugging his sculpted hips and water droplets sprinkling the muscles that flexed his back. Fencing equipment lay scattered across the end of the bed. I'd seen flashes of the blade in his living room earlier as I'd noshed on creamy risotto in front of the TV.

There must be music playing in his room because he shifted his hips side to side. Now I saw his lips moving. He was singing. And he wasn't aware that I was watching from my nest on the chair with book in hand.

He sorted through some books and files stacked on the night table next to the bed. He read before going to sleep; just like me. Tucking a file under his arm, he then scooted around the bed, performing a twirl that I'd be impressed to see on any dance floor. His abs flexed beautifully.

I sighed. Fencing had honed that man's physique. I wondered if he practiced any other sports? I wasn't in to sports, but I may have to search the channels for a fencing match one of these days.

I performed a little wave, but he didn't notice. He dance-stepped all the way to the door, gripped the doorknob—then paused. Twisting a look over his shoulder as if remembering to look across the street, he saw me, and smiled.

Whew.

Stepping up to the window he beamed at me and waved. Then he tapped his ears and pointed to the dresser, where I assumed he must have a stereo.

I snapped my fingers and grooved my shoulders in my best Beyonce impersonation—she had nothing to fear from me—then pointed to him.

He offered a sheepish shrug.

"Very sexy," I mouthed, knowing he wouldn't understand, but it didn't matter. I twirled my fingers in a circle.

He did another spin, ending in what was probably his best effort at a Michael Jackson sort of bent head, hand to the back of his skull pose. Stick with the fencing, I thought. I was thrilled to have seen that unguarded moment from him, though. Monsieur Sexy had some groove in those hips. And he didn't take himself too seriously.

Nice.

Reaching for the notebook he now kept on or near his bed—it was nestled under the discarded fencing jacket—he quickly wrote something, then pressed it flat to the window.

"Online business meeting with Tokyo," I read. "Ten minutes. Sorry."

Offering a consoling shrug, he dropped the notebook onto the bed. Turning back to the door, he again paused with the doorknob in hand. Setting the files on the bed, he then tugged off the towel, splayed his arms, and allowed me a look at the high and mighty erection.

If that was all I'd get from him tonight, I could live with it. Every seven or eight inches of it. Springy and hard, even doing a few dance moves of its own as he turned to the side to give me that view.

I gave him a thumbs up and blew him a kiss. He caught the kiss, smashed it against his heart, then grabbed the towel and the files. Two seconds later the bedroom light blinked out.

Online business meeting? I wondered if the people on the Tokyo end would be aware they were communicating with a man in a towel? And an exquisite erection beneath it.

Sighing, I picked up my book and plopped onto the bed. With hope, I'd get to the steamy parts tonight.

ÅÅÅ

It started to sprinkle outside while I was in the supermarket, loading my basket with fruits and whole grains. I was making a concerted effort at eating healthy. I'd already reduced my sugar consumption considerably, but grains didn't cut it all the time. Which is precisely why I'd nestled the package of dark chocolate beneath the box of barley.

I perused the wine selection, which was quite good, considering that it was sold in a grocery store. On the other hand, I was in France, and wine in a grocery store was akin to milk in the American grocery stores—*de rigueur*. I was in the mood for a sweet, peachy moscato. I'd broil another goat cheese tonight, and hide the barley at the back of the cupboard. I figured I scored points in the health column merely for the purchase.

That's my story and I'm sticking to it.

The male cashier was cute in a geeky sort of way, with green-rimmed glasses and a flip of blonde hair over one eye. He sat behind the register with bored disinterest, running my dozen items over the beeping scanner. He probably didn't notice how I stood taller, or that I'd combed my hair into a chignon this morning because it had emphasized my cheekbones. Or maybe he did and didn't care. Or he was gay.

That had to be it, because I was looking damn good today—if I did say so myself. Attribute it all to great fantasies about my sexy neighbor.

I slashed my credit card and stuffed the items into the bag I always carried with me.

Swerving to avoid the grasping, chocolate-coated hands of a toddler sitting in a cart, I approached the automatic double doors, but paused before I could activate the motion sensor embedded in the rubber pad.

Outside, standing before the store, speaking with another man gesturing as if giving directions, was...him. My window lover. The man with the steel cock, and the charming smile that started in his eyes before his mouth caught on and joined in on the fun.

My heart rocketed to my throat, then dive-bombed. I actually felt it land in my stomach and splash; the feeling was that visceral.

What to do? I didn't want to see him. Well I did. But—no. We'd agreed to the rules. No names, and walk away if we ever see one another in public.

I turned my back to the door, my eyes running over the store window littered with painted sales lingo. I stood before the only door. It served as both entrance and exit. Those who entered were corralled to the right to queue down the aisles of frozen foods. Those leaving filed out from the left.

If I walked out now, I'd have to pass by him, and I didn't think I could slip past without him noticing me.

I managed a sneaky look over my shoulder as I stood there, hoping others would assume that I was waiting for someone still in the store. He was fully dressed (I had yet to see him completely clothed, unless you count fencing gear) in slouchy gray jeans and a loose tee-shirt. Black tennis shoes graced his feet. Hmm... Didn't seem like his style. He gestured down the street, and the man he spoke to nodded. The glint of a gold watch on his wrist caught my eye.

He turned suddenly, heading toward the door.

Ack! I rushed away from the door, and past the cashier who'd checked me out earlier. He gave me a quirk of a brow, even as he slashed the next customer's lettuce across the scanner. Spying a stack of flyers, I bent and drew a finger over a picture of fluorescent oranges, while managing to sneak a look under my arm.

Black tennis shoes stepped on to the rubber matting. He stood there...

Just stood there. What was he doing? Looking at me? No, he couldn't recognize me from this angle—well, he had seen me bent over, my bare ass toward the window—but I wore a knee-length skirt now.

"Please," I murmured, picking up the flyer and turning my back to the door.

"Ah!" I heard him exclaim. The doors slid open and he strode back outside.

I made it to the glass doors before they even slid open. Impatiently, I waited for the sensors to react to my presence, and slipped through as soon as I could when they did. I turned the corner without thinking. Oh hell, this was the same direction he had walked. And he stood right there. Closing a car door that was parked at the curb, he turned and began walking straight for me, swinging a recyclable bag in one hand as he inspected his watch. He'd forgotten his bag.

And—wait.

"That's not him," I said on a gasp.

The stranger nodded to me. I must have looked like a fool just standing there checking him out. He was tall, with brown curly hair, but—nope, not my window lover.

Feeling a flush climb my neck and checks, I turned and jog-walked the other way. It was opposite the direction of my apartment, but I'd be damned if I was going to walk toward that complete stranger.

Releasing a huge breath, I paused before the window of a sweet shop three storefronts down. Eyeing the lush, matte-black boxes of pastel gumdrops in the window display, I ever so cautiously cast a look out of the corner of my eye. The sidewalk before the supermarket was void of people. Tennis Shoe Man had gone inside.

Pressing my forehead to the glass, I closed my eyes. "I let my imagination get the better of me again."

What would I have done if it actually had been him? I couldn't run away from him forever. I liked what we had started. It was new and adventurous and fun. And it was safe.

Safety felt right to me for now, though I'm not sure why. It wasn't as if I'd had a bad experience with a man. Breakups happened all the time. So did awkward marriage proposals. I didn't despise dating either. Not short term, anyway.

There was just something about Monsieur Sexy and his willingness to accept what we were doing as it was. He was a mystery to me, and the mystery was what attracted me to him. He was forbidden fruit, yet different. No one had told me not to touch; I simply could not touch. Therefore, I had to find new, more inventive ways to show him my pleasure, and hopefully, give him pleasure in return.

Noticing the snooty gaze of a bespectacled sales clerk from inside the sweet shop, I stepped back from the window. I decided to cross the street and walk another block over before turning in the direction of my apartment. Crisis averted. I had some window shopping to do. It would help me walk off my nerves.

A line queued outside Louboutin like usual. I wandered by, smiling smugly. I'd already claimed my extravagant prize. I overheard whispers from those in line that they were running low on a certain model of shoe. Oh, the harrowing travails of the Parisian woman and her quest for pleasure!

A fine leathers shop was located about six blocks away from my neighborhood. I always slowed when nearing its turquoise door and understated window display. The items inside were handmade; tooled lovingly, I assumed, by the elderly owner who always flashed a warm smile for those passing by the store window.

I stopped to take in the window display that featured some gorgeous, leather-covered notebooks. They were similar to the simple, moleskin notebooks I often saw in bookstores, yet were more elegant and lush. Smelling like rich leather, I imagined, and substantial to hold in hand. A simple bee, with wings spread, was tooled on the lower right corner of a creamy golden journal. A crushed-violets cover bore the iconic fleur-de-lis.

I wasn't much of a note taker or record keeper in my personal life, though it was probably because my job consisted of compiling notes for others. Something about that gold notebook called to me though. The bee was impressed within the leather, an imprint of something having once been there. Like a man's thumbprint upon a woman's thigh, or the slightest curve of a tooth left against the skin. I had a thing for bees. Once they left the planet, we humans would be hopeless regarding maintaining sustainable food supplies.

Save the bees!

I looked up, expecting to see the old proprietor standing there with his warm smile. Instead, I followed a dark gray business suit sleeve up, and saw a tall man talking with another. My heart gave a whoop. The tall man was *him*.

And then my heart shivered. The anxiety that I'd suffered at the grocery store returned, but much subtler this time because I'd been through this once already. It could be another case of mistaken identity.

What was it about manifesting that which you most desired in everything you saw?

"Seriously? Is it really him?"

Yes. I knew him well through glass. Even dressed in a suit.

I marveled at the suit, and thought through all the possible reasons that he, a man whom I had guessed worked from home, would be out in the city wearing said suit. And here we stood, closer than close. The risk of him walking out the shop door and right into me was great.

I felt confidant that should he turn toward the door, I could sneak around to the narrow alleyway not ten steps away.

It was a weird coincidence, us both being here at this particular time on this particular day. But then I reminded myself that there are no coincidences in life. Everything happens for a reason.

I believed in fate and destiny. That's why I didn't dash off. The universe had put us in close proximity for a reason. I had to stick around and see what developed. But I kept the alley in peripheral view.

He held up a leather-wrapped pen and was explaining something to the old store owner. Were they discussing the quality craftsmanship?

Monsieur Sexy seemed like a man who would appreciate fine tailored goods. Black tennis shoes. No way. Bespoke suits? Yes, please.

I could let those fantasies wander for days. I'd once read a meme online—likely at Pinterest—that went something like: as lingerie is to a man, a well-tailored suit is to a woman.

Meowr. Nummy.

Distracted by my thoughts, I wasn't even sure when he had turned to look out the window. Directly at me. His eyes widened in surprise, and then softened. His familiar smile lessened my skyrocketing anxiety, but not my thudding heart. I managed that silly little wave I did when I greeted him naked from my bedroom window. I was fully clothed now. So why did I feel more exposed than I ever had before?

Probably because he'd caught me staring at him unawares. Would he dash outside and speak to me? Demand to know why I was spying on him? I hadn't been, but he couldn't know that. He might think that I had followed him here.

What he did next set my heart to a crazy flutter.

He pressed his palm against the window, above the pretty hand-tooled notebooks. Right there, but a foot from my face. I'd never stood in such close proximity to him before. It freaked me out. My skin grew clammy, and then in the next second, flushed warm. Being this close to him unsettled me, and made me want to dash for cover. Yet my feet remained planted.

I lifted my hand and placed it against the pane, matching my fingers to his. The glass was cold, but I swear it heated so quickly it was as if we stood palm to palm. An intimate moment stolen amidst the mundane, while the ordinary world moved around us as voyeurs to our touch.

It was a touch. Our first.

I parted my lips to speak, feeling as if I should say something. Then words felt wrong, too intrusive. Just he and I, our eyes locked in a comfortable stare. A close gaze that read me like a book. His eyes were gray, but a bluish, end-of-day-sky gray. I owned a tee shirt that color. Faded and so comfy. I wanted to climb into those eyes, snuggle up and never leave. He'd welcome me in; I knew that he would.

The old man reappeared, and without removing his hand from the glass, my guy turned and said something to him. *My guy*. He must be making a purchase. He turned back to me, lifted a brow, and waited.

I felt as if he might stand there all day, his hand pressed against the window. I could, too. The world could fall away and we would remain, holding up the glass that wasn't so much a barrier to us, as it was an entry into our souls. But surely someone on the street would question sooner or later and ruin our moment.

Reluctantly, I took my hand away, then kissed it and blew him the regretful farewell. He caught it against his heart. The twinkle in his sky-gray eyes was there before his lips registered the smile.

I was undone. I wasn't sure my feet could move me away from such a sight, but I knew for certain that they would not walk me across the store's threshold. Nor would he come out. We had our rules.

The touch had been enough.

Smiling to myself, I turned and almost stumbled as I took that first step off the curb. Somehow I landed my other foot quickly enough, but I could still feel the mis-step in my heart. I knew some part of me wanted to turn back, to look over my shoulder.

I shook my head and walked onward.

I wanted to keep memories of our touch fresh and alive. I pressed the hand I'd held to the glass over my mouth. My lips were soft against my warm fingers, and a smile pushed up my cheeks.

My heart sang.

Eight

Sitting up in bed, I stretched my arms over my head, and winced at the bright sunlight. It was too early. Seven a.m. according to the alarm clock, but I couldn't sleep. I'd forgotten to close the curtains after spending the evening reading, while waiting for Monsieur Sexy to show in the window.

He had not. He must have had an entire evening of errands, or perhaps a visit to a friend's house that had kept him out late? Or maybe he had a business meeting given the way he'd been dressed? I didn't want to over think where he'd been. That way lie Crazytown.

I was due in at the map shop by nine-thirty, so I dragged myself upright and slid off the bed, expertly landing my feet in pink fuzzy slippers. I'd slipped on the soft blue-gray tee shirt after arriving home last night. The color of his eyes. Mm... I tugged it up and buried my face in the softness. A smile was irrepressible.

Leaning forward, I stretched out my arms, which tugged at my back muscles. The bed was comfy, but sometimes I slept on my stomach and that screwed up my body's natural alignment.

Glancing out the window, I noticed that his curtains were open. The way the sun avoided his window for mine allowed me to see well into his room, even without lights. He lay on the bed, his arms splayed, eyes closed. White sheets were strewn haphazardly across his legs. And...

"Wow." I pressed my nose to the window to get a better look at the upright action across the way. "Now that's some impressive morning wood."

Feeling not even a little guilty for observing his secret hard-on while he slept, I observed the natural phenomenon, teeth sucking in the corner of my lip. Men were supposed to have erections all through the night, but mornings were their peak 'wood' time. Or so I'd probably read in some woman's magazine. Who ordered a study like that? And could I volunteer to be a watcher throughout the night?

I wondered if he always slept naked? He usually walked around in his boxer briefs. I guess I hadn't paid attention to see if he put them back on after our window jack n' jill session.

Did it matter? Not in the least.

His penis jutted up proudly, tilted toward his stomach as the weight of it pulled it down. Oh, mercy, the weight of it. I could imagine taking it in hand, wrapping my fingers around it. The girth looked...substantial. I might not be able to touch fingertip to fingertip. I preferred a nice thick cock. Girth was far more important than length. I loved to feel the tug and pull of it sliding in and out of me, to sense that it was almost too thick to enter. Not that he was slacking in the length department at all. Far from it.

Curling my fingers against my chest, I sighed. "I'd like to grab hold of that and not let go. What you would feel like inside me, Monsieur Sexy."

I sighed again, because that's all I could do.

Well, I could jill off. My nipples were hard, and my pussy probably wouldn't need more than a few strokes to get wet. But it felt squicky to take advantage of him that way; to exploit his lacking awareness while he slept.

I blew his cock a kiss, then tiptoed to the shower. Now, far from the eyes of a man who may wake and grip his hard-on, I directed the shower stream upward and landed it between my legs. The massage mode thumped water against my folds and awakened all the important nerve endings. I hummed deep in my throat and tilted my head forward, catching my free hand against the slick tile.

Putting one foot on the edge of the tub, I focused the water on my clit. Pulse. Shudder. Pulse. Fingers curled against the tiles. It didn't take long to come. And when I did, I gripped the showerhead with my free hand and cried out.

Someday I would grip his cock instead of a bathroom appliance.

Richard beckoned me into the back room before I could flip the *Ouvert* sign on the front door to announce that we were open. I'd forgotten about the map. I'd printed the pictures from my phone, but then hadn't given them a second glance.

The old map still lay proudly displayed on the drafting table. Mint tea brewed nearby.

"Any ideas yet?" he asked eagerly.

"Nothing's come to mind, though I intend to search the internet for the symbol tonight."

I'd simply been too busy to think about dusty old maps. Especially with a sexy, naked man—with no compunctions whatsoever about flashing me—right across the street. Directing me to do naughty things. And joining in. And oh, that pretty morning wood.

My chest heated and I fanned myself. Summoning an excuse felt necessary. "A little warm in here this morning. You should call the air conditioning company, Richard. Customers will linger longer if it's cool in the store."

"I don't need lingerers who have no intention of buying and simply want to hang out in the cool air until they head off to the next tourist stand hawking cheap scarves and plastic key rings."

I shoved a hand in my skirt pocket, fondling the fob attached to my front door key. It wasn't plastic but it did read *I ♥ Paris*. I'd bought it at the shop two doors down.

"Besides, it's actually rather cool. You feeling okay?"

"Uh, yes," I offered. "Must be this warm sweater."

"Come closer." Richard beckoned to the map. "Take it in again."

I wasn't sure what I'd see this time, but I wasn't one to disappoint an old man. Though Richard wasn't that old. In fact, he couldn't be more than forty-five. While that was almost twice my age, he looked good. If it weren't for the futsy sweaters, wrinkled khakis, and leather loafers that were his uniform, I'd call him seasoned.

"Close your eyes," he suggested. When I balked, he added, "Use all of your senses. It's the only way to truly discover. Draw in the scent of the paper and the ink."

I guess it wouldn't hurt to humor him. I closed my eyes and leaned over the map, briefly imagining the man catching a good look at my ass. That sent another flush to my chest, so I averted my attention back to the paper. And...it did have a scent.

"Old," I confirmed. "Musty. Maybe...damp? And a little salty."

"Very good. Now feel the paper. Run your finger along the edges carefully and remember how I've taught you to respect the paper."

I carefully drew my forefinger down the serrated edge, expecting it to be soft and smooth like the deckled edges on the innards of a hardcover book, but instead it was brittle. I lightened my touch.

"Taste it," he encouraged.

Closing my eyes and leaning way over I stuck out my tongue—

"Oh, dear no!" He grabbed me back from the map by an arm. "I was kidding about that one. I don't want you licking my prized map. But you take directions well, eh?"

I flushed at that comment. I didn't think he'd meant it to sound sexual, but...

"Now!" He clapped his hands together. "More details to add to your quest for the map's creator, eh?"

"Yes. I sometimes forget how much the senses work in tandem."

"Oh, yes indeed. You can't simply stare at a thing and expect to truly learn anything about it."

Like staring through glass at a naked man? I'd learned a lot about Monsieur Sexy. He preferred body-hugging underwear, though apparently he didn't sleep in them. He could be playful and liked to dance when he thought no one was looking. He was proud of his body, but didn't seem narcissistic. And his eyes could devastate a woman's wanting heart.

"You need to incorporate all the senses," Richard continued, oblivious to my straying thoughts. "Immerse yourself in the subject. Make a sense memory of the piece."

"Sense memories." I nodded, liking the term. "I'll forever associate this particular map with mint tea."

"Not a terrible association by any means. Ah, there are customers peering through the glass. Go invite them in, will you?"

I turned absently, and wandered out to the front of the tiny shop to twist the bolt lock on the door. Two tourists entered, calling out the requisite *bonjour* and I offered to help them with anything they were looking for. They were just browsing. As usual. I left them to meander through the stacks of maps laid on cardboard and sealed in plastic, as well as the various assorted prints from old books on history, anatomy, and even flora and fauna.

Closing the front door, I pressed my hand to the glass above the vinyl stick-on letters detailing the shop's hours of operation. The surface was cold and flat. Not at all like a man's body; warm, curved, taut and muscled, and...

How could I know everything I wanted to know about him when I'd only been using the one sense?

ÅÅÅ

I didn't step out of the shower until after eleven that night. I'd stayed late at the store to help Richard go over the month's accounts, which he still organized on a paper ledger despite my frequent suggestions that he invest in a program like Quicken. I wasn't sure the man had even touched a computer. He didn't own a cell phone, or *mobile*, as the Europeans called it. He did all of his calculations longhand on paper; without a calculator. It was as if the man had stepped from a classic BBC television series.

Padding into the kitchen in a bra, panties, and robe—I was oddly chilled for some reason—I poured a glass of moscato. I'd had a glass with supper, which had been a prosciutto and mozzarella panini I'd picked up from a deli on the way home. Savoring the sweet, peachy bubbles of the sparkling wine, I wondered if I had any dark chocolate left in my stash.

The drawer beside the fridge did not offer up any hidden chocolate bounty. Not even behind the scatter of batteries that I never needed. Until I did need one, and then they were all expired. Time to restock. (The chocolate. Screw the batteries.)

I wondered where Monsieur Sexy bought his chocolate? Did he stop in for groceries after work? Where did he work? That suit he'd worn the other day had been an *I have to impress someone* suit. He seemed to always be at home, so I'd just assumed that he worked from home. He'd had the online meeting with Tokyo. I suppose he could have had a meeting in person the day we'd pressed hands to the glass. Hmm...

Wandering into the bedroom, I flicked on the light. The curtains were drawn. I'd open them, but first things first. I sat on the bed, and slid my feet into the Louboutins and tied the ribbons. Luxury, you are mine. Another sip of moscato, and I felt decadent in the lacy bra and panties.

I wasn't planning on sleeping for a while.

Goblet in hand, I drew aside one sheer to find him lying on the bed, a thick computer textbook in hand. Glasses were perched on his nose, and he was wearing the gray boxer briefs. Those were my favorites because the light fabric emphasized the outline of his penis. It appeared that the briefs were his 'lounging around the house' wear. I hoped the winter wouldn't bring on the sweatpants.

Would we still be playing the singular sensory game then? It would qualify as a long-term relationship if we were. It would also be plain weird if we were still just window fucking in winter.

He noticed me then and waved, setting the book aside and placing his folded glasses on top of the cover.

Tapping my lower lip with a finger, I wondered how tonight should go down. The mutual masturbation session was a sure bet, but how could I mix things up?

I eyed the chair. I'd left the book splayed open. Romance heroes always knew exactly how to please their women, which tended to bother me. I mean, really? Women are all so different. There's not a standard. No 'one method pleases all' that men can utilize. Each woman is unique, and must be discovered and learned.

I suppose that was the hero's draw. That he was capable of knowing exactly what the heroine needed from the get-go.

But how did the heroine continue to keep his interest? Because I was pretty sure long flowing locks and a relentless giggle would get tiring after a while. Even if the sex was great.

My eyes fell upon the iPod docked in the speakerbase on the nightstand. Striding to the bed, my walk sashaying me slowly before the window, I bent forward to play with the MP3 player. I knew he couldn't see the nightstand from his position, but he could see my ass and legs, so I gave it a wiggle as I selected a playlist.

Stretching back my arm to display the iPod to him, I peeked around the curtain and pointed to the tiny red music box.

He crossed his arms and nodded. It was my turn to dance for him.

I love heavy metal bands, classic 80s hair bands, and even Taylor Swift mixed in every so often. I can lose an afternoon listening to Paganini's playful concertos. I usually listened to French soundtracks while baking. Didn't understand a single word, but still—the French accents! Country music? Not so much.

I scrolled up to KD Lang's rendition of "Hallelujah" and pushed play. I found the song sensual and disturbingly sexy. Setting the iPod into the speakerbase, the music murmured out into the room. I trailed my fingers over the curtain as I walked by it and before the exposed window. Slipping the robe from my shoulders, I let it glide down my arms, and with a graceful flick, sent it wavering to the chair.

Closing my eyes, I swept my hands over my temples and through my hair, taking the music into my body and moving my hips side to side to the beat. Slow, resonant, abiding. This evening I was incorporating sound into our sensory-deprived liaison. The only way I knew how.

The singer's voice enticed me away from the mundane of my bedroom and onto a stage that glowed softly with the flicker of a thousand candle flames. The fire warmed my skin and I smiled because the fantasy felt so real.

And then I felt the crescendo of the music rise in my body, and I abruptly turned to press my palms to the window, smiling wickedly at the man across the way.

Attention captured, he'd assumed his usual position, elbow bent and palm to his head, leaning against the window. He watched my every move.

I bent forward, jutting back my hips, hands still to the glass. Licking my lips seemed an appropriately seductive move, even though it felt kind of silly. The French called window shopping *faire du lèche-vitrines*, which literally meant, to lick the window.

Realizing that he didn't have a good view of my wiggling derriere, I turned to the side and bent forward, gliding my hands down one leg to the black ties caressing my ankle. Thank you, yoga. I could stretch and bend with ease. I think it enhanced my libido as well. That's my story, and I did like to make up stories.

Ass in the air, I glanced to the side to ensure my audience was rapt. He was. And the bulge in his briefs had stood up to take notice as well. Good boy.

Gliding my hands back up my leg, I noted how smooth my skin felt against my fingers. Ah, yet another sense: touch. His skin would feel like warm suede, like a long afternoon spent toasting under the bold sun. His penis? Like soft hand-warmed leather wrapped about a solid sword hilt.

While my hips matched the beat of the music, I tucked my forefingers inside my panties and shimmied them to mid-thigh. I was mooning the man in the window and it felt...liberating. A bit anxious.

But more so? Surprisingly sexy. Dragging my fingers up my thigh, I dipped them into my pussy. Hot and wet. Juicy for him.

Peeking around my legs, I blew him an air kiss, then dropped trou, kicking off the panties. This time, as I glided upward, I trailed my fingers along the inside of my thighs, and when I reached my warm apex, I waggled my fingers so he could see them, before bolding sticking two deep into my tingling, moist depths. A gasp huffed from my mouth.

I'd stopped dancing and stood there, slightly bent forward, my fingers exploring my moistness and a delicious hum trilling in my throat. Glancing the fingers of my other hand out to hold on to—something, anything—they streaked across the window.

Oh yeah. I could get off like this. Just fingering myself, my side facing the window, knowing that he watched, but not needing to see that eager attention.

The song segued to another ballad, a sensual tune I didn't recognize because my focus veered inward. The velvet chair beckoned before me, and I put a foot up on it. That opened my pussy. I stroked my fingers over my clit, slicking it until it felt like a wet pebble beneath shallow waters. Balancing with one hand to the window, I worked at the pleasure point, tilting back my head and—

I'd forgotten I was performing.

Fingers unwilling to stop their quest to bring on the bliss, I deftly cast a glance over my shoulder. His body was pressed to the glass, all but his face. Palms formed blurred skin-colored impressions on the window. His chest made another impression, except it was ridged in a darker skin shade where the muscles banded about his frame. Gray briefs over that thick rod, he rubbed against the window. I couldn't be sure he was even aware of the slight, hip-rocking motion.

I winked at him and turned my focus inward again. Eye contact wasn't important right now. I was giving him myself. Allowing him access to my private world. Could he hear and feel me as I did?

To stand there and pleasure myself so blatantly felt more intimate than a kiss could be. Because the curtain had been pulled aside, literally, to reveal me. All of me began to shiver in anticipation of the orgasm that swirled in my belly and sparkled in my pussy.

I couldn't stand on one leg anymore, so I turned and settled onto the edge of the chair. Legs spread and fingers moving of their own volition, I tilted back my head and thrust up my breasts, still caged within the lacy bra. I imagined how I looked from the side, hard nipples poking up the lace, shoulder and arm working vigorously. Legs shuddering, knees wanting to move close together to capture the orgasm, but instinctively staying apart because to draw out the big bang would only make it bigger, better, raging.

My free hand clutched at the chair arm. I whispered, "Yes," and then louder, "Yes!"

Tectonic plates shifted as I came. All the stage candles blinked out. I stopped rubbing and buried my fingers between my swollen labia, pressing firmly against my clit to direct all sensation there, as if a magnet drawing in filings ignited with pleasure.

Crying out loudly, I ended the long moan with a lingering, wilting sigh and then another *yes*, and another, and once more.

I laughed. Softly. My chest bounced up and down to the rhythm of the gleeful sound. In the background, Bon Jovi crooned about 'being there for me'.

Squeezing my thighs together, I felt my fingers there and imagined them a cock, relaxing against my mons after the big event. Hot and slick, and belonging to him.

Across the alley, his hand was tucked down the front of his boxers but not moving. Just holding, then. Reassuring? I didn't know, and didn't care. I was blissed out. He could jack off if he wanted to.

Instead, he stared at me, his gaze soft, his mouth slightly parted. It felt like an admiring look. I stretched out a leg, stabbing the carpet with a spike heel, and basked in that admiration.

Kissing my palm, I blew him that morsel. He caught it, then tucked it down the front of his briefs. Sneaky man.

Oh, yes, some serious *like* vibes lasered back and forth between the two of us. They were what occurred before that other L-word, of which, it was far too soon to even think about.

"Sweet dreams," I said, and pulled my legs to my chest, curling up in the chair facing him.

He stood there for the longest time, just looking at me. I returned the admiration. I don't think I'd ever before looked into a man's eyes for so long. Sky-gray. Soft and gentle, yet lusty and wanting. I'd given him a part of myself tonight, and he'd accepted it.

Nine

The stack of research books toppled from the end of my bed where I lay sprawled on my stomach. I tended to move from my desk to my bedroom for a change of scenery during the day. I lunged to catch the timeworn hardcovers, but gave up halfway, and instead sprawled carelessly across the end of my bed, arms and boobs dangling over the side. I laughed, but the position made it tough.

With my top half angling toward the floor I decided to do an ungraceful slide off the bed, palms walking the floor—

Movement out of the corner of my eye paused me in a plank position. Across the street he moved about in his bedroom. It was early evening, but I didn't have the light on, so he couldn't see my bed gymnastics. Thank God. The setting sun always beamed on my window, which must grant him a glare from his view, but I could usually see into his room during that golden hour of natural light.

And what I saw, instead of Monsieur Sexy, landed me on my face, my legs tumbling off the bed behind me. Ouch. I didn't take time to mourn the rug burn. Instead, I curled to a sit, grasping a book and holding it before the lower half of my face. (Because, you know, disguise.)

A woman strolled ever so casually about his bedroom, stripping away her clothes! She flipped long, gorgeous red hair over a shoulder, and shrugged off a padded fencing vest, letting it fall to the floor. Beneath, she wore a sleeveless gray tank, which she pulled off to reveal—no bra, and huge breasts.

"What the—?"

I crawled toward the window, using the pulled curtain on the left side as my camouflage. I didn't want her to see me watching, but she was oblivious, wandering before the end of his bed, flashing the whole world her breasts. They were huge, and she cupped them possessively and smiled.

I turned my back to the window. Crazy thoughts assaulted my brain. His lover? Well, she must be. Who else wandered around in his bedroom half naked?

She'd been wearing fencing gear. Maybe they went a few rounds and then— No. He wasn't in the room with her, helping her to undress. Wouldn't a lover do that?

Maybe she was a student? He didn't teach. Hell, I didn't have a clue about what he did, except that whatever it was, it seemed to keep him around home most of the day. I didn't want to look like a Peeping Jane. I never observed his living room antics. At least, not for too long.

Seriously. I know, my logic is fucked.

I peered around the curtain again and caught Boobs pulling a tee shirt over her head. It fit tightly and she cupped her breasts again and smiled. Yeah, honey, they're nice, but....

But, I had nothing. Her double Ds trumped my demure almost-C cups any day.

Now the pants went down and I forced myself to look away because *no panties*. When would he come into the room? Was he in the shower? I pressed the back of my head to the curtain and glass. Damn it. How long had they been lovers? Was I a side order on the nights he didn't see her? But he was around most nights. Did they have a day-time fling? Was this Awkward Marriage Proposal Guy all over again?

It wasn't like we really had any sort of relationship. Me and Monsieur Sexy were window buddies. We got off while the other watched. There were no feelings, emotions, or partnership contracts involved. I had no say over whom he saw. Or what, for that matter.

Ugg. She could stop a crash with those boobs.

As much as I'd like to think that he and I were exclusive, it was silly to expect so much from a man with whom I'd never even held a conversation.

All right. Chill. I have to accept this. I wasn't sure what to do with this new knowledge, but I wasn't going to freak over it. I didn't do the commitment thing anyway, and I was perfectly happy with that.

And yet, I'd seen her for a reason. No coincidences in this universe. None, whatsoever.

I turned and peeked around the curtain. She was no longer in the room. Out to the main living area to seduce her lover and let him undress her? Why the undressing? She could have sauntered out naked. Planted herself on his lap and spilled her long red hair over his face as he kissed her...

But I wanted him to kiss me. To feel his mouth on mine, tendering slow, passionate kisses. And then devouring harder, deeper. Driving inside me, taking from me and giving, too. It had been a while since I'd been properly kissed. A woman couldn't do that for herself.

I realized that I cupped my breasts, and flung my hands to the floor in disgust. No, not disgust, disappointment. He had a lover. And I had been a fool not to expect as much. The man was handsome times ten. He was a Frenchman, which—in my fantasies—implied he would have lovers. Many of them. A woman here, a woman there. A woman across the street in the window.

A woman wishing she could erase what she had just seen.

Standing, I eyed the books scattered at the base of the bed. I'd had enough with Henri VIII tonight. There was another man who couldn't keep it in his pants. The Tudor king had taken a multitude of women, and had found despicable ways to dispose of them when he'd grown bored of their affairs. Was Monsieur Sexy an asshole after all?

I sighed and shook my head. Not quite willing to label him so harshly, but cut to the core at this stunning revelation.

Again, movement caught my eye. I didn't want to see that obnoxious red hair or those bouncing breasts.

I backed toward the window and thought I'd be able to pull the curtain closed without turning around.

"Just do it. You know you want to."

Compelled to look, my heart fluttered this time. He wandered into the bedroom, his eyes tracking the floor. He saw me and his smile grew to that easy natural curve I'd come to expect from him. He waved. Putting up one finger—wait a second—he then searched the bed, under the pillow and turned aside the comforter. His eyes wandered the floor, and then he dove, snagging something from under the bed.

He straightened, dangling a pair of pink panties. Waggling them toward me, he shrugged, then left the room.

I tugged the curtains closed.

"Asshole."

AAA

Work flew by like a wounded vulture bobbling over a barren landscape. It was only two when I'd looked at the clock on my computer's control bar—for about the fourteenth time. After four hours of my eyes tracking page after page, I couldn't get in to online research anymore. It was a beautiful fall day. The sun was high. I'd spent the morning listing the various forms of marble used for sculptures in the fifteenth century.

Stone was boring. I needed...I needed...a respite.

Sitting upright, an idea for a field trip blinked above my head. I'd head to the Louvre for closeup inspection of the marble works. That would prove much easier on the eyeballs than screen strain. And afterward, a leisurely walk in the Tuileries would serve me the sunshine I craved. Strolling down the alleys of carved trees, the rocks crunching beneath our feet...

I sighed and caught my chin in palm. I'd made the mental slip of including another, nameless someone in my fantasy. Yet if I knew his name right now, I'd probably scribble it on a piece of paper, burn it, and offer the ashes to some demigod in exchange for singeing off his pubic hairs the next time his redhead went down on him.

Chuckling at my devious thoughts, I closed the laptop and reached for my purse. A lightweight purple scarf for around my neck—*de rigueur* when in Paris—and a small notebook to jot notes while at the museum. Skipping down to the lobby, I waved to the doorman and headed out toward the Seine. I avoided looking in windows as my rapid stroll moved me south. Was it because I didn't want to see the truth?

Or was I worrying too much? Creating scenarios that couldn't possibly be true. I'd worked with fiction writers so much my mind was beginning to spin and concoct fantasies just as theirs did. Always thinking. Thinking far too much.

He'd flashed the panties at me as if a pink banner he'd wanted me to salute. What man would do that unless he meant to send a message?

I beelined it toward the right bank and the Louvre. "Just a couple hours," I promised my reluctant work self. "And then escape."

Wandering from the Richelieu wing, where the majority of the marble statues were displayed, I made way back toward the Denon wing, planning one quick stop before my escape into the park. Once there, I'd do the tourist thing and buy a Nutella and banana crepe from a food stand, and not care that it had more calories than an entire week's allotment.

And I wouldn't give him another thought.

The museum was packed to the gills with tourists. All scattering about like ants seeking crumbs, none clear on their direction. I tuned out the bustle and managed to walk relatively unscathed through the thickly populated hallways.

It was difficult not thinking about someone who existed in a section of my brain designed to always bring him to the fore. Like a filing cabinet that, when opened, had one pesky file always popping up. No matter how many times I tried to stuff it back down, or fold back the corner, it kept popping up and would sometimes jam the drawer so it wouldn't close completely.

My brain was not completely closed. He'd jammed a corner into the drawer. I kept seeing him standing before the window, his palms pressed flat, his body with the impossible abs and ridged muscles. Hand on cock, he drew my admiration. Our eyes holding one another's. His were sky-gray. Had he noticed that mine were blue?

I wondered if I had jammed his drawer? Did he think about me while doing mundane things? Jabbing a fencing foil into defensive poses? Concentrating on business?

Or was he fucking the redhead right now?

He was usually home. Which meant that he must go to her place for an afternoon liaison when I was working and not paying attention to the comings and goings across the street. And why the hell had she been fencing with him? She didn't look the type to be interested in the sport. Not that I knew what type that was, just...she wasn't it. She was too top-heavy. How did she keep the proper balance required for perfect footwork and form?

I had no idea what fencing form was, or if big boobs helped or hindered the sport. Certainly though, she must require a special vest with a larger bust.

Big Red fenced because it was how she'd snagged him. I was sure of it. Now that she'd caught him, she'd slowly wean him off the fencing by offering more sex. And he, being a lusty Frenchman whose cock never seemed to be lax, would take anything she offered.

I caught my face in my palms and growled. "Stop doing this to yourself!"

I turned down a crowded hallway and forced myself to walk into the room that displayed the most popular painting here at the Louvre. The *Mona Lisa*. The crowd before the small portrait had to be thirty people deep, so I stepped to the left and stood before *The Wedding Feast at Cana*, my back to the curious bustle of gawkers.

I'd never had a tendency for choosing the wrong men. The bad men. My dating history had been filled with normal, polite, reasonable men. Yes, even Awkward Marriage Proposal Guy had been nice (when he'd not been eating out other women).

Ugg. Normal, polite, and reasonable. Didn't that sound sexy?

My eyes strayed around the massive wedding feast that had been painted in the sixteenth century by Paolo Veronese. The largest painting in the Louvre, I could lose time looking over the crowds of people on canvas. I bet the painter had been polite and reasonable.

Argh!

Who was I? Why couldn't I be more like Melanie, jet-setting the world with a man in every port? Seducing with a red-lipsticked pout. I wasn't ugly. I could do pretty when I broke out the blush and mascara. I could have any man I set my sight on. Not that I needed a man. Men were nice accessories. But I simply needed to know that I had the power to captivate.

I needed to know that I could flip my hair over my shoulder, like the redhead had, and win my prize.

I'd been festering over this too long. I hadn't gone back to the window last night. And I had no intention of opening the curtains tonight. It was over. I couldn't do this with a man who—

With a man who what? A man with whom I hadn't spoken a single word? A man whose name I didn't even know? A man who had never agreed to window fuck me exclusively. A man, whom I had so much to learn about.

And I wanted to keep learning. I just...needed a breather. Yeah, that was it. A day or two to get the pink panties out of my mental file folder. I didn't care that his file kept jamming my drawer. I just wanted it to be because of his papers, and none of them pink.

It was clearly time for Nutella and bananas.

I turned, preparing to leave the room, when an aisle opened amongst the mass of people and I got a great view of the Mona Lisa. She smiled that knowing smirk at me. Winked even. She'd have window sex with a man first chance she got. She'd probably had sex with Leonardo da Vinci—

"Leonardo da Vinci," I breathed.

My heartbeats started to bust a move. I began to pant. I couldn't believe it. Could it be?

The symbol from Richard's map. I'd seen it somewhere in my research. I'd compiled a few pages on Leonardo da Vinci last year for an author who had been writing a travel exposé on Milan, Italy. It had been a fascinating mental tour into fifteenth century Italy and the painter's life. Except he hadn't been simply a painter, but also a sculptor, designer, engineer, and...he'd made lots of sketches. Including a folio of knotwork designs.

I rushed out of the room and headed for the exit doors. I didn't care about the crepe anymore, or the sunshine. I had to find that book.

Ten

The next morning I raced into the map shop. "Richard?"

"Tea's on," he called from the back room. He startled when I rushed into the tiny room, elation panting my breaths. Teacup in hand, his bright eyes waited my revelation.

"How did you know?" I asked. "And do you really believe the map was drawn by Leonardo da Vinci?"

A grin curled into his eyes. And I noticed for the first time the sweater he wore daily matched his pale blue irises. I wanted to hug him, but that would be pressing it. He was more of a handshake kind of guy.

"I was at the Louvre yesterday afternoon," I said, as I set my purse in the old locker designated for employee items. "And I think Mona Lisa told me the answer to your riddle."

"*La Joconde* can be sneaky like that. An epiphany, eh?"

"I did some research on Leonardo for an author last year. I recalled seeing the symbol, so I dug out my notes. Sure enough, it matched. Leonardo was into knotwork because of the pun on his surname. *Vinco* translates as *osiers*. Osiers is roundabout related to wicker, and the knotwork involved with that. He had a period in the early 1500s where he sketched some folios featuring interlaced knotwork. But really? If this map is an original—do you know how valuable it would be?"

"Priceless." Richard leaned over the map. "I've put a call in to a private authenticator out of London. He verifies the historical significance and origins of lost artworks. He said without clear provenance that he'd need the map for at least a year. I told him I couldn't part with it for so long."

"Richard. But if it's real? How will you ever know? Why does he need it for so long?"

He shrugged. "Who knows? To take little pieces of it and test the age and ink and all that? They use radiocarbon dating on the paper.

He also mentioned he'd have to send it to Switzerland for that. I know it's real." He tapped his chest proudly. "Isn't that all that matters?"

"Well." Sure, if he wanted to hang the thing on his wall and be done with it. But the map could be worth millions. Or we could both be wrong, and it could be a copy done by one of Leonardo's students, or even a clever forgery.

"What would you do?" he posited.

"I'd have it tested."

"And then sell it if it was genuine?"

"Perhaps. Maybe not. I don't know. The maps you sell in the store are gorgeous, and they have so many tales to tell. Since taking the job here, I've begun collecting maps, but only those of Paris."

"Milan wouldn't be of interest to you."

"No, but a Leonardo da Vinci..." I sighed and crossed my arms, joining Richard's side as we stared at the possible masterpiece. "He did draw maps. There's a picture of one he made of southern Tuscany in the book I have at home. How could this have gotten lost and then suddenly resurfaced? Where did you get it, Richard?"

"From an old Scottish family. They'd inherited their great-grandfather's castle in Peterhead, and set to cleaning it to the bare walls so they could fix it up and sell it. They found the rolled map in a storage room filled with dusty old prints and newspapers. They hadn't any idea what they owned."

"But you did?"

He shrugged. "I wasn't sure. I thought I recognized the symbol, but I'm no expert on Leonardo da Vinci. I've been doing my own research though. Paid two thousand euros for this."

"Wow. That's a steal. If it's real."

"Indeed."

Out front someone knocked on the window. I checked my wristwatch. Five minutes after opening time. "I'll get that. And I'll spend the day considering ways to convince you to have it authenticated," I called as I walked into the front of the shop.

"You can certainly try!"

I'd walked home in the light rain, forgoing the Métro because the air smelled electric and fresh. I loved skipping through the rain, and by the time I got home, I had to wrap my hair in a towel to leech out the wet. I slipped on my robe, sans wet underthings.

The stereo had been playing Def Leppard since supper. I'd enjoyed a savory leek and carrot soup that I'd made at the end of winter and had frozen in a few ziplock bags to serve later. I could do the Martha Stewart thing when I wanted to. But my domestic bone was rarely eager for exercise so I employed it with caution.

Sipping a deep red wine, I strolled through the kitchen, putting away the silverware that had air-dried in the sink, and the single bowl and glass I'd used for supper.

Def Leppard's lead crooner asked me over and over, 'Have you ever needed someone so bad?'

I nodded. "Why yes. How did you know?"

It had been two days since I'd opened the bedroom curtains. Surely Monsieur Sexy had gotten over my absence and was now firmly ensconced in a happy, touch-filled relationship with the buxom redhead. Including sex.

Pressing my forehead to the fridge, I thudded it gently against the stainless steel. I know. I'd tried to stop angsting over this, and had been doing well until I glanced toward the living room window. Seriously, could I avoid windows for the rest of my life?

I was being silly. And really? I could handle this. I am a grown woman. I'd had a fun fling. I would move on. First item on tomorrow morning's list? Shop for window blinds. Maybe something in black?

I didn't necessarily want to move on, though. Which is why I strode into the bedroom and over to the window. It was around nine in the evening and I could see the glow of his bedroom light through the sheers. I just...had to look at him one last time. To stare into his eyes and...know.

I pulled aside the curtain and stood there, drawing in a breath through my nose. Setting the wine glass on the night stand, I pressed my palms to the window and closed my eyes, concentrating on the coolness of glass marrying to skin. Even though it had hit the eighties today—unusual for Paris in autumn—the glass still felt cool. How quickly the shadows erased the muggy heat.

I wished they could erase what I had seen across the street two days earlier.

Opening my eyes, I observed. He sat on the bed, legs extended and back against a folded pillow, reading another computer textbook. The laptop sat open near his thigh. Those black, thick-rimmed glasses were so sexy. The man must do some kind of computer geek work. The appeal of a smart man ranked alongside chocolate and Louboutins.

I sighed.

When he finally noticed me, he jumped off the bed. Putting up both palms in a 'wait' gesture, he dashed to the nightstand for the notebook.

I sucked in another inhale, preparing myself. This was it. The big kiss-off.

Glasses tossed aside, he slammed the notebook to the glass. I didn't fuck her.

Or maybe it wasn't a kiss-off. He waited for me to meet his gaze, and so, I did. He shook his head fervently.

He flipped the page. Words had already been written. She's a student. I teach fencing part-time.

My shoulders relaxed. Heat coiled in my belly. For a moment I'd suspected he was a teacher. And then I'd started to think. Too much. Why had I let that first intuition slip away and become less important than imagining the worst, like him fucking her?

Crazy flirt, was the next message. He tapped his chest and shook his head. Not interested in her.

I chewed the corner of my lip. I'd moped for two days, only to find out that I'd let my imagination carry me away again. So foolish.

He flipped another page. Apparently he'd written this in preparation for when he might next see me. Had he waited both nights for me to show at the window?

I am an idiot.

I'm interested in you, I mouthed the next message.

I nodded and pointed from me to him to indicate agreement.

He flipped another page. We have something…

Page flip. Fun.

Flip. Intriguing.

A little odd.

Crazysexy.

He flipped another page. Amazing.

I caught my palms against the glass again. My eyes strained to fight tears. Heartbeats thundered. I didn't know what to say. It didn't matter what I said; he wouldn't hear it. A teardrop spilled down my cheek. I tasted salt at the corner of my mouth.

He turned the page, and this time picked up the sharpie and wrote. I swallowed, and swiped away another tear while his attention was on the paper.

I'm sorry.

I shook my head side to side. "No, I'm sorry."

I dashed to the nightstand to grab my notebook and wrote swiftly, then turned it to him to read, No reason 4 U to B sorry. I was foolish.

He shrugged sheepishly. Writing, he then turned it to reveal: Panties.

"Well, yes," I said.

He paged back. Crazy flirt. Then he underlined the word crazy.

I nodded, and let a smile overtake me. It gushed a wave of relief through my body that loosened my tightened neck muscles and spit out a few more tears. I'd almost lost him in my worried file drawer. But his corner was still bent.

He wrote again. This time I hesitantly took a step back after reading what he'd written: Will we ever go beyond the glass?

Yes, I immediately thought.

And then I vacillated, bouncing between all the problems that face-to-face could bring. We'd have to talk to one another and maybe I wouldn't like the sound of his voice. Or worse, maybe I wouldn't like *him* up close. He might smell wrong. Or his voice could be grating. Or maybe he'd be boring. Hell, what if he was married?

No. Don't go there. I hadn't seen a wife. Wasn't so easy to hide a wife, either. He was not married.

Up close, I could learn so much about him. Surely he had nasty habits and quirks, and— Oh, stop it!

Obviously I was a great pessimistic imaginer, and could create problems that didn't exist. Look what had happened because I'd allowed my imagination to construct an affair?

He wanted to know if we could move to a level most normal people hit on their first date.

I rubbed a palm up and down my arm. The room was not cold, humid, in fact. I shrugged.

He nodded, and wrote. 2 soon. I'm good with slow.

He was? That felt incredible to know. And it also felt binding. Like we were sealing some kind of deal between the two of us. I know, I'd just convinced myself that I didn't need a relationship. But what we had was a new definition of relationship. And I wanted to see where it would go. Slowly, and then, eventually—perhaps even soon—I'd feel comfortable with that next step up to normal.

I picked up the notebook and wrote. I pressed the paper against the glass. So you teach?

He nodded. Made a motion of *en guarde*, stabbing his opponent with an invisible sword. Then he held up three fingers. I assumed to mean three days a week.

Oh, my musketeer. How I adored him.

He grabbed the book from the bed and held that to the glass. I had no idea what PHP meant, only that it was some kind of computer stuff.

He wrote on the paper: Day job. Work online. Consulting.

In but a few words and gestures I'd learned so much about him. Things I had mostly guessed at, but now they'd been confirmed. A step across the threshold. A kind of welcome into his life. A semi-commitment.

He pointed to me and said, "You?"

We were upping the stakes. Moving beyond anonymity by doling out personal information. I teetered on the edge of slamming the curtains shut, and wanting to rush outside, run across the street and up the stairs to knock on his door.

Slow, I reminded. I felt as if I could trust him. And he had offered a genuine apology for a silly misunderstanding that I had blown way out of proportion. More and more, the serious like I had for him was settling into my pores and fixing in my bones.

I nodded, and wrote on the paper: Research assistant.

Then I quickly wrote: Enough chatter.

He lifted a questioning brow.

I tossed aside the notebook and let the silk robe slink from my arms to puddle about my bare feet.

His grin was the loudest yes I'd heard in days.

ÅÅÅ

Monsieur Sexy sat on the bed, naked, his cock in hand. If I thought about it too much—and you know I like to think—men liked to handle the main stick. Must give them comfort. And a hard-on.

He gestured that I sit in the chair, and I was happy to oblige, but once seated, I felt as if we'd done this one before. I needed to mix things up. Couldn't have this window relationship grow stale. I mean, wasn't variety the key to a healthy relationship?

I was not going to analyze whether or not I should have used the word healthy in that last sentence. It was what was working at this moment, and that was perfectly fine with me. And him.

Tapping my bottom lip, I made show of looking upward while I gave the notion of variety some thought. I wasn't much of an actress, so I wondered how he always understood my gestures and actions. Maybe I had a stage career ahead of me, after all.

A relationship built entirely on mutual masturbation had to be based on the fundamentals. How did I please myself when alone?

"Ah ha!" I put up a finger for him to be patient, while I dashed to my dresser and pulled open the top drawer.

Inside were silk panties, cotton boyfriend-short panties that sat low on my hips, bras, a garter belt that I'd tried on once and had decided I wasn't the type for, and pull-up stockings. And...

"The silver surfer," I said, drawing out the stainless steel vibrator that was waterproof as well as having three different speeds. The nickname was mine; I couldn't recall the original product name. I loved the coolness of it when it first came out of the drawer, but the slick surface always warmed quickly when in my hands.

Sashaying back to the window, I sat down and tapped the vibrator against my pursed lips.

He hissed a resounding, "Yes," and leaned forward, putting his elbows on his knees, now completely negligent of his erection. Though I was sure he wouldn't forget about it entirely. I mean, the thing was huge, and so hard and springy between his legs. How to ignore something like that? It put my silver surfer to shame.

I wondered what it would be like to have a penis. The principle means to pleasure dangling there, outside my body, constantly rubbing against clothing, reacting as if it had a mind of its own—and perhaps it did.

I think if I had a penis I might never take my hands off the thing. I mean, how easy to get off by simply reaching down and stroking the magic genie? It had to be much less complex than operating the clitoris, the finicky little button that, when I thought I was close to coming, would suddenly recede and attempt to hide away from my efforts. So fickle, my clit.

But a penis. Now that could take some wickedly good punishment, and still, it begged for more and more.

Of course, I'd have to give it a name. What did he call his? And the decision of whether or not to dress to the left or right? How novel would that be? Today I'll go left. Or *was* it a choice? Did most men's penises simply choose one way over the other? I realized this was an important detail I must research. That, along with possible penis names.

I caught his wondering look and started to laugh. Always cracking myself up. So easily entertained. I sighed, and leaned back in the chair, hooking my heels on the ends of the seat so my knees were bent. I sat slightly at an angle to the window so I wasn't splayed open as if an anatomy lesson for him, but close enough to give him something to desire.

Warming the steel rod by rolling it between my palms, I winked at him. He'd found his cock again, his wrist rocking rhythmically. Good boy.

Knowing that a sexy man was watching my every move super-charged my libido. When normally it took me a while to warm up, to get into the mood of things, now I grew wet the moment I laid eyes on the man. Now that was a valuable skill. Able to make a woman's pussy drip with a single look. I wondered if a cape came with that?

Another giggle. I tapped the vibrator against my nipple. Clicking the speed to the lowest setting, which was a deep, rumbly kind of cement-rotator speed, I arched my back and tilted up my breasts, seeking the titillating motion.

Looking aside, I ensured he was transfixed.

I squeezed my other nipple with my free hand, and the shock of sensation jolted in my pussy. I needed motion down there. I slid the vibrator down and gently rolled it through my lips, not resting on my clit, but sliding the vibrations over it in a tease that made me squiggle.

I lowered the leg closest to the window. I needed him to see me. Because while I'd always valued the privacy I took when masturbating, to share it with someone I knew doubled the pleasure. I'd never whipped out the silver surfer in front of a man before. Once again, I granted him access to something secret.

Gliding the tip of the steel rod to my opening, I slicked it with my juices, and dragged it along my clit. I clicked the speed to medium, which offered a lighter yet faster vibration. I pressed the rod hard against my mons, my pelvic bone drawing in the vibrations and distributing it throughout my core. I bit my lip and squeezed my nipple hard. Eyes closed, I focused on directing the sensations, on working each part of me to a precise harmonization. It was a delicate performance that required skill, a knowing of oneself.

I've always thought a man could never learn how to please a woman unless the woman first knew exactly how to please herself. For who would teach the man the path to that pleasure? Did women expect the man to step into our lives with a map of our pleasure spots in hand and the skill already mastered?

That's not how it worked. Believe me, I've been with men who thought they knew the directions, and who instead had gotten woefully lost. Men who then had decided to simply pump inside me, thrusting harder and harder, because most men thought we women got off on the pumping, the thrusting in and out with their erection.

That worked swell on occasion, but not the majority of times. We required finessing. And for me, I knew that involved attention to my clit, and only occasional entry.

I glided the shaft up and down, as if a penis rubbing against me, but not entering me. The strokes started high at my clitoris and slid down to my perineum. Slick, long, quick. Slick, long, quick. And then a focused pressure against my swollen clit.

I moaned. My chest expanded, warming as it opened. Orgasm approached. I could feel it in the expectant sensation that hummed within my core, that indefinable spot behind my pubis. I didn't know its exact position because the humming was intangible, but sure.

Another squeeze of my nipple heightened the intensity. "Fuck yes," I whispered.

I glanced to the side. He stood transfixed, his cock untouched yet high and mighty against his stomach. God, it was so beautiful. I wanted to slick that heavy rod against my folds, and press it hard against my clit. I needed to squeeze my thighs about it and hold it tightly, rubbing him off while the head of it poked and pushed greedily against my clitoris.

Mmm... I aimed the head of the vibrator against my apex, imagining it was him, poking me, prodding, melding his heat into mine.

"Fuck." I snapped my knees together, and bucked my hips, riding the steel column. Were I with him right now, I'd be pulling him down on top of me, forcefully, begging him to drag his cock through my folds.

The shuddery march of climax peaked at my clit and I immediately drew the vibrator away and clicked it off, hanging that hand over the side of the chair. I pressed my other hand over my swollen bud, hard, securing the delicious orgasm for as long as possible as it quivered through my bones and made me shout, "Yes!"

I dropped the vibrator and slid that hand gently over a breast, cupping it, holding it, wanting to connect with softness, the round swell of my skin. Breathing out, I rode the last waves of orgasm with a moan that fell into a silly smile.

Turning my head to him I found not a man vigorously jacking off, but instead, a man with a tender look on his face, as if adoring me.

I smirked and couldn't summon the energy to smile or raise a hand. Lax and exhausted from the delicious muscle-stretching bone-shaking orgasm, I was content to sprawl there on the chair, letting him experience my bliss.

He kissed his fingers and pressed them to the window. I pressed two fingers to my window.

"I want to touch you," I said, knowing he wouldn't understand.

He shrugged, confirming my guess.

I coiled my fingers and made a jack-off motion.

He shook his head, dismissing the need to pleasure himself. He'd had enough just watching me? Sweet.

Eleven

I'd spent the entire day researching Versailles for an author in the States. Field trip! I'd been there only once before, and much as I'd dreaded going when the tourist mob would be unbearable, I'd taken an early train out, and only had to stand in line half an hour for entrance. The author had needed the most research on the Petite Trianon so I'd rented a golf cart and scooted out to explore.

Such luck that an Angelina was actually tucked back near my destination! The chocolate high had fortified me enough to forge through the afternoon taking notes and pictures. I'd organize it all, and hand it in to the author within the next few days.

After a shower to rinse off the dust from the day, I strolled into the bedroom naked and slipped into my Louboutins. I seriously had to go out in these pretties one of these days. A fancy restaurant or maybe an art showing. But I wasn't much for solo date-night. I wondered if Monsieur Sexy liked to go out and do the fancy? To walk into an art gallery on that man's arm, wearing my shoes? A fantasy come true.

Strolling to the window to check on the neighborhood sex god, I found him walking into the bedroom, cupcake in hand. He peeled the paper away from one side, and noticed me.

I waved, then posed, hands on hips, one hip tilted out. Those cupcakes had nothing on my breasts. And he knew it. The cupcake fell to his side, and he forgot all about sweet treats as his eyes took me in from head to toe, then to my pussy, where he lingered. Finally he managed a leap to my breasts, where I could feel the heat of his want, and that tingled my nipples to tight ruches.

"Wow," he mouthed.

He'd seen enough of me lately that my naked body shouldn't surprise him, so I was gleefully thrilled that he reacted in such a manner. Though I had to admit, that cupcake looked damn good.

I pointed to it.

He'd forgotten about it, and lifted it to display. When tilted frosting side toward the window, I recognized the playful fondant flower design and the tiny *Bon Anniversaire* on it. It was from the patisserie down the street. It was the cupcake you could get free on your birthday. Just had to flash your driver's license or identity card.

"Your birthday?" I asked. Duh.

He nodded. He started to put up fingers, three on one hand then—he shook his head and decided against that. But I assumed he must be at least thirty. Three or four years older than me? Nice. I was so over younger men and their hurry to come so I can show you how awesome I am when I spurt all over act. Ugg.

Peeling back the paper, he made a slow show of it, a sort of cupcake strip tease to entice me. Bad man. Didn't he know that besides shoes, I would commit grave crimes for chocolate? And I had it on good authority the chocolate cupcakes from that particular bakery were dense and moist. The buttercream frosting was so fresh it probably mooed. To. Die. For.

It would have been amazing to celebrate his birthday with him. To sit across the table from him in a quiet restaurant (wearing the shoes!) and share a celebratory round of "Happy Birthday", then light a candle on his cupcake. And for a gift...

I wanted to give him something. He must be celebrating by himself. No friends to gather together? No date? Was he such a solitary man?

I grabbed the notebook and wrote, then turned the paper toward the window. No celebration with friends?

He nodded. "On my way," I read his lips perfectly. He pointed to me. "Wish you could be there."

I shrugged. Then I remembered something that could be construed as a gift. I put up a finger for him to wait for me, then dashed into the bathroom. Hell, after last night's exhibition session with the vibrator I'm pretty sure I couldn't find my inhibitions if I tried. Oh, you vixen!

I'd saved the silly door prize I'd won last year at a bridal shower. Didn't think I'd actually ever use it, but it had been pretty and... In the linen closet, I reached behind a stack of towels, sorting blindly past the cotton balls and stack of lemon thyme soap that I picked up at Le Bon Marché.

Plastic crinkled, and I drew out the garish pink box.

"Stripper pasties." I shook the box and the mylar tassels gleamed. "Why not?"

I peeled the cardboard backing from the plastic front and handled the pretty bits of pink vinyl and tassel. I had no clue how to operate these puppies, or how to attach them. No instructions on the back of the box.

I didn't want to keep the birthday boy waiting, but these were the only gift I had. And I wanted him to have something to think about while he was out celebrating with friends later. He'd invited me along, but had he expected me to accept? I sensed he was more eager to rush this relationship to the next level than I was.

Because what was the next level? Meeting? Shaking hands? Kissing? Finally hearing one another's voices? Going out on that date while wearing the shoes? It's what normal couples did. But we weren't normal. We were...beyond the ordinary.

And besides, who got to define normal? Maybe this was normal for us.

Upon further study, I discovered the backs of the pasties were sticky. I peeled off the thin plastic sheet protecting the sticky tape and then stuck it over my hard nipple. It took some molding, and I suspected this probably worked better with a soft nipple, but what could I do? These pointy things of mine were always ready for action.

I put on the other and jiggled my breasts, testing the movement of the tassels. I'd need lessons to make them spin. Glancing in the mirror and thrusting back a shoulder I gave myself a seven for success because one of the pasties was only slightly higher than the other. I tilted down a shoulder, which lifted a breast. Now they were even.

And I was the Hunchback Stripper.

Laughing, I sauntered back to the window and displayed my twirly attire to the birthday boy.

He paused mid-bite, a few cupcake crumbs falling down his bare chest. I jiggled my breasts, attempting to operate the tassels, and then decided a shimmy worked best. Didn't rotate the tassels but it did flip them into a sparkly dance. And then I realized I was trying too hard, my arms out yet hands tensed into fists, and my back arched. Surely, I looked like the hunchback stripper trying to do the limbo.

Bursting into giggles, I shook my head and gestured that I'd given it my best shot. He laughed, too. I could but stand there, admiring the utter joy that filled his face and squinted his sky-gray eyes. So sexy. God, I wanted him in my arms. I wanted his kiss. I wanted to trace those faint crinkles at the corners of his eyes that always showed when he laughed.

I simply wanted to hear his laughter.

He set the half-eaten cupcake on the end of the bed and clapped. I think he even shouted, "Bravo!"

Holding out my imaginary skirt I performed a curtsey, then flicked the tassels teasingly. "Happy birthday! Or should I say, *Bon Anniversaire*!"

He placed a palm over his heart, accepting the gift. And then he pointed to me.

"Yes, me," I interpreted.

He spread his arms wide then brought them together before him in a big hug.

And I felt those strong, muscled arms banded about my back and his chest nuzzled up against mine. I sensed the heat of his breath tickle my cheek as he pressed his face aside mine. The scent of chocolate and frosting wavered around my nose.

Catching a palm against the window, I curled my fingers, as if to grab that hug, that immense gesture, and make it real.

"Happy birthday," I whispered again. "Hope it's a good one."

I signed off by saluting him, performing one last twirl of the pasties, and stepping away from the window. I could see him turn to retrieve his birthday cake. And as I moved against the wall, out of his sight, I tugged off the pasties and tossed them onto the bed.

Bending my knees I sank to the floor, hugged my arms across my chest and around my sides. I bowed my head against my forearms and squeezed my eyes shut.

I'm not sure why I sniffled through tears. What I had with the man in the window was enough.

Maybe.

Twelve

What was I doing?

I couldn't even celebrate with the guy for his birthday. That was not a healthy relationship. Women took their men out for a birthday dinner or drink, or both. They didn't stand in the window teasing him with something he could never touch or taste, or hear.

Would he ever touch me? Would I allow it?

At times, I desperately wanted him standing before me, stroking his fingers across my skin, as if the glass had conformed to my body and he was silently speaking to me with his touch. To feel his hot breath whisper against my lips as he kissed me would send shivers up and down my body.

Other times it felt too safe what we had. And it shouldn't. I mean, he lived across the street. At any time, he could walk over and into my building, march up to the third floor and rap on my front door.

But he didn't.

Was something wrong with me?

Maybe something was wrong with him?

Last night had been the longest night of my life. I don't think I slept more than a few hours. I lay in bed with my eyes open, knowing that I'd see his bedroom light blink on when he returned home from celebrating with friends. That had not happened until well after three in the morning. The fact that I hadn't been out with the group implied that I was not a friend.

"Because I'm his lover. Right?"

Lovers tended to touch one another. To speak to one another.

I shouldn't feel so much angst over a man whose name was Monsieur Sexy.

"I'm tired. I'm over thinking this," I reasoned. "Stop thinking!"

Tossing my work blouse to the dirty clothes hamper, I unzipped my rayon pants and slipped them off into a puddle. They should be hung so they didn't wrinkle, but after a long day hunched over the laptop compiling the Versailles information and Photoshopping the pictures, I was wiped out.

Wandering over to the window, I peered out. It was still too light outside for him to turn on his lamp across the street.

In bra and panties, I sat against the iron support beam where the window fit into the frame and the wall ended, stretching my legs out before me and wiggling my slippers. I may dress for work, even at home—never knew when I might need to rush out for research—but I always wore my slippers, and these pink fluffed ones had seen better days.

Like me? Had I seen better days with real, tangible men who picked me up at the door for dates, took me out to entertain, then actually touched my body when they fucked me?

Leaning forward, I pressed my forehead to my knees. My hamstrings tweaked in revolt. I hadn't practiced yoga for weeks. Maybe that was it. I needed centering. A good yoga session to work out the physical and mental kinks.

I inhaled through my nose and let my shoulders relax, taking this moment to steal some personal tuneup time. When doing yoga one was supposed to clear their mind, think of nothing but the muscles moving within the body, and their breath. In and out. Allowing outside thoughts to interfere wasn't Zen.

I wondered if he ever practiced yoga? It would be a great accompaniment to his fencing.

There I go again. Letting my mind wander.

I chuffed out a laugh, and rose to my elbows, tilting my head aside to look out the window. A few raindrops spattered the glass. I loved the rain. Making love while it rained was the ultimate turn-on. A cool breeze whispering through the screen, a man's body above mine, his cock buried deep within me, and my eyes closed to take in the electric ozone scent wafting in from outside.

That was the only thing I did not like about this apartment. The only openable window was in the kitchen. No cool rain breezes in the bedroom. I guess a girl who could actually afford an apartment in Paris shouldn't complain too much.

I touched the cool glass, following a raindrop's downward meandering trail. It wasn't a downpour, just a few drops. The sun still shone on the horizon. I didn't think it would turn into umbrella weather. Unfortunate. I wanted to smell the rain tonight as I lay in bed.

And imagine him lying beside me, our hands entwined.

"What am I doing?"

Did I want to take it to the next level? To actually invite him into my bed? Yes!

I needed the man's touch.

Movement across the alley caught my eye. His bedroom light blinked on. I turned to catch his hello wave. He sat before the window, cross-legged, putting himself on my level. He shrugged and made a sad face.

"Yes, I'm...sad." I tilted my head, not wanting him to lip read that last word. Then I turned a forced smile back at him. He couldn't know the thoughts pinging back and forth inside my skull.

Or did he? Did he struggle with this weird connection as much as I did? Any sane man with half a heart would.

"Good party?" I asked, and made an elaborate finger walking show of going out, dancing, partying, hoping he'd get it.

He frowned, but then leaned over to grab the empty cupcake liner still sitting on the night stand. He held it up and nodded. "Very good." He pointed to me. Then placed a hand over his heart. "Missed you," is what I think he said.

I shrugged, and again, leaned forward, stretching my arms along my legs and turning my head to watch him through the rain spatters.

He retrieved the notebook and thumbed through some of the pages on which he'd already written. When he placed it before the glass, I re-read the words that had made my heart skip many a beat the first time I'd read them: Exquisite. Bold. Gorgeous.

It skipped another beat. He had a way of putting things, without even opening his mouth. He had more than half a heart, that was for sure.

It occurred to me, that I'd never replied to the compliment, so, stretching back an arm, I managed to slap the tips of my fingers on the corner of the notebook on my bedside table. It landed on the floor, and I had to stretch to reach it. I was kind of happy where I was, and yeah, a little lazy tonight.

Call it melancholy.

I wrote the first words that came to mind, and turned the notebook toward the glass in a spot where only a few raindrops dotted the window.

Fascinating. Kind. Sofuckingsexy.

He laughed, then shrugged, and splayed his palms upward, as if to say, eh, I try. Humble. And that laughter. If I ever did hear it, I was pretty sure it would undo me. Reduce me to a melty puddle on the floor before him. It might even be better than an orgasm.

It was probably a good thing we hadn't gotten together beyond the glass. I'd make a fool of myself for sure.

I wrote another line and showed him. Tired.

He pointed to his chest and nodded. Him too. Which meant, we were signing off for the night. And in proof, he blew me a kiss. I caught it, and smashed it against my chest, as he had done many times. I almost felt the second heartbeat, him thudding inside me. Such a sensory reward could only be mine if he lay above me, our bodies connected and not separated by glass.

Rising, he tugged off his shirt, and dropped it on the end of the bed as he walked away. He was headed into the shower. I could sit here and wait for the after-shower show, but the rain had picked up, despite my guesses it would not. Water blurred my view.

Perhaps that was for the best. I wasn't right with the world. Why was that?

I climbed into bed. It was only seven p.m. But I wasn't interested in anything on TV, or the half-finished book tossed on the easy chair. I tried not to think of his naked body under the shower, muscles pulsing with movement and his hard cock rising to dance in the pseudo-rain.

So to distract my thoughts, I repeated a mantra: exquisite, bold, gorgeous. And by the time I dozed off, I think I actually believed it.

ƛƛƛ

Richard had reached the waffling stage. Before leaving the shop for the evening, I peeked into the back room one last time and asked him again. "Will you send the map off for authentication?"

"You do test me at times, you know that?" But he smiled, and shrugged. "I'm at sixty percent now, teetering toward sending it off. You go home. Quit bothering me, eh?"

I told him I'd see him next week, hoping that the weekend would haunt him with a driving need to have definitive proof about the map. If it was an original Leonardo da Vinci—wow.

I hopped on the Métro and got off one stop early. I wanted to window shop. And I never missed a chance to catch some sun rays. I could have headed to the park at Les Invalides, but I wasn't in the mood for pushy tourists this evening.

I lingered over a window display of mod fashions in Tim Bargeot's shop. I wasn't keen on white vinyl knee boots, but I did like the slim-fitted mini dresses with the retro color blocking. A men's purple velvet suitcoat also caught my eye. I imagined Monsieur Sexy wearing it, me on his arm clad in the funky mini dress belted smartly with a string of wide gold hoops.

Ah—no. I didn't foresee him ever doing the velvet. Sleek tailored suits and Italian leather shoes all the way for him. He appreciated bespoke and would pay for it. Besides, I teased the idea that he had to have extra room sown in the front of his trousers to comfortably fit his penis.

Walking the sidewalk toward my building, I realized I hadn't worked on my personal list of penis names. Roger was so overused. Jean-Jacques, I suspected, was the common French nickname. The French slang for penis was *bite*, if I recalled some recent research. Wasn't sure how that was pronounced, though.

If I was a chick, who also had a penis, would I give it a female name or a male name? Oh, such wonders. I've always liked the name Chuck for reasons that baffled me. Me and my penis Chuck.

I giggled out loud, and was suddenly aware that I had to pass his building and cross the street to get to mine. Why hadn't I considered this earlier and swung wide, as usual, to detour around a few blocks? And now here I stood, at the corner of the block before his building, in the open for any man to see...

Waiting for the light to turn green, I grew aware that the man walking not thirty feet down the sidewalk had paused. I turned—and abruptly looked away.

"Fuck," I swore under my breath. "Really?"

The universe was going for its over-achievement badge working to get the two of us together. And since I didn't believe in coincidences...

He wasn't moving. I noted that much from the corner of my eye. This had to be the longest red light ever!

What should I do? Turn and wave, then dash across the street? I didn't know. All rational thought fled. I was stranded there, waiting rescue from a man I had never spoken to, but with whom I had shared some of my most intimate secrets.

I flashed him another look. This was the first time we'd seen one another without a sheet of glass between us. A glassless meeting. And it felt so intimate, much more intimate than the day I'd pressed my hand to his at the leather shop.

Heartbeats thudded against my ribs, pounding like an anxious child who wanted to be let out so she could run free. Fingers curled into my palms and they grew clammy. Never had I felt more exposed to him than right now. My skin folded back to reveal my crazy thinking innards. Alone on the corner, only a dash away from him. Desperately wanting to rush into his arms, but unsure how to turn and make that first step.

He stood boldly, arms at his sides, one slightly back, shoulders proud and broad like a warrior. The bespoke suit screamed sex and control. So fine.

My God, what kept my feet firmly planted?

Finally, with a nod, he put up a hand and backed away, offering that sexy smile honed with the ability to undo me.

I felt liquid, unsteady. How wrong was it to resist running up to him and jumping into his arms? To wrap my legs around his waist and kiss him deeply?

He gestured that he was going the other way. I nodded, offered a weak smile.

The light changed to the little green man. I stepped off the curb, then paused. I couldn't *not* look at him. It's what we did. Stare at one another from a distance. Speaking so much. His eyes expressed regret. I understood. He was some kind of gentleman to have not approached me, and that impressed the hell out of me.

A car horn honked, jarring me out of my staring session. Monsieur Sexy backed further away, and when he reached the end of the building, he turned down the narrow alley between buildings that hugged the wall of his bedroom. Perhaps there was a back entrance.

And I, seeing the car that had honked was waiting for me to cross on the now-red light, dashed across the street without looking back.

When I reached the opposite curb I felt as though I'd done something wrong. Passed up an opportunity that might never be offered to me again. Hell, I'd made a mistake.

I peered down the sidewalk opposite from me, and wondered if I should run after him.

I shook my head. No. Play by the rules. They were my rules. And I'd made them for a reason.

"And what reason was that?" I muttered as I walked onward.

The doorman held open the door. I thanked him and stepped inside. Avoiding the elevator, as usual, I trekked the three flights upward.

"Really, what *is* the reason?" I pressed as I hit the second flight of stairs. "Things have changed. The relationship has progressed."

Yes, it had. I could call it a relationship with confidence, and knew that he felt much the same. Sure, he may date other women. Though, after the pink panty incident, I had reason to believe he was not dating others. He'd been adamant in convincing me he was not.

I shouldn't expect him to see only me. Because that was the crux, wasn't it? He only *saw* me. It wasn't as though he'd ever heard my voice. He'd never felt my skin or my hair, the slide of my panties as he'd slip them down my thighs to my black leather Louboutins. He'd never tasted my mouth or smelled my perfume oil or even my subtle musk after a day spent slaving away over the keyboard.

As I had not heard, smelled, tasted, or touched him. I wanted to drag my fingers through his hair after he'd peeled off the fencing mask and tuck the wavy curls back over his ear. I wanted to touch my tongue to his skin, draw a trail downward to his stomach and then to his cock where I would lick it until he groaned and begged me to go faster, take him in deeper.

Gripping the doorknob, I inserted the key, and pushed open the door. Inside, I deposited my bag on the floor by the chaise, and marched immediately to the kitchen to pour some wine. I kicked off my shoes, and flicked on the music. A soft tune; Michael Bublé. The subtle melody gentled my thoughts from going over the edge, as they tended to do.

I wanted to touch him. I wanted to listen to him say whatever it is he thought I should hear. I wanted to know if he smelled like spices and musk, or maybe leather, or even fresh outdoors. I needed to know the taste of him on my tongue.

I wanted us palm to palm. With no glass in between.

I wanted him to not be so respectful of the 'rules', and to walk up to me, sweep me into his arms and kiss me deeply.

I tapped the goblet rim against my lower teeth. *Did* I want all that?

Sometimes I lied to myself. We all did it. It's how we made excuses for those extra pounds (I have heavy bones) or once again forgetting to take out the trash (I was too busy with work). I couldn't be expected to actually know how to navigate this crazy odd no-touch relationship without some floundering.

Wandering into the bedroom, I saw him there, dressed in the suit and looking ever-so-stylish...waiting. Waiting for me to make the first move?

I knew what it had to be.

Setting the goblet down, I wrote Thank you on the notepaper and held it before the window.

He nodded, seeming to understand exactly. He wrote something and then gestured with a finger between him and me. He turned the paper toward me.

"Trust," I read.

My God, I think I stumbled over serious like and into deeper, unsure territory. Another four-letter word that started with L teased my hard-crushing heart. He'd walked away from me on the street because we'd made a rule, and he'd wanted to respect that rule. The man was trustworthy. It was an immense gift.

I'd do my best to return the respect.

He scribbled another message and turned the notebook toward me.

Business trip to Berlin.Leave tomorrow morning.2 weeks.

Wait.

"What?" I blurted out. The world tilted. I spilled wine down the side of the goblet and my fingers.

That was...unacceptable. He couldn't leave me for two weeks. Didn't he realize I looked forward to our nightly window love? Didn't he understand that after promising me trust, this was some kind of slap in the face?

He wrote more. I realized I held the goblet so tightly I wouldn't be surprised if it broke. I set it on the night stand, licked my fingers clean, and waited with arms crossed over my chest as he wrote for some time.

Here it comes, I thought. The big kiss-off. I don't know why I expected that. I'd thought it coming after the Pink Panty Incident. It hadn't. A trip to Berlin did not require a man to break it off with his window lover. Unless he had another fling waiting in Germany.

The notebook read: I will miss you.

Oh, mercy. Was he for real? And would he ever know how insane my brain could get, zooming from zero to explosion in a matter of a few thoughts?

I pressed my palm to the window and said, "Me too."

More writing. Big question to ask.

I nodded. If he invited me along I'd say no. Naturally. That would rocket the no-touch status to full-out touch too quickly. I was only prepared for another street corner meeting right now. Not...everything. But I certainly did expect him to ask. It was the polite thing to do. The lover's thing to do.

I want to Skype you.

I read it twice, because the first time I read it, it sounded in my head like some kind of nasty sexual act that I certainly wouldn't mind exploring with him. Skype meant video and sound. The video didn't bother me. We'd built a relationship based on sight alone.

But the voice?

I sighed out a huge breath. Caught my hand against my chest.

He wrote more. Big decision, I know. I leave it up to you.

Oh, great. No pressure there.

The next page took a while to write, and it was actually three pages by the time he finished.

Will leave my email address (no name) with UR doorman. Sealed envelope. UR choice to open. UR choice to Skype me. Please confirm that is all right to do?

I nodded, without thinking. Yes, it was okay.

Because he was leaving it to me. I didn't need to make the decision right now. I was merely giving him permission to open the doors a little wider. The glass would remain.

He blew me a kiss and tossed the notebook over his shoulder. The glint in his eye told me he was ready for a bon voyage jack n' jill session. Much as I wanted to sit and ruminate over this huge development, I knew this might be the last time we communicated for two weeks. Indeed, we both needed a send-off.

Thirteen

I couldn't take my eyes off him. Because I reminded myself I may not see him for two weeks. Fourteen days. Half a month. One twenty-fourth of a year.

Or, I could take the dare, and open the envelope.

I didn't want to think about that imminent decision. He would be gone by morning. Tonight was for us.

On the bed, he lay on his side, naked, stroking his cock, his eyelids shuttering up and down as he increased the speed of his hand movements. Then he would slow for a while and allow his thumb to work around the base of the helmet-like corona. Most sensitive there. And steeped with spice and rich male musk. It was a place where I wanted to lash my tongue along the swollen vein, then press it under the fleshy ridge, feeling his pulse beats. Gauging his shallow breaths as they neared the edge.

I imagined him sinking into the tendrils of exquisite pleasure that accompanied his forthcoming orgasm. Fingers digging into the sheets. Thighs tightening. Jaws clenching as he anticipated the rush of oblivion. I hoped it felt as good for him as it did for me.

I still wore my panties and bra, the silk robe wrapped loosely around my shower-steamed skin. I leaned forward on the chair arm, attentive, a bold voyeur.

The strange thought that I could make a habit of this, walking by lighted windows in the night, observing the antics going on behind the curtains, made me smile. No. I was no Peeping Jane. I only had eyes for one particular man and his iron cock that could take a beating. He jackhammered that thing now. His neck muscles were tight, his jaw tense.

He was so close to coming. I noticed the subtle shudder in his shoulders. His leg jerked. Abdomen muscles ridged like washboards gleamed with perspiration. His cock head was maroon, swollen with sensation.

I clenched the chair arm and leaned closer to the window. "Now," I whispered.

Hips bucking, he spurt a trail of pearls onto his abs. His hand gripped the main shaft hard, as if pulling the brake and squealing the wheels.

He cried out, "Yes!" and rolled onto his back, arms splaying out wide. His chest panted. His mouth fell slack.

His cock was still hard, but as I watched, it slowly softened and finally wilted upon his thigh, exhausted, spent. And guess what? Uncircumcised.

He turned to me and winked. Rubbing the heel of his palm over his face, he shoved away loose curls. Working hard, and rewarded for his efforts.

I clapped. "Encore!"

Plucking the boxer briefs that lay nearby on the bed, he wiped off the cum from his belly. I wanted to do that for him, slowly, sliding over each slick ridge of muscle until I'd mapped the territory in my memory.

He pointed toward me then made a gimmie gesture with his fingers.

"Oh yeah? You want this?" I peeled away my panties, and tossed them over a shoulder. Heels digging into the floor, I slid my fingers into my wet pussy. "I'm so wet for you, Monsieur Sexy. I wish you could feel me."

But since he couldn't, and there was no point in dreaming, I would give him something to think about while he was on vacation.

My juices slicked around my forefinger as I pushed it as deeply as I could manage. Curling my fingers backward toward the top of my vagina, I felt the rough texture of my G-spot. I'd never been able to operate that spot properly. Someday, I'd find the guy with the skill. Drawing out, I slicked around my labia, dancing over the thousands of nerve endings that tingled with each wicked stroke.

Already breathing deeply, my breaths panting, I glanced out the window. He'd moved to the edge of the bed, sitting upright, focused hungrily on my moves.

"Yes." I slammed a palm to the window, while the fingers on my other hand drew expertly the path to an orgasm I already felt humming in my core. Sucking in the corner of my lip, I lowered my head and snagged his gaze through a flutter of lashes. He started to match my insistent rhythms, his hand stroking his cock, which hadn't stayed soft for long.

My thoughts were reduced to singular ideas and feelings. No ability to wax poetic now. Hot, wet, tingly, burning, aching, wanting, desperate…

Desperate to keep him right there. In my eyes. On my skin. At my fingertips. Because there at the tip of my fingers lived another realm. A world that I wanted to keep him in, even if it meant preserving him behind the glass like this forever.

I held his steady gaze, needing to imprint this moment of raw connection between two people while the exquisite hum of imminent orgasm drilled into my being, igniting every nerve ending, and painting a sheen of shuddering anticipation over my skin.

"Feel me," I said, and moaned raggedly. Head falling forward, my thighs clenched. So close. So close to coming. Just a few more slicks of my finger….

Never lose him. Make him wait.

I stepped back from the window, fingers slipping from my wet folds. My legs unsteady, I stumbled and landed on the chair behind me. My skin, moist and hot, *cushed* against the velvet fabric. Panting, wanting to press my clit again to set off the rocket-fire, I clung to the chair arms.

My gaze never left his.

Pausing his grip on his erection, his mouth fell open. Abdomen pulsing, his chest rose and fell rapidly. Stopped in the middle of something I never wanted to end.

Yet tomorrow it would. And I couldn't pause this feeling forever, wishing it would hum along at this perfection vibration, occupying our beings with a never-ending pleasure that spoke only between the two of us.

I'd found something I'd never imagined possible. A handsome man willing to experiment with this crazy sex scenario. A certain confidence that a relationship had begun. Trust.

And yet I didn't even know his name. Couldn't scream it out as the orgasm ripped through my body and I found ecstasy. I wanted to know it. I needed to have a name to whisper while I softly thumbed myself in the middle of a sleepless night.

I didn't want to grab the notebook and write out the question. My body panted, pleading I continue with the seduction. The singular mastery of the emotion he was sending through the glass. He wanted me. He wanted to see me come.

He splayed his hands out at his sides in a *what next* gesture.

I spread my legs wide. He nodded. *Please. Give me that. All of you.* The humid night air might have been cooler than the heat forged from between my legs. I slicked my fingers over the throbbing nub that demanded attention. It pulsed as if with a life of its own. If I should rub it much longer, too fast, or too hard, it would swell and retreat, a punishment for my greediness. Instead, I dipped two fingers lower, wetting them inside my hot pussy.

Across the street he licked between two fingers, mimicking what he would do if he had me in his bed, his face buried between my thighs. My God, I wanted him there right now. His moustache tickling my thighs and labia. My musketeer who could slay me with his rapier tongue.

My moan littered the room in aching, languorous tones.

I wanted him to hear my desire. To know how he made me feel. To understand that this—whatever it was—could go on forever.

I wanted to pull his head down and feel his nose nuzzle against my clit as he sought to tease me. And then the hot lash of his tongue was all it would take...

A flick of my wet fingers across my clit bucked my hips and shuddered my bones within my skin. I came hard, my breath forcing out in a guttural moan. My legs shook, shoe-tip pressing to the cool window, and my shout had surely been heard through the glass.

Fifteen feet away. Separated by two thin sheets of clear barrier. His eyes held me in an embrace. He'd wrangled me into his world. I didn't ever want to leave.

Sighing and allowing laughter to bubble up and shake my breasts, I tilted a glance to him. Waving, he then kissed his fingers and blew that morsel to me.

As I was going for the catch the craziest thing happened. Another wave of orgasm rippled through my bones, prickling my skin and shivering sweetly through my body. But instead of laughter, a teardrop trickled out the corner of my eye.

What the hell?

I stood and, waving behind me without looking back, retreated between the sheets on my bed where the teardrop turned into sobs.

ᏗᏗᏗ

I woke in the morning with a sense of dread. Springing upright in bed, fully awake and completely naked—shoes on my feet—I turned toward the window. The sheer was not pulled. Rain beat against the glass. I wouldn't see him for two weeks.

Last night had been incredible. And insane.

I'd cried. Because the orgasm had been that good? It had happened once or twice before. Sex was so emotional. And to achieve such a tremendous release as orgasm would sometimes bring up tears, a sort of joyous cleansing of the soul.

What we'd shared together last night had felt joyous. And sad. I hadn't been able to look at him once the tears had started. Hadn't even given him a wave goodbye.

"Two weeks," I muttered. "Oh hell."

Jumping out of bed, I pulled on the bee robe and spun to press my palms against the window. Dark across the street in the opposite window. He'd already left. Or was that...?

I saw the end of a cab parked at the corner down the street.

I rushed out into the living room, my heels clicking frantically, and bowed my head to the window. My lungs panted. Something in my core flip-flopped. The joy I'd felt last night threatened to implode in a burst of sad tears. So this was what it felt like to lose something. Unsure and sick in my chest. I wanted to shout or even punch something.

"Only a few weeks," I whispered.

It could have been for the rest of my life. It still could be. I held all the cards, apparently, in that call.

What if, while away, he found someone new? Or simply decided that sex through a window wasn't fulfilling for him? What if he decided to call it off?

"Stop thinking," I reprimanded.

A man walked across the street toward the cab, coming from the direction of my building. Monsieur Sexy had been in my building?

Of course, he'd promised to leave an envelope for me with the doorman. Who had he said it was for? He didn't know my name.

How I'd wanted to call out his name last night. Would I ever...?

Didn't matter. I wasn't going to let my mind wander when these may be the last few seconds I saw him for a while. Wearing a casual gray business shirt and gray slacks he strode across the street, unconcerned about the rain. Smart Italian loafers, I decided of the shoes. I couldn't see well for the distance and angle of the streets. But yes, that was his style.

He strode around the back of the cab, shoving a hand through his hair. Casual. So easy and relaxed. He slicked away the rain that must jewel in his hair like diamonds on this slightly foggy autumn morning.

I pressed a palm to the window, leaning forward and almost said, "Stop, stay," but that was a fantasy I made up. He had business. He wouldn't stop and drop it all because some nameless woman behind glass requested he do so.

I felt his absence creep into my heart and chew away a tiny black spot as he opened the cab's back door. Mouth open, the humid air felt raw against my tongue. He stepped off the curb—and looked up and across the street, directly at my rain-streaked window.

Be still, my heart. He had been thinking of me.

I waved, and cautioned myself not to bounce on my toes in an attempt to show him how desperate I was to keep him here. Here, not so close to me, but within eyesight. Fifteen feet away. Behind glass. Mine when I could see him.

And when I could not? He belonged to the world, and anyone else he should happen to glance at, casually chat with while standing in line at the airport, or share a funny story with his seatmate on the airplane. Not mine.

He blew me a kiss.

He could be mine.

I caught the kiss and crushed it against my heart with both hands before kissing my fingertips and returning the goodbye.

Standing there with a hand upon the cab roof, he held my gaze as surely as a man could hold a woman's heart. With a fierce conviction that I did not want to waver, no matter the distance he was putting between us.

"Yes," I whispered. It wasn't in answer to any of his questions in particular, only a promise to myself.

He slid inside, and the cab rolled down the street.

My heart stopped beating. That little black spot began to bleed out, growing larger—

"The envelope." I raced into the bedroom to slip on some clothes.

Five minutes later I had scampered down to the lobby, asked the doorman if I'd been left anything, and now held a small red envelope in my hands. And a book-sized package wrapped in red paper to match the envelope.

It was thick, beautiful paper. Couldn't have come from any stationary set I'd imagine a man using. Had he bought it purposely for this moment?

I pressed the envelope to my lips and closed my eyes. Berlin. For two weeks. And I held the key to taking our relationship to the next level. To open it or to tear it up and toss it in the trashbin without looking?

And this unexpected package. What could it possibly be? Felt like a paperback book. Did he want me to read something in particular while he was gone?

The package had nothing to do with the envelope, I reasoned. I could open it now and still leave the envelope as I muddled over whether or not to rip that open.

"Right. Save the envelope, but as for the package..."

I'd never been patient at Christmas. More than a few times, I'd convinced my parents to let me open a package a day starting a few days in advance because that would stretch out the joy all the more. (Because you know, childhood logic.)

And there was rule number three: never open the package. Which, by its very forbidding tone, demanded I break it.

Turning over the package to look for the taped seam, I found that it had been wrapped with such precision a professional wrapper would shed tears at the results.

"He must have had the sales girl do this."

If he had done it himself I wasn't sure if I should fall at his feet and worship his skills or maybe wonder if he had control issues.

I myself liked to control things as much as possible. It was the introvert in me that liked quiet and calm. Yes, even amidst my mess of stacked books and unmade bed and piles of clothing I maintained a certain order. It was all in my head.

Sliding a finger under the ends, they released and I carefully folded away the thick crimson paper. Inside, gold leather covered a thin notebook. I turned it over and gasped. A bee with wings spread had been hand-tooled onto the lower right corner of the cover.

"Oh, my God. This is the one. From the shop. From the day..."

I pressed the notebook to my chest as if it was my dream musketeer and I had finally been allowed to hug him. We'd touched for the first time that day at the leather shop. Never had we stood so close to one another.

Lifting the notebook to smell the rich leather I blinked away a teardrop. How had he known? Had he made a guess? I did have the bee embroidered on my robe.

"Monsieur Sexy, I..." I didn't know what to say. This gift was tremendous. It was everything.

It was a beckon.

Picking up the unopened envelope, I slid it over my lips and then, wandering to the kitchen table, I set it down, leaning it before a stack of research books. A question mark had been drawn on the front of the envelope with a black sharpie.

I walked backward, hugging the notebook to my chest, eyes on the question mark. Heartbeats thundered. Another tear fell across my cheek. Tilting my head against the window I reveled in the crazy anxious sexy warmth that flooded my soul.

Dare I open it?

Screen

Part 2

One

Let's begin with a bang, shall we?

Because right now my mind was not here in my living room, three stories above a quiet Parisian street in the 7th arrondissement. I had just returned from an evening shift at the map shop. I pulled my shoulder-length chestnut hair out from the chignon, smoothed my hands down my hips, and let out a sigh. You know that sigh. The 'I'm home and I can finally relax' sigh.

My thoughts, though, had no intention of relaxing without a little help. In my mind, I drifted through the window, grabbed the man in the sleek Zegna suit by the tie and tugged him across the street.

Mmm... If I closed my eyes and pressed my back to the wall I could picture him standing before me now. Tall, broad-shouldered, and possessed of an innate charm; he could seduce without uttering a word. His fingers slid down the charcoal suit coat, unbuttoning one, then the next steel disk. Sky gray eyes mesmerized me. The man's grin said 'I know things that you don't, sweetie, but if you're lucky, I'll teach them to you'.

The only thing on his mind was sex.

He strode toward me. I dropped my arms to my sides, my palms flattening against the wall. With an anticipatory inhale my chest lifted and my shoulders tilted forward. Aiming for him, wanting him to move faster, to make a connection.

To finally touch me.

He shrugged down the finely-pinstriped suit coat. Hooking a finger at the collar, he smoothed it in half lengthwise in a well-polished move. A man of style and taste. He tossed it aside, landing the expensive coat across the back of the gray velvet chaise where I had spent many an afternoon daydreaming about him.

I hadn't made it as far as the chaise today. The daydream bombarded.

I shifted, palms still against the wall, but shoulders moving me closer, bending me forward so my silk shirt fell open to reveal cleavage, which was pushed up nicely by the demi-cup La Perla hug of black lace.

"Tell me what you want," he said in a deep, masculine purr that skittered through my system, aimed directly for my core. "You want to fuck?"

I grew wet *like that.*

"I want you to touch me," I said. "I want to feel you. Finally. I want you to push me against the wall and—"

He seized my shoulders and pushed. My back hit the wall. Not painful, but rather, exciting. I bit my lip and flashed want at his stern but softening gaze. That curl of a knowing smile remained. I desired to lick the dash of stubble under his lower lip. Feel its roughness against my soft mouth.

"You want a lot," he said.

Strolling my fingers down the front of his crisp gray dress shirt, I made quick work of the pearl buttons to reveal the hard pecs and abs beneath. So hot, his skin seemed to melt beneath my touch.

"Mmm... I want this."

I licked an exploratory trail from the base of his neck to his chest. His encouraging moan hummed against my mouth as I dashed over to tongue a tiny erect nipple. Wide yet graceful hands moved to my hips, attempting to pull me against him, but I was too intent on tasting his skin to comply.

Hot, hard, and oozing a warm spicy scent, he smelled like a wicked treasure I wanted to hide away. A secret I could pull out of its hiding place to press against my nose and remember delicious liaisons past. And while I wanted to stash him away only for myself, he felt too dangerous, too combustible for any container to properly hold.

I glided a palm over the rugged landscape of his chest and squeezed a solid pectoral muscle, cooing in appreciation. "Fencing keeps you hard."

"You keep me hard," he murmured.

Then he whispered something in French, so softly, that I could only fall into the melody of the unknown because I didn't speak the language. But I fell willingly, seduced by the erotic foreignness of all that he was.

Willingly, but not quite compliantly.

I grabbed him by the wrists and thrust his hands away from my hips and down to his sides. When I slipped the dress shirt over his shoulders, it hung at his wrists; he wore cufflinks and I didn't want to take the time to release him. A chuff of protest huffed against my forehead, but I ignored his drama.

He wore no belt, and I quickly unzipped, unclasped, and pushed the dress trousers down his thighs. Gray boxer briefs greedily hugged his erection. I grasped the thick shaft, squeezing it with a possessiveness that one usually reserves for long-desired surprises discovered beneath bright wrapping.

"I know what I want more than anything right now," I said. "Keep your hands down. Let me have a treat."

Fingernails gliding against the tight curve of his ass, I peeled the briefs down to reveal the heavy prize within. His cock thrust up boldly, the smooth head of it capping a length that slapped up against his torso.

Placing my hands on his hips, I squatted down, bending so that my knees were to either side of his legs. The pleated black skirt rode up my thighs, revealing that I wore no panties beneath. The air brushed my juicy pussy, stirring me to a wanting moan. I admired his hefty rod, cooing in appreciation. With each encouraging utterance his cock jumped and his testicles tightened. The girth was impressive, a tight fit that I desperately wanted to try out. The foreskin was snugged down below the corona, and the entire package was a gorgeous sculpture of flesh, muscle, and steel.

I shifted onto my knees. Good girls wore scuffs on the toes of their Louboutins.

Rubbing my cheek alongside his cock provoked a moan from him. I noticed his fingers tightened into a fist near his thigh, and smelled salted musk sweetened with spice—that was his scent. I wrapped my fingers about the base of him, a good handful. So hard and heavy with promise. How he managed to pack all this into his pants and walk with a normal stride...well. I suppose he wasn't hard all the time.

Only for me.

Hey, this *was* a daydream. I could orchestrate it any way I wanted to.

Sweeping the maroon head of him across my cheek, I purred. While his cock was hard as steel, the skin wrapping it was suede soft to the touch.

I looked up. His jaw muscles were tense but his mouth was parted. When he opened his eyes to meet mine, I smiled and asked, "Do you know what *you* want?"

His heavy cock bobbed in my lose grasp. "Suck me," he gasped. "*S'il vous plaît.*"

"I do please."

Tonguing him from the base where dark hairs curled, I followed the pulsing vein on the underside upward to the corona. An intensive suck to the meaty ridge summoned a throaty, drawn-out moan from him. His fingers brushed through my hair, but just as quickly, dropped back to his sides.

I had directed him to keep his hands down. Good boy.

Taking him into my mouth, I glided my tongue about the crown. Lush and firm as a plum, I sucked softly, then more firmly. The man tasted exquisite. I took my time dashing the tip of my tongue about him, seeking the sensitive area just at the end of the vein that made him gasp and his fists squeezed even tighter. His hips bucked forward, insisting on my attendance.

One hand clasping his length, I pulled him closer and lashed the head quickly, as if a sweet treat, before sucking him in deeply. I could feel the vein thicken against my tongue; his shaft could not get any harder. His thighs brushing my breasts were tense, the muscles straining. He would come soon. I could sense it in his panting breaths, the minute tremor of his hips, the aching groans. His body raced toward release.

But not this way. I was in this for the bang.

Squeezing him firmly—*mine, all mine*—I stood, bent to suck him in for a last, long, squeezing kiss, and then dusted my hair over his cock.

I straightened, meeting him eye to eye. (Five-inch heels, don't you know.) "Get me up against the wall. Now."

Though he was a Frenchman, he understood English perfectly. My back hit the wall. His hands gripped my thighs and he lifted me as I spread my legs about his hips. His hot cock seared along my inner thigh. I sucked in air as if he had burned me. It was the sweetest pain.

Panting lightly, I was thankful that he had enough range of motion with the sleeves still wrapped about his wrists to manage this position. His mouth dove to my neck where he kissed me hard against the vein. Chills scurried up my throat and down my spine. We'd never kissed on the mouth, not even in my daydreams. The ultimate intimacy. The kiss was a prize I was reserving for real life.

I squeezed hard with my thighs and wiggled my hips until I felt the head of him nudge my labia. He shoved, seeking entrance. His hands were occupied holding me up, so he was stabbing without guidance.

He snickered against my ear. "Soon, *oui*?"

Such a tease! By the third poke the head of his penis coaxed my slick folds open, but instead of gliding in slowly, he hilted himself.

"Oh, yes!" I cried loudly.

I was pretty sure my neighbors were out of town. If not? Welcome to my daydream.

The kiss at my neck trailed to my collarbone and nipped the bone and skin none-too-gently as he pumped inside me with a determined insistence. The thickness of him gliding in and out pulled at my clitoris, teasing it with an intangible touch. The non-touch was more intense than direct contact. The combination of his spicy scent, his hot skin, the slam of my ass against the wall—it all focused the pleasure at my core.

"So hot," he uttered as he thrust into me. "Tight. *Mon Dieu*. You are fire."

Such admiration was received with an open-mouthed moan. I gripped his shoulders, my fingernails marking his skin with red divots that we would laugh at later.

And when he paused, fully hilted so that I could feel him in my belly, he nuzzled his face against my jaw. His body tensed against mine. His chest crushed my breasts. A shift of his arm pulsed his solid pectoral against my nipple. Still fully clothed, my nipples ached for the bare heat of him, but the lace bra delivered an erotic rub that hardened them to diamonds. His abs were slick with perspiration, and my silk shirt stuck against the ridges. His breaths panted against my throat. Counting. Waiting so he would not come too quickly.

Or perhaps a pause before the triumph?

Yes, I wanted him to explode within me now. (Who needs condoms in a dream?) I squeezed my inner muscles about him. He groaned and pumped again. Pushing his hand up under my jaw, he held me gently, yet firmly. Gray sky eyes fixed to mine. We were connected at hips, irises, and through anticipatory heartbeats.

His jaw tight, he gasped, and then with one final pump, he slammed into me. His cry of ecstasy was short, yet loud. A burst of pure adrenaline laced with the ultimate pleasure. And with that last rough kiss of body against body, he tweaked my clit and I had a contained yet deliciously molten orgasm.

I slipped down the wall, sighing. My legs bent, my hand slid between my thighs and found the swollen apex of my pleasure.

Opening my eyes, I blinked at the fading daylight beaming through the window. The man in the suit sporting the sexy grin was gone. A mere figment. Yet capable of inducing in me real emotion and physical reactions.

My finger rested on my slippery clit. The orgasm had been real.

"Monsieur Sexy," I whispered. "I miss you."

I sat there a long time, fluttering down from the dream. And then I remembered that though Monsieur Sexy was, in reality, far away, I had the power to bring him closer, as if reaching through the glass in a daydream.

I stood, shimmied down my skirt, and wandered into the kitchen. My thighs were hot and slick. Parts of me still hummed softly from the orgasm. My face and breasts felt flushed. I love a good orgasm.

A red envelope sat on the table, tilted against a stack of research books. The books were about Henri VIII. The envelope was from my window lover. (Yes, you read that right. There really was a man in the window.) He'd left the note with the building concierge for me early this morning before getting in a cab and heading to the Charles de Gaulle airport to catch a flight to Berlin.

I didn't know his name. I'd never heard his voice (save in my dreams). I couldn't begin to describe how he smelled or even know if he had a favorite color or sports team. I wasn't sure how old he was (my guess placed him at early thirties). I couldn't know if he was a steak and potatoes kind of guy or a vegetarian.

I'd never felt his touch upon my skin.

And yet we had shared an amazing two weeks of window sex.

You may wonder, what the heck is window sex? It's two people standing in their adjacent bedrooms before floor-to-ceiling windows, self-pleasuring as they watch the other do the same. Sounds weird, but oh, it has been a ride I have not wanted to end.

Separated by two sheets of glass and fifteen feet of alley space, we'd occasionally communicated with a few words hastily scrawled with black sharpies on spiral notebook paper. But mostly we'd spoken with our eyes, our hands, and the flex and shift of our naked bodies.

I knew he was ripped, that he had a sense of humor, and that he liked chocolate cake. He taught fencing from his home, wore expensive suits and boxer briefs. I knew he wasn't circumcised. When erect, his penis was thick and a nice handful. He liked to jack-off. Hard.

And I knew that I could trust him.

We'd made rules. No names. If we should meet one another on the street, we'd turn and walk away. We'd followed those rules. And they had been tested.

And now a new test. He taught some kind of computer mumbo-jumbo online, and had, just this morning, flown to Berlin for two weeks. Business trip. I wasn't sure of his exact job title. And he knew only that I was a research assistant.

Knowing more wasn't important at this stage in the relationship.

Now I must endure two weeks without seeing my window lover, whom I had christened "Monsieur Sexy". (I do live in Paris, and I did hope that he was French, though he always wrote me notes in English). Two weeks of wandering before my bedroom window and not seeing the light in his bedroom across the street. A light that had illuminated delicious scenes of skin, carnal lust, and pleasure.

While at work at the map shop today, I had muddled over what I would do with myself these next few weeks. Alone! Tragically abandoned by my lover. Our steamy relationship shoved to an abrupt halt.

Guess what? I have a tendency to think too much.

Around noon I'd gotten lost in a mental replay of our daring window antics. (Two customers all day; trust me, I'd had lots of time for mental wandering.) The first time I had bared my breasts to him. The first sight of his cock. Me using the vibrator while he jacked off.

By the time I'd punched out at five, I'd been horny enough to engage in a flirtatious exchange of glances with a blonde man in a business suit on the Métro. He'd clutched a leather valise and had paused from texting on his iPhone to wink at me. Thank goodness he'd gotten off at the first stop. I could flirt, but to actually follow through? Eek! I was more daring behind glass.

Anyway, the new test.

Before leaving, Monsieur Sexy had asked me (via a note scribbled with Sharpie) to Skype him. Innocent enough, right? He'd left his email address in the red envelope that now sat on the kitchen table. If I wanted to take our relationship to the next level all I had to do was open the envelope.

I was curious. Anxious. Eager. Frightened. Anticipatory. A jumble of nerves had me pacing before the window now. I glanced to the red envelope. Could I do it? We'd never spoken. And Skype would allow us to see one another much more closely than we had up until now.

I could handle that. I'd seen all of Monsieur Sexy, as he had of me. He'd watched me masturbate, and bring myself to orgasm with a vibrator, and I'd even done a silly strip tease for him while wearing mylar stripper pasties. The man—whose name I did not know—knew things about me that no one else did.

How's that for never having spoken a single word to one another?

The red envelope screamed with a loud, teasing silence. I turned away from its shout and hugged my arms across my chest.

I craved his touch. His arms around me. His cock inside me. I wanted to learn more about him. And yes, I did want to hear his voice. But I was a nervous wreck right now. It was a big step. I know, most people spoke to one another on their first date. It was sort of a requirement.

So I had done things a bit differently. Call me unconventional.

I picked up the envelope, weighing the thick stationery upon my palm. The paper had a rough grain and felt handcrafted. It was crimson. The color of a deep, velvety rose petal. It also reminded me of lushly painted lips pursed in expectation of a kiss.

Oh, a kiss. More than anything, I desired his kiss.

A kiss would claim me. Secure our weird relationship in a new and startling hold. A kiss would breathe his world into me. A kiss from him would melt my insides and make me cream down my thighs.

A kiss would be the most raw and intimate means of communication we could share.

But because I'd gone about this relationship in such a backward manner, I had yet to feel the heat of his mouth against mine. I didn't know if his mouth would be firm and commanding, or if he preferred a lighter touch before thrusting his tongue against mine.

I wondered if he thought this much about me? Did he crave the feel of my skin beneath his fingers? Did he wonder how my lips would taste on his? Did he ever daydream about licking my pussy and listening to my moans as I begged him to never stop? When he grasped his cock and slid his fingers firmly and furiously up and down did he imagine thrusting inside me?

Holding the envelope against my mouth, I closed my eyes. I stood before the living room window. It was around six p.m. and the apartment smelled of vanilla from the sugar scrub I had used in last night's bath. A precariously balanced mountain of research books sat on the coffee table behind me. An empty wine goblet held post on top of the books.

"Should I?" I whispered, and tapped the envelope against my lips.

I set the envelope back on the kitchen table and picked up the gold leather notebook lying there. It had been wrapped in red paper to match the envelope and had been delivered along with it. I'd broken down and opened it this morning because curiosity had won out. I still couldn't believe he'd gifted me the very notebook I had been looking at in the leather shop window a few days earlier.

I smoothed my fingers over the journal. The leather was silken and pliable. A bee with spread wings had been hand-tooled onto the lower right corner. Had he known I have a thing for bees? Or had it merely been a whim to pick up one of the notebooks from the window display before which he had seen me standing?

Heartbeats fluttered. I pressed the notebook to my chest as if it were him and I had finally been allowed to hug him. Days ago, I'd accidentally run into him while window-shopping outside the leather shop. He had stood inside chatting with the owner. When he'd turned to spy me, we'd held each other's stare. Never had we stood so close to one another. Yet still separated by glass.

It was the first time I'd seen the true color of his eyes. I owned a tee shirt that color and slept in it often. He'd pressed his palm to the window and I had placed mine over his. Our first touch. He hadn't rushed out to talk to me, to finally make real contact with the woman he had seduced through glass.

We had our rules.

Lifting the notebook to smell the rich oil that had been worked into the leather I blinked away a teardrop. I didn't know what to say. This gift was tremendous. It was everything.

It was a sign.

I exhaled, feeling my breaths flow out and my chest empty. A slow intake of air. A little yoga breathing always calmed my nerves.

"I'm going to do this. I have to. I'd be a fool otherwise."

Clutching the notebook, I grabbed the red envelope and sailed into the bedroom where my unmade, king-size bed welcomed my stomach-first plop onto its cushy, down comforter. The lamp by the bed glowed. If I wanted him to see me at night it had to be on. I'd performed as if on stage before the window, my audience rapt. And he had returned the performance.

Now...the next act.

I pried a fingernail along the sealed edge of the envelope. I wasn't going to open it without some damage to the fine paper. That upset me. I liked to keep things neat. The pile of clothes on the easy chair by the window didn't count. I didn't have a bedroom closet, so it was either the standing garment rack or...the toss. Neatness was more a mental control issue for me.

Rolling to my back, I unfastened the buttons on my blouse. The room was warm despite the cool weather beyond the window.

To tear or not to tear? I appreciated his exact attention to detail. If I wanted to venture to the next level with him, I was going to have to work for it. To pry things open and dive in.

I peeled at the corner, and since I'd already done the damage, tore it until I could stick my finger in and slide it along the uppermost fold. From inside, a piece of crimson paper half the size of the envelope dropped out and landed on my chest.

Anticipation tingled at the base of my throat. I sucked in the corner of my lower lip. Would his email address provide a clue to his name? That would go against our rules. I wanted to know his name. And I did not. The not knowing fueled this wicked fantasy that I currently cruised through reality.

Enough stalling. I flipped the card over and read the email address written with a black sharpie in neat, squared letters: *nakedfencer@email.com.*

I laughed. I'd never seen him fencing naked. But I had seen him moving about his living room wielding a rapier and clad in mask and padded vest. The way our buildings were angled, our living rooms were too far apart to see well. Our bedrooms, though, jutted up at a diagonal to one another, only fifteen feet from window to window.

The email address was the only thing written on the paper. No name. Whew. He'd stuck to our rule. The guy really was trustworthy. I sniffed the paper. No scent. No clue to his aftershave. I wanted him to smell like spices spilling from a terracotta jar.

Allow me my extravagant fantasies.

I held all the power now. I could Skype him. And we could continue our touchless liaison. But instead of being absent touch, smell, taste and sound, we would only be absent touch, smell and taste.

Sound.

I wondered what his voice sounded like. Was he the Frenchman I fantasized him to be? Or maybe he was some other nationality? He apparently understood English because we'd communicated in our notes that way.

Hooking up with a sexy Frenchman was tops on my fantasy list. It was one of the very reasons I'd moved across the ocean from good ole Iowa. I'd wanted to have a glorious affair with a musketeer—er, um, Frenchman. (But if he'd been a musketeer in his past life? All the better.)

Pinching the crimson card between my fingers, I tilted my head back to spy the gorgeous Christian Louboutin shoes sitting on the floor—black leather tied with black velvet ribbons about the ankles. The card was the same color as the shoe soles.

Coincidence?

I didn't believe in coincidences. Everything happened for a reason. And for some reason, Monsieur Sexy had tapped into my innate desires and touched me even while he was in another country.

"Naked fencer, eh?" A shiver of anticipation scurried up my neck and tickled my ears.

I eyed the laptop that sat on the vanity beneath a scatter of freshly-washed bras and panties I'd yet to put away. Contact with my window lover was but a few keystrokes away.

I grew wet thinking about how deep and sensual his voice might sound. Reaching down, I lightly danced my fingertips over my mons, the pubic hair shaved to a short and neat kinda-oval. I was still creamy from the daydream. I wanted to hear him whisper at my ear all the things he fantasized about doing to me.

Sitting up, I reached for the laptop and signed onto Skype. I typed in his email address, then back-spaced, deleting it completely.

"I can't use my regular email. It has my name in it."

Not cool. Names were everything. Names were power. Names...could be looked up online and a person's entire world could be discovered in less than five minutes.

I wanted to retain some mystery. It felt right. Besides, it was our rule.

It occurred to me that I didn't have a different email. A secret for-online-lovers-only email. So I browsed over to Google Mail.

What handle should I use? *Windowstripper* seemed too obvious, and not classy enough. Besides, it was taken. *Sexthroughglass* was just weird. Also taken. *WishingforaFrenchman*? Not taken, but again, reeked of desperation.

The notebook lay on the comforter next to my leg. I would never admit to him that I had a thing about writing in notebooks. I couldn't do it. Couldn't make a mark on that first pristine page. And I owned half a dozen blank notebooks to prove my strange affliction. I traced a fingernail along the bee's wing and got an idea.

I typed in *beesweetforyou* and, remarkably, that name was not taken. It was corny, but I liked it, so I registered, and headed back to Skype.

After I'd entered all the new info and added *nakedfencer* to my contacts list, my fingers hovered over the trackpad. It was nearing seven at night. Still early, yet if he'd worked since arriving in Berlin, he might like to get some sleep.

And you are making excuses. Do it!

I toggled from *call* to *chat*. A call would bring him up on the screen, and me as well. A chat would merely be like online texting. I knew he'd intended for us to video chat, but...

I clicked on chat. If he didn't have Skype open I could leave him a message, close the laptop, and bury myself under the sheets in embarrassment at having actually made the leap from window to keyboard.

But really? I had lost my inhibitions while doing the stripper pasty dance for his birthday before the window. The vixen I'd once kept secreted deep inside had skipped up to the fore and was eager for this next step.

So I typed:

Finally opened the envelope. Hi! *Bonsoir*, I mean. Uh, I'm a little nervous. Couldn't bring myself to video chat for this first contact.

I hit send.

The green light next to his name clued me in that he was online. A few seconds later, I got a reply. My heart dropped to my gut. "Holy shit." He was there. We were about to communicate in real time.

So pleased you took a chance opening the envelope. Chat is fine for tonight. I'm tired. Flight was turbulent and gave me a headache. Entertained clients all afternoon. Just arrived at hotel.

God, he typed fast, and I loved his typing voice.

Beesweetforyou, eh? I like it.

I typed quickly. Thank you for the pretty notebook. How did you know I like bees?

I've seen your robe. It was a guess. Pleased you like it.

I pulled the notebook onto my lap. I love it. But I don't know if I want to write in it. Wouldn't know what to write.

His green light flashed while he typed. Write in it all the things you don't dare type or say to me.

Oh, that sounded deliciously naughty. Notebook confessions? Salacious tidbits that I'd keep only for myself? I might be able to manage that.

I wrote: So how do we start? This is...different. I feel like I know you and yet not. I sound like a fool. LOL

I love your laugh, he wrote. You always laugh after you come. That is sexy.

Seeing those words on the computer screen set my heartbeats to a rapid thunder. The man could seduce with only the written word. I didn't have to see his pretty eyes or his gorgeous smile. This man could keep me up all night—

Yikes. The battery level was on red. I had but minutes remaining. Where was the power cord in this mess of a room?

Have to find power cord. Running out of juice.

Don't worry about it. I hate to make this quick but... I need to get some sleep. Six a.m. meeting tomorrow. Can we begin for real tomorrow night?

I understand. And yes, tomorrow night.

I'm so pleased you took the next step, *mon abeille.*

Mon abeille? What had he just called me? Dare I ask? No. I'd look it up. But that confirmed that he was French. Mostly. Maybe?

I typed: I'll look for you around seven?

Sounds good. But will you really look? Will I be able to see you tomorrow night, as well as hear you?

I exhaled heavily, and typed. Yes. I promise.

You make me happy. *Bonne nuit.*

Same to you.

I clicked to sign off then because I didn't want to do the drawn-out linger, and even as I clicked the laptop screen went black.

"Whew. I did it!"

I rolled to my back, trailing my fingers over the warm aluminum laptop body. The crimson card crinkled under my elbow.

"Mon abeille," I whispered.

I had to plug in my laptop so I could look up that word.

Two

My bee.

The next morning I dashed from the bed to my desk in the living room. First thing I did was go to freetranslations.com and look up *mon abeille.* I'd learned enough French to get by since moving here, but that was still barely *bonjour* and *merci.* I could definitely understand it more than speak it. And that was more important to me, anyway.

He'd called me *my bee.* How cool was it that he had a nickname for me? Had he mouthed it as we'd stood before the windows baring our souls through naked skin?

I wondered what he'd think about the nickname I'd given him: Monsieur Sexy. A guy could go either way with that one. He could be flattered, or he could find it ridiculous and condescending. I wouldn't worry about it. Because overthinking always tended to segue into worry, and beyond that, freaking out.

I tapped the keyboard, eyeing the Skype app. It was nine a.m. He was at work. As should I be.

Pushing the laptop away on the desk, I spun up and floated into the bathroom to brush my teeth. It's difficult to brush when your smile wants to stretch ear to ear.

"My bee," I said as I tapped the water from the brush and then replaced it in the medicine cabinet. "Oh, Monsieur Sexy, I can't wait to talk to you tonight."

And I would talk to him. I'd utilize the video chat. I made that promise to myself as I wandered about my bedroom, gathering up clothes for the day from the floor. It was Tuesday. I had a lot of research work to do. And yet, the messy floor scattered with skirts, shoes, and books coaxed me to pick up more than a few things.

Two hours later, I sat on the bed in the pink tee-shirt and grey yoga pants I'd excavated from beneath a pile and exhaled a satisfied sigh. "I have not seen this room looking so clean in months."

I'd even organized the books by subject stacks. And, I'd checked online for bookshelves from Amazon. They were due to arrive within the week. I'd acquired a lot of books since arriving on French soil. They seemed to breed. But somehow the idea of actually installing bookshelves seemed so permanent.

I'd only intended to stay in Paris three years. The standard time for the skills and talents residence card I'd applied for. I could re-up for a ten-year resident card if I wished. I hadn't given it much thought yet. I loved Paris, but it would never be my home. I was American to the core of my red, white and blue bones.

With my library organized, I felt as if I'd made great leaps for womankind. I skipped out to the kitchen to make a salad for lunch. Spinach, snap peas, cauliflower, sunflower seeds, and feta cheese crumbles. A few sliced olives on the top, with a drizzle of olive oil as dressing. Voila!

I sat down to eat and eyed the bee notebook sitting on top of a stack of client files. I didn't dare touch it without risking olive oil on the leather cover. He was so thoughtful. The man was too good to be true.

I sat back on the kitchen chair, chewing. Thinking.

What *was* wrong with him? Most men would never figure out something so personal about a woman's likes without even holding a conversation with her. It was as if he were super-perceptive. Or one of those creepy stalkers who had investigated his prey and now was cozying up to her before he chained her in his basement.

My fork clattered onto the table. I shook the horrifying image out of my skull. Did something have to be wrong with him?

"No, he's just smart. And attentive."

I plucked an olive from the salad and popped it in my mouth. Surely, he had noticed the embroidered bee on my robe and took it from there. Which didn't make him ideal by any means.

"He could still have bad habits. Like leaving the toilet seat up. But he is a single man living alone. Why put it down? Maybe he never washes his dishes."

I couldn't see into his kitchen from my view across the street. A huge plant hung near the window that blurred view of anything beyond. Who watered the plant when he was gone? If he had asked me and I would have gladly agreed to do so. Then I could have snooped about his place—no.

Stabbing a fork into my salad, I shook my head. I had no desire to snoop. I'd witnessed his most intimate moments. Anything else was just window dressing. Or stacks of dirty dishes.

Ah heck. Who was I kidding? I belonged to the female species. Snooping was encoded in our DNA.

After lunch, I opened the notebook and...taking a deep breath and wielding a pen, lingered over the blank page. And lingered. And...

"Oh, just do it. Write something about him."

Pressing the pen to page, I actually wrote something. Yay, for me! I'd marked the clean page with my thoughts.

Okay. Enough excitement.

I checked Skype—no messages—then was determined to get in four or five hours of research before breaking for a muscle-stretching walk along the Seine. It was fall, after all, and I wanted to take advantage of the dwindling nice days before winter swooped in on icy wings.

The lure of roasted chestnuts also drew me. Vendors set up along the river to hawk their sweet autumn wares. I bought a crinkly package and nibbled the warm chestnuts while watching the *bateaux mouches* glide tourists before the Trocadero's bombastic fountains.

When I returned home after dark, a message waited on Skype. Almost dark, that is. The sun had set and the sky was gray, but it wasn't the liquid night that filled the sky when there was no moon. The city never managed to grow completely dark for all the streetlights and spotlights focused on tourist attractions and landmarks. Paris did not sleep.

Nakedfencer had sent me a message five minutes earlier. You there?

I sat before the desk, fingers poised above the keyboard. It felt almost as nerve wracking as it had when lingering over the blank journal page with pen in hand. Hmm, this didn't feel quite right. If I was going to hold a conversation with him tonight it had better be where I felt most comfortable chatting with him.

I picked up the laptop and padded into the bedroom. And...decided to shower before settling in for a chat, that, with hope, may stretch into the early morning hours. It had been windy during my walk, and more than a few times I'd dodged puddles disguised with colorful leaves. I needed some freshening.

I typed in: Taking a shower. Ten minutes and I'm all yours.

The quickest shower in my life still managed to get my hair clean. I scrubbed the stick-straight strands with a towel and combed it. I was growing it out. Past my shoulders now, I envisioned it spilling down to my hips so I could braid it *a la* some Disney princess.

Oy. That was a random thought. I didn't want to be a princess. Princesses got stuck in dusty old castles spinning wool and tending dwarves. I wanted to be queen of my castle. And whether or not a king sat beside me was entirely up for negotiation.

Padding naked into the bedroom, I tugged on the silk robe and pressed my fingers over the bee embroidered above the left breast.

"*Mon abeille*," I said with glee. Jumping onto the bed, I settled against the pillows and pulled the laptop onto my thighs. The wallpaper on the screen featured Romain Duris grinning at me. (French guy. Look him up.)

My naked fencer had written: Long day at work. Look forward to talking with you. Showered. Wine in hand. Music on low. You like to listen to music?

I replied: I love music.

With that cue, I opened up iTunes and found something to set the mood. Elvis's greatest romantic hits. I sang along, "I want you, I need you, I love you." Perfect.

Listen to music often, I continued typing, except when I'm working. Research assistant, as I wrote to you before. Work usually ten to four, but sometimes add hours on weekends. Hi! It's so cool chatting with you like this.

He replied immediately so I knew he was there, reading in real time as I had typed. I inhaled, countering my thudding heartbeats with a calming breath. He was so close. Much closer than the window had ever allowed. Because he was right there, beyond the screen.

He wrote: Can we switch to video? If you are nervous, you shouldn't be. I've already seen you. All of you. I want to hear your voice.

He followed that with a smiley face emoticon.

I rapped my fingers next to the trackpad. I knew it was coming. I wanted it to come. (And, oh man, could he make me come.) I needed to hear his voice, too. To finally hear the gorgeous laughter that had reduced me to swooning sighs against the window so many times.

My toes wiggled nervously, the silver toe ring glinting under the lamp glow. My fingers actually shook a little, too. I glanced aside where the long mirror that leaned against the wall caught my reflection. The woman in the mirror with the wet hair and bright yellow robe nodded at me. She was the vixen within who had giggled and delighted when I'd initially flashed my breasts to Monsieur Sexy. She was the one who had the nerve to finger herself before the window as he watched, his hand firmly wrapped about his cock.

She was me. And I was in for the ride.

I scrolled across the Skype menu and clicked on Video. All I had to do was lift my finger from the trackpad...

The tiny green camera light on the laptop flashed on. The all-seeing eye. An entrance into my home, my bedroom, my very soul. A video box opened on the majority of the screen, hiding Romain's sexy smirk. And then *he* appeared, looking straight at me. He smiled, his eyebrows perking up in delight, and then waved.

I returned the silly little wave I'd perfected from behind glass. It was our silent greeting that we knew well. I was almost compelled to grab a notebook and scribble out a 'What now?' but I didn't have to. I could simply speak.

The ability to form words scrambled off into a shadowed corner. My tongue felt numb. The simple skill of speech I'd learned twenty-eight years ago up and abandoned me. Oh, Romain, what do I do now?

I turned the music down to a quiet background murmur.

"*Bonsoir*," he said. Nervous as well, I sensed. He rubbed a thumb across his chin and looked aside before meeting my gaze and smiling widely.

Oh my God, his eyes were so gorgeous. Framed within black-rimmed glasses. Grayish blue and deep, not pale. They held depth and...soul. A girl could navigate new worlds in those eyes and wouldn't protest should the adventure lure her to Wonderland.

"All right," he said. "I will speak first. We are both nervous, *oui*?"

I nodded. His voice was accented with the French tones I heard every day walking about the city. But he was speaking to *me*. And the accent was only for me. Here was the Frenchman I'd dreamed about. Had wanted to meet, fall in love with, and make passionate love to for days on end. Yet he spoke English well.

Because he was smart. Computer geek, remember? Oh, but I knew how to pick them.

"You are nervous, *mon abeille*?"

I nodded again. I could listen to him speak all day. And stare into his eyes. I almost reached to touch the screen.

Suddenly the vixen poked me and I cleared my throat. "Yes," I managed. "Nervous? A little. Maybe a lot. Uh, hi. Your voice."

"*Oui*?"

"It's so sexy," I offered with what I felt was a blush, but in reality, I think my entire body turned a rosy shade. I was growing warmer everywhere, especially between my thighs. It was his eyes. That soft yet penetrating gaze permeated my skin and heated my insides. "You speak English well."

"I speak English, German, and some Russian. But I am a Frenchman to the bone. Was born in Paris, actually. You are American."

He said it as if he knew it. I didn't need to confirm. Instead, I simply listened. His voice was some kind of magic. Deep and steady, no awkward attempts at English, yet so gorgeously edged with the French accent.

"I won't try to guess what state you are from judging your accent. There are so many American accents."

"Iowa," I offered. "Midwestern middle of nowhere."

"Iowa is below Minnesota, *oui*?"

I nodded, struck by the beauty of him. The exquisite sound of him.

"I have been to Minneapolis on business. Pretty in the summer." He pushed the thick, black-rimmed glasses up his nose. "We will continue with the no names rule?"

"Oh, yes. Uh...it may seem weird to you, but I'm more comfortable maintaining that rule. For now, anyway."

"It is not weird. It is unusual, but not weird." A grin broke in his eyes first and I caught my chin against my palm. Wow.

I couldn't take my eyes from his face. It was so close, and yet hundreds of miles away. And his voice. Honey and French lavender woven together. What a way to trap a bee.

"You are beautiful, *mon abeille*."

And he was sex incarnate. I wanted to grab him by the face and kiss him. French him. Moan into his mouth and melt against his body. This little bee's wings were humming for some action.

"You are not saying much. Is everything okay?"

"Oh yes," I said. "Uh, I mean." I sighed. "I'm just falling into your voice. I could get lost in it. Maybe even live there. I know that sounds silly."

"You forget I have seen you at your silliest," he replied.

"Yeah?"

"Your stripper dance on my birthday made me smile. Er, I hope that was the intention?"

It hadn't started that way, but it certainly had ended on a comical note. My attempts to give him a birthday present through glass by digging out a set of stripper tassels I'd won as a gag gift from a girlfriend's shower had resulted in an awkward display. I'd dubbed myself the Hunchback Stripper for my unskilled attempt at the dance.

"I hope you had a great birthday," I offered.

"A couple of friends and I went to a club in the 9th. You know the Pigalle?"

"Yes, the red light district." I'd been there once or twice with my best friend, Melanie. The neighborhood featured three and four-story sex shops, flashing pink neon signs shaped like naked women, discreet hookup clubs, and not-so-discreet sex clubs.

"It is touristy," he said, "but we danced and drank whiskey shots. It was a good time. It would have been even better dancing with you."

"I do like club dancing. But you have seen my dance moves."

His image tilted closer to the screen and his voice grew more velvet than it already felt. "You would dance with me, *oui*?"

If he continued to pepper in some French words? Oh, fuck yes. He didn't need to speak the language, the accent alone was melting away my clothing, tightening my nipples, and wetting my pussy. And I'd seen him doing a sexy shimmy wearing only a towel while dancing around his bedroom. Yeah, I'd dance with the man.

"*Mon abeille*, you are...falling again?"

I nodded. Always. "You're wearing glasses. I've seen you wear them to read."

He tapped the rims. "My long distance vision from window to window is excellent. But up close and for the computer? Not so good. They bother you?"

"No!" I rushed out. Hooking my little finger at the corner of my mouth, I blushed again. So different speaking as compared to gesturing. I had to rein it in. "The glasses are sexy. You're sexy."

He bowed his head and I think he actually blushed. I'd called him sexy what—two or three times already in less than five minutes? So smooth, Miss Cyber Virgin. Not.

But I was a cyber virgin so I had to cut myself some slack.

We got caught in a silent appraisal of one another. The silence felt comfortable, familiar, so I let my gaze soften on him. He wasn't blatantly tan, but he did have a healthy skin tone. And that mustache and the trace of a stubble smudge under his lower lip were perfection. Mmm... I often imagined him as a musketeer who would lift my skirts and go down on me, his tongue sinking into my depths and then twirling around my clit until my body shook beneath his command. All for one and...oh, yes, please.

A lift of his brow clued he was waiting for me to speak. Did I have to? Couldn't I daydream a while longer?

"So I haven't seen you dressed all that often," I said, sliding up my feet on the bed so my legs were bent. I adjusted the laptop so my face still appeared on screen. "You do clothing well."

He laughed, and I instinctively reached for the screen. Wanting to touch those crinkles at the corners of his eyes. To hold that liquid laughter that sounded as good as it had looked through the window.

"I could listen to your laughter all day," I confessed. We'd been more intimate than this. Bald truths should not be difficult from here on out.

"And you laugh every time you come," he said. "I love that."

"I don't think I do *every* time."

He tilted his head and nodded. "*Oui*. You do. It is one of the things that makes you sexy to me. That and your ease to walk before the window and show me everything. Your ecstasy. Your silly side. Even your sadness. You are a confident woman."

He saw all that in me? I guess I wasn't as much of a wallflower as I'd always thought. Introversion didn't mean shyness or even being a hermit. I simply guarded my privacy. Yet with him, I preferred to share, because I knew I could trust him. And there was a certain perversion of danger play that appealed as well.

"Tell me," I asked, "that day we saw each other on the street outside your building." It had only been three days since then. My mind had been wandering on my walk home from a shopping excursion and I'd forgotten to loop around his building so I wouldn't accidentally run into him. We'd stood but twenty paces from one another for breathless moments. "Did you want to walk up to me?"

"More than I needed to breathe, *mon abeille.* I wanted to crush you up against me and kiss you and... " He rubbed a thumb along his temple, casting that soft gaze upon me again. So much emotion in his eyes. "But I sensed you were still unsure. I didn't want to rush you. I never want to do that. What we have..."

He paused for so long, I felt compelled to fill in the silence. "It's different."

"It is. But not a wrong different."

"No. It's something we have created for ourselves, and we're figuring out how it works as we go."

"*Oui.* I like that. Figuring it out as we go. Because, uh...we are a *we*?"

Strange to hear a desperate kind of hope in that question. But then, it did match my hope. And that he felt the same made me giddy with singing bluebirds and sunshine beaming from all around my head.

"Yes, we are a we," I confirmed. "Yet I don't suppose I've a right to demand exclusivity."

"Demand it," he insisted. The shadow of a mustache above his lip looked so lickable. My God, I'm so glad I'd clicked on Video this evening.

"Very well. Let's call this a relationship," I said. "Just the two of us. No others allowed."

Not that I expected a third party, but there were some who trolled for online lovers. I'd done research on it for an author last year. Cyber addicts kept a list of hookups and rarely stuck to just one. A different cyber sex partner for every day of the week was the norm. And two or three at a time? The more the merrier.

"I can do that," he said. "I want to do that with you, *mon abeille*."

I let out a breath and simply smiled at the screen for a while, allowing my heart to slow to a casual pace instead of frantic. We were a *we*. How cool was that?

We fell into that easy stare that we had mastered from window to window. When his eyes averted downward, and a smile tickled the corner of his lips, he finally said, "You are wearing the robe with the bee on it. I can see the inner curves of your breasts. I want to kiss them."

Instant gush between my legs. I was so slick I wanted to reach down and test the waters, but instead I pressed my thighs together to focus the intense hum of pleasure. Mmm...yes. I cupped my breasts, the silk sliding over the nipples and revealing them fully to him.

"You want to kiss these?" I teased.

Drawing my fingers along the edges of the robe, I pushed it off my shoulders, and put down my legs, sitting up straight. I allowed him a good look at them.

He'd seen them before. From a distance of fifteen feet and through glass. In a manner, he was still looking through glass. But the distance was lesser.

He kissed the tips of his fingers and said, "*Foutre*."

I knew that meant fuck.

"Do you know how often I think about fucking you, *mon abeille*?"

I sighed and leaned forward. His eyes were blue and gray and deep and wide and, yes, I had taken the proverbial fall and was currently performing the backstroke.

"As often as I?" I flicked him a cheeky wink.

"I dream about you," he said. "I wake in the morning with you on my mind."

And, apparently, on his cock. I'd caught him one morning—spied him through the glass—asleep on his bed, naked, erect cock high and proud. But I had no intention of telling him that I peeped on him when he wasn't looking. That was just creepy, right?

And having a sexual relationship through glass wasn't creepy?

No, it wasn't. Voyeurism was a safe fetish when shared by two consenting adults. Besides, we'd moved on. Cyber sex was the hot thing.

The intimacy of such a situation moved beyond touch because it was all about the brain. And the brain was the biggest sexual organ in the body.

Sigh... We were almost close to normal now that we'd added voice to our repertoire.

"What are you thinking about?"

I dipped my head, because his question made me blush. I thought I'd gotten over my inhibitions by flashing the man through glass, but there were still things we could do that tested the depths of my intimate discretions. Like *talking* about sex. There was a hell of a lot more emotion involved in talking than going through the motions and watching without sound. Talking revealed more than sight alone with tone and rhythm. It was that brain thing. Voice engaged my imagination and at the same time connected me to reality. A heady new challenge.

"You don't have to tell me your thoughts," he said. "We can talk about anything. I like to listen to your voice."

"I'm sure the American accent has nothing on the French when it comes to sensuality. Your voice does things to me."

"Is that so?" Boyish glee glinted in his eyes. Mercy, I needed to touch my humming clit. "Like what?"

I tapped my chest instead. "I feel it here. The tenor of your voice stirs in me. Makes my skin warm, and..." I lowered my eyes, lashes dusting my cheeks. "...makes me wet."

"My voice does that? That is remarkable. So I wouldn't have to touch you, just talk?"

I nodded then offered a sheepish shrug. "You have something, Monsieur Sexy. Oh—" I pressed fingers to my mouth. I hadn't meant to tell him I called him that. Darn.

"Monsieur Sexy? Is that what you call me?"

Another sheepish lift of shoulder.

"You started as Mr. Sexy," I said, deciding I was in over my head, so I might as well go down and sit at the bottom like a properly chastised naughty girl. "But since you're French..."

"I see. I'm not sure I can live up to such a title."

"Don't worry about that. Your voice alone..." I purred a satisfied noise from the base of my throat.

"Now you are making me self-conscious."

"Really?" I perked up and searched his eyes. He glanced aside for a few seconds. "After all the times I've watched you jack off, a silly little nickname is what makes you nervous?"

He swiped a hand over his mouth and leaned back in his chair. A coffee cup went to his lips, and he sipped. "Tea," he offered. "Chamomile. It calms me after a long day at work."

"I prefer cinnamon myself. And you're changing the subject."

"So I am. We are testing the grounds, *oui*? This new medium of voice challenges our expectations of one another."

"*Oui*," I said. "Truth? I would feel more comfortable stripping off my clothes for you if we hadn't sound on these things."

"I can relate to that. This is more intimate than what we've done thus far. But I don't want to go back to the window. Not when your pretty blue eyes are so close to me now. Do you want me to turn off the sound?"

I actually considered it for nano-seconds. "No. We can do this. But is it okay if we go slow?"

"How slow?"

Splaying my hands over my naked breasts, I felt entirely comfortable sitting there. And I could see on the little screenshot of me that my breasts bounced up and down into the picture as I moved. I then wobbled my hand back and forth to signal middle ground. Then I realized I'd just made a hand gesture.

I wasn't standing before the window anymore.

"Let's play it by ear," I finally said.

"How does that mean? I'm not sure I understand that phrase."

"Oh. Uh. Let's go with however comfortable we're feeling. I'm flashing you my boobs. I'm comfortable with that."

"I am comfortable with that, too."

His sexy grin started at the corners of his eyes and curled his mouth. It was a comfortable place I'd peered into often. And now I'd taken a step across the threshold. I liked it there, standing in the foyer waiting to be invited further.

"I think your breasts are very sensitive to touch," he said. "You like to squeeze your nipples to get off, *oui*?"

"You noticed?"

"I have noticed everything about you, *mon abeille*. Your breasts are full yet soft like peaches. They are a handful for you."

I cupped my breasts before the monitor. Yep, he was right. Perfect handful. But what it would feel like to have a larger, more masculine pair of hands on them tickled at my core and tightened my nipples against my palms.

"Mm, I'm thinking about you touching them right now."

"Me as well," he agreed. "Your nipples are always hard. I could lick them for you. Trace my tongue along the soft undersides of your breasts. Taste your sweetness. Drag my tongue up to the rubies that grow harder in my mouth. Then I will slide my teeth along them in a tease."

I pressed my thighs together. The heat between them slipped moist and slick across my skin. What had happened to going slow?

Fuck slow. Seriously.

"You like me to suck them hard or softly?"

"Both," I answered immediately.

Hands still cupping my breasts, I tilted back my shoulders to lift the sweet treats he described for his tongue. I couldn't feel the hot, wet lash of him tasting me, but I did feel a satisfying tingle skitter across my skin when I tweaked both nipples with my fingers. I moaned and settled against the pillow, the laptop wobbling on my thighs.

"Mmm," he growled. His eyes were closed, one hand held up before his face, his fingers dancing imperceptibly. Imagining his actions. "I think you taste like honey, *mon abeille*. And you smell like a honey-soaked bee. Anticipation jitters your heartbeats beneath my mouth. Fast. You like it firm now. I suck in your skin and feed on your nipple. The texture of it against my tongue is fun to play with. I lick it and trace the rigid peak until I can memorize the shape of you. I could suckle from you forever. *Mon Dieu*."

The hand before him dropped to his lap. I couldn't see what he was doing, but I had my suspicions.

"Are you rubbing your cock?" I asked, tongue dashing to the corner of my mouth in anticipation.

He nodded. "Is okay with you? I can suck you at the same time."

"Very okay. I wish I could see you jacking off."

"I...uh..." He closed his eyelids tightly. Trying to maintain the sensual feeling, I'm sure. "Tomorrow I will adjust the camera for a better view, *oui*?"

"That's fine. Just take that pretty boy out of your pants right now, and rub it like you'd rub my breasts and nipples, please?"

"*S'il vous plaît*," he corrected.

"*S'il vous plaît*," I repeated. The French means to saying please was much more delicious on the tongue.

He stood and unzipped then shuffled down his trousers. "You like this?" He turned to the side, gliding his fingers down the hard shaft that was so close I could reach out and touch it.

I'd seen him handle the main stick before, so now I focused on taking it in, learning the color and shape of it. Deeper colored than his lightly tanned skin, the head of it growing darker as his fingers slid up and down, slowly, not rushed.

He turned toward the computer. The underside of his cock was thick, and I knew if my fingers were pressing on it, it would feel full and yet supple, filled with his need to get off.

"Squeeze your nipples," he said. "Let me watch you so close to me. Lick your fingers to wet them and make your tits slick."

I followed directions, my breast and hand becoming the star of the show. He bent again to watch me, and his hand worked faster up and down his cock.

"Tell me how you like it," he said, pumping at his cock. In the background a phone jangled.

No, don't answer it.

Another tweak of my nipple arched my back and I shoved my free hand between my thighs.

The phone again rang. He glanced to the side. "*Mon abeille*, I have to take this. It is work." He grabbed the phone and signaled for me to pause.

Pause?

But I was touching myself for him. We were having a moment here!

He spoke to someone, stood, and wandered out of camera range.

"Shoot." I exhaled and pushed the hair from my face. "Work this late?"

He flashed back into view, the phone tucked between shoulder and crooked head, and I saw him type. Words scrolled onto the screen before me.

Tech problem for tomorrow. Must straighten out. Will take some time. So sorry.

I typed: I understand. We did agree to go slooowly. We can pick up tomorrow where we left off.

Promise!

"Sweet dreams," I said. "Until tomorrow night."

His screen went black and I closed the laptop with a frustrated sigh.

Okay. So the something that had to be wrong with him had just revealed itself. The man was a workaholic. And he was far too casual about *coitus interruptus*.

I couldn't get upset about this. And I wouldn't. (Okay, just a little. I mean, come on!)

Setting the laptop on the floor, I pulled up the sheets and snuggled into the pillow. Slipping a hand between my legs, I replayed Monsieur Sexy's voice in my reverie as I brought myself to a soft, shuddering orgasm.

Three

I was responsible for closing the map shop this evening. Richard, the owner, was out of town for a few days on another map-sleuthing adventure. Tourist season was settling to a lull, and while the shop normally closed at seven, we sometimes kept it open as long as tourists kept stopping in to browse. We were featuring a ten-euro reprint of a 19th century Parisian map. Sales were moderately brisk.

At eight, I decided to turn over the closed sign, even though the boulevard still bustled with tourists snapping shots of Nôtre Dame, which loomed against the purple and gray night sky just across the river. Tourists passed by, browsing the nearby shops for scarves, keyrings and baby bibs that all touted Paris bedazzled in rhinestones.

One of these days one of those glittery tee shirts would be mine. I did like anything that sparkled. I still considered myself more a tourist than a resident.

But I did enjoy working at the shop, and adored my apartment, so I really should start thinking more in terms of resident. And now there was Monsieur Sexy. We'd known each other almost three weeks. But the notion that we could create something more permanent hit me like a burst of confetti. I wanted to do it. I was capable of doing it.

I was rushing into this happily ever after too fast.

"Slow down," I warned, as I wandered into the back room. "You don't want to marry the prince and get stuck in the castle cleaning toilets, do you?"

Right. Slow and easy was fine with me. For now.

Actually, since crossing the ocean I had become a bit of a short-term dater. A month or two had become my relationship max. Enough time to have some fun, some great sex, and learn a little about the guy, but not long enough to commit. And that worked swell for me. I had no plans to start thinking marriage and babies until after I'd passed the big 3-0.

In the back room, the map Richard had found on a previous expedition lay upon a wooden drafting table covered with linen to protect it. He believed it was an original map drawn by Leonardo da Vinci. And I was inclined to agree, having noted that the knotwork monogram in the key legend was exactly like another Da Vinci monogram featured in one of his published notebooks.

It was fun to imagine it could be something so valuable. And if it was, I was surprised Richard had left it here, lying out in the open. If I had been distracted out in the shop, any customer could have slipped into this small office and taken off with the map. Not that I ever lost track of a customer. The shop was small. Four people filled it.

Now, as I closed the safe and twisted the dial, I gently glided my fingers over the linen and recalled Richard telling me how a person never truly knows something unless they engage all their senses in the discovery.

I had engaged a new sense with Monsieur Sexy. And oh, what his voice did to me. The French accent made some of his words shorter than usual, a little uncertain before he spoke another word, but always correct in his choice of English words. He was smart. But I already knew that. The guy was some kind of IT genius. Geeks had never attracted me. But this geek wore his smarts with style.

Computer smarts were vastly different from street smarts, though. And sensual smarts. Just because a guy knew his way in and around a computer's hardware and software didn't mean he could do so with a woman. My software required a delicate touch. And when it did not, a firmer touch must be employed. But to know when which touch was needed? Definitely an art form.

He'd been doing all right thus far. Not that he'd yet to navigate any of my software. This no-touching business was admittedly weird. But then again, I had asked for it, and I liked it.

Yes, I liked the distance.

I sighed dramatically. Who was I kidding? No touching was for the birds. I needed stimulation that came from the surprise of a man's touch.

Flicking off the office lights, I walked through the shop, and once outside, locked the front door. I wasn't on the schedule for another three days. That was fine. I had enough research work at home to keep me busy for months.

Deciding against walking home, even though the night was bright and many tourists strolled along the river boulevard, I headed down the sidewalk and turned at the corner where a café sided in brown with gold embellishments mastered the corner. Set back in the intersection was a massive pink granite fountain that depicted St. Michael stabbing a downed dragon. Parisians were all about glorifying the macabre.

The Métro stop was tucked amidst the sidewalk café tables. Walking beneath the Art Nouveau-styled sign, I skipped down the steps, slashed my Navigo card, and hopped a train to the seventh where I lived.

Living only five blocks from the Eiffel Tower should be every girl's dream. Am I right? It was all fun and games until you had to battle the crowds in the Métro tunnels, and then the masses that queued up around the Iron Lady and stretched out for blocks in quest of historical sites and photo-ops.

My building sat at the edge of all of that madness. It was nestled in a quiet vee. That was how I'd met Monsieur Sexy. Our bedroom windows were positioned across from one another. And when the lights were on in our respective rooms we could see everything.

Now that the romance—and yes, I did consider this a romance—had graduated to the computer screen, I hoped to get to know him a lot better. Get inside of his brain and pick about. I'd always thought the way to learn a man was through the mental rather than the physical.

I entered my building, nodded to the concierge, and skipped up to the third floor. I never took the elevator. I had a fear of it stopping and me being trapped inside the two-person-only suspended coffin.

There were two apartments on the third floor. I'd met my neighbors last year, and hadn't seen them since. A young couple with accents I had assessed as Irish. I suspected that they traveled a lot because they were rarely home.

Walking into my home was always relaxing. I dropped my purse by the door, and aimed for the kitchen where I poured a glass of red wine, or moscato, if I had that on hand. Tonight it was a nice, sweet red. Heeling off my shoes in the middle of the kitchen floor, I padded into the living room to collapse on the chaise.

A day on my feet, even wearing the comfy kitten heels, always seemed to compress my spine. What I wouldn't give for a massage. Thing was, I didn't like strangers touching me, so I'd never paid for a massage. I relied on generous lovers to do the job. Too bad my current lover couldn't touch me.

Eyeing the laptop that sat waaay over there on the desk, I sighed. Should have grabbed that before I'd settled in, because now I was just too comfy. I did have my cell phone though. I pulled it from my pocket, and scanned through email.

Sitting up as I read, I landed on a particular email I'd been waiting weeks to receive and swallowed awkwardly on a quick sip of wine. "Yes! I got it!"

The job I'd applied for a month ago. The author had interviewed me via email because he was looking for someone to produce a bible for his ever-growing fantasy series. It would involve re-reading his six books, making character profiles, term lists, maps, and keeping track of all the elements in his stories for as long as the series continued.

"This is going to be fun."

I couldn't wait to get started. He'd emailed me digital copies of all his books, and wanted to see a first draft in three months. I could do that, as well as keeping my current research schedule. The extra income would be awesome. But more so, the experience would look great on my resume.

Sipping the wine, I wished Monsieur Sexy were sitting next to me so I could clink my goblet against his in celebration.

I cast a glance toward the desk. The laptop blinked at me.

"He works all day. The only time I get to chat with him is a few hours at night. I have to share this good news with him."

Dragging my weary bones upright, I wandered to the desk with goblet in hand. Hooking the laptop under an arm, I veered toward the bedroom and landed on the comfy velvet chair that matched the chaise. I hadn't realized just how much space there was on this chair until I'd picked up the other day. Bending my legs to sit yoga-style, I set the goblet on the floor beside the chair, nestled deeper into comfort, and then signed on to Skype.

A message waited. He'd pinged me half an hour ago.

Bummed I'd missed him, especially since he wasn't presently online. Looking for you, the message said. Had he given up waiting for me?

Sorry, worked late tonight. You out there? I have exciting news! I sent back, and hit the chime button that would alert him if he was near the computer.

While waiting I finished the wine. I wasn't a big drinker. A goblet once or twice a week was about all I indulged in. Though, since I'd met Monsieur Sexy I'd been imbibing more often. What was that about? Not like I needed the soft release of inhibitions to, er...release my inhibitions.

Or did I?

I tapped my lip, considering that one. No. I didn't need alcohol to feel relaxed and comfortable sharing my body with a man. Even if it had been before a third floor window, in which, at any time, a complete stranger standing below could have spied my naked antics.

Ok, maybe a sip now and then helped.

But now we 'd garnered a certain privacy communicating screen to screen. It was weird to consider. We'd gone from bold exhibitionism to more secretive play. Such a crazy ridiculous backwards relationship.

The computer pinged and I pulled the laptop back onto my legs.

"Hey," he said. "Wasn't sure I'd catch you tonight. Forgive me for abruptly ending our talk last night?"

"Of course. You had business. How did that work out?"

"I was on the phone for two hours, but we sorted out the problem. You look gorgeous."

"Thanks. I got home late from work. Kept the shop open until the tourist crowd slowed. Most of the day I worked on some accounting the boss left for me. He's old-fashioned and does everything on paper. No computer."

"Some people cling to what they are comfortable with. My father will never come into the computer age either."

That glimpse into his personal life made me smile.

"What's so funny?"

I shook my head and drew up a leg to my body, leaning against the chair back. "Nothing at all. I like hearing about your life. I only have my father, and he lives in the States."

"My father is in Marseille."

"Is that the seaside town where all the celebrities vacation?"

"I'm not sure about the celebrity quotient, but it is a coastal city. Pretty in the summer if you like to sit topless on the nude beach."

"Do you go to nude beaches often?"

He shrugged and leaned forward onto the desk, or whatever it was he had the laptop sitting on. "On occasion. I'm not much for letting it dangle for everyone to see."

"So then you don't strip for just any strange woman?"

"Definitely not. Only the pretty ones who peep in my window."

"I'm not a Peeping Jane."

"Oh, yes, you are. I recall it was you I caught looking at me as I strode about my room in only my briefs."

And oh, did I adore the boxer briefs he wore. Snug and hugging that nicely-sized package of his. Mmm...

"Yes, but you *were* walking around with the light on and the curtains wide open," I countered.

"Eh." He shrugged. I loved that sound. A Frenchman's concession to guilt. No biggie, it is just my nature, *mademoiselle*. "So what is your exciting news?"

I told him about getting the fantasy bible job.

"The bible? You know that has been done. And well."

"Not *the* bible." I giggled. "It's like a compendium of all the facts about the fantasy world the author has created. And if he likes my work, I can continue as long as he writes the series."

"Do you like his books?"

"I do, actually. It's sword and sorcery meets swashbucklers. And the women are strong and brave. It'll be fun being a part of it all."

"Then I am pleased for you. *Felicitations*!" He lifted a goblet and we toasted my success.

"I wish you were here with me so we could actually clink glasses."

"That is important to you?" he asked. "The clink?"

"No, but having you here is. I miss you, even though I see you every night. I miss...what I don't have from you yet."

Wow. Where had that come from? And had it sounded desperate?

"I think I understand," he said. "I don't know that I've ever had a woman miss me before."

"Really? I'd say I'm happy to be your first, but that sounds weird. And I'm all about not being weird. Oh heck, that sounded weird." I giggled again.

He leaned closer to the camera so his face filled the screen. "Your laughter is even better when I can hear it. I want to make you laugh again. Only this time it will be because you've just come, *oui*?"

"Give it your best shot, Monsieur Sexy."

I stood, and with a few steps, landed on the bed. I set the laptop onto the comforter and rolled to my side, head propped against my palm.

He shook his head and chuckled without sound. "That name you use for me. It is not right."

"You don't think you're sexy?"

"Eh."

Again with the agreement to not agree too much. I loved it.

"I don't know enough French to concoct a precious nickname like *mon abeille*."

"You are my little bee. Carefree and pretty to look at. But maybe you sting if not handled properly, eh?"

"I don't know about that. Do bees giggle?"

"This one will."

He suddenly stood, because the background on the screen changed and I saw him walk into the bedroom, which was plain white and had the standard fake, painted masterpiece on the wall. The curtains were closed and it was dark, so the screen went grainy.

A light flicked on and I saw him walk away from the computer and sit on the bed.

"I bought a webcam today," he said. "It picks up a wider range than the tiny computer camera. And I have a remote." He displayed the little silver device.

"That's cool. So you can walk around while we, uh, you know?"

"You know?" He tilted a castigating look at me. "You cannot say what it is we do?"

"We have jack n' jill sessions," I provided bravely.

Because mercy, it was more difficult to actually speak about it than to do it. Putting our intimate liaisons into words was bold. Raw.

"Jack and Jill?"

"You've never heard that term before? Men jack off, and women jill off."

"Ah, I understand. The term is odd."

"It's mutual masturbation."

"Screen sex," he said. "That sounds more sexy, *oui*?" A wink landed right in my heart. Stabbed by flirtatious sexiness.

Mercy.

"Screen sex is more sexy," I agreed. "Unless it's before the window, then it's window sex."

"Take off your top," he suddenly said. The tone was not a suggestion, but rather a subtle order. He slid back on the bed to sit up against the headboard and the requisite stacks of hotel pillows. "Show me those gorgeous breasts that I love to lick."

I sat up, and the image of me on the screen suddenly showed only my torso. That wouldn't do. I needed one of those fancy wide-range cameras.

"Just wait. I need to set the laptop on a table or something."

He spoke while I cleared off the vanity and organized my workspace.

"I thought of that when I bought the camera. I purchased one for you too," he said. "I've had it sent overnight to your building. I don't know your apartment number, so I put a note to the concierge that it should go to the woman who received the red envelope. Is that okay?"

"Yes, very clever. Though, the concierge will start wondering what the heck is up."

"Do you worry what he thinks about you?"

"No."

And yes. I always worried for reasons that were silly. And the more I thought about the thing, the bigger it became and then I really started to worry, and—I think too much. Plain and simple.

"My apartment is 3A," I provided. Because I had nothing to hide from him. He was in Berlin. Not like he could rush over and ravage me right now.

Oh, but please? Ravaging sounded like something I could get behind one hundred percent. Or in front of, or with legs splayed, or—you get the idea.

"3A," he said. "Good to know."

I tilted the screen and sat back on the bed. It captured me from head to knee. Perfect. "How's that?"

"*Bon*." He pulled off his business shirt and tossed it aside.

The movement of his muscles flexing over his rigid abdomen made me suck in a breath. Thanks to the fencing lessons he taught, his abs were ripped. From the bedside table he plucked up his glasses and put those on. I did love him in those specs. "Now you. But slowly, *oui*?"

"What? You don't like my silly strip shows?"

"Oh, yes. Undress however you like. I am privileged to watch you."

Good answer. But was he for real? I mean there had to be something about him that was just awful. What made me so special that he'd suffer a touchless relationship on the computer?

Stop thinking! The little devils on my shoulder were named Myself and My Thoughts. I could talk myself out of anything *like that* and convince my thoughts of any major disaster just as quickly.

"*Mon abeille*?"

Right. A sexy Frenchman waited to lust over my naked skin. I mustn't disappoint.

I was wearing a silk blouse that unbuttoned with a slide of my fingers down the placket. Beneath the silk, La Perla peeked out. The pink set today. I liked to coordinate underthings to outerwear. It made my day. Seriously. Don't tell me you don't do the same.

Shifting my shoulders shimmied the silk down my arms. I drew my fingers over the tops of my breasts. He'd clasped his hands before his mouth and ran a thumb along his lower lip. Focused and intent upon my moves, he remained a silent witness. The silence felt sexy. It was what I'd grown accustomed to with him.

Hearing his voice peeled away another of his layers, and yet, I'm sure his voice delved deeper into my layers as well. Did I want him to get to my core?

Oh God, yes. Again and again.

Cupping my breasts, I teased my fingernails along the lace that just covered my nipples. The demi-bra gave the girls an extra upward push. I released the plastic snap in front, and slowly peeled aside each pink lace cup.

My nipples were hard, diamonds awaiting the gemologist's approving eye. As his forefinger glanced over his mouth, behind it grew a smile. I watched his lips curve, the sexy crinkles at the corners of his eyes forming. He always smiled in his eyes first. Those gray sky eyes that seemed to reflect his moods brightly. I could stare into them all day. And now with the computer screen before me, he was close enough that peering into those eyes was possible.

And yet, with him sitting back on the bed, the distance felt familiar, as if we were once again separated by our bedroom windows and fifteen feet of air space. Interesting. What was old was new to us in ways that surprised.

I grazed my fingernails over my nipples and closed my eyes, moaning at the erotic pleasure of the touch. It would feel a thousand times more stimulating if he were actually touching me, yet the fantasy of imagining my touch as his worked. The skin on my breasts goosebumped and tightened. I arched my back, brushing my erect nipples against my palms.

"They are so pretty," he murmured. "Hard and tight. Can you imagine my mouth on them?"

I nodded. I had an excellent imagination. It got me in trouble at the worst times, like when I should get off the Métro at my stop, but forget to because the dashing musketeer was whisking me away from the villain on the back of his powerful destrier.

"Tell me how it feels," Monsieur Sexy purred. "Squeeze them and tease them as you describe the feeling."

I inhaled through my nose and opened my eyes. Confession time. I felt...a little anxiety. When once I'd stood behind the window and directed my own foreplay for him to watch, now he was orchestrating my moves. I shouldn't mind it. I didn't mind it.

But it was different. Describe things? A new challenge in this odd coupling of two who had never touched.

"I'm not sure I can do the dirty talk."

"Why does it have to be dirty? Just be honest. Tell me what you like."

Well, when he put it that way.

"I'm not sure how to describe it," I said, wishing suddenly we could go back to no sound. Sex shouldn't be a challenge, should it? I'd never talked dirty before. So sue me. "It's...so good." Really? Was that the best I could do? "But not as good as I imagine it would feel with your tongue licking my nipple."

I moaned then because I could feel the heat of his wet tongue lash over my breast. "You'd start slow, dancing your tongue over my skin. Around the tightened, ruched aureole. One side, then the other. Then you'd circle one so agonizingly slow—"

I squeezed a nipple and the sensation electrified a path down my belly and to my core. "I like it when you suck it into your mouth, taking it deeply, firmly. Like you need me desperately. You're hungry for me."

He murmured a satisfied noise that sounded like a purr from a wild animal.

"You suck hard on my nipple, sculpting it to a rigid peak. Your fingers work softly around the top and bottom of my breast. It's a combination of gentle and desperately wicked. Oh..."

Leaning forward, I caught my breast in a palm and squeezed. If only his mouth were right there, his tongue dashing between my fingers to claim the prize. His slickness would wet my fingers. I'd pinch them about my nipple and feed it to him, giving him myself, and demanding that he take greedily, roughly.

"I suckle the other one, too," he added. "Licking it until it is slippery between my thumb and finger. I pinch it hard, and you moan. Your back arches, seeking more."

I pinched my other nipple and—yep, the moan came unbidden. Now I pressed my thighs together. My pussy was hot and moist. This was all his doing. The tenor of his voice moved through my veins, the intensity of his gaze glided like touch over my skin. Mmm, I concentrated on the tingle at the apex of my labia that pulsed with want.

"Let me suck it in deeply," he whispered. His eyes were closed now. He was beautiful. A man following his desires, his fingers held before him instead of at his mouth. They pinched and caressed, and I could feel the tweaking touch at my breast. "Harder?"

"Yes," I said on a gasp. "Suck me."

His tongue dashed out and he pressed it between his fingers. The image ramped up my heartbeats. Wetness glistened on his fingers, his lips. My nipples ached, tingled, tightened impossibly.

I shoved my left hand between my thighs and pressed a finger against my clit. Not moving. The pressure was enough to stir the humming tendrils there.

"A little nip," he said. He made a biting motion, and then winked at me.

That wink. Mercy.

"Not too hard. But I want you to feel me," he said. "Be marked by me."

"Oh yes, mark me."

"I suck in the side of your breast," he said. "Hard. Tasting you. Feeding on you. Drawing a dark color to the surface. There, I've marked you."

I could barely speak. The finger at my clit had begun to wobble the swollen bud back and forth. Pacing slowly, intensely focused on luring forth the bliss.

"I'm going to come," I said on a breathy gasp.

"Yes." Sky gray eyes found mine. "Are you fingering yourself?"

I nodded.

"Good, *mon abeille*. Do it the way you like it. Fast then slow, then faster. I've watched you. I know how you like it."

"Are you jacking off?"

"*Oui*. All it takes is watching you to get off, *mon abeille*. And your face. When you feel a streak of pleasure your lips soften and turn into an O. I want to feel that O on my cock."

He growled then, head bowing and his focus turning inward, likely, toward the task, literally, at hand.

And I forgot about my own pleasure and leaned forward. The intensity of his expression, eyes closed and jaw muscles pulsing... That was a turn-on that required no touch at all.

"I like to watch you come," I said, giving him the honesty he'd requested.

I squeezed one nipple hard as my finger slicked faster over my clit. "Oh, so close."

He'd grown silent. And that silent observation put me over the edge. Climax emerged at my fingertips. I crushed a palm over my breast and cried out. A brief outburst as the orgasm shivered through my core and tingled at my breasts. It was a quickie, bursting in the space behind my clit and shaking my thighs and hips, but satisfying.

"Fuck," he said.

Lifting my head, I eyed the elegant Frenchman who held a loose clasp over his cock. I'd not heard him swear in English. I liked it. His accent gave it a nasty yet sensual tone that I'd never thought possible.

His cheeks flushed. He smiled and shook his head. A wag of his hand, the one that had been doing all the work, revealed cream slicked all over it.

"*Trés bien,*" he muttered, and sat back so I could once again, only see his face.

Something about a man's face when he is depleted, relaxed, and satisfied was so appealing. It softened him. Made him more human. Not that he'd ever come off as hard and inhuman to me. Just... All I could do was sigh, because that's what he now did too.

I laughed softly and pulled the laptop back onto my thighs. My chest panting, my breasts tingled and ached from my rough treatment. I cupped one and eased my fingers about it.

"I wish I could have had your tit in my mouth," he said.

"Me too, but this was nothing to complain about."

"One day I will mark you."

"You mean put a hickey on me?"

"That is what you call it? A love bite? Yes, a hickey. Right there on the side where it plumps so nicely. It will fill my palm." He cupped a palm to demonstrate caressing my breast.

I couldn't wait.

"You are so sexy right now, *mon abeille*. Your skin is flushed and your cheeks bright."

I touched my cheeks. I hadn't realized that happened after I came. Well, I'd never looked in the mirror after an orgasm before.

"*Trés jolie*. Tomorrow night, *oui*?"

"*Oui*," I agreed.

"Can we make it a dinner date?"

"Dinner?"

"I will arrange everything. Let's say eight p.m.?"

"Uh, sure." I wasn't sure what he intended, but was willing to jump in for the adventure. "I'll be out and about tomorrow. I've errands to run, but will plan to be home before then."

"You have a mobile with Skype on it?"

"I do."

"I take a lunch at noon. If you want to say hello to me then..."

"I will."

He kissed his palm and blew me the kiss. "Sweet dreams, *mon abeille*."

I caught the kiss, and using my pinched fingers placed it on the side of my breast, right where he said he'd like to mark me.

"Bravo," he said. "Until tomorrow. *Bonne nuit*."

"*Bonne nuit*." I clicked off Skype, suspecting that if I hadn't, we might have stared at each other until one made the first move.

I was still on a high from the orgasm, and now I fell back against the pillow and breathed through it, smiling.

I pulled up the laptop and clicked it off. Setting it on the floor, I picked up the notebook I'd left there and opened it up.

Time for another confession.

Four

Strolling down the mile-long-plus Champs Elysees amidst the pruned horse chestnut trees was always an exercise in credit card stamina. The shops lining both sides of the broad avenue boasted to-die-for high-end clothing, jewelry, gadgets, and foods. The tourists were swarming, even this late in the year. But the sun was high, and the air was warm, so I couldn't resist slowing my pace and taking in everything. I tugged the houndstooth scarf free from around my neck and stuffed it in my purse. I veered right to avoid a gaggle of teenagers cooing over their latest purchases stuffed into glossy pink bags.

I couldn't afford anything in the stores along this street. It was the history that often lured me here. Champs Elysees translated to Elysian Fields, the place of the blessed dead. The avenue stretched from the Obelisk of Luxor, which was way down by the Louvre, and up to the Place Charles de Gaulle, where the Arc de Triomphe held court.

Andre le Nôtre, the famous 17th century gardener who had designed the Versailles gardens, had had a hand in gussying up this once former stretch of dusty medieval markets. As well, many kings had contributed to its improvement over the centuries. By the late 18th century it had become the fashionable place to 'see and be seen'. If a 19th century girl were going to show off her new gown and diamonds, she'd hop in Daddy's open-sided fiacre with a handsome dandy, and tour down the wide street. Nowadays, the rich cruised by in Maseratis and limos.

Hey, if Romain Duris pulled up in a sportscar and gave me the eye I'd instantly forget my cyber affair and hop in. (It could happen.)

I'd once walked over to watch the parade on Bastille day, but the crowd was so thick I'd given up on seeing anything, and had instead spent the afternoon sitting down by the river daydreaming about musketeers and damsels in distress.

Maybe some day I'd write the great American novel. In Paris.

Or back in the States. Who knew?

There was something keeping me here now, but that may not last forever. And while I adored the city, becoming an expatriate did not appeal to me. I liked being an American, and well, the money my mother had left me after she'd died wasn't going to last forever. It paid rent and food and utilities. I could probably survive another six or seven years on it, but the idea of investing some of it also appealed.

I knew nothing about finance and investments, though. And I sure as heck was not going to hire a French accountant to handle my finances. The accent was strictly for my pleasure, not the pain of business.

My favorite place to window drool was Louis Vuitton, which sat a ways up the street. Slowing as I walked before a dress shop that screamed *you must have a black credit card to walk through our gilded doors*, I felt the phone vibrate inside my purse and tugged it out. Monsieur Sexy had Skyped me. Ah, it was noon. I'd lost track of time.

Walking up to the window to steal a little private time amidst the bustle of shoppers, I said hi, and he asked where I was.

"Ah, the shop on the Champs Elysees," he said. "I know that shop. You going in to buy a pretty dress?"

"Not on my budget." He knew this shop? Interesting. "But I do see a McDonalds up the street. It's been a while since I've stopped in for their macarons. They're no Pierre Hermes, but they'll serve in a pinch."

"Will you do me a favor?" he asked.

"Anything."

"Go into the shop. I want to buy you a dress."

"Uh..." I glanced through the store window. There were only a couple dozen dresses hung here and there because to actually display racks of them might crash the bank. And the clothes were black and white, no colors allowed. Too bourgeoisie, apparently. "They're pretty, but—"

"But nothing. I want to buy you a treat. Please let me spoil you, *mon abeille*?"

The idea of walking inside with my no-touch lover, literally, in hand, and buying a dress—excited me. It was so Rex Harrison and Audrey Hepburn, but with a cyber-twist. And heck, if he wanted to spoil me who was I to protest? I imagined this must be how my friend Melanie felt when her playboy lovers bought her gifts. Which was often.

"Okay, you twisted my arm," I said. "But the sales girls will think I'm crazy."

"I'm sure it is done all the time. You are old school, eh? This cyber relationship is popular nowadays."

Indeed, it was. There weren't many people I passed on the sidewalk who weren't chattering into their phones to someone. Could the elderly woman in diamonds and working the cougar print slacks be talking to her cyber lover right now?

All right then. Time to try something totally new and daring.

I strode inside the shop and said, "*Bonjour, Madame,*" to the red-headed saleswoman who returned the greeting. "*Parlez vous anglais*?" I asked. I could manage some French, but if they didn't mind English then I was all for that.

"A little," she said with a perky smile. Not the snobbish decline to knowing the language I usually got from salespeople. Refreshing.

Back in the corner another sales woman was showing a young blonde woman purses. I did feel her disdain even in the brief glance she cast my way.

"Something black," Monsieur Sexy said from the phone.

I turned the phone toward the sales girl. "Uh, my lover. He wants to spoil me." Just saying it shot a giddy streak through my system, but I kept from bouncing on my toes.

"*Ah, oui,*" she said, peering at my phone. "*Bonjour, Monsieur*!"

"*Quelque chose exquise pour mademoiselle. Peut-être noir*?"

I turned the phone toward me. "Hey, no flirting with the salesgirl."

He chuckled and any jealousy that had risen bubbled away on the gorgeous tones of his laughter.

"Monsieur wishes to see something in black for you," she said to me. "I have the perfect item. Your size?"

I told her my size, and she clicked off on her towering silver heels toward a back room.

"So what are you eating for lunch?" I asked as I paced before a display of white silk mini-dresses laden with pearls. The other saleswoman again cast me a snobbish glance down the slide of her nose.

Suck it, lady.

"The company caters the classroom, so I nabbed a sub sandwich and some chips. You know, I like chips. The plain ones. Nothing with fancy seasoning or those disturbing ridges."

"I'll remember that. Ridges disturb you. But to be honest, you strike me as more of a steak and wine kind of man."

"Ah? Not much for big slabs of *vache*—er, cow. Why do you think that of me?"

I shrugged as I drew a fingertip along a strand of glossy pearls. "When I've seen you in your suit you looked so elegant and classy."

"I do like to dress well when I am away from the home office. No use in putting on a suit at home, eh? But I have a certain image I must maintain for clients. And my appetite tends toward the American tastes."

"Really? We Americans love our big slabs of beef."

His laughter paused me in the center of the white marbled floor. I wanted to kiss the screen, but the saleswoman helping me had reappeared, sans dress. She gestured I follow her down a narrow white-marble-walled aisle toward the dressing rooms. I followed the click of her skyscraper heels.

"I'm going to change," I said. "You coming along?"

"That is the very reason I asked you to go in the store. So I could get you naked in public." He waggled his brows suggestively.

"Naughty boy," I whispered as the saleswoman opened the door.

"I've placed two items inside," she said. "I trust Monsieur will favor them both. I am Roxane. Call for me if you need..." Her lashes dusted over her bright green eyes. I got the distinct feeling she had just summed me up sexually. "...anything."

"*Merci*, Roxane," he said as I stepped inside.

Roxane closed the door behind me and I stifled a giggle. "Did you get that? Anything?"

"Anything can mean very much," he said. "Or you. Perhaps both of us, eh?

"That's just weird. I've never had a woman flirt with me before. I must be imagining things."

"If that is what you wish to believe."

The dressing room was lined floor-to-ceiling with pink chiffon and it smelled like candy. It was like standing inside a fancy purse. I set the phone on a tiny corner shelf. A pink and gray striped damask arm chair sat in one corner, next to a long mirror that was etched with arabesques around the borders.

"Can you see me?" I asked as I turned to study the two dresses hung before the chiffon curtain and shed my coat to toss on the chair.

"The back of you is as sexy as the front. So you would never consider a liaison with a woman?"

"Are you serious?" I turned, expecting to catch his teasing wink. No wink. "You are. Hmm... I've never thought about it before."

A person didn't have to be gay to be curious about their own sex. I wasn't curious, though I could admit that Roxane was gorgeous and her kohl-lined green eyes had been stunning. And okay, if that had been a flirtatious look she'd given me then I could dig it. I appreciated the attention. Made me feel sexy.

The first dress was silk with a lace cutout along the neckline and around the hem. I kicked off my shoes and pulled the blouse off over my head.

"Have you ever had sex with a man?" I turned to display to him the black bra I wore, and bent to slip down my skirt. "Would you tell me?"

"I will tell you anything you want to know. One time in college. It was curiosity. Not sex. We kissed. It was different than kissing a woman, but I liked it. I also like those lacy underthings you are wearing. You've worn them before?"

"They're my favorites. Makes me feel sexy. So you've kissed a guy. I find that incredibly sexy."

Because, okay, out of curiosity I'd cruised a few Tumblr accounts that featured softcore photos of men embracing. There was something so titillating about hard, muscled bodies pressed next to one another in the most intimate of clutches.

"I think watching you kiss a woman would be sexy," Monsieur Sexy offered.

"But a kiss is so intimate. We've never kissed."

"You think a touch would be less intimate?"

"Depends on where the touch is, I guess."

I unsnapped the front of the bra and flashed him my breasts. Then as quickly I reclasped it and looked toward the door. I knew I had privacy in here, but it still felt more daring than standing before a window naked. Because Roxane wasn't stupid. And she could likely be standing down the aisle, ten feet away, listening to everything we said.

I would, if I were her. Customer walks in with a man on her cell phone and he orchestrates the purchase? That one would be too intriguing to resist.

"You know," I said as I stepped into the dress. It felt like a cloud sliding over my skin. "This little tryst feels more intimate than some of the other things we've done. And sneaky."

"Do you think she is close by, listening to us?"

"I'd bet on it," I said quietly. If she was listening, I was going to make it a challenge.

"Maybe Roxane would like to watch?"

I didn't know what to say to that one so a smirk sufficed. I couldn't imagine undressing before another woman simply for her sexual pleasure. I'd never be able to look her in the eye, that was for sure.

"Look at me," I suddenly said, and paused, back of the dress unzipped, and stared into his eyes. "How often do you really look at your lover when in bed with them?"

"Depends if the lights are on or off. Do you prefer them on?"

"I do. But I confess that I am an eye-contact avoider. Unless of course, it's fifteen feet and behind glass."

"I like gazing into your blue eyes."

"Yes, but will you do it when we are having sex? When we finally lay skin against skin?"

"I will."

"I would like to say I will, but such intimacy is a little scary."

And where had that confession come from? Certainly not from my inner vixen. My introvert was showing. But that was okay. It had to be.

"You know you can trust me, *mon abeille*."

"I do know that." And the introvert relaxed a bit, willing to play this one out.

I left the zipper undone and turned to study the dress in the mirror. A little loose around the stomach and hips. And the tag claimed it required dry-cleaning. This dress would never survive my need for dropping clothing on the floor as I undressed. Then again, I wouldn't need to clean it often because I rarely went to any places in the city that required such fancy dress.

"What do you think?" I turned before the phone and stood on tiptoes to give him the complete view.

"Pretty," he said.

"Right. But not the best."

He wobbled his hand side to side and gave me one of those Frenchman's 'ehs' that I loved so much. "Next option."

I quickly made the change, loving that the all-lace version hugged my body and especially my breasts. It clung like a second skin and was discreetly lined with a nude fabric so it looked as though it was lace against skin.

A satisfied murmur hummed in his throat. "You should not wear a brassière with that."

"I won't. But say it again."

"What? Brassière? Do you make fun of me now?"

"No. Maybe. I love to listen to you speak. And maybe I like you telling me what to do. Just a little."

"In that case, no panties either. And make a note."

"What's that?"

"The first time we actually see one another and touch?"

I nodded.

"No panties or brassière. Promise me."

"I promise," I said on a breathy gasp.

Telling me I wasn't allowed those undergarments when around him did things to me. The dressing room suddenly felt smaller and warmer. I let my palm fall down the front of the dress, and stopping over my mons I put pressure there where my clit suddenly pulsed for attention.

Monsieur Sexy made a growling sound. "You are aroused."

"You're guessing."

"Your pupils have dilated."

I peered close to the phone screen. "You can't see that well through there."

He chuckled. "No, but your eyes have darkened, so it's a guess. Is it the dress or me watching you?"

"Both."

"*Bon*. That is the one."

I nodded. "You have great taste. But I would like to get it zipped up to make sure it's not too tight."

With my back turned to him I managed a sneaky look at the price tag. Mercy. Or when in Paris: *merde!* This one would set him back a month's rent on my place. My rent was not cheap. I couldn't let him do it.

"You like it?" he asked. "It is as if it were made for you."

Indeed, it was. The lace was so soft, a possessive hug against my skin. Oh, but it would be perfect with my Louboutins. And to imagine stepping out on the town wearing this dress, those shoes, and holding Monsieur Sexy's hand...

A knock on the door startled me from the delicious fantasy. "All is well?"

"She'll take it," Monsieur Sexy called before I could speak. And then he said to me, "Do you dare experiment with a touch?"

I spun quickly to face the door. I knew what he was asking.

"Mademoiselle, do you need assistance?" Roxane called from outside the door.

I glanced to the phone. He lifted his chin and tilted his head. Defying me?

Daring me.

"I do," I suddenly said. Panic quickened my heartbeats, but I remained calm on the outside. "You can come in. I would like to see the dress zipped up."

The door opened and Roxane stepped inside. Red hair spilled softly over her white satin shoulder. I hadn't noticed her soft floral perfume before, or how petite she actually was. Five-inch heels brought her face to my eye level. Once I looked into her eyes, it was difficult to notice anything else about her. Stunning, simply stunning.

"Zip her up," Monsieur Sexy instructed, "*s'il vous plaît.*"

"*Bien sûr, Monsieur.*"

She stepped around behind me. I faced the phone. Her hand glided down the opened zipper, the cool gloss of her nails skimming my skin. A flinch tickled at me, but I was holding my breath in an attempt not to show my sudden anxiety. She was a fast study. She knew what we were up to.

Thing was, could I do this?

I sucked in a breath as the zipper inched upward, hugging the fabric about my body. Suddenly the dressing room felt small and I felt...invaded. I pressed a hand over my stomach. My fingers quivered. I closed my eyes. I didn't want to look into his eyes.

"An excellent fit," Roxane said in her quiet voice. It felt like the elegant pearls displayed out front with the dresses and slipped around my senses. "Your figure is *exquis*."

I liked that word: exquisite. It relaxed me a bit. *Nothing to feel threatened by in here. Just you and your inner vixen trying something new and daring.*

I nodded. "I like the feel of it." Opening my eyes I noticed she stood beside me, facing the phone.

"*Ça vous plaît, Monsieur*?"

She'd asked if it pleased him.

He nodded. "The lace at her collar is not right?"

"Ah?" Roxane stepped around in front of me and checked the front of the dress, tucking her finger along the collar and slipping it between the lace and my skin. "Tucked under," she cooed. "I will fix."

Slowly she journeyed down toward my breast. I inhaled. The touch was so light and not at all tentative as it could be from a man. I wasn't going to stop her. I didn't want to. While slightly freaked, and at the same time a contained bundle of nerves, I felt the need to challenge my inhibitions yet again. My inner vixen was undulating her hips and cooing right back at Roxane.

And I wanted to show Monsieur Sexy that I was no shirking violet.

"You should not wear a brassière with this dress," Roxane said. Her eyes flashed up toward mine. Like emeralds. I bet her lovers stared at them as they made love with the lights on.

"I—I don't think I will. Your eyes are gorgeous." The compliment slipped out on a cool exhale. I had become the vixen.

Then she tilted up onto her tiptoes and touched my mouth. One glossy fingernail trailed along the upper curve of my lower lip. Exploring. Curious. She was going to kiss me...

"*Ses lèvres sont seulement pour moi,*" Monsieur Sexy suddenly said.

Pouting her mouth into a bright red moue, she nodded and leaned in to whisper at my ear, "He said your lips are only for him."

I lifted my chin and parted my lips, eyeing him slyly. *Thanks, lover.* At that moment I felt like his possession, and it was amazing.

Then Roxane kissed my earlobe. First she nudged my ear with her nose, then, her lips closed over the lobe. She tugged it gently and sucked it in. The sensation tickled along my neck and toward my nipples, which hardened beneath the lace. Her wrist brushed my nipple and she again cooed.

I noticed then that I squeezed my thighs together because...I was wet. And all I could think to distract myself from the feelings I should only get from another man was to close my eyes. My hand glanced across the front of Roxane's silk shirt. Her nipple was erect, and the surprise of that knowing came out in a sigh.

"You have never done anything like this," she whispered at my ear, so softly, I'm sure the man on the phone did not hear.

I shook my head subtly.

"Relax," she cooed.

From outside the door and down the hallway, a woman's voice called out for Roxane.

"My boss." Roxane stepped away from me, smoothing her hands down her blouse and then shrugging her fingers through her long, red hair. A glance toward the phone, and she nodded. "*Excusé moi.* I must return to the sales floor. When you've changed, call for me, and I'll bring out the dress for you."

I touched my earlobe as she left me alone in the room with my curious lover. Butterflies fluttered out of my stomach, leaving me feeling empty. I sighed heavily. Brushed my palm over a breast and felt my heartbeats racing.

"Talk to me, *mon abeille*."

I didn't know what to say. It hadn't been a blatant encounter. No kiss. I was glad for that. But the contact with my ear had been intimate, invading, and yet, I'd savored the feel of it. If Roxane had stayed any longer, might I have placed my hand on one of her breasts?

I think so.

"I need to think about this," was all I could reply. I turned my back to the phone and slipped out of the dress.

Five minutes later, after I'd handed the phone to Roxane so Monsieur Sexy could give her his credit card number, I expected to be handed a bag with the dress in it.

"It will be delivered to your address this evening," she informed me while escorting me toward the front door. "Instructions from your lover."

Her boss, a grand dame in diamonds and tweed was talking to another customer within hearing range. No sneers this time, I noticed.

Roxane's bright red lips curled into a knowing smile. I nodded, allowing the moment to sink in. Yes, I had a lover who liked to buy me pretty, expensive things, and who could seduce even a French woman over the phone.

And she had seduced me.

"*Merci*," I said, holding her gaze for too long. I would always associate emeralds with Roxane.

She blushed. "Return whenever you wish. Both of you."

And it felt like the perfect moment for a goodbye kiss—so I dashed for the door.

Once outside, the cool fall air brisked my face, and I tugged the scarf out of my purse before putting the phone to my ear as I walked. "That was too generous."

"That was the beginning of our evening."

"Even the touching?"

"No, that was an enjoyable aside. You liked it?"

"It was new for me. I'm still processing."

"I could sense your dis-ease, but as well, your curiosity. You know how hard that made me?"

"I can imagine. Men are all about the visual. Okay. So it did feel good in a forbidden fruits kind of way."

"We will return to the shop some day. Together."

"Uh..." I couldn't agree. Maybe? Still processing.

"My lunch is over," he offered. " I have to return to class. I will see you at eight for our date?"

"You will see me."

"In the dress sans panties and brassière."

"Anything for you."

Anything? Even sex with another woman? Oy. Let's not get ahead of ourselves, shall we?

"*Ciao, mon abeille.* I will think of nothing but fucking you in black lace for the rest of the day."

And I stumbled on the curb and bumped into the person in front of me as he clicked off. The woman I'd crashed into turned around and cast me a nasty glare. I couldn't even be ashamed.

I had become a well-kept woman.

Five

I took the Métro home. The moment I'd clicked off with Monsieur Sexy the sky had darkened and tourists had scampered for cover. It began raining cats and dogs, and I'd worn kitten heels today. The train stopped three blocks from my apartment building, so I still had to jockey for the wall and under awnings. By the time the concierge greeted me and handed me a dress bag I was soaked, but very happy not to have walked home in the rain with the expensive contents.

A package emblazoned with Amazon's cheeky smile waited for me as well. The box was too small for bookshelves, but through a pitiful sheet of wet hair spilling over my face, I thanked the concierge, slipped off my shoes, and padded up the stairs to the third floor, leaving puddles in my wake.

I deposited the box on the chaise in the living room then veered toward the bedroom. I hung the dress from a hook beside the mirror, and then stripped away my wet vestments. I had gone from feeling like a million bucks to feeling like a miserable wet puppy.

A hot shower stirred up the feeling in my fingers and face.

Wrapping my wet hair in a towel, I wandered into the bedroom naked and glanced over the dress bag that held the promise of romance within. As well as the memory of the illicit touch in the dressing room.

I glanced in the mirror, tugging the earlobe Roxane had kissed. "Who are you?"

Who had stood in that dressing room getting turned on by another woman's touch? A complete stranger had put her lips on my ear. And I had liked it so much that my pussy had grown warm and moist.

I could never walk by that store again. And yet, the idea of returning, on Monsieur Sexy's arm, intrigued. Did my future hold a *ménage à trois*?

"Roxane, eh?"

Sting's longing chorus about Roxane keened into my thoughts. I wasn't even sure how the logistics of such a combination could work. Yep, that's me. Vanilla to the core. But if truth be faced, I decided that if there was ever going to be three naked bodies in my king-size bed, I'd prefer it be myself and two other men. Because really? I had no intention of sharing my man with another woman.

I pulled the towel from my head and patted my hair with it. "Dinner with Monsieur Sexy. I wonder how he's going to pull that one off?"

Would he send me to a restaurant and once there I'd have to communicate with him via cell phone and Skype? It would be weird, but I was up for anything he had in mind. But if he asked me to kiss anyone nearby I would call foul. One daring new encounter for the day had been enough.

Crossing my fingers that if he did send me somewhere it would be with front door taxi service, I fluffed out my hair, then decided to blow dry it with a flip to the ends.

Next up, the dress. He'd seen me in lingerie, my robe, and nothing. A few times I had stripped off my clothing for him before the window as he'd watched. And I guess last night I'd done the upper strip for him. Mm, that had been a good one. It upped the erotic level when he told me what to do. And challenged my ability to release inhibitions and really trust. I'd almost panicked in the dressing room. But I think he'd realized that.

Or maybe not. He had said we would return to the shop some day. I liked that he thought in terms of us going places together in the future.

I sorted through my underwear drawer, my fingers browsing over lace and satin and a few cotton pieces—then I remembered. He'd requested me sans underthings tonight.

A sensual tingle scurried up my stomach and tightened my nipples. I was submitting to his will. And I liked it.

My fingers traced down the lace dress. Snagging the price tag, I almost pulled it off, but stopped myself. I scampered into the bathroom for a nail snips to do it right. Didn't want to risk snagging the fabric or putting a run in the lace. Not after that credit card bill.

"He has to be rich," I said as I pulled the dress up around my naked thighs. "How many guys can lay down their card like that for a little bit of lace?"

Had he done it to impress me? At this moment was he lamenting the bill he'd receive next month and wondering how he would cover it?

I shook my head as I reached behind to tug up the zipper. (Yep, I could have zipped myself at the store.) Monsieur Sexy wasn't the sort to do such a thing. He didn't need to impress me. And judging from the fancy suit I'd once seen him wearing, he appreciated fine clothing and could afford it.

With the dress hugging my skin, I smoothed my hands up to cup my breasts. The lacy neckline dipped low and accentuated my almost-Cs. A pushup bra would have really worked the dress, but no. I turned to the side and admired my silhouette in the mirror.

"Not bad. Have I lost weight?"

Because I used to have a nudge of a muffintop going on, but even in this body-hugging dress I couldn't see a nudge at all.

"Nice."

I hadn't been paying attention to what I ate lately. Any poundage that had slipped away had to be because of the hot new love affair. I'd take it.

With an excited shimmy of my hips, I glanced at the Louboutins holding court before the foot of my bed. The black leather beauties tied around the ankle with velvet ribbons.

"Fingers crossed the rain stops."

Sitting on the gray velvet chair, I pulled on the supple leather shoes, and tied them about my ankles. I tilted my head to look out the window. Though he'd left the curtains open, I couldn't see into his bedroom across the street. Rain blurred the view, and the lacking sunlight sheened his window with a white glare.

We'd come a long way. Voyeurism across the street from one another to cyber-sexing. I sighed.

I couldn't understand how some couples actually engaged in cyber relationships for long periods of time. It was only so satisfying. And more and more it was growing frustrating. If I was honest with myself, cyber sex was unfulfilling. Left me empty even though I wanted to believe it filled me. Sure, it fulfilled my need for mental connection. But the physical contact?

"Hardly."

We were still watching one another. Participating, but only with ourselves.

The doorbuzzer rang. I wasn't expecting anyone so, engaging a cautious stride, I slunk up to the door. Weird, right? I didn't think a serial killer would knock first. On the other hand, what a perfect way to gain entrance into the unsuspecting woman's apartment: knock and greet her with a smile.

Oh, my God, I think too much.

Peering through the peephole I spied a man dressed in a white chef's uniform and holding an armload of bags and boxes. I opened the door and he introduced himself in French.

"*Parlez vous anglais*?" I asked.

"*Non, Mademoiselle.*"

He barged past me and looked about, his arms loaded with goods, and headed into the kitchen. From what I could guess he was saying, and the delicious scents that emerged as he began pulling things from the bags and boxes, he'd brought dinner.

Yay! Now I didn't have to brave the weather in my pretty things. And how cool, Monsieur Sexy and I would have a private meal together.

The chef sneered at the kitchen table scattered with books, files, and other assorted ephemera that basically lived there because I had too much stuff and not enough storage. I sensed his disapproval.

"I'll get that." I rushed to clear the table, grabbing heaps of stuff and...swinging around, I eyed the floor before the living room window. I got that far before books starting falling out of my arms.

An annoyed 'tut' echoed out from the kitchen. The fridge opened and closed. Plates and goblets were retrieved from my cupboards. A strange Frenchman shuffled about in my kitchen setting up a meal for me, and I was thrilled. Who cared if he was the cooking serial killer? At least I'd leave this world with a full stomach.

After a plate had been set on the table with a silver dome over the top, and silverware placed in the proper setting, he poured wine and then gestured I sit. "*Mademoiselle.*"

I sat and he pulled up the chair.

He checked his wristwatch and nodded. Satisfied. "Eh...er...Skype?"

"Oh, yes!" My dinner date began soon. "*Merci, Monsieur.*"

He bowed and then pointed to the fridge. "*Le dessert. Au revoir, Mademoiselle. Bon appétit*!" he called as the front door closed.

And I sat in wonder before the table, my fingertips playing with the silverware. They'd never gleamed so brightly. Must have something to do with being positioned in the proper place settings.

I sipped the wine. "*Mon Dieu*. This is..." I grabbed the bottle and scanned the French label. "I don't know what this is, but it tastes expensive. Amazing."

Note to self: look up this wine online later.

I could get used to being spoiled. Yet no lover waited for me to wrap my arms around and kiss in thanks. At the very least I needed to blow him an appreciative kiss. Which I wouldn't be able to do if I didn't get my act together.

Dashing into the bedroom, I retrieved the laptop and turned it on as I returned to the table. Setting the laptop at the top of the table setting, I seated myself.

Skype pinged and Monsieur Sexy's face flashed onto the screen. "*Bonsoir*," he greeted me with goblet of wine held high.

"*Bonsoir*." I tapped the screen with the goblet rim, and he did the same. Cyber-toasting at its best. "This is amazing. I can't believe you planned all this."

"The dinner has arrived? Excellent. I was worried it would not happen for the timeline. Ah, I see you have your food before you. And I have mine."

I could see him from head to tabletop. Before him sat an elegant dining service and a bottle of wine. He was suited up. A thin violet tie filed down a gray shirt and a darker gray suit. He looked like a GQ model. Seriously. I'd seen him walking down the street in a suit, and if the man didn't belong on a runway, then neither did Naomi Campbell.

"Are you pleased with the selection?" he asked.

"I haven't looked yet. The chef just left." I took the silver cover off my food and it released a gush of savory scents. Tiny ravioli and white sauce accented with carrots and something deep red, probably peppers. "I love shrimp."

"And the chef, did he leave dessert in the fridge?"

"Yes. Do you want me to—"

"No, leave it for later. Let's enjoy our meal and chat. Ah, you are wearing the dress. The neckline frames your breasts perfectly. I wish I were there to kiss around the lace. Stand up and let me admire you."

I did so and turned, propping a hand at my hip. Then I leaned forward to give him a better view of the lace-surrounded bosom he so wanted to kiss.

"No underthings?"

"Just the lace and my skin," I said. Then the vixen in me inched up the lace hem, slowly gliding up my thigh until—just as the dip of my labia were revealed I tugged the dress back down. "Does that please you?"

"I have just received a sneak taste of dessert. I told you I would think about you today and I did. But I tore the lace in my fantasy."

"Really? Where?"

"Where was I fantasizing about you?"

"No, where did it tear?"

"Ah." A smile glinted in his eyes. "At the hem of your skirt. I tugged too quickly and hard. Needed to get my hand between your legs to feel you wet and hot on my fingers."

I clamped down on my lip with my teeth. The man was too much. But just enough for me.

"Let's eat before we start ripping any lace," I suggested. "This will be fun. Sort of like a dinner out. You sitting across from me, me from you."

"Except I can't smell your perfume or stroke the back of your hand, or even move closer to slide my hand up your thigh under the table."

I paused with a fork full of tiny shrimp and white sauce suspended above the plate. He had such a way with words. And here I'd been worried about eating quickly before the food got cold. He was thinking only about me. And how he would touch me.

"You do that very well, you know?" I said.

"What is that?"

"The interested lover part."

"I am interested in everything about you. Will you allow me to tease out more details tonight?"

"Go for it."

"Excellent." Propping his elbows on the table, hands steepled before him, revealed the diamonds in his cufflinks. Small and set in brushed silver. Classy.

"I do want to know about the bees," he said. "If you will indulge me."

"Yes, the bees." I set down the fork and toggled the stem of the wine goblet between my fingers. "My grandfather's farm was sold at auction last year. He grew red clover on a small farm in Iowa. Honeybees have become so scarce they no longer pollinated his plants and his crops had become worthless. The bees are dying out, and when they are gone, our food sources will suffer."

"France has the same problem. I watched a documentary on it not long ago."

"You watch documentaries?" I wiggled on the chair, thrilled to learn we had a common link. "You like learning new things?"

"Always." Sexy Frenchman's smile directly ahead. Crinkle at the eyes. Glint in the irises. And... Direct hit to my heart.

I sipped more wine so my goofy smile wouldn't break out. I loved chatting with him via Skype, but I seriously needed to turn off my window on the screen. I could see myself, and I was always checking to make sure I didn't have food in my teeth or was sitting slumped. I had a tendency to slump.

Pushing my shoulders back, I reminded myself about the newly absent muffintop. I looked great this evening, and I intended to work this dress for all it was worth. (Which was quite a lot.)

"Did you know the *Jardin des Plants* has a bee exhibit?"

"They do? I haven't yet stumbled onto it when I visit. I love that garden. That one, and the Luxembourg in the 6th. I love espaliered trees and carved shrubbery."

"I like a nicely trimmed bush myself." Frenchman's wink.

Mercy. I was undone.

A waggle of his brow pushed me closer to the edge and I wanted to abandon the meal and just fuck. But...no. I took a deep breath and relaxed. Though I must say I was pleasantly moist between my legs right now.

I traced a fingertip around the goblet rim. "So tell me what you are passionate about. Beyond the work you do."

"I like to stay fit. That is why I teach fencing. I used to fence competitively, but I injured a muscle in my leg and now I'm useless for the intense competition. I like to cycle."

"Really? Around the city?"

"No, too many tourists. I have a mountain bike that I take out often with friends. We bike hundreds of miles, crash down mountains, and get horribly banged up. It's a riot."

I suddenly felt so out of his league. The man was sexy, a computer brainiac, and he participated in sports that pushed him to the limits and chewed him up and spit him out. How cool was that?

What did I do for exercise beyond rushing to the Métro in kitten heels and struggling with women in the line before Louboutin? (Well, and masturbating. Orgasm counted as exercise, right?)

"The mountain biking explains your tan," I said.

"It is fading. I haven't been out since before the move. Been too busy with work. I'm training new employees here in Berlin. It's intensive stuff, but the guys seem to pick it up easily. They're a smart bunch. I will be pleased if one or two learn enough to promote."

"Promote? Are you like the head honcho?"

"Yes, I own the company. We're small, but within a few years I plan to take on the world."

"More power to you, boss man."

"*Merci.*" Another tilt of his goblet toward the screen. "I am the most competitive with myself, I admit."

"I can relate. I have a type A side that comes out when working. But I counter that with my type C side."

"Type C?"

"Comfort whore."

"I'm not sure I understand, but I suspect it is a good thing for you."

"Oh, it is."

I finished the shrimp pasta and set down my fork. "So, I know what sports you like, that you're smart, and that you like to dance around in a towel when you think no one is looking."

"Eh. I am a terrible dancer."

"I wouldn't say terrible. I've seen your hip action. So what else? Tell me what TV shows you like?"

"I don't actually watch more than an hour a week."

That made me sit up. I noticed my dropped jaw on the tiny screen and closed my mouth quickly. Wow. That said so much about him. But it figured. If he were owner of an up and coming business when would he have the time? Competitive and determined. Love it.

"I like to read," he offered. "When I'm not cramming new information into my brain from the latest software and systems updates, I have my nose stuck in historical fiction."

"What's your favorite book?" I asked.

"The Three Musketeers, of course."

"What?!"

He sat up abruptly and glanced around, tugging at the knot of his tie. "Did I say something wrong?"

Poor French dude. I'd freaked him out.

"Nothing wrong," I hastened out. "You just said your favorite book, and it's one of mine, too."

"Is that so? Dumas created classic heroes. I reread the story every few years. It is the reason I took up fencing. When I was a kid I wanted to be a musketeer."

"Oh, you are," I said before I realized I was speaking about my fantasies and not real life.

"You think so?"

"I know so. If I can make a confession?"

"Please do. I love it when you reveal your secrets to me, *mon abeille*."

His sexy accent stirred beneath my skin and warmed me everywhere. If he knew I was wet for him right now... Well, I'd let him know about that soon enough.

"When I first saw you moving in..." I pushed aside the plate and pulled the laptop closer. "You were carrying a box with your fencing foil sticking out of it."

His eyes softened, admiring me. I soaked it in like a sponge.

"First, you need to know my mind wanders. A lot. I can go from reality to fantasy like that." I snapped my fingers in example. "Anyway, that day I saw you moving in, I started thinking about swords and musketeers. And then I imagined you as a musketeer. On your knees. Licking my pussy."

"Is that so?"

I nodded. I couldn't be embarrassed with him. This was a step deeper into confidence.

"Did I push my way under your skirts?"

"I think I was on a bed, lying back. You pushed up my skirts and I spread my legs for you." I hadn't gotten much farther with the fantasy at the time, but I sure could imagine things progressing now. "You want to know how it felt?"

"Of course, you must tell me. How do you like me to tongue you?"

The lace dress was suddenly far too stuffy for this warm room. I tugged at the neckline then cautioned against ripping the lace. Only he could do that.

"All over at first," I decided. "Tasting me, slipping up and down along my folds to learn my structure."

He closed his eyes and his lips parted slightly. "I can imagine that. Tucking the tip of my tongue between your folds and tasting your sweetness and heat." He flashed open his eyes. "Are you hot right now?"

"Oh, hell yes."

"Lift your skirts for me, *mon abeille*. Let me glide my tongue over your treats for dessert."

"But what about the dessert in the fridge?"

"You are still hungry? Go get it. But I will be displeased if you do not return naked."

"Is that so?"

Such a demand would have normally had me snappishly refusing to play along with any man's silly desires. But this man was different. He was mine. And I wanted to please him. And I had been thinking this dress was getting too hot.

"Be right back."

I took the supper dishes away from the table and set them in the sink. Unzipping the back of my dress as I pulled open the fridge door, I let the sheath fall to the floor around my heels. Comfort whore, remember? I stood there in the light from the fridge, allowing the coolness to waft over my warm skin. It tickled. It teased. It was weird, I know, but hey, I was working with what I had. And that was a laptop, and an eager Frenchman whose voice could bring me to my knees.

I wasn't about to disappoint.

A small white box sat in the fridge, labeled *dessert*, as if the White Rabbit had been in here while I wasn't looking. If it had said *eat me*, I wouldn't have blinked at doing just that. I took it out and stroked my fingers over the box. It was a nice box, not like those flimsy takeout boxes. Something designed to present a gift.

I recalled the red envelope and wrapping paper he'd used to send the bee notebook and his email address. Fine. Elegant. He was a discerning shopper. Dare I believe his discernment went as far as the woman with whom he'd chosen to engage in an affair?

I almost didn't need the treat inside the box. The thrill of knowing he liked to spoil me with fine things was more than enough. Seriously. A man who took the time to attend to the small details?

There had to be something wrong with him. Sooner or later his warts would show.

"But hopefully not tonight," I whispered.

I pulled off the box top. Inside sat an exquisite little cake topped with an artful arabesque that had been dusted on the creamy surface with what looked like dark chocolate powder. Drawing it out, I set it on the counter. The dessert sat on a gold circle of cardboard. I think it was ganache or maybe mousse. Three layers, starting with dark brown on the bottom, a lighter brown in the middle (probably milk chocolate) and a creamy white vanilla section on top.

I dashed my finger down the side, swiping all three colors of the cool, whipped delight onto my skin, then licked it off.

"Oh, heaven."

"*Mon abeille*?"

I peeked around the refrigerator door. He couldn't see me from this position.

"No sneaking a taste until I see you naked," he called. "Come, my cyber lover."

He wanted me to come? All in good time, my sexy musketeer. All in good time.

Sliding my tongue along my lips to thoroughly clean away evidence of sneaking, I closed the fridge door and skipped back to the kitchen table with dessert in hand. I stood before the laptop with the smeared side facing me and performed a Vanna White sweep of hand beneath the plate.

"Is this what you've been waiting for?" I asked sweetly. I even batted my lashes. Yeah, I could work the corny seduction like a pro.

"All day. But you look even better than I imagined. Lower the dessert. Lower. *Bon*, just there."

I held the treat below my breasts now so he got a view of my torso topped by hard nipples, a sweet treat, and my trimmed pussy.

"Want a taste?" I cooed.

"You've already tasted it," he decided smugly.

"Who me?" I swiped a finger along the corner of my mouth. Had I a telling smear of chocolate there?

"You see? The guilty party tries to clean away the evidence," he said. Waggling a finger at me, he chastised, "I caught you."

I shrugged and then dashed a finger across the top of the dessert and displayed it to him. "You got me. It's incredible." I licked off the cream and chocolate powder, following with a moan. "Did you get one for yourself?"

"*Non*. You are my dessert, *oui*?"

"Yes."

"Did you get the camera I sent for you?"

"Uh...you sent me a camera?" Right. The box from Amazon. I'd forgotten all about it. "I haven't had time to open it. I'm sorry. I'll do it later. This is good though? I mean, you can see the important parts, right?"

"I like to see your face and your reactions most of all."

I dashed another finger through the creamy white section, and just before putting it in my mouth, on a whim, I traced a line down from my bellybutton to my mons. "You want to lick it off?"

"I wish I was there to smear that over your skin and then eat you until you shove your fingers through my hair and tug."

One ticket to Berlin, please?

Dipping a finger into the darkest chocolate layer, I pulled up a wodge and bent so the camera could capture my face as I waggled the finger at him. "Lick this, lover boy."

I bit off a portion of the wodge, moaning at the exquisite dark sweetness and the whipped creaminess that melted over my tongue and drizzled down my throat. I wandered my hand lower, gliding it over my breasts. My nipples were so hard.

"You following me with your tongue?"

"Yes. There. Show me where you want my tongue."

I slid the chocolate over my mons, drawing a line across my skin that spread as heat melted the dessert further. By the time my finger eased over my clit there was no chocolate. Didn't matter. I wasn't sure of the efficacy of chocolate mousse as a lubricant. Surely a little food down there wasn't going to hurt anything, though.

"Lick me," I said in a groaning, achy voice that surprised me with its wanton tone. "Give me your tongue. Deeply."

"Yes, slow and all over your skin. You taste sweet, better than the chocolate. Mmm, can you feel me nudge my nose against your pussy? I like how you shave that narrow strip there. It is inviting, and the hair is soft and smelling like chocolate. Can you feel my tongue press hard against your clit? Tell me how you like it. Softer? Harder?"

"Mm, yes, firmer. And hold it there," I said as I pressed my fingers lengthwise along my clit and held firmly. It hummed, pleading for movement, yet at the same time my entire system enjoyed the intense pressure and the wanting scream for more.

"More," he said. "Paint your pretty pussy with more sweetness so I can devour you."

Oh, fuck, devouring sounded exquisite. His tongue taking all it desired, his fingers pressed against my ass, digging in as he crushed my mons to his face and ate me, licking me so no dessert remained.

I plunged my fingers into the creamy chocolate, thinking it felt a little dirty, and imagining that it was some kind of sexual toy. I licked some from my fingers (because seriously, I wasn't going to let it go to waste without eating some of it). Then wantonly rubbed my fingers over my mons and along my folds, sliding the instantly liquid chocolate over my skin.

"Eat this," I said, and noticed the scene on the monitor. Just my torso and crotch showed, and my hand, rubbing the dark treat up and over my skin, between my legs. It was erotic to watch it. For a moment it wasn't me, but some sexy porn actress putting on a show.

"Put your fingers on your clit and squeeze it," he said. "I need you to feel me now. I wish you had that silver vibrator. I want you full of me, *mon abeille*."

Mention of the vibrator elicited a gasp from me. Just thinking of having something hard inside me as my fingers worked at my slippery clit paced my breaths faster. I squeezed my thighs together and drove my fingers over my clit. I swore because orgasm was close, so close.

Glancing up, I saw his gorgeous eyes fixated on me. The messy chocolate smears that glistened on my skin. My fingers rubbing vigorously.

With orgasm racing through my core and aiming for my pussy, I slammed my hand on the table. "Fuck. I want your tongue on me so badly."

"You can feel it. Close your eyes."

I did so, and the wet chocolate was so slick as my fingers slowed over my clit, teasing up the release. And finally with a firm squeeze of my thighs, I came. Thrusting my head back and shouting, I—I had never come standing up before. I wobbled, and landed on the chair behind me, knowing his view was only of my face. I swept away the hair from my eyelashes and laughed then because I caught my face on the screen. A smear of dessert dashed under my eye like a footballers' sunscreen.

The giddy wave journeyed through me and left as quickly as it had arrived. Panting and pleased, I leaned an elbow on the table and inspected the mess of dessert remaining. Fingering up a thick wodge I licked it off.

"*Vous êtes es dans un bel état*."

"Whatever you just said, I agree."

He laughed. "I said you were a gorgeous mess."

"I'm just getting started."

"How so?"

"It's time to suck you."

"Yes?"

"You have your hand on your cock, lover?"

"How did you know?"

I dragged my fingers through the mousse. My body was loose and warm, my breaths panting from climax, and I couldn't wait to make him feel the same.

"Let me see that big boy," I demanded.

He stood and stepped aside the table, revealing his hard-on on the screen.

"Mmm..." I pushed my fingers into my mouth, licking the sweetness. "I'm going to lick you now. Watch me."

Using my fingers in the best estimation of his cock as I could, I licked along their length slowly, then nibbled the sides, delighting in the chocolate taste.

"Faster," he gasped.

At that demand, I stopped and curled a smile beside my fingers. With my other hand, I grasped the base of my fingers. "This is your cock," I said. "You feel that at the base?"

His hand had wrapped about the root of his gorgeous erection, squeezing. Eyes closed, he nodded.

"You want this?" I teased.

"Yes—no! Go slower, *s'il vous plaît*," he groaned.

He was so close. Even while he slowly hugged up and down his length, I noticed the signs of imminent climax. He always closed his eyes tightly. His hips shook, pending explosion. And his muscles tensed all over, tightening the fingers of his free hand, the powerful muscles strapping his thighs, and banding fiercely across his abs.

"I want to know your name," he said with a gasp.

"What?"

"So I can call it out as I come."

"Uh..." Weren't we busy with something here? Why the sudden need for my name? I wasn't ready for that. Maybe? I needed time to think about it.

I'm sorry, I am a woman who likes to think over her options and not jump into anything.

While I struggled with that simple yet monumental request, Monsieur Sexy came, his tension releasing in a long, winded groan. And instead of crying my name, he made do, "*Mon abeille*!"

I sighed. I was depriving him of something necessary to a healthy relationship. But I didn't want to do the guilt trip right now. All I wanted was to be there, standing beside him, running my fingers through his hair. Kissing his mouth as he gasped through the last tendrils of orgasm. And slicking my fingers through the cum on his thigh.

"Tonight has been lovely," I said softly. Because to tell the truth right now would spoil the sensual mood. Truth being that he'd just thrown me for a loop.

"Your name," he said in panting breaths. "Will I ever learn it?"

I nodded. Brushed the hair from my face and caught my chin in hand. "When I'm ready."

"Fair enough. *Bonne nuit*."

Six

I had to be at the map shop in an hour, so I downed a breakfast of black tea, a crumpet spread with chunky almond butter, and a peach I'd found lurking amidst the lettuce at the grocery store. Peach season was past, but this little gem tasted sweet enough to make me pine for a summer's-end orchard visit.

Clearing away the dishes, I also cleaned up from last night's sexy dessert debacle. Chocolate was smeared on the table, and I found traces of dried vanilla mousse on the chair, laptop and—

I swiped the dishtowel over the creamy dash on the wall by the table. "How did I manage that?"

Laughing, I tossed the towel in the clothes hamper, reminded myself to do laundry later after work, and then headed out for a half shift at the shop.

Richard greeted me with a gleeful glint to his eyes. The Mister Rogers sweater he always wore was buttoned up to his proper plaid bowtie. He held up a receipt that wasn't one the shop issued with purchases.

"Look what I've done," he announced, his British accent making every word a delight to listen to.

I peered at the receipt, and saw that it was for an authentication firm in London. "You sent off the map?"

It was possible the man just may own a work by a renaissance master, but he had to send it away for authentication to be sure.

"The courier picked it up before you got here," he said. "Did I do the right thing? I'm not sure."

"Yes, you did, Richard." His reluctance was because the authenticator may keep it up to a year. The process involved was long and arduous. "Having definitive proof is important."

"Yes, but *I* know it was drawn by da Vinci. That should be all that matters."

"Not if you intend to sell it for the big bucks." I strolled into the back room and stuffed my purse into a cubby. "*Are* you going to sell it?" I called out, as I bent to exchange my walking flats for the Louboutins I knew I could endure for the four-hour shift.

Richard's eyes fell to my shoes as I strode into the shop. "I'm not sure what I'll do with the map, authentic or not. Those are some seriously sexy shoes." His gaze wandered up my legs, and the black pencil skirt, topped by a snug—but not blatantly tight—pink sweater with three-quarter length sleeves and a deep vee neckline.

I'd been dressing a bit sexier lately. And why not? I felt great about myself, and the confidence I'd gained from my window and on-screen affair with Monsieur Sexy was manifesting in my attire.

My boss's mouth dropped open, his tongue teasing at his upper lip. His gaze was riveted to my chest. And that lascivious stare lasted much longer than was comfortable.

"Is something wrong?" I had the audacity to ask, jarring Richard's attention away from my breasts. "Were you going to head out now that I'm here?"

"Uh, yes." He snapped his eyes onto mine, but he couldn't hide the barest blush that rosed his cheeks. "Pretty shoes," he offered.

"Thanks." Though I was pretty darn sure he couldn't tell me their color. As for my cup size? He'd probably made a healthy guess. Weird. I'd never received such a blatant once-over from him in the two years I'd been working at the shop.

"Would you mind hanging a new map for me today? The one on the wall there." He pointed to the map of Turkey. "It's been up for years and is starting to fade. Find another map that'll fit the frame, will you?"

"Of course."

Thrilled to actually have something to do beyond dusting and strolling the eighteen by twelve square foot shop over and over in wait of a few curious customers, I waved him off as he exited out the front door.

Richard waved through the window as he passed. I suppressed a frown. Normally, I'd be a little freaked that the boss had given me the eye. And I was.

Yet I also wanted to bask (just a little) in the knowledge that I had captured another man's interest. Not like it was difficult to do. Just, well, when a woman was seeing someone and another man looked at her?

That was some kind of sneaky sexy thrill, if you ask me. And I was willing to take the shoe compliment from my forty-year-old boss. It was the breast leer that made me uncomfortable.

Shaking off the weird shiver of squickiness, I clicked back into the office to go through the stack of stock prints and maps.

Amongst the maps were floral prints, some botanical diagrams revealing the inner workings of various plants, and—a nude. Wow. I had no idea Richard's tastes ran toward male nudes. He'd never sold anything like this in the shop before. It had to be an item included in a larger lot he hadn't noticed.

Then again, I was newly aware of Richard's lusty interests. Hmm...

I stroked a finger along the sketch of the man's thigh. He lay in repose, arms behind his head, while his legs were crossed at the ankle. His penis had been drawn slack, the head of it snugged inside the foreskin.

I wondered about the artist who had drawn this. Male or female? Sketching to learn anatomy or simply a study of a beloved man? I wondered if it was recent or centuries old. Difficult to determine by the paper, which did sport a tea-stain on the corner and frayed edges.

My thoughts strayed to the model's mindset at the time of posing. He'd either been relaxed, near falling asleep after a long sitting session, or so bored that his penis had taken a nap.

Had I been the artist, I'd want to draw that particular piece of anatomy at full mast. Could a person sketch fast enough to capture a man's woody? I mean, even if aroused, eventually it would take a break once it realized it wasn't going to get any action behind intent observation. Of course, that could prove a mighty turn-on. Just lying there, unmoving, while someone else observed every portion of your being.

Yeah, that would get me wet if I had to lay naked before a man and allow him to study me. I'd have to close my eyes and think of something else. The man's eyes in the picture were looking beyond, it seemed.

If I were the artist I would sit close to the subject, eyes on that steely prize. The model would have to remain still while I studied his penis. Subtle inhale, and...a gentle increase in musk as his heartbeats pounded. Anticipating my touch, the heat of my breath. A hot, wet kiss...

My pencil would make soft sounds, imbuing lead upon the paper. I'd probably have my tongue stuck out the corner of my mouth. The model would clench his fingers as he eyed my tongue, wishing it could be utilized for more than a thought crutch.

I'd look up and catch his hungry look. "Please," he'd moan. "Come closer so your drawing has the detail you desire."

Oh, yes, I desired the details.

Gliding my chair forward, I'd lean over the paper, pencil turned to catch the heavy weight of the model's erection on the thin wooden utensil. I'd lift it slightly and stretch my eyes up and down the underside of it. His balls would be tight and high, hugging the base of his penis. His inhale as I slid the pencil along his shaft toward the base would please me. But my goal wouldn't be pleasure. My objective was to learn every intricacy of this body part that I could never own, and only play with when given opportunity.

I fell deeper into my fantasy, becoming one with the stage I had set. I noticed I had drawn the object of my scrutiny too narrow, so made some quick strokes on the page to widen it. More than a handful, should I grasp it, my fingers would not touch to my thumb.

Allowing myself to get lost, I engaged my senses. My fantasy man smelled like he'd been walking naked through a pine forest after a rain storm. I liked it. Drawing the pencil downward, I tenderly traced the golden stick along one tightened testicle, inducing yet another gasping breath from him. He needed me to touch him with my hands, to learn his shape and size as if a blind woman.

I wasn't going to give him that pleasure. His restraint and utter need were thrilling. My heartbeats had grown so loud the sudden call of "*Bonjour*" went unnoticed.

And then a woman stood directly behind me, her head tilted in question. "Paris?" she repeated.

"Penis," I whispered and spun around to face her.

The customer's gaping red mouth ripped me out of the fantasy and back to real life. I stood with chin caught in palm, one hand stroking the air before me.

"Uh, oh, sorry." I dropped my hands and tucked them behind my back. "Paris, you said?"

Nodding cautiously, the woman stepped back as I strolled out onto the sales floor. She'd heard me say penis.

I wasn't going to apologize.

"What's your favorite sexual position?" Monsieur Sexy asked from the computer screen as I made the bed in full view of the wide-range camera I'd set up after I'd gotten home from work.

I'd explained to him that I had fresh, warm sheets from the dryer, and wanted to get them on the bed. He'd said to go ahead and do a little housekeeping—so long as I did it naked. And wearing the shoes.

Bless the man, he adored the shoes.

So while I wasn't paying particular attention to him, he shot out a few questions. Did I enjoy my job at the map shop? Yes, but I never wanted a full-time job away from home. My research work kept me satisfied and independent. I didn't mention the weird pass from Richard. Sexual harassment? I didn't want to think about it. Besides, I'd probably overthink it so I had decided to give my boss a pass. This time.

Monsieur Sexy asked: Did I drive? Yes, but I didn't own a car. Paris was a walkable city; impractical for driving the short distances a resident usually had to traverse. What was my favorite color? It varied from purple to pink to yellow. Had I ever had a pet? I declined telling him about the hamster that had died a slow death due to my neglect when I was a teenager.

"My favorite position?" I stood from smoothing my palms over the bottom sheet that stretched tightly across the king-size bed and eyed the gorgeous Frenchman watching me from the computer screen. The thick black glasses increased his sexy geek appeal exponentially.

Sitting on the bed and spreading my legs boldly, heels to the floor and back arched to thrust my breasts forward, I teased a finger along my mouth to illustrate deep thought. Or maybe just sexy wondering.

"I like so many," I decided. "Is a man's head between my legs considered a position?"

"*Oui, mon abeille.* You like a man who can lick you to orgasm?"

"Mmm..." Just thinking about it made me wet. I slid my fingers down and put gentle pressure over my clitoris. "Yes, please."

"I will put you in that position," he suggested.

"I certainly hope you will. I also think I like it bent over and wiggling my ass for you to come inside."

He had a delicious purring sort of wanting growl that seemed to birth deep in his throat. The tone of it always hit me directly in the pussy and I loosened considerably, leaning back to prop an elbow on the bed. But I wanted to see him, so I slid my legs up to lie on my side and talk directly to the camera, which I'd positioned beside the laptop on the night stand.

"What about your favorite position?" I asked, drawing my fingers lightly along my thigh.

"You wiggling your derriere for me is perfect," he said. "Bent over the back of my sofa, your long legs parted, and those shoes. I'd like to stand back and look at your peach bottom and that soft place in the middle that is like the center of a fruit."

I bit the side of my lip. The words were seductive and alluring. But when spoken with a French accent everything about his words increased my desires tenfold.

"I'd like to slip my fingers into your fruit, and slick them across your clit until you drip down to my wrist. You want that?"

"Yes, please."

"Then I must slide my cock into you. Slow and deep. That is why I like this position. I can go so deep and hold your hips, controlling you."

I pressed my cheek against the clean white sheet and rolled onto my chest, my ass high as I knelt forward. I imagined leaning over the back of his sofa, my ass exposed, waiting for him to touch me. But instead, he stood there, looking at my most private places. Studying me. Deciding how he would touch and lick me. And whether or not he should shove his cock in slowly, or perhaps slam it in hard and deep to make me cry out in stunned, yet delicious surprise.

He groaned. "You are *très jolie* like that. Your breasts against the sheet and your ass in the air. Are your nipples hard?"

"Yes," I gasped.

The subtle wiggles of my hips moved my nipples across the sheets. I lifted slightly to make the connection a little softer, brushing my skin, ruching my nipples tightly.

I gripped the sheets near my head and spread my knees out wider. The position was vulnerable and unsure. It upped my desire. I wanted to feel him enter me. The molten heat of him gliding into my tight opening, slick with my juices, and his thighs slamming hard against mine.

"What's your favorite secret place to make love?" he asked.

I tilted my face toward him and rolled to my side, sliding my fingers between my legs. "Like in a car or in a public restaurant?"

"If that is your fantasy?"

"I don't know that I've considered it before. The window was pretty daring," I decided. "But I think I'd like to do it in the winter, in the snow."

"Really?" He mocked a shiver.

"I love snow. I am from Iowa. We do good snow there."

"Can't say I can understand the thrill in that. It would be very cold."

"Not if I had a warm body hugging close to mine."

"True. But I'm not sure a man could maintain his hard-on in the cold."

"Are you saying you're not up for the challenge?"

His dark brow quirked beneath a spill of tousled hair. I loved his curls and the way his hair always looked as if he'd just stepped out of bed, yet not.

"Anything for you."

"Really?" I leaned forward on my elbows, studying the man on the screen. Sometimes he said things that sounded so devoted. Like we were in a serious, committed relationship. That thrilled me. And it surprised me that a man could think in such terms about a woman he hadn't yet touched or kissed.

"Anything," he repeated.

"All right then. I'll put snow on our list. What about you? What's your fantasy place to have sex?"

"Ah, I know this one. The Louvre."

"In the museum?" Astonished, I could but gasp. "Or you must mean outside, maybe behind and in a corner somewhere?"

"*Non*. Inside the room with the Mona Lisa. Perhaps back in the corner somewhere, away from the crowd, but right there, close to everyone."

"You want to have sex during the day, in a crowded museum, where everyone can watch?"

He nodded.

The voyeuristic little pervert. I creamed between my thighs just thinking about taking the man over my knee and spanking him for such thoughts.

"With you," he said. "Promise me we'll do it some day?"

My jaw dropped open. I certainly dreamed of having real, full-contact sex with this man some day. But in the Louvre?

"Are you afraid?" he taunted. "We could be discreet. You would wear a skirt and I would stand behind you. Slip up the skirt and jam myself up inside you."

I bit down on my lip when he said jam with the appropriate emphasis, so that I could literally feel him jamming his cock into me. Breathing heavily, I nodded in agreement. I couldn't imagine doing such a thing in a public place, but I didn't want to disappoint him. And we were strictly talking fantasy, right? Fantasy implied things that weren't real. Things that would never happen. Because if they did happen, then they couldn't be called a fantasy. Like studying a model's cock in detail while drawing it was never going to happen.

Right?

I nodded. "I'm in."

"Yes!" He raised his hands in triumph. "Soon, *mon abeille*. Soon."

What had I just agreed to?

Ah heck, why not?

Sitting up and eyeing the top sheet that was no longer warm from the dryer, but still needed to be placed on the bed, I tugged it to me and leaned forward, one knee pulled up to my chest. I recalled a silly thought I entertained when thinking about Monsieur Sexy and his hard and always-eager cock.

"Do you have a name for your penis? I mean, I think a lot of men do name it."

He bowed his head. Was that a blush? Oh, that gleeful smile crinkling at the corner of his eyes. It mastered me. It wrapped me in wide arms and pulled me in for a hug. And I lived inside it, a willing prisoner.

"I do," he said. "You will not laugh?"

"Hmm, well, I think I should be allowed to laugh if it's something like Crazy Larry or Big Boy."

He chuckled. "Close. I call it Monsieur Eiffel."

"Is that so?" I pressed the sheet to my mouth and nose, hiding a giggle that wanted release. Well, it wasn't like any man was going to name the thing Spot or Little Guy. "Appropriate," I finally managed to say with as straight a face as possible. "It is imposing and steely hard."

"Like iron," he said. Then he stood and displayed Monsieur Eiffel, whom I hadn't realized had been bared all this time. Indeed, like the iron statue, he thrust up erect and proud. A monument for sure. But I wouldn't allow anyone to buy a ticket to this exhibition. He was all mine.

Had he been stroking himself as he'd been watching me gyrate on the bed? I certainly hoped so.

"I have a name for mine," I said.

"Your pussy?"

"Now don't think I'm crazy, but I have a tendency to think about odd things a lot."

"So you've explained. You are the woman who thinks too much."

"Exactly. And one day I was wondering what it would be like to have a penis. And if I did have one, I'd have to name it."

"That is odd, but not crazy. Er, maybe. What would you name your penis?"

"Chuck," I announced.

His laughter was better than I had ever imagined it could be when I'd only been able to witness it through glass. To never hear it. And now that I could, it intoxicated.

"Monsieur Eiffel and Chuck," he said, finally coming down from the explosion of laughter. "Quite the pair. You, *mon abeille*, are *exquis, gras, magnifique*."

I knew the one word, but... "What does that mean?"

He held up a finger to wait, and he walked over and picked up a notebook. I watched him write something on the page, then he turned it to face the camera.

I read the words he'd first written about me when our window affair had been new and burgeoning. "Exquisite, bold, gorgeous."

The man had a way of saying things without even speaking.

I rolled to my back on the bed, closing my eyes as I thought those words over and over. Had I ever been in a relationship that had made me feel so good about myself? I don't think so. I'd been in some great relationships, and some not-so-great ones. I had even taken a monthly lover since moving to Paris.

Which reminded me... I had to break my standing date with the Brit. It was due this weekend. He'd understand. We hooked up when possible. He'd gotten serious about a woman for half a year and we'd been cool with not seeing one another. But we were always there for the other when the relationships grew stale.

I turned and gazed into Monsieur Sexy's eyes. I didn't want this one to stale.

"Look out the window," he suddenly said.

I twisted my head, but my view out the window wasn't great because I had the bedroom light on. I reached up to switch it off, and propped up on my elbows. I gazed out the window at the full moon sitting high in the sky above his building across the street.

"That looks like a werewolf moon," I said. "I wonder if they'll howl tonight."

"You are into the werewolves and vampires, then?"

I rolled to my back again, content to lay bathed in the moonlight, legs bent and hands on my stomach. "No. Not like the stuff on TV and in the movies. I researched werewolves for an author a few months ago, and I never could understand how a woman could be attracted to the big hairy lugs. All that back hair. And can you imagine the hairs left behind in the shower?"

"Ah, give the guy a break. Someone has to love him."

We both laughed, and he prompted whether or not I was a dog or cat person. "I love dogs," he offered. "Someday I'll own land and will have a mastiff."

I knew mastiffs were huge and hairy, but very lovable. "I'll go with a cat," I said. "They don't jump on you or slobber all over you."

"I see." His voice took on a serious edge. "Then we are at a crossroads, *mon abeille*."

"What?" I turned onto an elbow and flicked on the light switch so he could see my confused look. His expression had grown so serious I suddenly felt as if I was standing with a rapier before my opponent.

"I am not sure I can be in a relationship with a woman who does not like my pet." He held the serious moue for about five seconds before cracking and offering a smile. "I kid you. I don't have a pet, but I'm sure I could like a little kitty cat."

"We don't have anything to worry about. It's not like we're living together."

"Exactly. But maybe I should find out what religion you are."

"Is that important?"

"It's not a deal breaker, but I don't know if I could accept an atheist into my heart. I said that wrong. I could accept the person, I just wouldn't feel comfortable with them."

"Don't worry, sweetie, I'm Catholic to the bone. Got the guilt card to prove it."

"Catholic girls masturbate before windows while strangers watch?"

"Only the ones who are going to hell. I intend to bypass purgatory and hell and make a break for heaven."

"Sounds like a daring plan. I was raised Catholic as well."

"I stop in for a service at Nôtre Dame every month or so," I offered. "I can understand most of the Latin because I've been listening to it all my life on Sundays. So reverent. Even with the tourists banging about in the aisles. I can stare at the rose windows endlessly. I marvel over any cathedral that was built so long ago and without the technology that builders have nowadays."

"It is awe-inspiring. This is nice, *mon abeille*."

"Us chatting?"

"*Oui*. I want to talk to you as you fall asleep."

"Mmm, well it's going to happen soon. I washed my sheets with lavender. The scent always makes me sleepy. And it's nice and cool in here tonight."

I shook out the top sheet that I'd yet to tuck in and pulled it over my naked body, while shuffling out of the shoes and dropping them to the floor. Lying back and closing my eyes, the next question he asked surprised me.

"Tell me something deeply personal about you."

Okay, I could play with that. I wanted to grow this relationship. So I'd haul out the big one. Because talking to him felt safe.

"After my mother died I was inconsolable for months. I didn't think I'd ever rise above the pain of her loss. She was too young." A looseness of emotion heated the corners of my eyes and dampened my throat. "She had been taking college courses and was working toward her Masters degree in historical literature. She never got a chance to leave her mark on the world."

I clutched the bed sheets. My mother had died six years ago. There wasn't a day I didn't think about her bright smile. Would she have smiled to learn of my liaison with Monsieur Sexy? Yeah, I think she would have loved to hear all the details.

After what felt like a forever of silence, Monsieur Sexy looked up and straight into the camera. "She left her mark on you."

I huffed out a gasp. Teardrops spilled down my cheek. He was right. My mother was indelibly embedded within my soul. And that acknowledgement felt immense.

"Thank you," I said. "No one has ever said anything so simple yet so meaningful to me. It means a lot." I sniffed away the tears and laughed to disguise my sudden descent into memory. "I don't usually cry when I think about her. But the confession felt intense. So what about you? Let's divert to you. Are both your parents still alive?"

"Yes. My father—eh. We are not close."

"You mentioned he lives in Marseilles?"

"Yes, I have not seen him in years. We never talk. He is not interested in me, but rather his young paramours who like to party and spend his money."

I sensed his distinct dislike for his father's apparent playboy lifestyle. So I wouldn't press. "Your mother?"

"She is, hmm..." He tapped his temple. "In India right now. The last picture she sent was over a month ago. We try to see each other once a year, but her travels keep her away. She wants to see the entire world, and she's having a great time doing it with her latest lover du jour."

"She must be proud of her son? You owning a business and all?"

"She is. We may not see each other often, but when we do it is as if it has only been days. Though she would be startled if I told her I have an American lover."

I pulled up my hands to my chest, cuddling myself at mention of the title lover. It felt so cozy and exclusive. So what I asked next really surprised me. "Do you think this is real between us?"

"Yes." Again, that clear and intense stare. "More real than other relationships I've had."

"I want it to become more real when you get back to Paris." I just said it. I don't know where the words had come from.

Yes, I did. They'd pushed up from my very soul (via the tiny vixen). And really? It was time.

"More real?"

"In person," I said. "Touch. Eye to eye. Skin against skin."

His tone softened. "Yes. Sure." His gaze flickered to somewhere off screen. I sensed, hmm...reluctance.

No, I was tired. And he was as well.

"Good night, lover," I said. "To getting real."

He nodded, but again did not meet my gaze. "*Bonne nuit*."

Seven

Panting, I fell back into the pillows and stretched my arms out to my sides. That orgasm had been phenomenal.

To my side, I heard Monsieur Sexy moan as he rode out the climax in Berlin. So far away from me, yet right there, able to connect to me with only a few spoken words and a lot of hands-on.

Too bad the hands-on had been from our respective hands; mine on me, his on himself. As I lay there, conscious of his presence, yet in my own world—because I was alone—I began to reconsider my need to keep this relationship so far from me. Distant. Safe.

Safe wasn't so fun when all I could do was wish and wonder how it would feel to have the man's hands on my skin. Sure I could get myself off. And that felt great. And with him watching? All the better. But I was ready for touch. Seriously.

For more than three weeks we'd shared looks, gestures and moans. And we were at it again. I'd fallen asleep talking with him last night, spilling some dreams and learning a few of his. Morning sunlight had woken me twenty minutes ago. I'd noticed the laptop was still on, the camera light flashing green. And there he was, watching me.

He'd woken five minutes earlier, and before heading to the shower, had sat down to watch me a while. When I'd woken, he'd suggested a jack n' jill session. And due to a particularly delicious dream about sketching Monsieur Eiffel, I hadn't refused.

"What are you thinking about?" he asked from beside me.

I wished I could roll over and kiss him, there in my bed. Stroke my hands over his chest, hot and moist with perspiration, and glide them down to his semi-hard penis. I'd take it in hand, bend down, and kiss the head of it. Taste it. Devour it.

Own him.

"I'm thinking about sucking you," I said, and turned to face the computer screen. "How good it would feel to have your skin under my fingers. To feel your heat. To put your cock in my mouth."

He groaned and nodded. "That seems to be a common thought between us. I think about licking your pussy. Pushing my tongue inside you and tasting you. And your nipples. I want to suck them until you come."

"I think I've reached the pinnacle of frustration. When do you get back from Berlin?"

"I've another few days here."

Just a few days. Did I really want to do it? Finally meet him?

Yes, and ah, hell no.

Fine. So I'm a waffler, switching sides like a disk of baked flour and water that gets flipped in the pan. I should demand the man return to Paris immediately, walk up to my apartment and sweep me off my feet and ravish me for days unending.

It would happen. It must happen. But thinking about it made me more nervous than that first moment when I'd finally heard his voice across the cyber waves. And—wait. I wasn't the only one. Hadn't I heard reluctance in his voice last night? I had. I know it. When I'd suggested we make things more real, he had, well, waffled.

"What will be the first thing that you do when you see me in person?" I asked.

I reached out to touch the screen and traced along his chest. He sat against the pillows on the hotel room bed. The camera captured his whole body, yet a smirk was the sexiest thing he wore.

"I would like to say I'd tear away your clothes and fuck you."

Sounded like a solid plan to me. "But?"

"But. I think I'd like to take it slow. Maybe talk like we did last night. And then we should kiss. Do you know how often I think about kissing you? And then I wonder: will you like my kiss? Will I do it right? What if it is wrong?"

I nodded. I'd had the same thoughts. Would he be boring in person? Maybe he'd smell? What if he wasn't so deft with handling a woman as he was with handling Monsieur Eiffel? And yes, the all-telling kiss. A kiss could make or break a relationship. Seriously. If the twosome didn't kiss well, then why bother?

"We're a couple of flakes," I decided.

"I don't understand that reference."

"You know, kind of stupid about some things, yet not about others. We're engaged in an intense relationship, yet we can both scare ourselves thinking about that first real connection."

He nodded. "You do tend to think too much."

"You've noticed, eh?"

"I'd rather you be a thinker than someone who jumps in no matter the consequences."

"That sounds good. In theory. But isn't jumping in blindly fun once in awhile?"

He nodded, tilted his head in thought. He wasn't completely agreeing with me, and that made me wonder what had scared him away from the blind jump. He came off as an adventurous sort. Mountain biking with his friends on the weekends, and dancing naked before windows? The man was fearless.

But perhaps less so than I imagined. Fine with me. He had his layers, and I was slowly peeling them aside, learning them, running my fingers lightly over his many intricate surfaces.

I really needed to touch his surfaces. Like all over, and most especially, inside those boxer briefs. Cripes. When had I become such a horn dog?

They say knowing how to love oneself via self-pleasuring was the kindest, most nurturing thing a woman could do for herself. But there was a point when all that self-stimulation wanted to scream for a wing man.

Monsieur Sexy looked aside. He reached for a bottle of water and tilted back a long swallow. I noticed the books splayed open on the table next to his bed.

"What are you reading?" I asked.

He held up a staying finger as he finished the water. Then, with relish, he brandished the book before the camera.

"Mapping The Woman?" I read.

"I found it in a drawer here. Do you know the woman's clitoris is actually shaped like a wishbone and extends down both sides of the vaginal opening?"

I did know that. And hallelujah for random book finds.

"I cannot wait to experiment," he continued, paging through the book. "Fascinating stuff."

"Well, if you need a volunteer...?"

"But of course! I can't believe this is so new to me, and yet it is exquisite knowledge. We men think it is just that precious little button between your legs that must be coaxed and licked and teased."

"Coaxing, licking and teasing works for me."

"Yes, but all along the sides as well! Certainly, I tend those areas, but I've never known they were so rife to receive exquisite sensation. *Mon Dieu*, you women are a marvel."

I could really get behind his enthusiasm. Rather, spread my legs for it. "So you'll be taking that book home with you?"

"No, I have the diagram memorized. I will leave it for the next man."

"The clitorises of the world will be so happy," I sang.

"Indeed!"

I sat up on the bed and stretched, thrusting up my breasts just because I knew he was watching. "I suppose I should get dressed. Lots of work to do today on the fantasy bible job."

"Yes, I must head out soon. But I have a favor to ask you," he said as he walked about the hotel room. "I've been gone over a week. I did not consider this before leaving. But the picture above my bed reminds me of it."

"What?"

The screen panned about the room and landed on the picture above his bed. I was a froth of green fronds, a closeup of a palm tree or somesuch. Gorgeous and lush, it reminded me to lament the passing of summer.

"They are the only living things I own," he said, turning the camera back toward his naked torso. Monsieur Eiffel was taking a much-needed rest. "I have some plants in the loft. I forgot to water them before I left."

"You want me to run over and take care of them? I could do that."

And what joy. I'd get a look inside his domain. His home. Most importantly, his bedroom. Cue the secret agent music!

"Would you do that? I'll email you the building code, and my front door has a code as well."

"Of course. It's right across the street. Although I have to warn you, I am a snoop."

"I am okay with that. Look around all you like. I'm pretty sure all the pink panties are gone."

He had to bring that one up? While engaged in our window tryst, I'd witnessed one of his female students changing from fencing gear to street clothes in his bedroom. I hadn't known she was a student at the time, and my crazy, think-too-much brain took me there. Yeah, that he was fucking her.

He hadn't been. But then, he should have never waggled those pink panties she'd strategically left behind at me, either.

"I kid you," he tried. "Sorry?"

"No need for apologies. Another example of me thinking far too much and concocting the worst out of nothing. Maybe I'll plant some of my panties for you to find."

"*S'il vous plaît*?"

He was so cute when he begged. I kissed my fingers and blew him the kiss. He caught the morsel and cupped the hand over the head of his lax cock.

"Someday I will kiss you there," I said.

"Promise?"

"Promise. See you tonight?" I asked.

"Sure. But you can Skype me during the day to let me know how it goes with the plants. Remember, I usually take a break around noon."

"Sounds like a plan. Have a great day at work, Monsieur Sexy. Give Monsieur Eiffel a squeeze for me, will you?"

He squeezed his cock. "Do the same for Chuck, eh? Rub her slow and soft as you think of me."

So he thought to call my pussy Chuck? It worked for me. Because it was our secret, my confession to him, and I loved that he knew that little oddity about me.

"*Ciao*," I said.

And the strangest word lingered on my tongue. But I wasn't silly, and I hadn't known him long enough to say that particular L-word.

Right?

"*À bientôt, mon abeille.*"

ÅÅÅ

Nakedfencer's email arrived after I'd eaten yogurt and granola for breakfast. I printed up the entrance codes he'd sent, and stuffed it in my purse. I slipped on a loose red blouse and a pleated skirt, and then tucked my feet into the Louboutins. Dressing up merely to walk across the street and make facetime with some plants?

You'd better believe it. I was entering his domicile. His lair. His private world. I wanted to do it right. As well, if anyone in the building saw me, I wanted to make an impression. The third floor resident's sexy lover? I could work it.

I made it through the ground floor door to the building with ease. The concierge nodded, acknowledging that I had used the code. He could assume I was a client of one of the businesses or the third floor occupant's lover. Made me feel clandestine.

The lobby was accented with brass Art Nouveau touches, and housed two businesses, one on each side of the building. The elevator was a narrow number with a brass door. Me take the elevator? Nope. I took the stairs up to the first floor (which was actually the second floor to us Americans; the French count ground floor, first, then second). Another dash up to the second (third) floor.

Holding the digital code to access my cyber-lover's home felt like I'd suddenly won the lottery. Seriously. My heartbeats hadn't stopped thundering. It was as if I were going to meet him and touch him and...

I knew that was fantasy, but my heart and clammy hands were certainly in for the adventure. I'd brought along the tin watering can I used for my plants. Very well, my *plant*. Which was close to dead.

I'm pretty sure Monsieur Sexy had no clue he'd asked a plant killer to tend his precious greenery. It may be best if I merely glanced at them and not touch them at all. What could another few days without water do to them?

"No, you can do this," I muttered as I punched in the six-digit code. "You will impress him with your nurturing abilities."

And if I possessed any such skills, would they please step up now?

The door opened to a large, quiet room. It was late morning. Gray clouds surfed the Paris troposphere. The weathergirl warned we'd be pummeled this evening. I was sick of the rain, but it was still better than snow. I liked snow, yet the city proper rarely got anything beyond a quick shovel. But when my principal means of navigating the city was on foot, I preferred as little as possible, pretty please.

The vast room was not decorated, not even a picture on a wall. Up near the front windows a mountain bike sat parked, waiting another adventure down a muddy, steep slope. A set of weights and a pull-up bar held reign in the far left corner on a rubber mat. Beside that on the wall were hooks garnering two fencing masks and padded protective vests.

So this big room must be where he practiced and taught fencing. It was a good space for dashing about.

I wandered to the equipment hung on the wall, and tapped the fencing foil with the red button secured on the end to prevent an opponent from getting pierced. Taking the weapon by the grip I was surprised at how light it was. And not bent, as had been the sorry equipment I'd used in high school. I'd only taken fencing for a few weeks to get the physical activity credit. I hadn't enjoyed the sport. What high school girl could suffer the indignity of the sweaty vest and stinking mask? I had just been thankful it was the last class of the day so I could tug my messy hair back into a ponytail afterward.

Remembering the *en garde* position, I tucked my arm against my body, pointing the weapon at my invisible opponent, while my other arm I bent upward, hand relaxed. And in my imagination he stood before me: Monsieur Sexy. Make that *Musketeer* Sexy. He wasn't wearing the bespoke suit that screamed sex monster that promised a breathtaking roll in the sheets. No, he was wearing a black musketeer tunic trimmed with silver lace, and a beaver felt hat sporting a frilly red plume that dusted the air with each stride of his bucket-topped boots.

"*En garde,*" I declared, walking around my invisible opponent.

He daren't raise his weapon to me, a woman. The man was honorable and chivalrous. He lived to serve the king. Instead, his sly smirk told me he considered all the ways he could defeat me with a sensual touch.

I swept my blade through the air between us, dismissing him with a bow.

Yeah, so my fantasy life was fulfilling. What was new?

Only a little sad that I didn't hang up the foil next to an actual musketeer's rapier, I left the equipment and wandered to the far end of the practice space where a leather sofa demarcated the living area. I set my purse on the floor. His flat was a big open space, but he'd set up a sofa and two chairs before a small television. He owned an old tube version.

"What the heck?" I didn't think they actually made TVs in cabinets anymore.

I looked about for the remote, but decided by proof of the apparent relic that a person probably had to walk up to the TV and turn the knob to bring it to life. I couldn't remember a time when I had ever physically touched a TV to make it work. I did recall though, my mother regaling me with tales of her childhood when her parents had used her as a human remote control by directing her to switch channels during commercials.

I dismissed the antiquity with a shake of my head, and wandered into the kitchen, which, in keeping with French standards, was small and a mere stretch of counter along the wall which boasted glass-fronted cabinets overhead. The fridge was short, the stovetop petite. A two-person table sat in the middle of the tile flooring that designated the kitchen area. The table was clear of all personal or business detritus, in vast opposition to my disaster at home.

Could I ever allow this neat freak to venture into my messy yet lovable domicile? A distinct twinge of doubt niggled at the back of my neck. So out of the man's comfort zone.

Ah there, hanging before the kitchen window, was a gorgeous froth of greenery. Vines and leaves climbed over the pot edges, spilling three feet down until it nearly touched the floor. Beautiful and full and so green. It even smelled like summer.

Pressing my palms to my stomach, I approached it with caution. The last thing I wanted to do was kill my lover's plant. A symbol of his care and attentiveness. I had never been able to nurture a green thing.

Did that make me lacking in the ability to care and be attentive to others? I swallowed. I wasn't an ogre. I could care for living things. It was just the silent green ones that gave me challenge.

"Do you really need water?" I asked timidly.

I reached into the pot and tested the soil with a finger. Yep, it was dry.

Blowing out a breath, I filled the watering can at the sink. While standing there I browsed over the fridge surface. No magnets. No kitschy towels or cute tchotchkes that would grant me a clue to his personality. The entire fencing/living/kitchen area was bland. There weren't even colors. Save for the green plant and the brown sofa, everything was gray.

So was this to be the ugly in the man I'd feared was too perfect? He had no decorating sense? What man did? And yet wasn't a man's home a reflection of his personality?

"No, he's a fun guy. I've seen him dancing naked with a cupcake."

It was then that I noticed the laptop at the end of the sofa and the thick book on top of it. Must be one of those computer manuals I'd seen him reading. Was that it for his office? Besides the sofa, coffee table, chairs, and TV, there was no other furniture. No desk or office cupboards.

"Maybe in another room."

Clasping my arms across my chest, I exhaled.

We were seemingly so completely opposite it made me wince. But then, if his place had been a disordered mess like mine, would that have endeared me to him? Doubt it. I could not tolerate a slob, or a man who couldn't, at the very least, clean up after himself.

I decided that I liked his clean control because I knew that wasn't completely him. I'd seen his fun side.

I would give him a pass on the decorating since it had only been a few months that he had lived here.

Tilting the watering can over the plant, I set upon killing it. I spied another plant sitting in a big pot at the corner of the room, a sort of marker dividing the kitchen from the living area. I filled the can and gave it a generous sip, crossing my fingers all the while.

He'd said *plants* when we'd talked. This could be it, but I'd better check all the rooms. I hadn't seen any when we'd been looking at each other through our respective bedroom windows. Then again, I'd only had eyes for him.

Again filling the can, I then wandered down the hall and tried the first of two doors. It opened into the bathroom, which I knew must also have a door on the opposite wall because he could enter it from his bedroom.

I flicked on the switch. More gray walls, but the tile was gorgeous. Clear green and blue that resembled sea glass lined the wall behind the vanity mirror and in the shower. It glinted under the light. Atypical for Paris, it was a good-sized bathroom that two people could easily navigate together.

Well, you know, I had to consider options for the future. It's how women think. I know you'd do the same.

Another plant hung near the shower door, so I gave it a sip. I strolled my fingers over the white towel hung from the rack and imagined it wrapped about his hips, his erection tenting the terrycloth from beneath. When his cock grew harder and thicker it would stretch at the towel and...finally tug the tucked corner away, dropping the towel to the floor at his feet.

I would curl my fingers about that demanding rod. Tugging him close to me I would give it a squeeze. He'd suck in a gasp, his eyes shuttering in pleasure. Kneeling, I'd stroke a fingernail along the bulging vein on the underside of his thickness, following it down to cup his testicles. Heavy and snugged up against the base of his cock, I'd lick them, tasting his faint salty flavor and the clean wet droplets from the shower.

The watering can clanked against the tiles. I stood suddenly upright, realizing I'd bent forward and was gripping the towel hanging before me.

"Wow. I so need to get a real boyfriend," I said. "One that I can touch. And lick. And...

And just everything.

I wandered into the bedroom, my heels clicking the hardwood floor. No plants in here.

I strolled along the end of his king-size, which sat low because there was apparently no box spring. I hadn't noticed that when looking through the window. Interesting. On the table beside his bed sat a digital clock and a stack of books.

Leaning over, I pressed my palms onto the mattress. My fingers sank deeply into the foam surface. Nice. I'd like to snug into this temperpedic and roll up against his strong, muscled back, pressing my bare breasts to the heat of him. Slide up a leg and hook it over his thigh while I rubbed my clit against his ass...

Oh yeah, this chick was frustrated.

Standing abruptly, I twisted around, fanning my face. Standing in his bedroom did things to me that I liked. A lot. My heart raced. My skin flushed. Arousal came so easily when considering Monsieur Sexy.

A dresser sat against the wall. On top sat an iPod dock similar to the one I kept beside my bed. No iPod in it, though, so I couldn't snoop through his playlists. Bummer. He must take it along when traveling.

I tugged open the top dresser drawer and glanced over my shoulder toward the closed bedroom door as I did.

Silly, girl. No one was looking.

Inside the drawer lay his boxer briefs, each spread out flat and neatly stacked and—they were in order from lightest color to darkest. A control freak's wet dream.

I ran a palm over a gray pair. Soft. I loved how the briefs snugged his erection so possessively. Almost as if a tease to me. *Ha, ha, look at this. I am right here, against his skin, hugging this nice thick cock you desperately want to touch.*

Wishing there was a hard cock beneath my hand right now sent a shiver of desire through my system. I squeezed my legs together and the bows on my shoes tickled my bare ankles. Mmm...

The lower drawers contained some folded tee-shirts, jogging pants, and socks. No pink panties, thank God.

"But wait."

I shimmied down the panties from under my skirt—completely planned—and pulled off the black lace bit of nothing. Tucking it between the stacks of his underwear toward the back, I closed the drawer.

Then I tugged the drawer open again and snatched the gray pair. I'd left my purse in the living room on the floor beside the sofa. I scrunched them up in my hand, but then...

I held them before my hips to check the size. "Why not?"

Bending, I stepped into the boxer briefs and pulled them up my legs and under my pleated skirt. They fit loosely, and the seam of the flap in front was a different feel against my shaved pussy. I wiggled my hips, moving subtly within the male undergarment. Did guys actually use the flap to whip it out and take a pee? Seemed like it would be just as easy, if not easier, to pull the things down.

I was wearing his underwear. It felt sneaky and naughty. I giggled and pulled my skirt down, smoothing over the pleats. I'd tell him about it later.

Maybe.

I wandered to the closet and pulled open one of the French doors. Inside a half a dozen suits hung neatly on wooden hangers that smelled of cedar. I strolled my fingers down the fabric and inhaled.

"OhmyGod." For the first time I smelled him. And it wasn't spicy, as I'd hoped, but instead a sort of sable, bay rum scent tainted with the overwhelming cedar. Sweet and, mmm...

I pressed my nose to the suit, aiming for the collar, where I knew the fabric had lain closest to his bare skin. There the scent was stronger. I inhaled deeply. Drowning in the imagined feel of his nose against my neck, his scent caressing me, I hummed with pleasure. "Mmm, yes."

The white and gray shirts also smelled faintly of him, as did the purple silk tie I drew out to rub against my cheek. Turning, the tie still pressed to my face, I climbed onto the bed and stretched out on my back. Thinking to turn my head into the pillow I was rewarded with more of his delicious, sensual fragrance.

"Nummy."

I curled up my legs and tugged the pillow against my face, burying myself in his essence. A wiggle of my hips rubbed my pussy against the soft reminder of his closeness.

Eight

I slipped into a reverie. In my dream, I walked out into Monsieur Sexy's living area, strolling my hand along the back of the leather sofa. It was brown and worn, like a seasoned cowboy's chaps. It smelled as if it belonged in the corner of a bookstore, comfy and welcoming to anyone who cared to settle in for a long read.

Someone cleared their throat. I turned in a spin, hand going to my mouth that had opened in a surprised O. Before the window, he sat on a chair, one ankle propped across his knee. Bespoke Italian leather shoes gleamed in the sunlight beaming in from over his straight, broad shoulders. An arm was draped across the back of chair. A curl of brown hair tickled his ear. He sat in arrogant expectation, those sky-gray eyes taking me in as he had done so often through his bedroom window.

No glass this time. Not even a computer screen. *Just a dream.*

Here's to not waking too quickly.

"Did you leave your panties in my bedroom?" he asked in that French-laced deep voice that had the capability of making me wet *like that.*

"I uh..." Feeling almost guilty, I gave a sheepish shrug. "Yes." A little defiance in that reply. And why not? I couldn't wait to see what he would do next.

"Then you've no lace on under that flirty little skirt of yours?"

My hand slid across the pleated skirt hem that stopped high on my thighs. A curl of wanton need shivered in my core. The room was not hot, but I was suddenly warm and moist between my legs.

I shook my head no.

"Then what are you wearing?"

"Your briefs."

His eyebrow lifted. A tilt of his head. He caught his fingers against a temple. "Good girl."

The approval should have felt juvenile and silly, but instead it caused my shoulders to shift back, lifting my breasts with a confident inhalation.

"Slide the skirt off and let me look at what you've done."

Tongue teasing at the backs of my teeth, I nodded and unzipped. I'd undressed before him; this was nothing new. The skirt dropped at my beribboned heels and I flicked it away with a foot. Standing there in his boxers, my blouse spilling over the waistband, I felt ashamed only briefly.

Then the tiny vixen within me pushed up and giggled. I tilted forward a hip, boldly displaying what naughtiness I'd gotten up to.

"You like the feel of my clothing on your skin?" he asked.

"Oh yes. Makes me feel as if you are right here. Standing before me. Will you—"

"Not yet. I want to look at you," he said. "Turn around."

Telling me what to do? Yes, please.

I turned away from him. The boxer briefs hung loosely at my hips yet they did caress my derriere. I teased a finger at the corner of my mouth, wanting to peek over a shoulder. Feeling a bit like the student forced to stand before the front of the classroom with all eyes on her, I was suddenly nervous.

"Slip them off," he said.

Expose myself before the whole classroom? Eek!

Wait. This was not a nightmare, but a daydream. And the only one watching was someone I trusted completely. I wiggled down the briefs and with another flick of foot, relegated his underwear on top of the puddle of my skirt.

"Now bend over the sofa."

Oh, mercy. Heat traced my neck and up under my jaw, quickly overcoming my cheeks. He'd told me the other night during a Skype session that his favorite position was with the woman bent over before him. Giddy glee echoed out a shiver within my core and to my extremities. My nipples hardened, and it was all I could do not to brush my fingers over them as I bent over the back of the sofa.

I ran my hands down the aged leather and caught my elbows against the back. (You won't see this in any bookstore.) I tilted a look under my arm at him. He'd leaned forward, hands hanging slack between his knees. His gaze was intense. And it was focused on my bared derriere.

"Spread your legs," he directed, "a little."

Want swirled at my pussy. I'd grown so wet I wouldn't be surprised if I creamed down my thighs. The lace bra teased at my erect nipples. Every molecule in my body hummed, alert and wanting.

Wiggling my hips as I spread my legs, I guessed he could see my asshole and the swell of my labia. His silent perusal only increased my breaths and my heartbeats pounded to match the quiet strains of some pop song that I now noticed playing in the background. Not loud; barely there. Dream music. The bass had been turned up. Each beat permeated my skin and glided through my veins.

Anticipation made me squirmy. I wiggled my hips again and stretched my arms along the back of the sofa to tilt up my ass. For as flushed and hot as I felt, the air cooled my skin as if a lover's breath seeking the heated core of me.

He growled an approving noise. Chair legs scraped on the wood floor. Italian leather shoes strode toward me.

It was all I could do to not turn and look at him, or to plunge into his embrace. I wanted this surrender to his control. It felt intimately exquisite. And dirty.

The lightest touch trailed up the back of one of my thighs. Slowly. Lingering. It felt like a breeze that had a focus. He drew his fingertips over my ass, tracing the curve of it from one side to the other, then down the opposite thigh. And when he ventured upward again, and his fingers paused at the crease where the curve of my ass met my leg, I sucked in a breath, and clutched at the leather with my fingers.

His crisp cotton sleeve cuff brushed my bottom, and dusted in the direction of my pussy. I closed my eyes. Heartbeats raced. I hadn't realized how tightly I held my jaws, and when I did, I dipped my head and gasped to release that tension.

"You want me to touch you?" he asked. "Where you are wet?"

I nodded. "Please."

"Spread wider," he insisted calmly, firmly.

My feet stepped outward, the heels of my shoes clicking on the wood floor. I arched my back and thrust my ass as high as possible, seeking the promised touch. I needed him against my skin. I wanted him to feel my wetness, to push his fingers inside me.

To own me.

Exploratory fingers paused just below my derriere. Two heartbeats. A shallow breath. I bit my lower lip. And then...

His fingers ventured between my legs and over my pussy lips. Burying my face against the leather, I sighed at that first deliciously intimate contact. So light and barely there, I couldn't be sure he would commit to the touch. It was frustrating, until it was not. And the tease urged me into a wanting moan.

When his fingers parted my labia and slicked my wetness, I felt his other hand grip my hip and hold me firmly. One finger slid inside me.

"Oh, fuck," I groaned.

"You're so wet," he said on a controlled tone. "And tight."

I rocked my hips, pumping on his finger, seeking the rhythm that would get me off. A greedy little underwear stealer, am I.

"You want more?" he asked. "You want it deeper?"

"Yes," I demanded, and slammed my hips back to his hand. "Give me more. Two fingers."

The entrance this time was slow, yet insistent. He stroked me inside. Deeply. It felt exquisite. Naughty. Bold. Yet the skim of his sleeve over my skin was the most erotic sensation, and every time it happened I gasped, surprised at how my entire system clenched up in anticipation.

"More," I said. "Fill me."

"Yes." He groaned as he slipped three fingers inside me.

Filled with him, so exquisitely pierced, I thrust my hips backward, seeking the stretch, the wanting moans that came from him. The smell of his cologne, wild and fresh. The hand at my hip gripped hard, almost painfully. He wanted to go so deep. I wanted to take him all in. This was deliciously merciless. I felt controlled, yet in control. Mastered, yet able to break my reins should I wish.

"Show me how you like it," he whispered. "Faster? Slowly?"

I rocked my hips, pumping on his fingers slowly, deeply. I wanted to feel all of him and know he felt me. Too fast, and the spell would be broken.

"You like to be filled," he commented. "*Je suis annulée.*"

Oh, delicious Frenchman, fuck me with your words.

His fingers slipped from me and I heard him unzip. His pants dropped to the floor. A hot, swollen cock slapped against my ass. Hard and steely, it slipped up and down, teasing me, but not yet venturing near my aching wetness that desired only to be filled by him.

Both hands to my hips now, he directed me forward so I felt his cock glide between my thighs. The head of him nudged at my clit. *Let me in.* And then it slipped away. *No wait, I'm just teasing.*

I sucked in a breath. Wanting to reach down, to grab hold of him and press him against my clitoris, I instead clung to the leather. One of my heels scraped the wood floor. I was his to control. And the agony of not getting what I wanted was too perfect.

"You want me inside you? You think you deserve that after you've been snooping about my place?"

Oops. But I had told him I would snoop. Of course, that didn't mean he would approve, or that he wouldn't want to punish me by withholding his cock when I needed it ramming inside me. Right now. Come. On. Give it to me!

One hand slid up and clutched my breast through the blouse. He pinched my nipple hard. I cried out. Nudging my ass against him, I hoped the pressure on his cock would get to him and he wouldn't hold out much longer...

The sudden entrance of his hard shaft felt as if I'd been pierced by molten lava. In the best way.

"Yes!" I slammed my hips backward, pumping against him. The friction tugged at my clit and hummed around the entrance of my vagina. "Harder. Deeper," I insisted.

He complied, his hands at my hips not so much commanding, as directing my movements. And when he did finally slam into me—and stay there—I felt his shudders in my bones. He reached under my stomach and pulled me upright against his chest. A hand clasped my breast, but didn't squeeze, only held me, claiming me. He thrust once again and cried out, his orgasm spilling into me in a hot gush.

"Fuck yes," he murmured near my ear. "*Très bon, mon abeille.*"

I woke on his bed, heartbeats racing and stomach panting. My hand shot instantly to my crotch, pressing the soft gray boxer material against my clit. Fuck, it was there, the climax that I'd had in my dream, waiting, so close to fruition...

I pulled down the boxers and jilled off there on his bed, my head pressing back into his pillow, my legs stretched across the white coverlet.

The scent of him drowned me, and the feel of how he had touched me captured my imagination and made it real.

I came hard and shouting out in triumph. Body shaking and arms splaying out to my sides, I chuckled softly as I panted through the delicious reward of my naughty dream.

On my cyber lover's bed. Alone. With no one to touch but myself.

Nine

"*Merci*," Monsieur Sexy said as he pulled off his dress shirt to reveal abs that demanded some serious licking.

"Hold off on the thanks until you see if the plants survive," I offered.

I, too, was stripping down. It was late, and we'd both had long days at work, but there was no way either of us could come down from the adrenaline of nine to five—or one to eight as it had been for me—without a tension relieving jack n' jill session.

"Your apartment is huge. The rent must be ridiculous," I said. "And you must be rich."

"A man with money means so much to you?"

I cast a glance at the computer screen. He'd asked with such concern. Had I sounded materialistic? "Uh...no. I'm not a gold digger. I know it's not cheap to live in Paris."

"You live in Paris. In the 7th, which is notoriously snooty and old money."

"In an apartment a tenth the size of yours. I have a trust fund that will see me through a few more years, if I decide to stay."

"*If* you decide to stay?"

"Been here almost two and a half years. Once my three year Visa is up, I'll have to decide whether or not to stay."

"Any thoughts on that?"

"Not really." Seriously, I hadn't thought that far in advance. I liked to live day to day. But that he seemed so concerned for my future tickled me. Did he want me to stay?

I paused before slipping down my skirt. This naughty girl had almost forgotten her daring steal.

"Did you find the plant in the bathroom, as well?" he asked.

"I did. Your plants are all very healthy. You must have a green thumb. Ohh... That's not green."

He stood before the camera, in close range, slowly easing his fingers about his cock, polishing the cylinder for some piston action. When he was completely erect the deep maroon head of it gleamed. And the vein that ran along the underside of it got engorged when he was close to coming.

Yeah, I noticed things like that. Hard not to when it was all on the screen, right there, for a girl to study. Talk about in your face. I wasn't beyond licking the screen. If I recorded him I could sit back, at my leisure, pause the video, and zoom in on Monsieur Eiffel. But we'd made a rule. Neither of us would record these conversations, not the video or the audio.

Did I trust that he wasn't secretly recording our antics and posting at some skeevy online sites?

I had to. Wasn't like I had a choice. Actually, I did have a choice. I could not be doing this. But that was as ridiculous to consider as not breathing.

"You are not going to undress completely?"

I teased a fingernail at the corner of my mouth, approaching the camera cautiously. "I have a confession to make."

"Good, bad, or naughty?"

"Naughty." I blushed because the tiny vixen within me wished to be chastised for her wicked deed. "I uh...left you a present in your underwear drawer."

"Is that so? Was it pink?"

"Never." Because pink panties reminded me of Boobs, the fencing student I'd witnessed undressing in his bedroom. That image of her huge boobs and self-satisfied smirk would never leave me. "I prefer black lace," I said.

"Mm, I can't wait to get home."

"And..."

"And?"

"I may have borrowed something of yours." I unzipped the skirt at the back and let it fall down to the floor to reveal what I wore beneath.

"Are those...?"

I nodded. Managed a sheepish smile. Then I jut out a hip and wiggled my derriere to model the stylish yet masculine wardrobe choice.

"I like them on you," he offered.

"I prefer them on you." I smoothed a palm over the front of the boxer briefs, poking a finger in along the flap. "You fill them out much better than I do. But it has been an enlightening experience putting on men's underwear for the first time."

"How so?"

"This flap is just decorative, isn't it? I mean, you usually just tug them down to go pee, I'm sure."

"Unless a guy is standing in a public bathroom before a urinal and doesn't want to flash his ass to everyone."

"Ah. That makes sense." I slid my hand inside the opening, tickling across my mons. "Here I thought it was easy access to the main stick. You guys do like to touch it. A lot."

"A reassuring grasp every so often is warranted," he agreed. "What can I say? Monsieur Eiffel has been with me all my life. We are close."

I giggled. "I'll return these, I promise."

"Only if I get to take them off you."

"Deal." I slid down the underwear and kicked them aside. "Better?"

"Let me look at you bent over," he said.

"What?" I approached the camera and made comical show at peering into the lens and tapping it. *Is this thing on?* "Have you been following me in my dreams?"

"What do you mean?"

"I uh..." Finger to the corner of my lower lip, I teased at confessing my maneuvers in his home. Hell, why not? Stolen underwear and daydreams, here I come. "When I was in your place today I told you I snooped."

"Right. What does that have to do with me wanting to stare at your gorgeous derriere?"

I wiggled the body part mentioned because his compliments always gave me a giddy thrill.

"Confession number two coming right up. After putting on your underwear and snooping in your closet and sorting through your books—I love that you read, by the way."

"All the time. It keeps me vital. And I learn how to operate your clitoris."

"Yay, for reading! So, I laid down on your bed and smushed my face into your pillow."

His cock faded into the background as his face appeared on the screen. One dark brow arched curiously.

"I wanted to smell you. And you smell..." I sighed, clasping my hands to my breasts. "Wonderful. Like leather and whiskey, I think. I've never tasted whiskey, so it's a guess."

"Rum," he said. "And something else, but I don't recall. It's a scent that was...given to me a few years ago. I like it."

"So do I. Anyway, as I was lying there, soaking in your scent, I closed my eyes and started to daydream about the things you would do to me if you were home."

"Yes?"

"And..." I sat on the bed so he could see all of me. "I fell asleep for a bit. And you were in my dreams, looking so handsome in your suit. I love you in a suit. Anyway, you told me to bend over the back of your sofa for a good long look."

"Ah, I understand. Did I like what I saw?"

I nodded. "Then you fucked me hard."

"I fuck you hard all the time in my dreams. Do you still have that silver vibrator?"

I sat up, my nipples tightening expectantly. "Of course."

"Retrieve it, and let me fuck you."

Five minutes later I was bent over the bed, my ass facing the camera, and the vibrator wedged between the mattress and my pussy. I came hard and cried out, clutching the sheets as my insides quivered and my thighs shook.

Behind me—I couldn't see him from this exposed angle—Monsieur Sexy was jacking off. He said, "Fuck yeah," and came as well.

My cheeks were burnished rosy and my breasts sheened with perspiration. I rolled to my back, the vibrator clattering to the floor. I laughed at the silliness of this American twenty-something chick living in

Paris, alone, getting off before the camera for a man she had never touched or kissed.

I trusted him enough to do things like jill off, ass toward the camera. I stole his private underthings. And I may have killed his plants.

I was so not myself anymore. Who had I become?

"*Tu me manques*," he said.

I turned to face the camera. His profile faced me. Eyes closed he smiled widely.

"What does that mean?" I asked.

"I feel you are missing from me."

Wow. That would carry me for days. Seriously. Such a statement landed right in the pleasure center of my brain, and felt as good as an orgasm.

"Damn, that was good," he whispered. "But it will be better than good when finally it is you on my bed instead of the laptop, *oui*?"

"*Oui*. Soon yes?"

"Er, soon?"

"For us to get together?" I reiterated.

"You are not pleased with what we have now?"

Again with the weird reluctance. I leaned up on my elbows and stared at the screen. He'd been saying all along that he couldn't wait to meet me. To fuck me. Was I imagining a change of heart from him?

"Of course I'm pleased," I said. "But I want to touch you. You...don't want to touch me?"

"I do, *mon abeille*." He studied my face, his eyes intent. "I think you are getting upset?"

"I..." I sighed. Maybe I had taken it wrong. He was still eager. Perhaps just exhausted from our jack n' jill session. "No, not upset. We'll meet in good time. I'll give you a call tomorrow at lunch? That reminds me I have to plug in my phone, which...is in my purse."

I sat up on the bed. I didn't recall coming home from his place with purse in hand. I'd left my apartment door unlocked so hadn't needed to sort around in the depths of it for a key.

"I think I left my purse at your place. Is it okay if I run over there tomorrow morning to get it?"

"Of course it is. You locked the door behind you when you left?"

"Yes. I still have the codes written down, stuffed in my skirt pocket. I'm sorry. That was stupid of me."

"Don't worry about it, *mon abeille.* If I could have you in my place all the time I would do so. Perhaps it was for the best so you can do a plant check while you are there? Make sure your administrations didn't serve them a fatal dose."

"If they did, I'll have to do a quick replacement on all of them before you return. But I'll never tell if I do."

"If the plants seem a little smaller, perhaps even different than the ones I have now, I won't ask. Promise."

"You're too good to me." I pulled up the pillow to prop under my head. "Why are you so good? What is wrong with you?"

"Must something be wrong with me? I adore you. Isn't that what a person does when they like a person? Treat them well? As well as I can when we are separated by this distance and a glass barrier."

"When do you return?"

"Four days."

I considered asking to meet him the moment he returned, but stuffed the urge away. Instead I nodded. I'd wait for him to broach the subject of a meeting. I felt a little off about his reluctance. Was it something I had imagined? Didn't think so.

Though, there was something I could do to urge him along. I remembered the invitation Melanie had sent me. The party was days away on All Saints Day. I would never miss one of her shindigs. And this year, it was going to be the best, because I'd already ordered my costume and couldn't wait to slip into that fantasy.

"I'm going to send you an email," I said. "Forward you something, actually. It's...something we might use to get together."

"Yes? You want to meet when I return to Paris?"

I touched the screen. It was warm, and yet, not at all like living, breathing flesh. It couldn't react to my touch, nor could it move closer, hush a soft breath across my cheek, or wrap an arm about my waist and pull me closer.

"Hell yes, I want to meet. But I'm sensing you're reluctant."

He shrugged, smoothed his hand along his jaw. Avoided looking directly at the screen. "You going to be waiting at the curb as soon as I arrive?"

Tension in that question. He was trying not to say something. And whatever it was, I didn't want to hear it. "No. I'll wait for you to say when it feels right. Would you prefer that?"

"Yes. Uh, don't think about it too much, though, okay? I know how you like to think."

"Promise." But that was a lie. Really? He couldn't commit and say 'Yes, be there waiting for me'? "I'll send the email."

"You make me curious."

"Good. I like to know a man is wondering about what I'll do next. Until tomorrow?"

"*Bonne nuit, mon abeille.*" He kissed his fingers and blew me the kiss.

Tonight I grasped the kiss and sheltered it in my cupped palms for the longest time, holding it below my face as if I'd trapped a firefly and the glow could actually warm my face, the wings fluttering the sensation of his kiss across my lips. "Until tomorrow."

I signed out of Skype, then found the email Melanie had sent me. Attached to the email, a gif featuring a sugar skull blinked its eyes at me. The French were not big on Halloween, but they did do treats and costumes for the kids. The adults were more into All Saints Day, or the more popular name for it, Day of the Dead.

If I clicked the 'send' button then there was no going back. I was committing to a meeting. Would the invite please him or push him farther from me? I couldn't shake the odd feeling that he had just taken a step back from me, farther from that curb.

Hmm...

No waffling! the tiny vixen screamed inside me.

My finger hovered over the return key, but not for long. I clicked send, and quickly close the laptop.

"Four days and he's back," I muttered.

And then?

"And then," I said with a smile, and crawled between the sheets.

And I was instantly transported outside to the curb, clad in a body-hugging dress and my ribbon-tied shoes, waiting expectantly with hands clasped. The wind burnished my cheeks rosy. My heartbeats fluttered.

A cab arrived and the back door opened. Out stepped an Italian leather shoe. He rose before me, so tall I had to look up to capture that sexy sly wink.

"*Mon abeille—*"

Pause. He should know my name for that first auspicious meeting. Yes?

Yes, I needed to do something about that.

Okay, in my dreams (for now) he called me by name. Then he whisked me into his arms. One strong arm banded across my back. I tilted forward on my tiptoes. Our eyes closed.

The kiss was inevitable...

Ten

I found my purse sitting on the hardwood floor before the leather sofa where I'd left it. Noticing the hanging plant in the window still looked as vibrant and alive as it had before I'd gotten to it yesterday, I decided I had done no harm. A quick trip down the hallway to peek in the bathroom... Lush greenery.

"Whew."

Turning on my heels, I sashayed back to the living room. A glance to the sofa stirred up a thigh-squeezing twinge of desire. I ran my hand along the aged brown leather as I walked by.

"Soon. Three more days."

And then what? His odd reluctance during our cyber-chat last night bothered me. I had initially been the one a little freaked about bringing our relationship to the next level with the video and voice. I mean, after all, I'm the chick who starts looking for the door after dating a man for a month.

But now? I was glad I had succumbed. And I was ready to rush toward the next level: touch. I needed it. I wanted to feel his skin, to know his breath against my cheek, to shiver under the lash of his tongue as it explored my body.

I wanted to stand at the curb, waiting for his kiss.

But was he having second thoughts? Pulling back from something he'd initially encouraged?

Or was I over-analyzing life once again?

"I am," I admonished as I opened the front door. "And he avoided the rich question too." I remembered that as I stepped out from the massive flat.

That must have been what switched him over to cautious mode. I'd asked about money.

"Stupid," I muttered.

And yet, the man had freely bought me a dress that had boasted a four-figure price tag. And he'd ordered an exquisite meal, hand-delivered by the chef that must have also set him back a fortune. Weird. Well, he probably didn't like to define himself with a dollar figure. I could dig it. But my curiosity wouldn't rest. I knew that.

Locking the door behind me, I strolled leisurely down the stairs to the first floor, and down again toward the ground level. (The *rez-de-chaussée* if you're following if French.) I could so handle living in this building. The space was much bigger than my tiny closet. I'd have to share the space with Monsieur Sexy, but that would be cool. I'd watch him fence with his students and cook him simple meals served with wine and love. I'd launder his sheets and underwear, then slip on a dryer-warm pair and tease him with my semi-sexy stripper moves. We'd be such a happy pair.

I laughed because this time I didn't mind following my wandering thoughts into a future I could definitely entertain. I just hoped he wasn't seriously rethinking what he'd gotten himself into.

At the bottom of the stairwell I met an elderly gentleman whose bright green eyes were sheltered beneath a froth of bushy gray brows. The scent of cherry tobacco filled his airspace as if an invisible cloud.

"Ah, Madame!" he declared. "English, yes? It is so nice to finally meet you."

"Madame?"

"You descended from the upper flat? You are Monsieur's wife, *oui*?"

My heart dropped to my toes. The fantasy shattered like black glass, cutting through my skin as each piece fell around me. I gripped the wood handrail to my right, leaning hard onto it.

Monsieur's *wife*?

The man must be mistaken. Yet there was only one resident living in the upper flat. In the entire building, because the rest was all designated to business space.

"I am Francois DeCardes. The builder owner." He bowed with a nod of his head. "When Monsieur signed the lease he mentioned his wife traveled too often. Makes him very sad. But we were pleased to have a married couple occupy the flat. You are enjoying the space?"

"Uh, the space?" Dizzy, I clenched the handrail. Cotton crowded my mouth. Heartbeats thundered at the back of my throat. I nodded. I didn't know how to launch into an explanation that I was not who he thought I was. I wanted to race out of there and scream at the top of my lungs. "Yes, the space. It's nice."

Nice? It was occupied by a freaking married couple! Oh hell, what was happening?

"Is Monsieur home?" the old man asked. "I've an insurance form I need him to sign. Subtle changes to the building policy. Nothing terribly unpleasant."

"He's away," I provided rotely. Not really in my body at the moment, I took a step away from the stairs, yet turned back to look up at the old man. "In Berlin."

"Ah, your paths do not cross then?"

I shook my head. Looked away. How to breathe?

Crossed paths? Only last night I'd wanted to reach through the computer screen, grab the man by his face, and plead with him to touch me. And now? I could no longer sense my heartbeats, though something pounded like tribal drums in my ears.

Married? The man with whom I had thought to be firmly ensconced in a relationship with, was married? Fuck me.

No, fuck him!

"He'll be home..." I couldn't speak without revealing the shake in my voice. I managed a fleeting glance upward. "Have you his email?"

"*Oui.* I can forward the documents that way. Just thought to stop in while I was in the neighborhood. Are you well, Madame?"

I nodded but it came out as a sort of head shake rotating Exorcist pea-soup-spewing movement.

Fuck. Me.

"I was headed out for some air." I patted my purse, hugged tight to my gut as if I were trying to fend off an oncoming battle spear with the flimsy armor. The armor had failed. I'd received a direct hit to the heart. "Is that all you need?"

"*Oui. Bonjour, Madame.* I will walk you out?"

"No, *merci.* I'm in a bit of a rush. I'll tell Monsieur you stopped by."

Really? I was out of my head. I couldn't think. I could barely stand. I needed to move.

I rushed past the concierge and out into the October air where I gasped in the afternoon chill edged with the crisp, lingering remnants of rain. It should have felt refreshing, but instead I choked and clutched my throat. I pounded my chest. Where were my heartbeats? I...I...

Fuck.

Not looking for cars, I raced across the street on a red light.

"Married," I muttered, over and over.

I passed by the concierge, his usual friendly greeting a garble of nonsensical syllables vying against the pounding in my ears. It was the rushing blood. I couldn't hear over my own need to keep breathing, to stay alive.

Yes, I was being dramatic. But hell. Really?

Once inside my apartment with the door closed, I didn't scream, as I had wanted to. Instead, I tossed my purse aside to the floor, slammed my back to the door, and squatted, sliding down until I sat with my legs sprawled before me.

I gasped in a chuffing breath, holding back tears.

The bastard was married.

And I had been a fool.

Eleven

I couldn't work. It felt ridiculous to sit before the computer and attempt to ignore the fact that a month of my life had been sacrificed to a man whom I had thought to trust. A man to whom I had exposed my deepest secrets. A man—a nameless man—who had forgotten to mention that he was married.

But had he really forgotten such an important detail regarding his life? Doubtful.

How had he hidden a wife from me?

The building owner had mentioned to me that *Madame* traveled a lot. Had she been away so much that she hadn't even been to his new place across the street from me? He'd lived there almost two months.

Yet, I realized I hadn't paid close attention to the comings and goings across the street. Out of respect. We'd kept our voyeurism to the bedroom windows. Occasionally I'd caught a glimpse of him fencing with an opponent across the street in the area I'd decided was his practice space.

Had I completely missed a wife going in and out, suitcases in hand, a kiss to her husband's cheek as she waited at the curb for the cab?

Or was I blowing this out of proportion? I was, by nature, a great imaginer. An accidental fantasist. I thought entirely too much. And my thinking often veered me away from reality and into fictional territory. I know it's a problem. But it's the way I was. Everybody daydreamed.

This was more than a daydream. Daydreams were generally good. This was a reality nightmare.

So was I concocting a wife for him? Perhaps the old man with the insurance papers had heard Monsieur incorrectly? Or if he was married, maybe it wasn't a happy marriage? Were they on the skids since she was away so much?

Could I hope?

I covered my face with my palms. I'd lain on the gray chaise in the living room since returning home from collecting my purse. Rain poured outside, battering the window. A reflection of my inner war? Of my inability to accept this one as a loss?

I sat up and shook my head. "I have to keep a calm head about this. I owe it to him. I owe it to myself."

Right?

I could do this. I had to get the facts before jumping to wild accusations.

I'd lain on the couch through his lunch break, so a lunch chat was out of the question. I'd sign on to Skype tonight and we'd talk. And I would ask. Just put it out there. *Do you have a wife?* I'd know if he lied to me. I just would.

He'd been so kind and good to me. He couldn't be married. Married men who cheated kept their mistress a secret, bought them expensive bribes, and—oh!

"Fuck!"

I had to stop thinking about it or I'd have a raging migraine by the time the sun set. I hadn't eaten lunch. Making something to eat would distract my thoughts. Or better yet, I'd run down the street to the grocery and look for some fresh salad items. The walk in the rain would clear my thoughts.

A man's hand reached for the fuzzy peach the same time I'd grasped the plump fruit. He playfully tugged, then relented.

"You have taken the best one," he said in what I guessed was an Irish accent.

Oh, but European accents were always my undoing. Hell, I was already undone. In the worst way possible.

What had the Irishman said? Indeed, I had taken the best piece of fruit. And I wasn't about to give up my booty. I'd just had something very meaningful ripped out of my life. I was keeping the damn peach.

"Naturally," I said, and looked up to fall into a pair of dazzling blue eyes.

He was older, probably pushing forty to judge the gray tufts above his ears and the creases on his forehead and at the corners of his eyes. Black hair had been shaved closed to his scalp and a short-trimmed beard framed his face and eyes. His handsome quotient was equal to the foreign accent quotient—killer.

My wounded heart managed a weak flutter.

"Could I trade you two plums for that one peach?" he said, plucking up two dark purple baubles and juggling them in his palm.

"I'm afraid I have my heart set on braised peach with goat cheese," I offered.

"You tease me with your culinary machinations. You are dining alone?"

An odd question. But I decided he was being flirtatious. And guess what? I liked it. I *needed* the release in my tight and tense shoulder muscles. While Monsieur Sexy's image had staked claim in the frontal cortex of my brain, I was desperate to paper over it with something different. Something kinder. Something not French. And not so...married.

My eyes veered to the man's fingers. No visible gold band or a tan line indicting a missing wedding ring.

Monsieur Sexy did not wear a ring either. Sneaky.

"Yes, alone," I finally answered. "I don't share my peaches with just anyone."

That got a blushing tilt of head from him. "I would hope not. Do you live in the area? I have not seen you before. I have lived in this neighborhood for five years."

"I do, but I'm not looking to share," I reiterated. I may have slipped into desperation but I wasn't certifiable. "*Bonsoir, monsieur*. I do thank you for surrendering the peach."

"Any day, *mademoiselle*."

I strolled toward the front of the store, plastic shopping basket hooked on one moist arm. It was still pouring outside, but I'd worn a scarf over my hair for the dash to the store. Tilting a look over my shoulder, I discovered the Irishman watching me. He tossed a plum in the air, and winked.

I returned a warm smile. Mercy. It had been a while since I'd flirted. The detour had been necessary.

As I paid with a credit card, and slipped the few items into my reusable bag, I tendered one last look back into the store before leaving. The man was nowhere to be seen. I couldn't manage a regretful sigh. Probably for the best. I didn't need him following me home or becoming a stalker.

The concierge had carried up two huge boxes from Amazon and leaned them against the wall outside my apartment door.

"The bookshelves. My books will be so pleased."

I dragged the boxes inside and found them a home against the inner wall, then made supper. Cut in half and pitted, the peach braised under the broiler and topped with softened goat cheese and a touch of brown sugar made for a delicious meal. A frisky white moscato and half a baguette topped it off.

Barefoot and clad in comfortable jersey slacks and a tee-shirt, I wandered into the kitchen, depositing the dishes in the sink. I'd wash them in the morning with the breakfast dishes. I had to work at the map shop tomorrow. Would I want to? Much as a distraction appealed, the idea of sinking into myself and wallowing lured more strongly.

Skyping tonight felt ominous. But necessary. I had to know. One way or another. I hoped for the best, but my heart was already picking out mourning black.

Really? Me, the girl who agreed with her best friend that the shortest relationships were the best? The one who had laughed off a desperate marriage proposal from a man whom she'd caught with his head between her BFF's legs? The one who wasn't ready to settle into anything except a sexy pair of high heels?

I tugged up my tee-shirt, prepared to slip into the yellow silk robe before opening up Skype. I pulled the shirt down. I didn't want to do this half-dressed. I would feel more confident with clothes on.

Actually, I'd gained a lot of confidence by basking before Monsieur Sexy's gaze while completely naked. I had become a goddess comfortable within her skin. It felt empowering.

Now the sigh did escape.

"A spurned goddess," I muttered.

Didn't all the pissed-off goddesses usually retaliate with hellfire and unspeakable punishments that lasted a thousand lifetimes? Monsieur

Sexy should be glad I hadn't done research on Greek goddesses. I was out of my element regarding revenge.

Eying the laptop sitting on the end of the bed, I decided to take it out to the living room, away from the camera setup. He'd have to do with my face before the screen. And if I had blown things out of proportion, and it turned out Francois DeCardes the building manager was delusional, I could always move back into the bedroom to end the night in the usual manner that involved much heavy breathing and an orgasm, or two.

Setting the laptop on the coffee table, I then paced before the window. Still raining. Every-so-often lightning crackled the black sky. Nights like this usually put me in a smoldering, romantic mood. I loved to have sex while the rain pattered the windows.

I touched the cool glass. Beyond the water streaks, his building loomed. Would this be it? If he really was married, that meant I'd never see him, never touch him, never... Why did it bother me that I wouldn't be able to fulfill that need for touch?

Because! I am woman. Feel me breathe, sigh and desire. And oh, but I ached for contact.

It was about twenty minutes past the usual time we connected. I'm sure he'd already pinged me.

"Just get it over with," I coached.

The getting it over with part felt so...final. Would this be our last conversation? Ever? It could be if he was married. Because how to get beyond something like that? It would make me the other woman. I was no man's other woman. That was so not cool with me. I would not inflict that kind of pain on another woman.

But I may have already done so. Would she find the credit card receipt for the dress? Surely, he kept a private account for his liaisons.

Liaisons? Kill me now.

How could he do that to his wife?

I was working myself up again. My pacing had increased, as had my breathing. Stopping to inhale deeply, I concentrated on the in and out, in and out of my breath. It brought me down, but could never completely tether me to calm.

I leaned over and opened the laptop cover. Skype automatically opened when I signed on, and it pinged, indicating he was online.

Waiting. Completely unaware of what I now knew. Last time we'd chatted I'd confessed my underwear theft and we'd had a rousing cyber-sex session that had left us both panting.

My God, I'd sent him the All Saints Day party invitation. Damn it.

"Be cool," I cautioned. "He's playing reluctant anyway."

Was his reluctance due to the fact that he was married? Of course! Why else would the guy not want to meet me? Ugg. I so had not seen this coming.

I signed on and the video stream displayed the side of his face. Glasses on, he was reading, which he did when I hadn't made it to the computer before or at the same time as him. He held a newspaper, and I could make out the headline but couldn't interpret the German. Did he speak German? I think he had mentioned as much. He must if he were teaching in Berlin. Talented man.

There was so much about him to admire.

"Hey," I said, sitting on the couch and leaning forward, elbows on my knees. "Did you have a good supper?"

"*Bonsoir, mon abeille*. I did indeed eat well. McDonalds' big cheeseburger and fries."

That startled me. He was pretty health conscious. I mean, a guy who fenced regularly and sported washboard abs probably didn't touch the greasy stuff.

"Seriously?"

"Yes. I don't normally eat the fast food, but I walk by McDonalds every day on the way from work to the hotel and—I don't know—the smell lured me in. It was good. Though I may regret it soon enough."

"I guess a greasy, carb-loaded meal should be considered a necessary treat every so often."

"I had the chocolate milkshake, too. I haven't had one of those since I was a kid."

"Really? My favorite as a kid was a rootbeer float."

"I've never tasted rootbeer."

"Never? That's absolutely scandalous. I'm going to have to find you some rootbeer and STAT."

"Is it better than a chocolate milkshake?"

"By leaps and bounds. I promise you, after you've had vanilla ice cream mushed up in a glass of rootbeer you will have dreams about it."

"I dream about you."

I caught my chin in palm and smiled at his handsome and sincere visage. "I dream about you, too."

"About me fucking you?"

"All the time. All day. Every night."

"Did you run over to my place to get your purse?"

"Yes. Oh." I sat upright. My heart dropped to my gut. *Ker-splash.*

I'd forgotten. Seriously forgotten. I'd fallen into his sky-gray eyes and the surprise of his fastfood foray, and the utter shock of the man never having tasted rootbeer, and—had completely forgotten.

I clenched my fingers before me and looked at them. The knuckles turned white. I suddenly felt defensive. For no reason. He should be the one on the defense.

"I got the invitation," he said. "A costume party?"

I stared at the screen, hearing, but not processing his words.

"Two days following when I return? I suppose we can manage that, eh?"

He could *manage* that? What was that supposed to mean? Did he even care? Or would he have to schedule it around his wife?

"So what is it tonight, *mon abeille*? Shall we fuck together or can I watch you do a strip tease?"

"Are you married?" I blurted out.

I caught my fingers against my lips. My heart jittered as if it had just been poked with a cattle prod. I exhaled through my nose.

"Wh-what?" He leaned forward, catching a palm against his temple.

"You heard me. I asked you a question. You need to answer it truthfully. I need to know."

"*Mon abeille—*"

"Please! A man spoke to me after I left your flat. The building owner. He needed you to sign some insurance papers."

"Ah, yes. His email did not mention meeting you—"

"He called me Madame. Thought I was your wife. The wife you'd told him travels a lot and who isn't around much. What. The.

Hell?" I gripped the computer screen as if it was his face and I needed to hold him there. To make him feel my consternation and pain. "Are you married?"

He bowed his head, rubbed his lips with his fingers. Looked aside, then directly at me. I couldn't read his expression. He conveyed no expression. His eyes were flat and his mouth straight.

Yet when he winced, I knew the answer before he plainly said, "Yes."

"Oh, fuck no." I stood and paced toward the wall.

"You need to listen to me. Let me explain."

"Explain?" I rushed back to bend before the screen. "What explaining is there to do? You're married! I've been having an affair with a married man. I can't believe this. I trusted you!"

"*Mon abielle*, you cannot do this. Do not rage as you are doing. Be calm and listen to me."

"Fuck calm." He was telling me what to do when he should be apologizing? "How can you do this to your wife?"

"Sit down."

"No. I'm not going to do anything you ask me to do. This is insane."

"You have to be calm."

"I will not!"

"Really? So you are going to stomp your pretty little shoes and pull out the dramatics?" He made that innately French phawing sound of disgust. "I thought you were different."

"What?" Heartbeats thundered now. And my fists were clenched so tightly I wouldn't have been surprised to feel blood drip from my palms.

"You heard me. Different," he reiterated sharply. "Not like other women who rant and toss out dramatics when they are upset."

"Oh, I'll give you dramatics, buddy."

"Why do I have to do this with you acting the child?"

"Child? How dare you accuse me, when you are the one who is in the doghouse, mister?"

"I do not know what that means."

"Oh, yes you do. You're just playing the French card to piss me off."

He waggled an accusatory finger at me. "You are annoying when you are like this. I will not listen to you until you are calm. And then we can talk."

"If we don't talk now, it's never going to happen. You explain yourself."

"Will you listen calmly?"

He was playing for time. I knew it! He was an asshole of the finest water. He'd confessed. Straight out said yes. The man was married.

I paced again, furious.

"Don't be stupid about this," he said. "You have a tendency to blow things out of proportion. You and your thinking too much. You know that!"

So I did just that. It wasn't his place to point that out. Especially now. I suddenly wished we could go back to how we'd started. With no sound, just gestures and movement. I had a hand gesture for him.

"Asshole!" I couldn't control my anger. I had to say it.

"You think I'd invest my time with you just to have it end because of this small detail?" he countered.

Small detail? The man was delusional.

"No," he continued. "I have spent the past month getting to know you. Learning you. Enjoying you. Hell, I don't even know your name, and yet I count the minutes when I can next see and talk to you. Is it fair to fall in love with someone and not even know their name?"

"Love?" I sat before the laptop, my body so tense my fingers hurt. "You have no right to use that word about us. You can't love a woman when you are married to someone else."

"Is that so? Who are you to tell me how to think and feel? How to love? Who to love? When to love? This is what I feel about you, *mon abielle,* and I mean it."

"You do not. You are tossing out that word to try and win my sympathy."

"I cannot do that. I have always been honest with you."

"Honest? Really? Seems like you forgot to be honest about something very important in your life. Would you have ever told me you had a wife?"

He exhaled. Ran his fingers roughly through his hair. Normally I would have creamed my panties at the gesture. Now, I wanted to punch the laptop screen.

"Honesty?" he finally said. "Being married is not a fact a man leads with when he's in a new relationship."

"I can't believe you."

"*Je t'aime, mon abeille.*"

I scoffed loudly. Wasn't knowing you are in love a very specific point in a relationship when a man should reveal the wife? Aggh!

"Ah, but maybe you do not know the meaning of the word," he insisted. "Is it that you are one of those women who string a man along for a few weeks, perhaps a month, and then you dump him and on to the next lover?"

I breathed out. The exhale hurt at the back of my throat. Had he heard conversations I'd shared with Melanie as we extolled the virtues of the quickie relationship as opposed to investing more than a month's time in any particular man? We were right at that one-month expiration date.

And right now, this thing we had felt oh, so beyond the use-by date.

"I won't listen to you put me down to defend your betrayals."

I slammed the laptop shut and slammed my back to the chaise. A wave of tears spilled down my cheeks and I rushed to the bathroom. Turning on the shower and undressing, I stepped under the water so my neighbors wouldn't hear me bawling.

Twelve

I stared at the closed laptop for five minutes. Maybe it was ten? Could have been longer. Right now I wanted to talk to him as much as I wanted to physically hurt him. Much as I hated him, I had invested in him. The man had become a part of me in ways I couldn't define. He was Monsieur Sexy. *My* Monsieur Sexy. The man knew things about me I rarely shared with anyone.

Love? I wasn't sure. But I felt strong *like* for him most certainly.

Did he really believe he loved me? Some hearts worked that way. It wasn't my place to judge if the velocity with which he ransomed his heart was true or false. But if true, the idea of him loving me also sickened me. What would Madame think?

Madame.

Kill. Me. Now.

I had every right to rage and slam the laptop shut. Every right. But had it been the grown up thing to do? Definitely not. And hadn't I decided before signing on to Skype tonight that I was going to listen calmly? If I thought that I could think myself into all sorts of crazy scenarios, real life had a way of trumping that tenfold.

I touched the brushed aluminum laptop surface. I'd seen hurt in his eyes. And anger. Anger at me for the way I had reacted. He had no right to claim anger.

Maybe a little bit. I had acted like a child. Tossing out the dramatics, as he had said. But his comment about me dumping a man after a month had hit too close to home. I'd needed some distance. I'd cried all the tears I could manage in the shower. Afterward, I'd sat on the edge of the tub sobbing quietly into the towel.

Now, a half hour later, I'd settled. I was calm. I was ready to listen if he was willing to talk. Because I couldn't let it end this way. Despite his lacking scruples, I would not let him remember me as the crazy one.

Opening the laptop, I signed onto Skype. He was still there. In fact, his video feed showed the top of his head. He'd put his head down on the table before the computer. I felt instantly guilty.

Wait! No, I didn't. Monsieur Sexy was a big boy. He could take a few angry words from a woman.

Right?

I tapped the alert tone. He looked up. No smile, just a resigned moue as he rested his temple against a palm and waited for me to speak. His eyes showed traces of red.

"I'm sorry," I said. "For reacting the way I did. I'm not sorry for my anger, though. I can't be."

"I understand. I said some harsh things that were used as defense not in an understanding means. And for that I apologize. *Desolé*."

"Thank you."

"You...rubbed against an open wound."

Seriously? He had opened a wide, gaping wound in my heart. What was he going to do about that?

Sighing, I nodded and shoved my hands under each of my thighs. Calm, remember? Hear him out and then walk away from this mistake.

"I'm ready to listen," I offered. "I need to hear everything you want me to know. You should probably tell me the stuff you'd not intended me to know as well."

"*Merci, mon abeille*. I will say it all." Sitting up, he placed his folded hands on the keyboard, and began. "I haven't been married, in my heart, for a year. We've been separated that long."

Separated? That was a good thing. Well, from my point of view. Maybe. He could merely be referring to her lengthy business trips away from home.

"I confess I lied to the building administrator when leasing the flat. They were looking for a quiet, married couple, not a single man. And I was married. On paper. It was easy enough to embellish the story about my wife being away on business so I could snap up the place. I've always wanted to live in Paris near the Eiffel Tower. I couldn't let the apartment fall out of my hands."

"Where did you live before moving here?"

"Uh, here. In Berlin."

I felt my jaw want to drop, but I didn't allow it. Had he a home with the wife in Berlin? Is that what he'd left only two months earlier to move here?

And he was in Berlin now.

My stomach did a flip-flop. It was increasingly harder to remain calm and detached.

"We've been married for two years," he said. "This past year we've been separated. I had my own apartment in Berlin, but the building began refurbishing in August so I was forced to move. She does travel extensively. But trust me when I say we have not been intimate for the past year. We are separated in every definition of the word."

"I'm sorry." Really?

Huh. I actually was sorry for him. My parents had divorced four years before my mother's car accident. No matter that the love had been lost, it was still a difficult and abrupt shove-off into the single life for any person to manage.

"You mustn't be sorry for me," he said. "I thought I loved her. I would not have married her had I not been in love. Unfortunately she was a bad choice. I learned about her frequents affairs—maintained while traveling—after our first anniversary. I'd installed a new email program and initially set it up with both our emails. For two days her liaisons were revealed in my in-box before she realized the *faux pas*. I tried to hang in there, to give the marriage my best shot. She promised fidelity. That lasted less than two months."

I could actually see the pain draw his face into a solemn mask. A mask to protect his feelings? I hated seeing his eyes so sad. He was the smiling Frenchman across the street who liked to eat chocolate cupcakes and shake his hips to music.

I couldn't help asking. "So you think the separation will help...what?"

"Nothing. It is not a means to think things over and perhaps get back together. She asked for a divorce. I agreed. We are separated while the divorce proceedings are underway. It could have been so simple. Sign the documents, say goodbye. Forever. But she's being a..." He sighed. More of that tense shoving of fingers through his hair.

He'd relented from calling her a nasty name. He must still hold some love for her in his heart. I could sense it. As he should. Shouldn't he? He'd fallen in love, only to realize she had not been as in love as he.

"She's asking for too much," he continued. "Much more than I want to give her. Thus, we've been embroiled in a drawn-out war over property and assets."

"That sounds like an awful thing to experience," I said. "Especially since you must have loved her once?"

"I did. I tend to fall in love easily."

He'd said he loved me. I know everyone loved in their own way and time. Some fell in love at first sight. Others could be friends for years, then date, then live together, before they finally realized the spark that kept them going was love.

As well, there were all kinds of love. Family, friendship, respect, honorable. So his confession of love for me could be entirely different than the kind a man feels about a woman he's asked to marry him.

Ah hell. I was thinking again.

"As you have already guessed," he provided, "I am comfortable. Financially. She strives to take what was never hers in the first place."

"That's got to be tough. Now I'm really sorry for getting so upset," I offered. And I was. Poor guy. I wanted to pat him on the head like a puppy then pull him into my arms.

"No, I should have said something from the start."

"Really?"

He shrugged. "Perhaps not. How does one gesture 'I'm married but going through a divorce' through a window?"

I smiled, as did he. The levity didn't last though.

"I am skittish about women, if truth be told," he said. "That's why, at least I think, when you showed up in the window it was like the right woman in the right situation *à la bonne heure*. You weren't right there in my face. We took our time. We're still taking our time. I feel comfortable with you."

Wow. Our situation really did suit him. For a man who may be leery about dating a woman, sex through glass as well as online was the perfect means to test the waters. And that explained the reluctance I'd sensed from him. What man wanted to jump into a full-on touching, hearts-crashing sort of relationship while also involved in a bitter divorce struggle?

But I couldn't be smart and dismiss the fact that he was legally married. And whether or not he still loved her was not the point. The fact remained, there was another woman in Monsieur Sexy's life right now. And until she was satisfied enough to sign the papers and walk away from him, I didn't believe the two of us could move forward.

Maybe? I don't know. I needed to think about this. To dissect my feelings about the whole thing. And to do it rationally, and not let my thoughts push me over some ridiculous cliff of no return.

"I don't want this to change things between us," he said, "but I'd be a fool to believe it will not. What we have? It means something to me. It is not a fling. I meant it when I said I love you, *mon abeille*. You are the only woman I care about right now. I just wish I hadn't said it to you in a moment of defensive anger. Love is gentle and sexy with us. You have to believe that."

"I actually do. And I promise I won't overthink that. You love me. But..." I sighed and caught my head against my palm. We both gazed at the screens as if we were watching the other walk away, never to return. "This does change things."

"If I had the signed divorce papers in hand would that make a difference?"

"Probably. Then I'd know she was officially out of your life. But, then again, I don't know. I need some time to roll this one over in my head."

"Yes, you do. I suppose this means the party invite has been rescinded?"

The costume party at which I'd hoped we could finally meet. Touch. Kiss one another. Hug. Begin what we'd been slowly working toward over the past month.

I did still want to meet him. Wife or not. Was that selfish of me? Or human nature?

"I sensed some reluctance from you regarding our finally meeting."

"And now you know why," he said. "But I was actually allowing myself to breathe easy and get excited for the party. A costume party appealed. I wouldn't have to think about any of this mess. You would be the only one in my thoughts. I understand though—"

"No, it's still an offer," I interrupted. "But I think we should go to radio silence for a few days, to give me some time to muddle this over. Is that okay?"

He nodded. "I will miss our conversations, but it is what I want you to do. I don't want you investing any more time with me unless you can trust me."

"I do know that I can trust you." Strange as that sounded it felt genuine to say it. I wasn't compromising my beliefs just to placate the man, or myself. I had spoken truth.

"I fly into Paris tomorrow evening."

"The party isn't for three days."

"I'll look for you in the window."

He kissed his palm and blew me a kiss. I closed my eyes, feeling that kiss upon my eyelids. When I finally opened my eyes, his screen was dark.

And my heart felt as if a dark cloud had settled above it.

Thirteen

I checked the incoming flights from Berlin to Paris and found only one arrived this evening at six p.m. It wasn't as though I eagerly awaited his return. Or that I wanted to rush to the window to watch him step out of the cab, suitcase in hand, and have him turn and wave to me.

The fantasy of meeting him at the curb for a kiss? Shattered.

Actually, I wanted to not be home when he arrived. I added in an hour and a half for arrival and cab ride home, and decided I'd do something this evening that would keep me away until at least nine.

I wasn't acting childish. I was protecting my heart. I needed to armor up. It was the only way I could get through this day.

I had a half shift at the map shop, so hopped on the Métro to the fifth, and was thankful Richard wasn't in. The awkward pass he'd made at me returned to memory as I exchanged keys for the cash register with Vincent, one of the full-time employees, and waved as he left for a family reunion in Rome.

What was it with men acting strangely lately? If they weren't flirting or making passes at me they were making me their illicit lover in the shadow of their wife's absence.

No, that was harsh. He was separated. A fact that would surely serve the survival of this relationship. Maybe?

Alone in the shop was not as peaceful as you would imagine. Sure, it was nice to sit amongst the old maps and prints and browse them, letting my mind wander to the times in which they had been made, and visualize myself wandering a cobbled street and in elaborate clothing. (I was usually a well-off aristocrat or royal in my imagination. Why not?) But just thinking about my imaginary riches swerved my thoughts around to the conversation with Monsieur Sexy last night.

He'd said his wife was trying to take too much from him. How much was too much? He'd confessed to being well-off financially. Was he a millionaire? The neighborhood where we lived wasn't upper-crust, but it certainly wasn't the ghetto. It was upper middle income, I'd guess. Snooty, as he'd mentioned? Perhaps. Yet his apartment hadn't advertised excess or riches. Heck, it had been stark, lacking in decorations or anything of value. Though he did wear fine suits.

I should have asked for clarification about his financial status. We'd come far enough into the relationship that I had every right to be curious. He didn't have to give me a bank statement. I'd be cool with a 'well off' or 'filthy' in reply to how rich.

No, he wasn't filthy rich. It didn't fit him. Perhaps he merely made enough to live the lifestyle he chose, and fill his life with the things that pleased him.

Like me? Did I please him?

He'd said he loved me. Why was I finding it so difficult to accept that declaration?

"Because that will make me the other woman," I muttered. I shook my head. "He doesn't love her. Accept that."

How could any woman married to Monsieur Sexy have an affair? Let alone, many? I couldn't figure it. Apparently there was something about the man that had made the woman turn her head from him.

I shouldn't be dissecting their failed marriage in an attempt to pin down what was wrong with him. That only proved what was wrong with me. That I liked to dwell, and couldn't let things go.

But I had to admit this situation demanded curiosity. And I'd told him that I needed to think about it. So that was what I was doing. Thinking, thinking, thinking.

I rapped my fingers on a stack of mail placed beside the cash register. It was one of those old wooden jobbies with the number keys and the prices on metal tabs that clicked up to show total sales. Richard was old school tech all the way.

I thumbed through the envelopes and one in particular stood out. The clear address window showed a pink paper inside with the shop address on it. When I lifted the edge of the window I could see the red 'urgent' stamp inside.

I had opened the shop's mail on occasion. Richard appreciated finding his mail neatly stacked on the desk in the back room. So I didn't hesitate to open this letter.

I should have left it sealed.

It was an eviction letter. The shop, apparently, was six months behind on rent. Two previous letters had been sent. This was the final notice. The owner had thirty days to vacate the premises.

"Oh, Richard, why didn't you say something?"

I couldn't envision the shop closing. This neat little nook tucked amongst the tourist shops and Greek restaurants was a piece of Parisian history that needed to exist. It had been selling maps and historical prints for four decades. It provided a cultural respite from the kitschy tourist shops in the area.

He would probably be furious that I'd read the letter. Not because I'd opened it, but because I now knew.

I shoved the pink sheet back in the envelope and considered re-licking the envelope, but it had torn halfway across when I'd opened it. Impossible to make it look unopened.

I'd tuck it amongst the other mail and leave the whole stack on his desk. And hope he had a plan.

Two elder women shared tea and conversation at the table next to mine in Angelina. They were seated before a six-by-six foot mirror that reflected the full house on this lazy autumn evening. I hoped that I would look as regal as they did when I was that old. Worn around the edges, and certainly faded, yet still harboring a bright spark in my eyes.

I bet those women could tell the stories. Love lost and gained, travel, adventure, grief, and heartache, surely. I longed to listen to them, but I didn't want to appear as if I was trying to listen in on their conversation, so I lifted the fork to my mouth for one final bite of decadent chocolate mousse.

Too bad Melanie couldn't have been here. This had been an emergency trip to Angelina for hot chocolate and more chocolate layered on top of that. My soul had required the infusion of decadence. And I'd gotten my period this morning. Four days early. Funny how startling life events tended to queue that sneaky cycle to the fore. Hence, the chocolate was necessity.

A family with two little girls dressed in costumes that vaguely resembled something from the eighteenth century were seated near the elderly women. The costume party, I thought with a sigh. Would I see Monsieur Sexy there? I'd sent the invite with the address, and had not reneged when he'd given me opportunity. It was his choice to make the connection that night. If we happened upon one another, it was meant to be.

I think I could overlook the wife for that auspicious meeting. At least to experience the initial thrill of finally standing before him, smelling him, touching him, feeling his presence call out to me and draw me toward him.

But I shouldn't overthink the meeting. It could never be as good as I could dream it to be, so no sense in going down that path.

Heh. I was proud of myself for stalling what could have resulted in another trip to crazytown.

Another sigh was unstoppable. Okay, so I was obviously swaying toward forgiveness and understanding. I had to. I really liked the guy.

And I was suddenly struck by a desperate unknowing. "What *is* his name?"

If we were to be open and truthful with one another, names were a necessity. But was now the time to ask for his name?

"More than important," I murmured. Because seriously? It was time for this chick to do some cyber-research on the man in the window.

I toyed with the dark brown folder in which the bill had been delivered. *Angelina* scrolled in copper letters across the front. Getting an idea, I opened the folder to reveal the copper-colored insides. With a dark pen, I scribbled my most urgent thoughts on it, then tucked it in my purse to take home with me. I counted out some euros for the bill, then checked the time on my cell phone. 9:30. Excellent timing.

I headed out, intending to walk home. The night was chilly, so I pulled my thigh-length sweater coat tight about my body and fluffed up the red scarf I'd tied around my neck. Mittens and knee-high riding boots had been necessary, as well.

It was late, and the tourists were sparse. I could enjoy the walk down the sidewalks without having to dodge a group posing for a picture or someone walking backward with camera in hand. And yet I felt disappointed with myself. Really? Trying to avoid the man like some kind of schoolgirl hiding behind the big oak tree to dodge the bully?

A wrench had been jammed into our relationship. Now I had the choice to grab that big ole clunky thing and run, or try to figure how to make it function within the mechanism that surrounded the two of us.

We were an *us*. Well, we had become an us. I wasn't sure if we still were. We stood at a crossroads, held up by a flashing red light while a high-speed train whooshed between the two of us. When the crossbars finally lifted, would we reach across and grasp hands?

I paused before his building entrance. The concierge inside nodded to me, and then indicated he was locking the door. I signaled him to stop and handed him the Angelina folder.

"For Monsieur," I said. "On the third-er, second floor. Would you mind?"

"I will run it up now."

"Uh, no. Er..." I wouldn't have time to explain I wanted to give him the same choice to open the envelope as he had given me. "Can you leave it in his mailbox, *s'il vous plaît*?"

The concierge nodded and bid me *bonne nuit*.

Before entering my building, I glanced up and across the street. The light was on in his kitchen and bedroom. As I climbed the three levels of stairs to my apartment I wondered if, after crossing his threshold, he had walked immediately to the window to look for me.

I hoped he had. Because the only other option was to not look for me, and that would be so sad. Yet I'd not been there to offer a welcome home wave.

Or a kiss at the curb.

I was being irrational about this. So he had a wife. He didn't love her, and he was in the process of divorcing her. That made him virtually single. And if she were off having affairs with other men then what did she care if I pulled him into my arms and gave him the love he deserved?

Is that how the other woman always thought? Was *I* the other woman? Mercy.

"No, I'm not," I muttered, stepping across the threshold and setting my purse aside. "I am his cyber girlfriend."

Just speaking it made me smile. And something inside me shifted. I decided at that moment how I would proceed. I was willing to continue our relationship because I wanted to. Because I was emotionally involved, and didn't want to let this detail of the soon-to-be ex-wife destroy something that wanted to grow and flourish, and perhaps even be great.

We had to reach across the tracks and join hands. It was inevitable.

He was mine. And I was willing to fight for him.

Shoulders settling back and spine straightening, I strode into the bedroom and pulled my hair free from the ponytail binder. Toeing off my riding boots, and tugging the scarf free to fall down my chest, I paused and glanced out the window. The sheers were pulled back, but I hadn't turned on the light, so he couldn't see me in the dark. His bedroom was revealed like a diorama, sans sexy fencer standing in his skivvies.

Fine. I had told him I'd need some time to think about this. And I entirely expected him to understand, should I not sign in online or go to the window.

But I had just decided to fight for him.

And I would.

I tapped the laptop, vacillating my next move. I'd asked for radio silence. And yet an email was necessary. I typed up a note. Left a note scribbled on Angelina folder for you in your mailbox. My name is inside. Open if you wish. I need to know your name. It is important. I hope you feel the same.

I didn't sign off with sincerely or even goodbye. Just left it like that. Business-like. It felt right.

Slipping off my clothes and leaving them in my wake on the bedroom floor, I wandered into the bathroom and turned on the shower. While I waited for the water to grow hot, I brushed my teeth, and winked at the chick in the mirror. She'd grown bold over the past month. Doing things the introvert in me would never have dreamt doing.

I'd let the tiny vixen run free. I loved her now. I embraced her willingness to try things that might scare other women. I was the sexy vixen who strode before the window in five-inch heels wearing nothing but a teasing smile. I could jill myself off to exquisite orgasm while posed before a camera in order to allow my lover to watch.

I had accepted a man's confession to loving me. And I was graciously accepting him into my life, warts and all (and man, those were some big warts).

And Monsieur Sexy had been the one to tease out that vixen.

"I'm going to do this," I said and my reflection nodded in agreement.

Hopping in the shower, I soaped up and lingered under the stream. The hot water beat against my stomach and mons. Gliding my hands down my slick skin, I closed my eyes and imagined him standing before me, his fingers mapping out my curves and glides and even my nooks.

He dropped his hand and slicked it over my skin. He kissed all along my labia, down one side and up the other, until he reached the pinnacle and there, he dashed his tongue against my clit.

The fantasy was too good. I reached back and above and detached the showerhead from the wall hook, bringing it down to focus exactly where I wanted to feel his tongue. Pulsing, swishing, tasting me. Lapping at me as if starved for sustenance, and then softer, a reverent sort of touch that stirred my insides to a writhing, wanting hum.

I wanted to spread my fingers through his hair. The showerhead was not Monsieur Sexy's head. So I made due with the fantasy of feeling his wet hair against my thigh as he supped upon me. And as I came, I cried out loudly and gripped for the shower curtain to steady myself as I wobbled forward, catching the clenching waves that tensed my pussy in delicious climax.

"Oh, yes." I laughed and dropped the showerhead to the floor of the tub. Then, kneeling, I caught the upstream against my pulsing pussy.

Round two? "Why the hell not."

ᐃᐃᐃ

Ten minutes later I wandered into the bedroom, the robe open, my hair toweled off yet hanging wet and heavy across my shoulders. Two orgasms had worked nicely to relieve my cramps. I peered out the window. He sat in bed, the sheets over his lap, reading one of those thick computer manuals that would probably render me into a catatonic state before I reached the bottom of page one. I preferred romances, thank you very much.

I loved when he wore those stoic, black-rimmed glasses. Sexy geek fencer guys did it for me. And to think on it... He was going through a tough time right now, struggling to get a divorce from a wife who had cuckolded him, over and over. (Yes, I'd just thought the word cuckolded. I'd been doing too much historical research lately.)

Poor guy. He needed tender loving care.

I leaned over and clicked on the lamp sitting on my nightstand. He instantly looked over, dropping the book onto his lap.

I waved. Yes, I was being a tease, standing there exposed. I was pretty darn sure he could deal with it.

He held up the brown Angelina folder and winked. Picking up his notebook he wrote, then turned it to me. You will always be mon abeille.

Sigh.

So he now knew my name. We were in it to win it. Or something like that.

He wrote on two more pages: Mon nom est

"My name is," I interpreted, thinking it funny he'd just written in French. I flexed my fingers in anticipation.

Jean-Louis

Another sigh. A breathless fall into romance and wonder and all that good stuff a girl should feel when in a relationship.

"Jean-Louis," I whispered. It fit him perfectly. "My Frenchman."

I gave him a thumbs up.

Emboldened by our confessions, I grabbed the spiral-bound notebook from the nightstand and the sharpie marker. I wrote something while he waited, hands to hips. How much did I love the gray boxer briefs that conformed over that thick erection?

I wonder if he'd found my panties?

"Jean-Louis," I whispered again. My Jean-Louis.

Having written the three most daring words I'd probably thought about our relationship lately, I hesitated turning the notebook around. I could chicken out, tear off the page and toss it over my shoulder. I'd wave him off, click off the light and crawl between the sheets. 'Nuff said. The relationship was on wobbly legs at best.

But...

No. I'd decided to fight for him. And this chick wasn't about to go down easy. (Unless he wanted me to go down on him, then...)

Okay, right, stop thinking. Focus!

I pointed from me and then to him. He nodded. I could feel his anticipation permeate the glass and burst in my heart. And that is what endeared him to me. He was honest and open and trustworthy, and he'd given me his all. As much as a man is capable of giving in the sort of hookup we had.

I turned the notebook around. Let's do this.

Head bowing for a moment, I imagined he must be relieved, his heartbeats thumping and his anxiety settling down on the scale. He gave me two thumbs up, then blew me a kiss. Then he grabbed something off his dresser. It was the laptop.

I shook my head. "Not tonight."

I wrote more, then turned the notebook around.

Party in two days. Still need time. Just the window until then?

He nodded eagerly.

I wrote again: I can't wait to touch you.

He pressed his palms together before his mouth and bowed, perhaps overwhelmed by my confession. It was the truth. I wanted—no needed—to touch him.

Finally.

Skin

Part 3

One

Have you ever so desperately wanted something to happen that anticipation jittered in your veins? While at the same time, if it really did happen you felt sure you'd pass out?

Been there, doing that right now.

Tonight promised to be an auspicious night. I would finally meet my lover face to face. No windows separating us; not even a computer screen. We would finally stand before one another. And for the first time, we would touch.

That is if he chose to show. The party had been going strong for hours. I was beginning to worry that my coach might transform to a pumpkin in a sparkling of faery dust.

Very well, I highly doubted my ride home, the Paris Métro, would suddenly morph into mice and gourds, but that was the way my brain tended to work. If not properly engaged, my imagination got carried away.

It was November 1st, and my best friend Melanie hosted her annual bash celebrating All Saint's Day, or *La Toussaint*. The French were more into this day than Halloween. Even though it was officially a religious holiday, Melanie encouraged the costumes and fun. (And gallons of champagne.) Costumes ranged from the standard spooky Halloween fare: vampires, ghosts, witches, and blood-dripping zombies, to some historical figures, and the classic Day of the Dead painted faces or even entire skeletons, as well.

For my costume, I'd gone with my favorite time period, the seventeenth century. And while I'd vacillated over the skull paint for my face, I'd decided to go glamorous and as historically accurate as a costume rental would allow. Clad in a poufy skirt and tight corset, this was the closest I'd ever get to time travel.

All I needed to fulfill one of my recurrent fantasies was a handsome fop in a damask frockcoat.

The party was in full swing. Dance music bounced off the walls fueling the exuberant crowd. Around eleven, I pulled myself away from the black-and-white harlequin dance floor to seek refreshment. Humungous crystal chandeliers floated over the ballroom and smaller versions queued down the sides of the room. Underwhich, I found Melanie and gave her a giddy girlfriend hug.

"Is he here?" Melanie's question bubbled up gaily. I suspected it was due more to the Krug than a party high.

Melanie wore a sexy Alice in Wonderland costume that revealed her bosom almost to the nipples, and she clutched a stuffed white rabbit. A curly blonde wig hid her bright red hair. An ace of hearts temporary tattoo dotted her right cheek below her green eye. Lush lashes fluttered expectantly. I bet Alice had never shown the Mad Hatter so much cleavage, or had flashed Wonderland with frilly, red, ruffled panties when she bent over.

"Haven't seen him," I provided, but coached my tone to remain chipper. "He may not have found a costume and decided to stay home. I did only give him a few days notice."

I'd met the man I waited for a little over a month ago, via our bedroom windows. We'd teased one another with flashes of skin through the windows. Then we had taken it to full-on mutual masturbation while communicating via notes on paper smashed up against the glass. Because we'd agreed not to share our names, I'd christened him Monsieur Sexy. When he'd left for a two-week business trip to Berlin our sexy liaison had graduated to cyber sex. As well, we'd shared details about our lives. And I'd heard his voice for the first time. Sigh...

Jean-Louis was his name. I'd only learned it a few days ago (via Skype) after also learning a devastating detail about his personal life—that he was married.

But I wasn't wearing the Other Woman crown. Not officially, anyway. Jean-Louis was in the process of getting a divorce, and had been separated from his wife for a year. All that was required was his wife's signature on the divorce papers. So we were cool to continue with the relationship. Maybe. Mostly.

Hell, I didn't want to think about such things as other women and wives tonight. Everything was daisies and sunshine and baskets full of puppies. And one extremely sexy Alice in Wonderland.

I'd dared Jean-Louis to meet me tonight (before I'd known he was married). It was high time I felt the man's skin against mine. And I wanted this first meeting to be perfect.

If it even happened. I wasn't sure what I'd do if he didn't show.

"You need more champagne, *mon amie*," Melanie offered.

She wasn't French, but she could speak the language smoothly. I could still barely understand it, even after living in Paris for over two years. It was absolutely bliss-inducing when Jean-Louis spoke to me in his French, husky, sensual voice, and my being completely oblivious to the meaning, allowed for me to simply savor how the tones glided across my skin and stimulated my desires.

"I'm good for now," I said to Melanie. "I'll swing by the bar in a bit. I'm headed toward the balcony for some fresh air. My stays are tight."

"Yes, but they push up your boobs nicely."

"You think?" I caressed the boobs in question and wiggled. "So that's why all the men have been bumping into walls and marble columns when I walk by."

Melanie and I shared winks. When in Paris, flirt like you mean it, but never let them take you home.

"There are so many people!"

"Hundreds," Melanie said over the sudden racket as a popular song thundered from the speakers. The elite crowd cheered and pumped their fists to the beat. "I have to find Rene," she said. "He wants to show me his Tweedledee." With a wink, the sexy Alice slipped into the crowd, assuming the beat with her body and dancing out of sight.

"She's so good at that," I muttered.

Mingling was not my thing. Crowds made the introvert in me shudder. If it weren't for anticipation, I would have ducked out of the party an hour earlier. But I remained hopeful.

My breaths stopped as I turned and spied a musketeer in a blue tunic trimmed in silver lace standing before the neon-lit bar. My heart performed a kickstart, stutter, and then stalled. I clasped a hand to my chest. My breasts were exposed by the low-cut bodice but not so much I worried my nipples would perform a peep show. They used to wear their dresses much lower to expose nipple back in the seventeenth century. So I was actually a prude tonight.

Prudishness aside, I wove through the crowd toward the musketeer. I wasn't sure what I'd say when finally I stood before Jean-Louis without a window or a computer screen to separate us. Hi, seemed inadequate. Grabbing him and making out with him was long overdue, but inappropriate for this crowd.

Maybe not. Tonight I'd seen more risqué embraces and tongues lashing one another than an actual sex club might feature. I was surprised I hadn't seen full-out sex yet. Maybe I wasn't looking in the right places. There were some shadowy corners. And I'd wondered about the coatroom when I'd arrived. If the attendant were on break....

Oh, the thoughts my brain entertained. It was a riot up there in my cranium.

I neared the blue tunic and spied the black beaver hat that sported a swish of red plume. He'd actually dressed as a musketeer! The man knew the way into my fantasies because he had stood inside them, dallied about, and mastered a few of his own.

When a bunny hopped out of my way to reveal the musketeer completely, I stopped where I was. The musketeer turned to me and nodded. I smiled, and swallowed my rising heart.

Not my musketeer.

For starters, he was too short. I'd once seen Jean-Louis standing out on the sidewalk, but thirty paces away from me. He was tall, fit, and had a way of standing that held his shoulders back, his arms hanging freely at his sides. Like a fashion model showing off his wares.

The next point that clued me in that this particular musketeer wasn't here for me was his rich, caramel skin color. I turned away quickly and closed my eyes. Idiot. I had almost flung myself at a complete stranger.

Okay, so not exactly *flung*. I didn't do the fling. I could stand naked before a window and jill-off in front of a man with whom I'd never exchanged a spoken word, but I most certainly would not humiliate myself with the submissive fling.

Smiling now, because my thoughts were too silly at times, I glided through the vast ballroom toward the balcony. A jester in green and red bowed grandly to me, and I nodded a courtly acknowledgement. This was fun, but I felt painfully alone. Most were coupled up or standing in groups laughing and dancing. I'm sure there were also many standing on their own, but of course I didn't notice the wallflowers. That would be too reassuring.

Many sets of two-story double doors stretched along the curved end of the ballroom. Elegant, red damask curtains plunged to the floor, framing the balcony doors. Outside was sure to be chilly. The thermometer had dropped to fifty degrees this evening. Still, as a native Iowan, this weather felt balmy for November. I craved a few moments away from the couples and laughter, and wanted to see if the view provided a glimpse of some of the Parisian landmarks.

And if I happened to stroll past the dessert table along the way, I wouldn't allow anyone to talk me out of chocolate. Chocolate consumed while partying had no calories. Because, you know, dancing and the energy of the evening jittered it all off. That's my story and I'm sticking to it.

The music was loud, but it was a slow dance and the lights had dimmed measurably. Spicy cloves and sweet pumpkin emanated from the lit candles on the tabletops. Bright orange candles nestled inside miniature pumpkins bedazzled with rhinestones. The French could dazzle up any holiday.

I bypassed a particularly large sheet-covered being who had drawn dripping blood from the corners of his ghostly sheet eyes. Did ghosts bleed? The semantics of every costume would drive me batty if I thought too hard. Which I did.

I always thought too much.

My costume, on the other hand, was as historically accurate as it got when a girl had but three days to find a rental close to the biggest costume holiday of the year. I wore an elegant seventeenth century gown. The hips were wide, but not plumped out with wooden panniers. I hadn't wanted to struggle in the crowd with that impediment.

The fabric was pink silk damask that sheened silver under the light. The three-quarter-length sleeves were dusted with white lace. And the stays, or corset, were laddered from gut to breasts with white velvet bows that matched the bow I'd pinned in my hair.

Yes, I'd gone to the salon and had the stylist curl my hair and pin it up. When I'd told her about the costume party, she said she could do the flour-puffed look, but we'd decided against that after seeing how pretty my chestnut hair had turned out. Simple, elegant, and with a few ringlets dangling down my neck and near my ears.

I felt like a princess. But I wasn't wearing the glass slippers, or my sexy black beribboned Louboutins. The costume shop had offered matching shoes that resembled the seventeenth century style. They were actually comfy.

Take that, bleeding sheet ghost man.

A line queued along the wall and I decided that must be where the dessert bar hawked its sweet temptations. Indeed, orange neon pumpkins suspended from spiderwebs lit the chocolate fountain below, behind which zombies served up chocolate treats as fast as their shambles would allow.

I scanned the line for the end, and as I turned, I gasped. Standing not ten feet away—before the line, but not in it—was a real musketeer. Framed by the vast opened doors that led to the balcony, his silhouette stood out. He didn't wear the tunic with the cross and fleur de lis emblazoned on it. Instead he was dressed in a rich black damask doublet and breeches. Beneath the unbuttoned doublet peeked a silver threaded waistcoat, and the spill of white lace from his shirt sleeves hit me *right there* where my geeky love for historical fashion bounced for joy. Brown suede bucket-topped boots slouched below his knees. And at his waist and across his shoulder slanted a leather sword belt. I wasn't sure if the sword in the sheath was real, but who the hell cared?

It was him. Monsieur Sexy. The man who had seduced me through a window. The lover who had claimed me via Skype. The man who had seen me at my most vulnerable, and yes, even at my silliest. I knew things about him. We'd shared our most intimate selves with one another.

"Jean-Louis," I whispered. I didn't know his last name. Didn't need to. As if some kind of mantra, I'd whispered that name countless times over the past few days.

Never had we stood in a room so close and without a barrier between us.

I met his gaze. His smile was already there. Bright in his sky-gray depths and nestled in the faint lines at the corners of those eyes. His grin was capped by a moustache, and beneath his bottom lip a triangle of stubble heightened the musketeer appeal. Dashing, slightly curly, dark hair had been pushed over his ears with a hand, as was his habit, and an unconscious movement I knew he often made.

"Oh, my God," I whispered. The world slipped away. Sounds ceased, save for the thud of life gushing through my veins.

My hand soared to my breast. Trying to stop my thundering heartbeats? Or maybe even holding the stays in place for fear that those crazy heartbeats would burst through and bleed all over the costume.

There he stood.

And here I stood.

We'd done it. We'd shattered through glass and computer screen to bare ourselves before one another. Nothing remained but to touch.

Could I do that? Actually touch a man whom I'd known for over a month, but had yet to know so intimately? I didn't know what he smelled like. I didn't know if his skin was soft or roughened from the sun. I did know the scent of sable and spice lingered on his clothes (I'd watered his plants and snooped about his place when he'd been in Berlin). But that scent had only offered a pale remnant of him, not the actual man.

I'd been standing there for two or three minutes, considering him. He must think me mad. Well, he knew I thought too much. But could he be aware of the thoughts racing through my mind? Maybe the same nervous thoughts stormed his brain?

When he held out a black-gloved hand, trimmed in white lace, I sighed. A fantasy stood before me. The unattainable image of a musketeer I'd often used to stir my nights into deliciously sexy dreams. Only this one was real in a way I could not explain to anyone else. Because I knew he had a thing for musketeers, as I did. As a kid he'd fallen in love with *The Three Musketeers*, and now read it once a year. He'd taken his first fencing lesson because he'd wanted to be a musketeer when he grew up. Now he gave fencing lessons. And while he'd never dash away at an enemy in real life, I knew he was fierce and would protect me should I require protecting.

I should walk over to him. Take his hand. Begin the next chapter in this weird and slightly abnormal relationship that had started without sound, smell, taste or touch—only sight—and had now slowly worked its way to the beginning. Where normal couples began. Standing before one another, delving into each other's gazes.

Do it. Move your legs. Walk over to him!

I...couldn't make my legs move. My stomach flip-flopped. And I was thankful for the gown because it concealed my nervous compulsion to imitate a statue.

I held out a hand and stretched my arm as if that could bring us together. It activated something, because he walked toward me. Eyes fixed to mine; he breached the distance in seconds. Stopping before me, he tugged off a glove and slipped his bare, warm hand into mine.

"Hey," he said.

I sighed out a heavy breath. I'd spoken to him for hours at a time online. Hadn't stopped gabbing, except to strip and have hot and sexy mutual masturbation sessions with him.

Everything changed with a few steps of his boots and the slide of his hand across mine. The glint in his eyes reassured my silly nerves. He was real. Warm and alive. Reality felt so right. Yet, I admit, it was also a little scary.

"Hey," I managed.

He took my other hand, the glove still on his, and held them between us. He leaned in, not to kiss, because his trajectory moved his face alongside mine. And there, his nose nudged my earlobe. Shivers traced along my neck. My nipples grew so hard I thought they would burst through the fabric. The hush of his warm breath along my neck where the hair had been pulled up felt like a summer breeze. But even more? I wanted him to invade me, to completely own me.

"I'm glad I decided to come here," he said. "I was nervous about this."

"You were?"

"After all that has been revealed between us? *Oui*."

And his nose nuzzled along my skin. His subtle moan crept into my soul. His hands squeezed mine. I closed my eyes. I couldn't fight the crazy thunder of my heartbeats, but I did have to stay focused so I wouldn't crash and faint in his arms.

Because of all that had been revealed.

He was a married man. Albeit a married man in the process of getting a divorce. More on that later. Right now I didn't want anything to taint this moment.

"You smell better than I imagined," he said at my ear. "Vanilla. I had expected honey, *mon abeille*."

His pet name for me. It meant *my bee.*

Focus. Don't pass out from utter joy.

I tilted my head toward his, our noses moving closer, our lips still too far away to kiss. The cloves I could smell everywhere hung on his hair and skin. I didn't know if it was his cologne or this ballroom's sensory milieu. I'd take it. A spicy scented man was my favorite kind of treat.

When he moved his face away from mine, I released a murmur that I hoped he hadn't heard. A greedy noise. *Don't take my treat away from me, please.*

But he didn't step back, and stood before me, my hands in his, his thumbs gently stroking my skin.

"I could stand before you all night," he said. His eyes twinkled and his smile seemed irrepressible. "Just drink you in. Your skin is so soft." He lifted my hand and kissed the back of it. The warmth of his mouth and the tickle of his moustache would undo me.

Would? Hell, I was undone. Falling. Into him.

"You okay?" His eyes narrowed as he studied my face. "Your cheeks are flushed."

Did I look like I was ready to faint? Probably. I think I could faint. The corset had grown tight. But no, I wasn't about to topple.

Maybe.

"I'm good. It's just..."

"Overwhelming?"

I shrugged and nodded. "So real. Here you are. Standing before me. My musketeer."

"You like the costume? We match, eh?"

I realized this was the first time I'd heard his voice right next to me and not filtered through a computer speaker. It was richer, more full and deep. The French accent felt like a decadent arabesque upon his exquisitely seductive tones. Mercy, but he could fuck me with that voice.

He had fucked me with that voice.

"*Mon abeille*?"

I had to stop letting my mind wander. He was here. Now. And we had to begin.

I confessed, "I think I'm a little lightheaded."

"Let's go out on the balcony, *oui*?"

"Yes."

He clasped my hand and I followed him up four stairs and out through the two-story-high glass doors. Three other people stood on the balcony, all quietly chatting near a table that glittered with pumpkins and rhinestones. I didn't notice the fall chill. My body was on fire. Because Jean-Louis held my hand.

Pausing before the balcony railing, he turned, and again we held each other's eyes for long moments of silence. It was something we were accustomed to, for we had established this relationship through glass, silently observing one another. Speaking with our eyes.

I stroked my fingers along his cheek. "You are my musketeer, and I am your lady." He dipped his head into my palm and kissed the center of it. "No tunic?"

"I couldn't find one. And I wanted it to be authentic, not like that other musketeer I saw walking around earlier."

"Wrong style," I agreed, sharing a knowing nod with him. The musketeers had worn black tunics for a time, not blue. "This is you." I swept my gaze down the rich damask coat. Gold buttons dotted one side of the opened coat. "I..." Should I say it? I'd been brazenly open with him online. Why edit myself now? "I want to take it off of you."

His smile grew and he bracketed my face with both his hands. "There's my sexy Hollie who tells me what she wants. I was wondering for a moment if I had lost you. Nerves, *oui*?"

I nodded and clasped his wrists as he held my face. Would he kiss me? I desperately needed to know his kiss. His mouth on mine. I'd dreamed about it so often I suddenly wondered if the real thing would be a letdown.

And then I realized he'd said my name. It was the first time I'd heard him speak it. And he'd only learned it a few days ago as I had his. I'd left him a note in his mailbox. My name scribbled on a piece of paper. It had been his choice to look at it. And he had.

"Jean-Louis," I whispered.

"Hollie." He tilted his head down and our foreheads met.

This closeness was exquisite. He smelled like my dreams. His warmth lured me closer as if a river current. I wanted to dive in and float with arms spread out to my sides.

I also wanted to run my hands all over his body, to finally touch every part of him. I needed... I needed privacy where I could rip off his clothing and explore and taste and touch and suck and...

"I want to kiss you," he said. "May I?"

I nodded, and my reply came out as a wanting gasp, "Yes, please."

My heart thudded. My toes became springs as I bounced subtly, wishing I was as tall as him to be able to meet the kiss. My hands glided down the front of his damask coat. The fabric was rich and authentic to the time period, which made the whole experience surreal and so, so exciting.

I opened my eyes as his mouth landed on mine, and closed them just as quickly. Focus zoomed to my mouth. The light, yet sure, brush of his lips. Testing. That first tentative touch. Yes, I am here. Yes, I want to taste you. Yes, yes, and oh...yes.

He tilted his mouth against mine and the kiss grew more confident. It was rich and exquisite. Sure. Like he'd been there many times before and knew his place.

The tickle of his moustache teased my upper lip. I gripped his coat with my fingers and clung to him, standing on tiptoes because he was taller than expected. And he swept an arm around my back to hold me against him. To claim me.

I had dreamed about this kiss. And then I had tried not to imagine what it would be like because I feared I'd concoct a fantasy that couldn't possibly be recreated. I needn't have worried. Jean-Louis's mouth on mine was heaven. His breath tasted like the champagne I'd sipped upon arrival at the party. His body heat lured me closer. The smell of him sank into my very soul and found its home.

And then he opened my mouth with his and danced his tongue along my teeth, the inner sides of my lips, and to my tongue. Mmm, I loved this. Falling into him. Losing myself in this exquisite connection.

I reached up, spreading my fingers through his soft, dark hair and felt a curl tickle about one of them. He groaned into my mouth and held me tighter. As if he never wanted to let go. I breathed his air, taking life from him and giving back my own.

And then he gently, slowly begin to pull away, he kissed me quickly at the corner of my mouth, then yet another deep and delving kiss, and then one to my lower lip that suckled for a moment. He pressed his forehead to mine, and we both must have sighed.

"That was..." I realized there was no way to put it into words. And why should I? So instead I kissed him again.

I've placed Angelina's hot chocolate on the top of my favorite treats list. No more. Jean-Louis's kiss was number one. I devoured it, feasted upon his sensual taste and the smell of his skin against mine. Mmm...

Happy All Saints Day to me.

"*Mon abeille*," he breathed against my mouth. "*Très bon.* You cannot know how long I have desired this."

"As long as I have, surely. You taste so good. Don't let me go."

He still held me in a tight clutch, our faces but a breath away from one another. We'd fallen into one another's eyes, the music in the adjoining ballroom but a distant melody to our thumping hearts. In my peripheral vision the city lights twinkled, a glamorous backdrop to our embrace.

I was in Paris standing in the arms of a sexy Frenchman who had kissed me silly. And all I wanted was another kiss.

"Another?" he asked, but didn't wait for my approval.

He kissed me soundly. Then a dash of his tongue teased my mouth open and I felt so light and free that I must have grown an inch because I didn't have to reach so far to meet him. The curls at my neck were clasped in his fingers. His leg pressed against my skirts, a solid stance that claimed me, held me.

Owned me.

I had become the musketeer's woman.

"Let's find a private corner," he whispered at my ear.

My heartbeats skipped and the vixen inside me sang like some kind of love-struck heroine in a Disney cartoon.

His hand stroked my cheek and down my neck to land on top of my breasts. "There is somewhere else on you I wish to put my mouth." He leaned in to whisper at my ear. "I crave to taste your pussy."

The giddy nerves I'd felt upon first sighting him had simmered to a steady gush of urgent need and desire. Fuck the looming divorce situation. We'd been good. We'd denied ourselves one another for too long.

The time had come for touch. And to give him the taste he craved.

I gripped his waistcoat. "I know the perfect place."

Two

Jean-Louis grabbed my hand and we dashed through the crowd of revelers. Light falling from the chandeliers glimmered on masks and painted faces. Champagne glasses tilted into melodious *tings*. Lush spice and musk tainted the atmosphere. Together we rushed toward adventure and the erotic play that we'd been feeding for too long. It had boiled to the top. Time to let it spill over.

The coat check was a vast closet walled in red velvet. Rows upon rows of coats held court. Jean-Louis spoke to the valet in French, who then handed him a key. My cyber lover tugged me inside the room. The valet called out something.

"What did he say?"

"He's taking a break," Jean-Louis said. "He'll be back in half an hour. There's an employee room here."

We navigated the tight rows of coats hung on a rotating track such as you'd see at a laundromat until we spied a door. Jean-Louis stuck the key into the lock. Boots lined the floor. Cubbies held street clothing. Employees must change in here. He turned the lock on the door and tucked the key into a pocket in his musketeer breeches. (Okay, so pockets were not period correct but I couldn't argue that faux pas.)

I had to take a moment to succumb to a costume orgasm over the two of us. He in his damask coat and breeches a la the seventeenth century, with lace dripping from his wrists and tied at his throat, plus the billowing ostrich plume on his hat. It screamed swashbuckler!

And I in my silk dress cinched tightly to push up my breasts. We made a dashing pair.

Bracketing my face with his palms, he kissed me again. Too quickly, he pulled away to gaze into my eyes. His breath, tinted with champagne, hushed over my mouth. The spices on his skin mulled the champagne into a sweet treat.

I wanted him to touch me. Everywhere.

"I know where I'd like you to put your mouth," I said. The vixen that had blossomed within me over the past month fluttered her lashes and stepped back from the musketeer. My skirts shushed the carpeted floor.

"Tell me, Mademoiselle. I am at your command." He swept a dashing bow that would have reduced any damsel to a swoon.

I turned and strolled to a long table set along the back wall. It was half-covered with purses, backpacks, and messenger bags. They could be easily moved.

Walking up the fabric of my skirt with my fingers, I smiled to myself. Desire rushed forth and pushed away any niggling reluctance. Because, yes, I was nervous. Here I stood in the same room as the man I had only communicated with via window and computer screen. It was real now. Nothing to hide behind. And my heart burst from the chrysalis to flutter its wings.

Turning to him, I lifted my skirt high enough to reveal my thighs, on which I wore not-quite period appropriate white silk thigh-high stockings. Pink bows tufted at the tops, inviting his eye. And a little higher....

"*Mon Dieu.*" He brushed the hair from his face, his eyes glued to my nethers. "*Mon abeille*, you did as I asked."

He'd once requested I not wear panties the first time we were to meet. Who was I to disappoint a musketeer?

He dropped to his knees and took off his plumed hat, tossing it aside with a dashing sweep. That move made me suck in a breath. Damn, but I had such control over him right now. And he was my willing sycophant, walking up to me on his knees. He ran his palms up my thighs, looking over my neatly trimmed pussy. He took his time. I could feel his eyes on me, much as I had come to feel his desire through the window, and to sense his arousal while he sat in a Berlin hotel room and the computer screen had provided but a facsimile of sensual awareness.

Hot breaths hushed on my thighs where the pink bow had first drawn his eyes. Then the heat whispered higher and moved to the apex at my mons. His unabashed study of me swirled a delicious tingle up my spine and I clutched the skirt fabric expectantly. I grew so wet; if I'd been wearing panties, I would have creamed them.

Eventually, he looked up to me. His eyes were the color of the sky after the rain. Gray-sky eyes. Though the room was muted with low light, his pupils glinted. I ran my fingers through his hair. The soft curls slipped about my fingers like ribbon.

I gripped a hank and gasped, "Yes, please."

First press of his mouth to my pussy stirred up a moan from me. His heated breath tickled sensation across my skin. He kissed down the patch of hair that didn't form a pattern so much as I liked to keep it short and neat. A kiss there, another kiss next to it. The pressure of his hands at my thighs pulsed my muscles there. The rub of the gold buttons on his coat tickled aside my knee.

I'd once fantasized about him dressed as a musketeer, kneeling before me to sup between my legs. Seriously. Talk about a fantasy come true.

Reality was much better.

The point of his tongue dashed out and licked along my labia, tasting me, slowly tendering a line from top to bottom of the slit. Then he journeyed along the outside, up, down, and up again. He'd drawn a line around the most sensitive parts of me. Yet when he pressed his tongue against my clit, where the tiny bud had already begun to swell and seek sensation, I gripped his hair tighter and bit down on my lip. "Fuck yes."

"I have wanted to taste you for so long," he murmured, pressing his cheek to my trimmed thatch and glancing up. "*Exquis*," he said. He tapped my labia and slicked my juices teasingly along the seam. "May I go further?"

"Uh-huh," I managed, though truly, my gasps should have been invitation enough.

His finger glided inside me, and I moaned at the delicious intrusion. How many times had I fingered myself for his viewing pleasure, brought myself to orgasm as he had done the same to himself so far away from me? Now it would be different, and the same, and so, so right. It was fifty ways to heaven to feel him inside me. Invading me in the most desirable way. When he curled his finger forward and brushed my ridged G-spot, I cried out.

"Ah... That is the place," he said as he kissed my clit and worked his finger slowly, expertly, within me. A hush of hot breath against my swollen bud clenched my stomach muscles. Moans gasped out unbidden. My skin heated and breaths panted. Mercy.

He stroked my inhibitions away, drawing up the vixen until my entire system tingled in anticipation. My cheeks flushed, as did my breasts. I clutched at the fabric and his hair, seeking stability, yet desiring to soar unbound. His kiss deepened, his tongue manipulating the swollen head of my clit, while his finger inside me danced me closer to the edge, to a wicked fall that I wanted to take, nets be damned.

This man could make me soar.

"Hollie." His whisper fluttered through my being. A harmonization to the intensity of the imminent orgasm.

I was so close. Right there. I squeezed my thighs together, but not for long. Didn't want to stop him from doing as he pleased with me. And when he suckled my clitoris and brushed it ever so lightly with his bottom teeth, I surrendered. His heat, his mouth, his fingers. The tickle of his hair against my thighs. The press of his bicep along my leg. Oh, but he owned me as I shuddered and threw back my head, not crying out, yet moaning deep in my throat as orgasm won.

He wrapped one arm about my hips, pulling me hard against his mouth; that wicked tongue still teasing at my throbbing clit. It was almost cruel to attempt to prolong the exquisite pleasure, but that didn't stop me from tilting my hips toward him to keep him there. Hot and wet and so hungry against me.

"Yes," I murmured. Breaths panting, one hand fluttered down to find landing on his shoulder.

He glided up along me, kissing my breasts that heaved up and down within the confines of the dress. Oh, yeah, real heaving bosoms. Take that romance chicks! His tongue tickled my flushed skin as I gasped, flying on the orgasm that had rocketed me through the stratosphere.

I usually did not come so easily or quickly. It was because this had been our first touch. Our first intimate connection. Without removing a stitch of clothing, the man had mastered me.

Now he sought my nipple with his tongue, though the dress stays were tight and not eager to give up the prize so easily. I hooked a leg about one of his and pulled his hips against mine, my mons still bared.

The rub of the rough, damask fabric breeches against my skin teased at the fading orgasm.

"Your orgasm is even better up close and in my face," he said as he nipped the crest of my breast. "You taste like my fantasies, *mon abeille*. But I need more. All of you."

The musketeer hiked up my leg and levered me onto the table behind me. Would he fuck me right here in the closet? Had it been half an hour? I didn't want us discovered. And yet I wanted him to fuck me. To shove his cock into me and fill me—but no. We could wait. We had to.

I pushed him back and yet clung to an intricate button on his coat. Pulling him to me, I kissed him hard, deeply, tasting my own salty flavor and mining a desperate groan from him.

"Take me home," I said between quick kisses. "I want you to fuck me, but not here. In private. Yes?"

He pulled my hand down and pressed it over his breeches. My God, his cock was hard. Thick and sturdy, as I knew from witnessing his erection many times through glass. I squeezed my fingers over it, eliciting a strained moan from him.

"You want me to go down on you quick?"

"No, not quick," he said. "You are right. We must leave. Now."

He grabbed my hand, and I shuffled down my skirts as we headed out the doorway. Perfect timing. The valet caught the key Jean-Louis tossed to him, and he winked, sliding me a sidelong assessment as we rushed by.

Let him look and wonder. What else did he think we had been doing in the coat closet, eh? The guy probably had a small side business going renting out the room to horny lovers while he went on break.

We glided toward the main foyer, but I abruptly pulled Jean-Louis to a stop. "I have to say goodbye to Melanie. The party hostess. She's my best friend."

"Very well. I'll hail a cab. You've five minutes before I—" He slid my hand over his erection again. "—take care of this myself."

"Oh, no, you don't. Monsieur Eiffel is all mine tonight." Monsieur Eiffel is what he called his cock. Yeah, I know. But so much better than Roger, right? "I'll be out in four minutes."

He kissed me hard and held my stare for so long I whimpered as I felt my pussy moisten to flood level. And then I shook my head, and with a giggle, took off toward the main ballroom to find wicked Alice and thank her for inviting me to her Wonderland.

ÅÅÅ

The cab ride, which was only ten minutes long, was a lesson in self-restraint. At first I didn't care what the cabbie saw. I reached for Jean-Louis's lap, aiming to get a good grip on his main shaft, yet he tutted me and waved an admonishing finger.

"Patience," he said with a delicious little-boy smirk. "We are almost there."

I think he tipped the cabbie generously. I'm sure that had been a fifty euro bill he'd handed over. Jean-Louis was comfortable financially; at least that's as best I'd been able to determine. A few weeks ago he'd enticed me into a high-end shop on the Champs Elysees (via Skype) and had bought me a two thousand euro dress without blinking. And his apartment, situated in the snooty 7th arrondissement, must cost twice that every month. Yeah, he was rich.

But the money didn't matter. Seriously. I wasn't a gold digger. I didn't need much in this life. Books, a cool peachy moscato, and some fancy Louboutins were the things that made me happy.

And one sexy Frenchman.

We sailed up the stairway to the third floor where, at his door, I took the initiative and punched in the digital code.

"I remember the code from when I watered your plants," I provided. It had only been a few days since I'd done so.

That had been the day I'd learned he was married.

No, I wasn't going to think about that right now. He was in the process of getting a divorce. And I was too horny to rationalize the good, bad, or downright wrong regarding this hookup.

It was all good. It had to be. It would be.

I entered his apartment, which was dark save for a narrow golden beam cast across the hardwood floor from a nearby streetlight. As soon as I heard the door lock click behind me, I was spun about. My back hit the door. He held me by the wrists, gently, yet with the promise of control. I gasped in a breath, my breasts heaving up from the tight stays.

"Hollie," he said. "I love your name. It is you. It pleases me to finally say it to you. Hollie, my pretty window lover who likes bees and fancy shoes."

"Jean-Louis," I said as if savoring a treat. "My Frenchman. A man who teaches computer mumbo-jumbo online and loves a great chocolate cupcake."

"You also like to watch me jack off."

"I could say the same for you."

"*Oui*. You know how to stroke yourself until you cry out. I adore the expression on your face when you come. Eyes closed, mouth open. Mm... Your breasts are so pretty." He kissed the top of each one. "And your pussy is what I want always."

He lifted me into his arms and carried me across the vast room that wasn't furnished because this was the spot where he taught fencing to students. An aged brown leather sofa delineated the living area from the practice space. We passed by the sofa, of which, I'd once had a delicious dream about the two of us having sex on.

He set me down briefly then lifted me in his arms, sweeping up my legs and managing to get a good grip despite the heavy and cumbersome skirts. "The men in the seventeenth century certainly had a lot of dress to deal with," he said.

"Yeah? Well, I'm thinking those buttons on your coat and breeches are going to take far too long for my urgent needs."

"You want me, eh?"

I kissed him when he paused in the doorway to the bedroom. Our mouths fit perfectly. Was it cliché to think we were meant for one another? Hell, we'd had practice getting to know one another over the past month. Now was for exercising all the unrealized desires that had been building to a head.

Once in the bedroom, he deposited me on the bed and I landed on my back, finding it hard to pull up to sit with the tightened corset. The costume had taken some time to lace the corset up the side, which was positioned thus only to make it easier to dress alone. I could understand now how the women from the past had required maids to help them dress.

"Help!" I cried and motioned my inability to sit up.

Jean-Louis laughed then leaned over me, placing his hands to either side of my shoulders. "You are stuck? That puts you at my mercy, *mon abeille*." Eyes crinkling, he smiled slyly. "I like you this way."

And I liked his easy closeness, and the ease with which we'd accepted this new experience of togetherness.

"Oh, come on," I pleaded. "I thought it was my turn to undress you and finally..."

"Finally what?"

"I want to suck you," I confessed. I'd mastered speaking my sensual needs while we'd enjoyed cyber sex. It had initially been uncomfortable to say words like pussy and cock out loud, and to put my desires into voice, but now I was a pro. "I want to hold your gorgeous, big, thick cock in my hand. You want that, don't you?"

"*Oui*. But I must have one more look under your skirts while you are at a disadvantage."

My skirts flew up, the hem landing on top of my face. His mouth found my tender bits, and the sure glide of his fingers slicked my labia. The sudden entrance of his fingers inside me captured my breath. I gripped for something, anything to tether myself to this world, but the heady gratification of feeling him within me would not allow such safety. And so I let my fingers relax, as well as the last tendrils of inhibition.

"I love you there," I uttered, abandoning the idea of giving him a hand job for now. He was focused on me. Why should I distract him?

A curl of his finger inside me hit the super-sensitive G-spot. I thanked all the deities whenever a man was lucky enough to happen upon it. Which was rare.

Jean-Louis, on the other hand, had found it immediately in the coatroom. And he now returned to the spot as if a favorite refuge often visited. A practiced man?

"Oh, yes, yes, yes," I hissed, clutching my skirts. My hips bucked upward, seeking the hot, firm wetness of his tongue on my clit while his fingers stroked me intently. The man was so focused.

"You like my tongue on you?" he asked in a husky tone. That French accent scurried shivers under my skin. The good kind that heightened my arousal even more. "Or inside you?"

"Both," I said on a gasp.

His tongue thrust inside me then darted here and there, lashing my skin and suckling it.

I dug my fingers into the sheets. The damned skirt lay over half my face, and when I inhaled, it sucked into my mouth. I tugged it down quickly, which covered his head. His firm hands parted my legs gently, wider, as he concentrated on my clitoris. Sucking slowly, teasing the firm tip of his tongue over my slickness.

My heartbeat raced. Breaths panted. A sheen of perspiration glistened on my chest. I could feel my heart in my throat. And his mouth at my core. His intent desire to pleasure me overwhelmed. Sweet, sable-tinted aftershave mingled the air to a delicious aroma. My thoughts swirled into that deliciously vast and giddy stratosphere that preceded orgasm. Nothing mattered but the sensations coursing through my body.

Our connection. We had come together. At last.

My hips bucked as the orgasm burst to fruition. Jean-Louis kissed my inner thigh and laid his head on my leg. Head pushing into the mattress, I surrendered to the Frenchman.

The night was just getting started.

Three

"Tell me what's going on in your brain," I asked as I rolled to my side on the bed next to Jean-Louis. Head snuggled on the pillow, his eyes heavy-lidded.

"It's ten in the morning on the day following the first night we touched, kissed, and made love," I continued. "You're lying here like some kind of sex god, your penis at half-mast looking ready for more action. You smell like my wildest sex dreams. You feel like heat and stone. And I need to know what you think of all this."

He tapped my nose then leaned over to kiss it. "I think when I told you a few days ago that I loved you that wasn't a mistake."

Indeed, he had confessed to loving me at a particularly harrowing moment in our video conversation: after he'd revealed that he was married. I'd initially felt it was a defensive 'I love you'. Yes, those are possible. But then I'd settled, thought about it, and decided that maybe he was the kind of person who fell in love quickly. That was possible, too.

It sure sounded good right now, as I lay in his bed, soaking up his warmth, deliciously exhausted from our exquisite lovemaking.

"I also think you are one of the most genuine people I've known," he added. "You are what you present to the world, *mon abeille*. No mask. No fake. All...this."

"What you see is what you get."

"I admire that about you. I also admire this." He leaned in to suck one of my nipples into his mouth. As much as they were tender from his all-night attentions, I again felt the sensual tug at my insides and arced my chest toward him in a quest for more. "Your nipples are so sensitive."

"Let's not get distracted just yet," I said, gently extricating myself from his soft, hot mouth. Because I did want to talk.

There was much I already knew about him, and so much I did not. I didn't expect to interrogate and learn all of him in one day. That's what relationships were for: learning about one another. I imagined a couple could be together for years, decades even, and still never know everything about the other.

"You're not disappointed?" I asked the one question that every woman probably thinks after their first night together with a man.

"In what? I told you that you are genuine. If you are talking about the sex, then no. All is *très bien, mon amour.* I sense self-conscious backtracking in that question?"

The man was perceptive. "It's a girl thing. I think. Do men ever worry about their performance?"

"Every time."

"Really? Because you rocked my world, lover. And now I need to do something I've only been able to dream about."

"What is that?"

I reached down and secured a firm grip about his penis, which was still a little soft, but at my touch, it flinched to attention and quickly grew harder.

"I'm going to lick you, and suck you, and..." I slid down on the bed, and cooed sweetly over the hard object. "You okay with that?"

He put his hands behind his head and settled into the pillow, his taut, muscled body stretched out before me. Oh, those tight abs. They really were rock hard. "*Bien sur.*"

I'd had my hands on his penis all through the night. I'd stroked and sucked and licked it in between tending his abs, nipples and mouth. But I hadn't taken the time to give it my full attention. A devoted undertaking that I now took to with glee.

I've never considered a man's penis a thing of beauty. Nor was it ugly. A penis was sort of an alien life form sprung from the edge of a man's torso. Surrounded by a thatch of curly dark hairs, Monsieur Eiffel grew up strong and straight, naked and veiny, with a thick maroon cap that pushed back the foreskin the more erect it grew. If I compared it to a mushroom one might find deep in the middle of some enchanted forest, it could only be that rare species the lost forest maiden sought out in a quest to discover true ecstasy. Once located in the center of the woods, she'd pull up her skirts and lower herself onto the rigid phallus, and piston herself madly until she creamed and fell to the lush mossy ground in fits of sighing pleasure.

I did mention my wicked imagination, yes?

Putting myself eye level to Monsieur Eiffel, which indeed, sprang up as straight and proud as the landmark, I hushed a breath over the column. His penis responded with a tightening flinch that bobbed against my lips. Without using my hands, I mouthed him, teasing my tongue along the suede-warm skin and tasting the sweet saltiness of him.

I shifted my body, straddling his legs. My breasts settled against his thighs. My nipples tingled expectantly as the fine hairs on his legs tickled them. I glided my feet along his, our toes dancing as I wedged my biggest toe between two of his. I did love having my feet touched, and his were soft, the skin on them ridiculously smooth. He never walked barefoot in the woods, I guessed. Socks on always. A city boy. Nothing wrong with that.

I liked the weird connection of toes entangled within toes. And don't get me started on how eagerly I wanted to bring up my fantasy of him licking my toes. That could wait for another day.

Clasping his cock firmly, I traced a zigzagging trail up the side of the column, dancing back and forth over the engorged vein. Drenched in musk and yes, traces of me, the scent of him appealed to the animal center of my brain that simply wanted more, more, and more.

His hips pushed upward in a greedy plea. His breathing was measured, yet deep. I managed a glance up over the landscape of his abs and chiseled pectorals and saw his eyes were closed, his jaw tense. Yet I sensed a certain relaxed expectation that made me grin against his cock. The man enjoyed my performance.

I turned my head, rolling the hard column over my cheek. This part of a man may not be the prettiest, but it was fun to play with, to touch and admire. To see how it reacted to a quick lick or a lingering draw of my tongue along its length. It bobbed and thickened, and the vein on the underside swelled. So intricate, and it was mine. All mine.

Feeling frisky, I nipped the side of him, using my teeth, but not biting hard. He flinched and tutted me playfully, which was quickly followed by a long moan. I loved the sound of his moans, and the gasping pleas that generally accompanied them. He wasn't a silent lover, and I found that strangely appealing considering I had preferred no chatter in the bedroom in the past. Perhaps it was because the last two weeks of our relationship had been fueled by talk. We knew how to ask one another for what we desired.

"You are hungry?" he asked on the end of one of those exquisite moans.

"Yes, I want a mouthful."

I tilted his cock downward, taking the head of it into my mouth as deeply as I could, and then sucking hard until his hips pumped in a pleading rhythm. Using a firm grip about the base of his cock, I cupped his testicles with my other hand, all while sucking him in and out of my mouth, licking around the firm edge of the corona, then past my lips until I felt him against the roof of my mouth.

His balls were so tight against his body I knew he could come at any moment, but that didn't stop me from tracing the oval curve of them down and around to the back where the skin met body. I traced quickly about his asshole, and then tickled my way up to the testicles again, cupping them gently.

The art of sucking cock was to not ignore your own pleasure. I was so wet. I rubbed my pussy against his knee, grinding the sweet spot with delicious friction, and encouraging him to nudge up hard against my clit. Oh yeah, that was what I wanted.

I quickened my speed, slicking my hand up and down his shaft while alternately licking the head, and then sucking it like a lollipop. His hips shuddered, as did his thighs, and he'd forgotten about giving me pressure with his knee. I didn't. I wriggled my mons against his leg to finely tune my burgeoning climax as I sucked him.

"*Oui*," he gasped. A hand gripped the back of my head, urging me gently, yet insistently forward.

A tilt of my hips intensified the teasing connection of my pussy to his knee. I could get off...just... A. Bit. More. Pressure.

Two more strokes and a deep, drawing suck at his cock head released Jean-Louis from the expectant, tight anticipation of orgasm. An explosive but brief shout burst from his lungs. The hand previously at my head beat the bed with a triumphant fist. He came in my mouth and down my chin. And I shifted on his knee, tendering out the softest yet sweetest little flutter of orgasm I could manage.

I slapped my palms to the bed on either side of his hips. With cum dripping down my chin, I licked at it, wiping most away with the side of my hand, and winked at him. The man's face was flushed. His eyes smiled brightly. He leaned up and pulled my head to him and kissed me hard, deep and long.

The taste of his cum, the wine we'd indulged through the night, and his salty essence mingled in a heady cocktail. My clit twitched and I squeezed my thighs together to capture the last twinkle of orgasm.

"Your cock is mine," I said into his mouth.

Then I collapsed beside him and drew up a knee to rest on his hip beside his lax penis. I spread my fingers across his hot, panting chest. We hadn't slept all night. It was probably close to noon.

Within minutes, we drifted off to sleep in each other's arms.

ÅÅÅ

It was morning. Again. Had we really spent two days in bed having wild, passionate sex with one another?

Oh yeah. Save for a few bathroom runs and a couple trips to raid the fridge of plums, wine, and cheese, the bed had been our island of exotic pleasure. Proof of our extended liaison lay in the parts of my body that were sore and achy. But it was a good kind of ache that made me smile so broadly I feared cracking my cheeks.

Jean-Louis sat on the opposite side of the bed, facing the window. Rare November sunshine beamed across his shoulders like white heaven on a god's physique. He was checking email on his cell phone, so I scampered into the bathroom, completely naked, and sat on the toilet to pee.

Not ten seconds later, the door opened, and he strolled in and over to the vanity to pick up his toothbrush.

"Hey, hey, hey!" I cringed forward on the toilet, protecting my breasts, feeling more exposed than I had the past two nights. "Peeing here."

"I can see that. I want to brush my teeth."

Seriously? "Nope. Peeing is sacred. Well, it used to be. Could you please leave me alone?"

He paused with the toothpaste oozing onto his brush and eyed me in the mirror. Had I just yelled at a puppy? A nod of his head and he headed out of the bathroom, toothbrush in hand, and eyes cautiously diverted from the crazy woman sitting on the toilet.

Whew. I wasn't crazy. Was I? No, not crazy. Sharing bodily functions was pushing the closeness. I could suck the man for hours, and spread my legs wide to allow him to do the same, but I wanted to keep tinkling private. It was not too much to ask for.

So, Jean-Louis's evil side had finally appeared. He was Share Too Much Guy. Or maybe he was into the golden stream? I cringed as I stood and flushed. Please, don't let him have that particular kink. I didn't understand the appeal. I erred on the side of vanilla sex, after all.

So I wasn't adventurous between the sheets, and did not need to explore my darker side with whips and chains. Just because everyone was reading about it didn't mean I had to be comfortable with it.

I eyed the shower then glanced to the closed door. Poor guy. He could very well be standing out there with a mouthful of toothpaste. Maybe *my* evil side had reared its head? Crazy Yelling From The Toilet Girl.

I opened the door and popped my head out. He sat on the end of the bed, toothbrush in hand and mouth suspiciously full.

"All clear," I offered. "Want to take a shower together?"

With a nod, he charged into the bathroom to spit. Toothbrush rinsed, a sip of mouthwash gargled, he then spun and pulled me into his arms, kissing me silly.

The kiss was a good, fresh, minty one. It involved a firm, commanding pressure that skittered tingles all up and down my sex-achy body, and focused in my nipples. I moaned and rubbed my breasts against his chest. Digging into his skin with my fingernails, I wanted to keep him there, and also to mark him. *To make him mine.* And when he stopped the kiss it felt as if he'd taken the air from me and replaced it with a heady hit of adrenaline.

"You should patent that one," I said.

"Which one?"

"That kiss. The silly kiss."

"I thought it was a You Are My Woman kiss?"

"Ooh, I like that even better. I am your woman. And you are my musketeer. Oh no."

"What?" he asked as he flipped on the shower and tended to the temperature. Standing there naked, his cock erect, he embodied casual sex god.

"I just realized when I finally leave and go home—because we have to work eventually—"

"Not until tomorrow."

"Right. But I will have to go home sooner or later. And it will be in my costume. That'll be an interesting walk of shame, even if it is only across the street."

He took my hand and we stepped into the shower stall, which was held us both without having to shuffle for the water stream. He stood with his back to the water and bracketed my face with his hands. "It is not shameful to be my woman. Or to walk across the street." He kissed me and it was a wet, slippery treat that ended too quickly. "But yes, it will be a silly walk in that dress."

"You are so not nice," I said, and playfully slapped his chest. "I've been waiting for your edges to show. You've been pretty open with me. I don't know what could possibly be wrong with you. Oh. Wait. I forgot. You're married."

"That is something we'll have to deal with. Everything out in the open, *oui*?"

"Yes, but let's not consider that chat until after the shower. I want to stand under the hot water and let it soothe my achy muscles."

"You are sore? Where, *mon abeille*? Here?" He stroked a finger over my lips.

"No. You could kiss me forever and a day and I'd still beg for more."

"How about here?" He bent to kiss my neck where I was pretty sure I'd find a hickey when I looked in the mirror.

"Nope."

He tweaked each nipple with his fingers.

"A little," I offered. "But don't let that stop you from anything you might have in mind."

His hand glided down my stomach and smoothed over my mons. I shivered, despite the hot water beating against our sides. He slicked a finger between my labia and ever so gently tweaked at my swollen clitoris. "Here?"

"Yep." I nodded against his chest. "It's a good ache. But I think it needs a little rest."

He dropped to his knees and kissed the achy part in question, then rose and pulled me into a hug. "Thank you," he said. "For making this real."

Four

Je m'appelle Jean-Louis!

Sorry. I will use English. Now that I am seeing an American woman my English is getting a workout. I generally speak my native French. I also speak German and Russian, and strive to begin learning Japanese soon. If I intend to make a mark in the International business world, I'll need an Asian language under my belt.

Yes, it is me, Jean-Louis. Dear Reader, you did not think you would ever get inside my head? *Bienvenue!* It is a good place to be. Especially after the past few days.

After the shower, Hollie had spread out her costume on the bed to study it. Volumes of pink satin and lace covered nearly the entire bed. I could sense her anxiety over having to wear it home. She lived across the street from my building. It would be a quick walk. I might have to snap a picture of her while doing so. Just for memory and, you know, possibly blackmail material. (I kid you. Maybe.)

All good things must end eventually. It was Monday. And work demanded my attention. I stood before the closet. I had a lunch meeting at the Hotel Regina with a client. He was considering investing in my company.

From behind, Hollie hugged me. I closed my eyes and took in the warm pressure of her body nuzzling against mine. Breasts against my bare back. Nipples hard upon my skin. Her breath flooding my pores. Soft hair spilling over my arm. Could I stop this moment forever?

How lucky am I to know this woman.

She stroked her fingers down the gray suit hanging prominently in view. "This one," she said. "It's perfect."

"Zegna," I confirmed, and pulled the suit coat out on the hanger. "This is my lucky suit."

"Can I dress you?"

My naked lover bounced on her toes, her blue eyes sparkling with glee. I had but an hour before I needed to meet the client. I couldn't refuse her playful suggestion.

I handed her the suit, pulled out a white dress shirt, and before I could select a tie, she reached in and tugged out the purple silk.

"I love this color," she said, smoothing the end of the tie over her lips. "It's sensual. Like you."

The woman said all the right things to polish up my bruised ego. Trust me, before I met Hollie, I'd been pretty low about myself. But I did not like to wallow. And how could I with a pair of perky breasts rubbing against my chest?

"Okay," she said, stepping back and tapping a finger to her lower lip. "Boxers!"

She bounced over to the dresser and pulled open my underwear drawer. In which, I had found a pair of her black lace panties the other day tucked amidst the boxer briefs. Left there when she'd visited to water my plants, apparently. I'd drawn them out and pressed them to my face. The soft fabric hadn't given up any scent of her, but the slick silk had prompted me to shove them down my pants and over my cock.

Monsieur Eiffel stood upright now to remember the feel of the cool fiber sliding over my erection.

"Oh, I see he's ready." Hollie bent to sweetly kiss the head of my cock. I shivered as the wet morsel sent a frisson of sensation throughout the erect shaft.

When Hollie knelt before me and asked me to step into a gray pair of boxers, I complied. She jutted up her derriere first, and I leaned forward to smooth a hand over her bottom. A quick smack produced a surprised cry from her.

She stood upright, dropping the boxers at my feet. "What was that for?"

"Couldn't resist." I winked. "I have to leave in less than an hour," I reminded. "Dress me quickly."

So maybe that slap had been too much. It had taken her off guard. Surprised her. And I wasn't sure if it had been a good or disturbing surprise. I'd had to try it, though. I wasn't into the rough stuff or spanking, but who could resist that gorgeous ass? It demanded the spank test.

She pulled up my boxers, and when she got to my cock she first shifted it to the left then thought about it and shifted it to its more natural position at the right.

"You dress *vers la droite*," she decided.

"I do. And look at you, Mademoiselle I Speak French Now."

She shimmied her shoulders and shrugged. "I know a few things. But prepare to be underwhelmed by my pitiful command of your language." She adjusted my cock slightly. Her attention only made it harder.

"It's going to be difficult to keep the fellow contained. Monsieur Eiffel doesn't like it when you cover him up."

She bent to kiss my cock through the gray fabric, and then gave it a firm squeeze. I groaned at that pressure. If I didn't manage a quickie before I left, I'd have to sit through lunch with an erection.

"Pants," she said, seemingly without regard for my obvious arousal. "No, shirt next." She turned and retrieved the shirt from the bed and I pressed my hard-on against her naked derriere. "I thought you were in a hurry?" she sweetly asked over a shoulder.

"I am. Fine. Shirt."

I stood back and held out my arms. Pulling it up each arm, and beginning to button it from the top, Hollie tilted forward, skimming the front of my cock with her hip.

"You are teasing me," I warned.

"Yes, well, if you are patient, I might do the dressing part quickly and then we'll have time for a quickie before you leave."

The woman was a mind reader. I did appreciate her hidden talents. As I also appreciated her full breasts, so I gave one a squeeze.

Despite the distraction, she landed the bottom button in the buttonhole then slid her fingers up the front of the shirt. "This is nice. It hangs perfectly and emphasizes your biceps. I do love a well-tailored man."

"Does it turn you on?" I wondered, eager to catalog her turn-ons.

She nodded. "To me, a man in a suit can be sexier than a naked man."

"Is that so?" I nudged my hard-on against her hip. "So you really prefer me clothed right now?"

The tip of her tongue peeked from the corner of her mouth. "Yes. No. Maybe."

A naked woman was dressing me, and I found it most titillating. Her nipples were tight and hard, a deep rose blossom against her pale skin. Sucking them put me on another plane. It was like a Zen act that calmed me, yet aroused at the same time. The jewels bobbling on my tongue were more delicious than any treat.

She lifted my trousers from the bed and I noticed the fabric skimmed her breasts and she hissed out a delicious sigh.

My cock prodded against the boxer briefs. It wanted attention. But in denying it gratification I was amping up the adrenaline. Anticipation heightened my senses and the citrus shampoo that lingered in Hollie's hair and on her skin teased at my nostrils.

Stepping into the trousers she held for me, I allowed her to pull them up. Carefully she zipped, though I winced, worried she might pinch something valuable—until she did not. A tight fit. It would be obvious over lunch.

"*Très bien,*" Hollie observed. I did love it when she attempted French. Even if sometimes she didn't quite get the pronunciation correct or the right words. "Are you meeting a man for lunch?"

"Why?"

"I'd be jealous if a woman got to enjoy all this sexy."

"I cannot leave with a hard-on," I protested, and pulled her into my embrace. I pumped my hips against hers. "Please, Hollie?"

She ground her loins against mine, and my eyelids shuttered. I tightened my jaw, riding the heady trip of want that shivered through my system. My cock pulsed. It was molten hot, and the building tension had already tugged up my balls.

"Mmm...do not tease me, *mon abeille*."

"Coat!" she declared, and shuffled from my grasp. "Arms behind you," she ordered, and again, I fought the growing frustration and complied.

"You should do the tie first," I suggested with the coat sleeves halfway up my arms.

"Oh, right." Moving around in front of me, Hollie slid the tie under the stiff shirt collar. Stiff? Oh...my aching cock.

What happened next surprised the hell out of me. Hollie secured my tie neatly and correctly in less than thirty seconds. It was as if she was a man and had been knotting ties for years. But even those of us who had been doing it forever usually struggled with length and knot fifty percent of the time.

"You make me curious," I said as she stepped back to admire her handiwork.

"I think I'll keep the reason to that particular talent a secret."

Really? Now this one would bother me. Had she dated a man so long and tied his tie for him every day? I didn't know Hollie's dating history. I'm sure she had dated a few men. She had once mentioned something about dating short-term since moving to Paris.

Eh. It was her past. It shouldn't be important. And hell, my past was still clinging to me, so I did not have a right to be nosey about hers.

"What's going on in there?" She twirled her finger before my forehead.

Caught in the act. "Just trying to figure if it was a lover who taught you."

"Secret," she said with a wink.

She adjusted the suit coat onto my shoulders, smoothing her hands down the front and the arms. I did have my suits tailored for me and spent a fortune on them. I appreciated a slim, clean line and a charcoal gray fabric.

"God, you look good in a suit. I could eat you."

"Still hungry?" I pumped my hips forward.

"You are a naughty boy."

"And you are a naked woman."

"Fair enough. Do you have a briefcase?"

"That's old school." I grabbed my mobile from the dresser and tucked it inside the coat pocket. "Everything I need is in there." I checked my watch. "Half an hour. I need twenty minutes to make the trip. That gives me ten right now. But I only need two."

"Two?" She teased a fingertip across her lower lip and fluttered innocent lashes. The sneaky vixen knew what I was talking about.

I swept her about the waist with a hand and turned her around to push against the dresser, which topped out level with her breasts. Pulling up her hands, I placed them on the dresser top. Then I unzipped, tugged down, and out sprang Monsieur Eiffel.

She wiggled her tight ass against my freed cock. I didn't bother with foreplay. The foreplay had been her hands gliding over the shirt, watching her eyes take me in as if her own creation, and in the surprise of discovering her tie mastery. She'd stirred me to a boil and now I had to spill over. I knew she was wet. I could smell her need.

One hand grasped her about both wrists, the other I used to guide myself between her thighs and enter her from behind. She jutted back her hips, opening herself to me. I thrust into her hard, quickly. Fuck yes, she was hot and slick and tight. Always ready for me.

I bowed my head to her shoulder and pumped fast, then slow, wanting to linger in her, the hot, slick, smothering, squeezing, sweetness of her. Bliss inside Hollie.

"Two minutes," she reminded softly.

Slamming hard to hilt myself within her, my muscles tensed and I fisted a hand against her stomach, holding her against my rigid, shaking body as I shot into her. A shout of triumph burst out.

Fuck, I'd never been so satiated in my life.

The walk of shame from Jean-Louis's place to mine wasn't terrible. I had only to cross the street, slip into my building, shrug at the concierge's raised eyebrow, then battle three flights of stairs in a long, wide-skirted seventeenth century dress that wasn't completely laced up the side because I'd never get out on my own otherwise.

Once at the door to my 3A apartment, I slipped the key out of the pocket handily sewn into the bodice, and spilled into my apartment with a greeting to the furniture that surprised me. I didn't usually greet inanimate objects. Today—thoroughly fucked as I was—I felt awesome.

So, hello, chaise! Hello, desk with a stack of work waiting for my attention! Hello, kitchen table!

"Hello, fridge!"

I swung open the refrigerator door and nabbed a bottle of water. Jean-Louis had only wine in his fridge, and his tap water had never cooled more than lukewarm. I tilted back a healthy, molar-twinging swallow then pressed the crinkly plastic bottle to my breasts as I sighed.

I hadn't been in this apartment for two nights. I was home. And no matter how much I wanted to rush back into Jean-Louis's arms, home always felt great. Here was my place. My things. My soul. I breathed here.

I am here.

Too philosophical? Hey, I had my moments.

With a few tugs at the laces, I deposited the dress on the bedroom floor and stepped out of the mass of fabric. It was a rental, but I didn't have to return it until Tuesday, which was tomorrow. I'd probably swing by the store with it tonight.

Casting a look out the bedroom window did not result in spying Jean-Louis in his respective bedroom. He had left long before I'd shuffled into my dress. After lunch with the client, he planned to collect some groceries for a meal he'd make me later. He was going to cook for me! I couldn't wait. I loved to sit down and be served by a man. What woman didn't? While there was always a chance he was an awful cook, did it matter?

Nope.

Pulling on a pair of soft brown leggings, I twirled about looking for a pretty top in the scatter of clothes on the easy chair by the window. That quick dash across the street had been unrepentantly nippy. I think the temperature had dropped twenty degrees since the night of the party. Time to start wearing sweaters and thick, cozy socks.

So not sexy. But it seemed whatever I wore around Monsieur Sexy wouldn't stay on for long anyway. Or for that matter, neither would his clothes stay on long, even in the process of dressing. That fast fuck up against the dresser hadn't given me an orgasm, but who cared? His cock pistoning inside me was enough. And really, I may be orgasmed out after the past few days.

Was that even possible? I hoped not.

I plucked a hip-length, pink, rayon top from the clothes rack near the chair. Elaborate brown embroidery around the sleeves and hem gave it a bohemian flair. There were little silk tassels at the vee of the neckline. I pulled it on and then eyed the Louboutins. They would look smashing with the outfit, but I didn't need to wear them around the house. I'd slip them on later, when I returned to my lover's home.

ÅÅÅ

Lunch went well. I believed the client would invest, but he was going to give it a day or two to think it over.

My company, VSquire, taught clients how to use virtual machines. It's all about cloud computing and virtualization today. And someone has to train the big corporations how to manage the infrastructures built on a virtualized platform. That's where my skilled trainers stepped in. Currently, I employed a small crew of a dozen trainers, but I was hiring every month. Eventually, I hoped to step away from online training myself, and sit back and watch it all run like a well-oiled engine. It would happen. Sooner, rather than later.

I hoped to bring in the investor to expand our reach to military bases and such locales as Afghanistan and Japan. If it was meant to happen, it would.

After filing the groceries away, I shed the Zegna suit and put on other clothes. I strolled through the loft in a pair of jersey pants and no shirt. I liked to be comfortable at home, save for when I work. Even teaching online, I strived to wear a business shirt and comfortable slacks. I have to look professional. I am the boss, after all.

Snagging a bottle of water from the fridge, I tilted back half before sitting at the kitchen table and pulling out the iPad to look up the recipe I intended to make for dinner. When I have the time, I love to cook. It relaxed me, and as well, allowed me to tap into the creative part of my brain that demanded attention.

I paused to glance out the window. Hollie was across the street in her building. The living room windows were too far apart to see well into each other's lives, and the manner in which the sun gleamed onto the side of her building sheened a gloss over the windows on her second floor apartment.

The walk of shame? Wasn't that what lovers called it when they had to sneak out of a hookup's bed and stumble home while wearing the previous night's clothes?

Hollie had no reason to be shameful about our relationship.

I smiled to myself. A relationship. One that had only just moved to the touch level the other night at the All Saints party. Until then we had been staring at each other through windows and a computer screen.

I had needed that slow approach. My life was complicated right now. And Hollie added another kink to that complication. But it was a kink I was willing to embrace. I had to. I had fallen in love with the woman.

I have a tendency to fall in love quickly. Call it a fault if you want to, but I never would. I didn't need to learn everything about a woman immediately. It was all in the eyes, the mouth, and the movement of her body. I could get lost watching Hollie move. The shift of her hips as she strode before me in those beribboned high heels. The swing of glossy chestnut hair across her shoulders. The shudder in her body that jiggled her breasts as she came after fingering herself for my pleasure.

"*Merde.*"

I grasped my cock through the jersey. It was hard. Didn't take much. Thinking about Hollie's breasts and how I had slammed her against the dresser earlier this morning turned it to stone. Her moans and her insistent rocking hips had pleaded for me to thrust harder. Faster.

And earlier than that, as we had lingered in bed. Mm... My tongue dashing into her pussy, licking, teasing and going deeper to taste her sweetness and salt. I could eat her every day. All day. Whenever she offered. And if she did not, I'd slide my hand down her stomach and tickle her clit until she squirmed awake and then I could spread aside one leg and lick her until she panted. And then laughed.

She tended to laugh after an orgasm. I loved the sound of it spilling up after a shout of joy. There was nothing else like a coming, laughing woman who was happy because of something I had done to her. And not just any woman; I preferred that woman be Hollie.

We men might come off as confident and know-it-alls in bed, but trust me, the only way to know we were doing it right was through a woman's approval, be it vocal or the physical squirming and uncontrollable shudders.

I think I found Hollie's sweet spot, too. Right to the side of her clitoris. I just had to rub it gently and keep it slick with my tongue. And then press against the bone beneath her skin. It was like operating a finely-tuned machine. One wrong touch and she'd never make it to climax.

I squeezed my cock and realized the hard-on was not going away unless I took care of matters. Sliding down my pants and right there, with one hand against the wall, the other greased the main shaft.

First I imagined Hollie's delicate hand wrapped about my thickness and mimicked that motion. Her fingers couldn't meet at the base, and that decreased the tightness I enjoyed when she slid down that far. I squeezed and slid up higher, slowly, and then faster. Imagining Hollie's tongue circling the head of it...oh, yes. Slick, slick, slick. Long, drawn out pressure of tongue to my cock head. Her mouth would be so hot against my skin. And tight. She knew how to suck me.

My pace grew rapid and firm. I stiffened my legs, thighs tensing as I felt the tremendous surge building along my length. So hard. So fast. Her mouth on me. Her sighs hot. Blue eyes looking up at me for direction. Faster. Don't stop...

I gasped out a throaty noise as I came and my fingers slicked through cum. My hips thrusted, my shaft swishing the air as I rode the intense pleasure.

But too quickly, I crashed. Without Hollie's hot mouth on me it had felt less than. Empty.

Fuck, I wish my life wasn't so complicated right now.

I hadn't expected to be at this particular crossroad so early in my life. I'd thought by now I'd be raising a family. Married to a loving and faithful wife. Looking forward to a cozy cottage in the country with a tire swing that I could push the kids on over the backyard pond while the pet dog scampered nearby.

It was a dream that had been with me for years. I strived for it. I needed that comfort and peace of family and a loving wife.

Pulling up my pants, I wandered to the kitchen sink and rinsed off my hand. Then I splashed my face with water.

Finding Hollie in the window that September day had been what I had needed at the time. A gorgeous woman who had shown interest in me, but yet, who had remained at a distance. Hell, she'd been across the street in an entirely different building from me. We hadn't touched, but we had shared a kind of trust through mutual self-pleasure. I'd needed that odd connection.

I tend to thrive when in a relationship with a woman. There's something about sharing my life with another and also about being monogamous that appeals greatly. I'm not the kind of guy who can do one-night stands, or sleep around with a new woman every other week.

I'd intended to keep the distance while I had been on work assignment in Berlin, even when Hollie and I had graduated to cyber sex. But to finally hear her voice, that confident giggle that always followed her climax, had struck me hard. I had fallen in love.

Yes, I was in love. You either enjoy spending time with a woman and being friends with her, or you only want the sex. I wanted sex, friendship, and a relationship with Hollie. But how to manage that with a wife still on the line? *Mon Dieu*, the woman was insisting on taking half of everything I own. We had been married two years. The last year we'd been separated. And as far as I knew, she'd only been faithful to me those first few months of the marriage.

Leaning over the sink and catching my elbows on the cool porcelain, I caught my face against my palms and rubbed my temples.

Was I doing the right thing by encouraging this relationship with Hollie? Was I right in the head? What sane man hooked up while still married? (Don't answer that.) Maybe I should put this relationship off until the divorce papers were signed and I could focus completely on Hollie?

I glanced through the window and across the street to the gleaming reflections on my lover's windows. She was like that. Bright. Always upbeat and gleaming. Like something I needed to survive.

Sunshine.

"Fuck."

Five

I caught myself humming as I sorted through the dresses hung on the rack at the back wall of my bedroom. It wasn't a song, just a happy melody.

I had good reason to be happy. I'd spent the last two days with Jean-Louis. We had kissed. We had touched. We had fucked. (Oh, baby, had we fucked.) We had lost ourselves in one another.

Yeah, it had been that good. And it was going to stay that good. Right?

I could dream. I wasn't going to let my mind go there. You know that there. The there that warns that nothing good can ever last for too long. The there that makes you question everything you do. Is it for real, or is something wrong with him?

There was nothing wrong with him. Sure, he wasn't perfect. No one was. Hell, he had a wife. But they were in the process of divorcing. And I was not going to hold that against him.

Instead, I'd hold my breasts against his bare, hot chest and breathe in the sable rum scent from his pores. I'd hold my fingers against his skin. I'd hold that nice handful of a cock that, even now, I could imagine pumping inside me, seeking my depths, filling me, owning me...

I groaned, catching a hand at the top bar of the clothes rack and leaning into the dresses. Biting my lip, I closed my eyes and slid my hand between my thighs to press against my clit. That pressure captured the hum of desire and intensified it. I ached for the man.

I don't think I've ever ached for a man before. I liked it. I wanted to feel this way all the time. Whirling about in a constant horny state. Ready to get off with a flick of his finger. Alive.

That's what the feeling was. I felt alive and vital, and yeah, sexy.

I know, I know. This was a new relationship. First-time sex and kisses always giddied about in a girl's system and made her feel as if she was a princess floating above the clouds. And then familiarity sank her into the clouds, and eventually the princess fell to earth.

That was fine by me. If I landed on earth then I'd grab Monsieur Sexy's hand and lead him into my bedroom.

So tonight I was dining at his place, and he was cooking. That thrilled me, and made me curious. He could not be kind, a great lover, *and* a good cook. It didn't compute. I'd have to be careful not to make a face if anything he made didn't taste right. I could fake pleasure, if need be.

Here's to never having to fake it in bed. I didn't believe in that. If a girl faked an orgasm she only enabled the guy. He thought she was having a great time? He'd continue with his lackluster attention to her pussy, or whathaveyou. Men only learned by being taught. And faking it was the worst lesson. I cared too much about my personal pleasure to sacrifice it in a misguided attempt to make the guy look good.

I ran my fingers down the black lace dress Jean-Louis had bought for me. He'd instructed me to go into a ritzy shop on the Champs Elysees while I'd chatted with him on Skype via my cell phone, and had helped me select a dress. There had been an incident with the sales girl. Roxane. She'd...touched me, and had almost kissed me. And I had let it happen. All while Jean-Louis had looked on.

The encounter had confused me, as well as bolstered my confidence. I had no desire to have sex with a woman, but that moment in the dressing room when I had allowed myself to feel a woman's touch on my skin had been incredible. And to know that my lover had been possessive enough to tell Roxane not to kiss me—because my lips were for him—had been an exquisite claiming.

He'd seen me in this dress, so I pulled out the red one. It wasn't silk, but it looked like it. It had been cheap. I'd probably gotten it at Nordstrom Rack back home in Iowa. But it was low cut with spaghetti straps, and the body-hugging shape of it stopped above my knees with a tickle of fringe. Seriously, it had three-inch long fringe. I loved the eclectic vibe. Hippie chick meets sex bomb.

I slipped it over my head and pulled it down. There was no zipper. No bra and no panties. (Because he liked me that way.) Just thinking that thought flushed my neck with a shivering blush.

Flouncing over to stand before the floor mirror, I inspected the look. My hair was loose and wavy thanks to the tousle it had received in the sheets the past days. I'd wash it tomorrow morning.

The Louboutins would be perfect with the dress, so I sat on the chair and strapped into the sexy. Black leather with velvet ties about the ankles. They were not slip in and slip out shoes. These were designed to make a statement and to attract the eye. The soles were the color of my dress, which made everything perfect.

"I've got to stop thinking that word. Perfect," I muttered. "No one or nothing is perfect."

If I set myself up to believe in perfection, I would only be let down. Instead, I'd settle for happiness. It definitely rocked my world.

ÅÅÅ

Hollie was refreshing. A whispery summer breeze curling into my life. A red-hot fringe tickling at my libido. She ate heartily of the food I had prepared, and hadn't stopped complimenting me. She was too good to be true. What was wrong with her?

I finished the broiled sole and ran my finger through the lemon and capers sauce for one last taste. Then I sat back on the kitchen chair and made a dessert out of watching my lover eat.

All women were prone to some bad habits. As were we men. But as a man, I have to say that women were more of a struggle to understand than we men. And yet, Hollie read like an open book. Bright and cheery, a bookish sort with a wild inside that she didn't mind letting out for me. She was smart, but didn't flaunt that. And she was sensual without (I suspected) realizing it.

Like right now. She leaned forward on an elbow and trailed her finger through the lemon sauce, licking the finger slowly afterward and smiling to herself, unaware that I observed. Or maybe she was aware?

No, she was lost. And I wanted her to stay lost so I could accidentally stumble upon her.

My eyes played at the red fringe dusting her thigh, then glided down the sleek length of her long leg. She was shorter than I, but perhaps it was the shoes that made her legs look so long. Those sexy black shoes with the ties caressing the ankles. Women swooned for those red-soled objects of desire. And put out a pretty penny to obtain them.

"Was that the first day you'd gotten those shoes?" I asked. "That day I saw you putting them on in front of the window?" I had watched her take them out from the box and, indeed, swoon over them as she slowly tried them on.

"Yes. I'd raided my mad money for these pretties. They spoke to me."

"They did?" Her blue eyes widened as she nodded in confirmation. My cock, which never truly relaxed when she was near, hardened. Because that blue sparkle always got me. Her eyes were true. They would never lie to me. "What did the shoes say to you, exactly?"

She pushed the plate away and dabbed her lips with the napkin. It was a paper towel from a roll but I'd hadn't anything fancier. Propping an arm on the back of the chair, with a tilt of her hips, she crossed her legs, displaying both with that accidental seduction I so loved to fall prey to.

"They said, 'Mademoiselle, you must ave zee shoes. *Oui*?'" She laughed, and sipped wine. A nervous reaction, I sensed, to her often-sudden humor. "Sorry," she added. "I shouldn't attempt to sound like a French person. But I was impersonating the shoes. They sounded like that. I swear to it."

"Is that so?"

I slid off the chair and knelt before her legs, stroking down the soft length of her calf to the velvet ribbon that encircled her ankle. Drawing her leg out and lifting her foot to eye level, I ventured my gaze along the sleek anklebone, down the exposed heel, and studied the slender curves and lines of her foot.

"My shoes have never spoken to me," I said. I kissed the top of her foot and she cooed and wiggled on the chair. The fringe danced and fell between her thighs, distracting me from the footwear.

Holding her by the ankle, I drew my nose up her leg and to the side of her knee where I caught the scent of vanilla. It was her signature scent, and when warmed on her skin it was as if a hot treat from the oven was luring me to take a bite.

I licked the inside of her knee and felt tension tighten the muscles in her leg. She was ticklish, and wanted to pull away, but was resisting the urge because... Because Hollie loved it when I licked her. Her sweet moan was all I needed to hear to know that.

"That was an amazing supper," she said on a breathy gasp.

I nuzzled my nose along her skin, moving slowly up the inside of her thigh. Silk against my skin. Vanilla silk. I moved her leg to the side. Her palm pressed against the edge of the table.

"Where did you learn to cook like that?"

Smiling, I paused and toyed with the fringe using my nose. "I was either going to become a chef or an IT tech after my *terminale* year of school. I took the *bac* and followed the money." Instead of the passion, is what I didn't say. I did love my job. But cooking? That was something else entirely. It satisfied my creative side.

"What's the bac?"

"Baccalaureat. It is an exam we take in order to go to university."

"Like the SATs in the States."

"Similar, I'm sure."

"So what's for dessert?" she managed as I blew at the fringe, aiming toward the apex of her thighs. She wasn't wearing panties. Good girl.

"You," I said plainly.

"Mmm, I like the sound of that. Ooh..."

I followed the vanilla musk scent of her to the shaved design decorating her mons. I could smell her, moist and wanting, and I didn't have to hold her leg to the side anymore. She slid it over my shoulder and I tilted up that shoulder to widen her for me.

Kissing her thatch of soft hairs, I nuzzled into them. I loved losing myself between a woman's legs. Hollie's pussy most especially. An intriguing place to explore. I teased my tongue down the soft, hot slit between her labia, nudging her open. My tongue entered her, and teased upward where her clitoris swelled up from the top of its shaft.

I'd learned something about a woman's anatomy from an abandoned sex manual I'd found in the hotel last week while in Berlin. The clitoris wasn't simply that little bud at the top of a woman's labia that I liked to tease with my tongue, but rather extended down like a wishbone along each side of the inner folds. So I parted those folds and pressed my tongue firmly along and down one side to trace those clitoral legs I could not see, but knew—from Hollie's moan—that I had found.

Her bottom slid forward to the edge of the chair, and I pushed my face in close, my nose nuzzling her clit and my tongue lashing down the other side. Firmly, as if licking the best and last juices from a delicious dessert, I consumed her. I sucked at the tender labia, and then dashed my tongue inside her, mining her incredible heat. Indulging in her salt and sweet and sex. My goal: to make her come.

Grasping fingers slid over my scalp. She tugged at my hair, and I answered her insistence with deep penetration from my tongue. Her thighs shivered aside my cheeks. The leg over my shoulder tensed, and then it relaxed. My erection strained against my pants. But I wouldn't unzip. The denial of such pleasure as feeling her skin against my hard-on would be as exquisite as if I'd been naked.

Flicking quickly at her swollen bud, I teased it this way and that, licking around it and sucking gently and then more firmly. Careful not to use my teeth, yet so eager to draw up her panting moans to a climax that I could now feel shudder within her hips and pelvis.

"More?" I asked.

"Don't stop," she hastened out. Her thighs squeezed against my head.

"Maybe I am finished?"

"Oh... Jean-Louis!"

I should not tease, but it was a way to extend the pleasure. "Very well. I cannot resist diving into you."

I pushed two fingers into her tight, enveloping depths. Hollie shifted on the chair, encouraging me with a guttural sound from her throat to go in deeper. I pressed my tongue to her clitoris. Curling my fingers forward, I found the ridged G-spot. One touch jerked her hips up against my face.

I controlled her. And yet she controlled me, because all I wanted was to win her release. I wouldn't be satisfied without hearing the sound of her surrender.

The toe of her foot nudged my groin. I gasped against her pussy. My breath hushing over her juicy slit must have been the catalyst. Hollie gripped my hair and cried out. The leg over my shoulder straightened and then relaxed, dangling down my back. Her breathy gasp accompanied a shimmy of shoulders to work through her bones. And her body slunk down the chair to where I had to pull her forward and onto my lap.

She collapsed against me, head falling forward, our foreheads meeting. Her panting breaths dusted my cheek. Her body clenched and then she relaxed into me, giggling.

I tucked my face into her neck where vanilla blossomed. "*C'est bon*," I muttered.

"You're telling me? Jean-Louis, I..." She sighed, and didn't say anything else.

She didn't need to. I still held a hand over her pussy, one finger against her clit. Her muscles contracted again.

ÅÅÅ

After supper and dessert, I ran home to slip on some boots because Jean-Louis suggested we go for a walk. I pulled on some leggings and my long, black, wool coat, too. It was nippy out. A scarf tucked around my neck repelled the cool kiss of November as I landed on the sidewalk before my building and sought my lover.

He stood across the street from his building, next to an elder gentleman in a beret. At sight of me, he handed the man back a cigar, blew out the smoke, and gestured for me to come to him. The air around him wafted sweet tobacco. He wrapped an arm about my shoulder and leaned in to kiss my cheek as we walked.

"I didn't know you smoked," I said.

I had a thing about smokers. I could not stand the smell of smoke on their clothing, in their hair, on their breath. I had thought Jean-Louis cared for his health, as well.

"I don't. Well, I did in school. To be cool, *oui*? Never did like to inhale though. But I never refuse a puff on a good cigar now and then."

Pleased he hadn't hidden an addiction, I hugged him with both arms and we strolled to the Avenue Floquet that paralleled the Eiffel Tower. A jogger passed by, singing out loud to the tunes piped through his earbuds.

Jean-Louis, surprisingly, picked up the catchy tune. "We are...wild."

"We are like young volcanoes," I replied, matching him with the next line. Then I skipped happily. "I love Fallout Boy."

"So do I." He squeezed my hand and we shared that thrill of knowing your lover had the same taste in music. For the one band, at least. "They are a good band for singing the lyrics loud in the shower."

"Yep. So is Pink."

"*Oui*, she is another of my favorites."

It was after nine in the evening, and despite the chill air, tourists flocked about the Iron Lady. Sharing a few more band favorites, we walked along the Champs-de-Mars on the left side facing the Seine. It was one of the largest open spaces of green in Paris, and I often spent afternoons sitting here, inhaling the scent of grass while I proofread work.

"I can smell what I want," he said. Gripping my hand, Jean-Louis quickened his steps.

I crossed my fingers he had a craving for the banana and Nutella crepes they sold at the base of the tower. Even though supper had been delicious and had hit the spot, I hadn't had my dessert yet.

My core still tingled to recall Jean-Louis with his head between my legs, tendering me to a rousing orgasm with such ease. I had the thought that my dating history since arriving on French soil had been to love them and leave them after a month. We'd already stretched this beyond a month. And I didn't want it to end.

Ever.

Did that mean I was falling in love with the guy? He'd already confessed love to me.

Nah. I was still a bit skittish about that word. It felt so permanent and honest to me. And reciprocating by saying the word just because a man had said it to you was not smart thinking. I wouldn't do that to myself.

But I could admit to serious like.

Jean-Louis stopped before a food stand that sold roasted chestnuts. Not quite as ooey and gooey as the crepe I'd craved, but I could dig it. He bought a paper cone of chestnuts and nodded for me to follow him. We skipped down the stairs leading to the docks where countless *bateaux mouches* waited passengers. Striding past the boats, he commandeered a bench, and I snuggled up next to him and dipped my fingers into the warm chestnuts.

"These remind me of when I was a kid," he said. "My grand-mere Beatrice had a chestnut tree. She'd roast them in the evenings over a hearth fire. Makes me nostalgic, and want to buy a cottage."

"Really? You want to live out in the country and roast chestnuts?"

"*Oui*!" he said enthusiastically. "It is a goal of mine. But perhaps I will find a larger chateau so the children have space to run about."

"And how many children do you intend to have?" The chestnut was sweet, having been roasted with honey, and it crunched softly between my molars.

"*Un ou deux*?"

"A couple kids? You have plans, my man."

"I'm not getting any younger."

I turned on the bench, crossing a leg, and studied the side of his face. The barest hint of gray tufted above his ear and those crazy-sexy laugh lines that crinkled out from the corner of his eyes got me every time. His prominent brow was a European thing, I think. And that triangle of stubble beneath his lower lip? Mercy.

"How old are you?" I asked.

"*Trente-quartre*."

I translated in my head. "Thirty-four? Hmm, I suspected you were in your early thirties."

"And how old are you, Mademoiselle?"

"Twenty-eight. But I don't have plans for marriage and children until I'm in my thirties."

"Seems reasonable. Get your career established and figure your life, then bring in others to share it with you. To enhance it."

He made it sound so simple. And yet, his first attempt at marriage had been a disaster. If it had been his first attempt. "You've only been married once, yes?"

He leaned in to kiss me. "*Oui, mon abeille*. I am not so terrible used goods."

"I don't think you are used goods. But so you know, I feel for you. I can't imagine any woman screwing around behind your back. But with that said," I added quickly, "I don't want to talk about her. Your marriage is your business. I'm glad it's out there, and I know about it, and..."

I sighed and reached for another chestnut to pop into my mouth before I said something stupid like 'tell me everything about her!'. I wanted to know everything. But I sure as hell didn't need to know a single tidbit if I wanted to maintain my sanity.

"I think it better we not discuss it too much," he said. "With luck, the divorce papers will be signed soon, and I can put that mistake in my past. But tell me. You have never made a mistake in the romance department before?"

"Oh, please. How much time do we have?"

I laughed then, and he joined me, and it wasn't necessary to detail any of those past mistakes. We were human. We all struggled and made mistakes, and learned from those mistakes. The key was in recognizing the lesson and moving on.

Sheesh. I was starting to think all new-agey and Dr. Phil-like. Enough of that plunge into Responsible Living 101.

Grabbing Jean-Louis by his coat collar I pulled him to me for a chestnut- and sugar-laced kiss. He pushed me down and rolled over me on the bench and deepened the connection. The taste of him was ridiculously sexy. The feel of his body over mine reassured me of his strength. The cool night heightened the brisk wind on my face and the tickle of his hair over my forehead.

"Love you," he murmured against my mouth. "And I mean that."

I knew that he did. But I couldn't return the compliment. Like was enough for me right now, and I sensed he wasn't worried that I couldn't say the L word to him yet.

"You should learn French, Hollie," he said, sitting up and offering me another chestnut. "Would you take a class?"

"I, uh..." Hadn't the desire to sit in a boring classroom learning whether or not words were masculine or feminine. I'd read enough Learn To Speak French books to fill an entire shelf. To no avail. French words didn't stick to my brain cells. "You want me to?"

He nodded. "You live in France. You have a French lover. You should learn the language."

"I suppose." I had a French lover! I would never get tired of hearing that statement. "I wonder if there are online courses?"

"I'm sure there are. But I suspect a classroom approach might be easier to comprehend."

"Maybe. I'll look it up online and see if there are classrooms in the area."

"Excellent. Let's go to your place," he suggested. "I want to make love to you in your bed. I've not yet been in your home."

"Hmm..." I made a show of considering the suggestion. Really, I was trying to decide how messy the place was, and if I'd left any heaps of dirty clothes lying on the floor in the bedroom. Heck, when weren't there heaps of clothing on the floor? "I think it'll pass inspection."

"You do not keep your place tidy?"

"I'll leave that for you to decide. But I'm hoping you'll be so eager to get under my skirt you won't notice the mess."

He pumped his erection against my hip. Yep, the guy was ready to go. "Well, if you think it is too messy we can always have sex right here?"

"You and your fantasy about public sex."

Once he'd confessed he wanted to have sex with me in the Louvre. And I'd agreed because I was pretty darn sure that was never going to happen.

I pushed him up and he relented. "My place it is."

"Let's take *un asenceur,*" Jean-Louis suggested as we filed into the lobby of my apartment building.

I tugged him toward the stairs. "No. I'm sure it's broken."

He cast a summary glance over the elevator doors. Heavy iron Art Nouveau curves worked about the small, and deceptively innocuous mechanism. "There is no sign."

"I like the exercise."

He tromped up the stairs behind me. "You are afraid of elevators," he stated. As if he was perfectly correct.

And he was. Mostly. Not *all* elevators. I liked the vast elevators in the States that could fit a car and a half dozen people in them with doors that opened on both ends. But these tiny little coffins in Paris that often came with a warning that no more than two—sometimes only one—could fit inside? *Non, merci.*

A roaming hand found its way up the back of my thigh and under my skirt as I reached the second floor (make that third in America). Jean-Louis pulled me to him and kissed me. "Why are you afraid?"

"I'm not afraid. I just... I don't like the small space. And walking up stairs is good exercise. And as a writer stuck behind the desk all day I don't get nearly enough—"

Another kiss silenced my superfluous excuses. The man knew exactly how to tame me. He lifted me into his arms with an ease that had me thinking I had recently lost more weight than I'd thought, and carried me to my door.

I wiggled the key in the lock and pushed in the door as he carried me over the threshold. Which I didn't want to overthink, so I let that one go.

"I am surprised you are not more bold with the lift," he said. Still on the elevator topic? "You are so daring, Hollie."

"Me?" I slid off my coat, took his from him, and...tossed them over the back of the gray chaise. "I'm not so daring."

"If that is so, then how is it a shy, unassuming woman fucks herself with a vibrator before her bedroom window for the man across the street? You still have that vibrator?" He was already unbuttoning his shirt and pulling it from his pants.

"I do."

He pulled me to him by the neckline of my red dress. Clutching the fabric so it tightened across my nipples, he eyed me with a sensual look that said *obey me if you want to get lucky*. "Go get it."

The words 'yes, master' formed on my tongue. But instead of speaking, I nodded and scampered—yes, scampered—into the bedroom. Toeing off my boots, I parked them at the end of the bed, and then pulled off the dress and the leggings, which rendered me naked. I shivered, but not from the chill in the air, rather in anticipation of standing before the Frenchman who waited out in the living room.

"I like this chaise!" he called. There was no bedroom door, and the living room was but twenty feet away. "Sexy. I want to make love to you on this chaise."

"I'm cool with that!" I pulled open my underwear drawer. "Where is it?"

Not tucked within the La Perla lace and Target cotton. So my taste in underwear was eclectic. And if a girl was going to invest in La Perla, then she had to save pennies by balancing out her wardrobe with the Tar-jay stuff.

I veered toward the bathroom, glancing out to the living room as I passed, and caught a glimpse of Jean-Louis pulling off his shirt. The side view of his abs resembled a climbing wall of rock. Each flex bulged the muscles and altered his landscape remarkably. Sweet mother, let me find that thing.

Ah, there. Sitting on the back of the tub. Where else?

I grabbed it and headed out to the living room, but by the time I paralleled the kitchen, I slowed and assumed a less eager facade and more sensual stride.

Jean-Louis had unzipped his pants, and at sight of naked ole me, he dropped them and kicked them off. For some reason, spying his erection beneath the boxer briefs, thick and bulging for release, was initially more exciting than seeing the actual thing.

I ran my tongue along my upper lip and waggled the silver vibrator, then drew it down between my breasts to my stomach. I had not perfected my seductress moves, but with practice, there was always hope.

"Is this what you want?"

He pushed down the boxers and kicked those aside, as well. His cock was big but not monstrous like those freakish things I sometimes read about in tales of lust and sex. It was just right; with enough extra girth to make me appreciate the ride.

He sat on the chaise, stretching his arms along the back of it. "Come sit down, *mon abeille*." A tilt of his hips made his cock pendulum back and forth. "Right here."

I leaned over him and kissed his nose, then dashed out my tongue to lick his upper lip. A wiggle of my mouth over his mustache tickled. I loved the sensation. He cupped my breasts and squeezed my nipples luring me to lean in for more. More, and more. Straddling him, I hovered, my pussy close to his cock, yet not touching.

"Let me have that." He took the vibrator, and as I kissed down his neck, he tested the single button on the end that slid to three different speeds. Slow, nicely faster, and oh, yeah, baby. He clicked it to slow and I grabbed it from him. "No, no, I want to try it out," he protested.

"Exactly." I touched the slick silver tip to his chest and he smirked and made a little grunt. "You've never had your hands on one of these before?"

"Not exactly my style."

"Then I need to give you a lesson." I roved gently to his nipple and pressed the vibrator against the tiny jewel that tightened even more.

"Oh," Jean-Louis said on a curious tone. "That's...mmm..."

"Feels good, doesn't it?"

He nodded, closed his eyes and tilted his head against the chaise. Arms stretched out across the gray, tufted velvet, he took in the sensations. I held back a giggle. This was fun trying something new. And he was willing to let me explore.

I tickled the tip of the Silver Surfer across his chest to his other nipple. Between my legs, his erection lodged against my thigh, hard and hot. I nudged my leg to rub it while carefully tending his nipple. He squirmed subtly, discovering the newness of the vibrator's touch and, perhaps, enjoying it.

"You like that?"

"It is different."

"Good different?"

He nodded. When his vocabulary decreased, I knew he was lost in pleasure.

I kissed his skin and trailed my tongue down the ridges of his abdomen, drawing the vibrator in the slick wake. His stomach muscles tightened and relaxed as I tested each roll of hardness with the silver tip. And down, down, gliding through the dark curls until I circled the base of his cock with the instrument.

Jean-Louis lifted his head, eager to watch what I was doing. He gasped in a breath. Exhaled. Stomach muscles clenched again. A satisfied moan.

"How about this?" I laid the silver rod against the length of his penis and held the two together, the vibrations shivering in my fingers. Drawing in the corner of my lip, I realized how wet I had become. Mmm... I pressed my thighs together and rotated my hips.

"*Mon abeille...*" he whispered on a lusty shiver.

He loved it. I could tell from the smile on his face. And when he grabbed my hair and clasped it as if to hold himself to something sure, I tilted my head to rest on his hip while I drew the vibrator up and down and all around his exquisite cock. A dip down to try at his testicles, but not long. I wasn't sure the vibrations would be as appreciated on those tender bits. But Jean-Louis did not protest. He opened his legs and then closed them. Untethered and unsure, but willing to take the ride. I could see the pending orgasm flush his skin, engorge the vein beneath his penis, and rise in the glistening pre-cum that spilled from the crown.

His fingers massaged in my hair, grasping, clinging, wanting, and then...he gripped the back of my head and pulled me up to sit on him again. An urgent kiss landed on my mouth. He grabbed the vibrator and pressed it between us, wedged between my labia and his cock. I rode both, rocking my hips as he kissed me with intensity. I wanted him deep inside my mouth, his tongue dancing with mine. I couldn't get him deep enough.

As well, I couldn't press hard enough against the double pleasure of hot cock and trembling shaft of steel. But I tried. I ground my clit against them. Fuck, that was good. It was all slick and juicy and hard and—fuck!

Jean-Louis moaned into my mouth. His clutch at my hair hurt and then it did not. He gripped my hips and pulled me down and back and forth.

I arched my back, which pushed everything tighter, closer, firmer. I grasped at air, seeking stability. But I craved the lost flutter of surrender.

"Yes," he hissed. His body trembled beneath mine.

The duel play of hardness and the added vibration worked its magic on me. Aware my lover was coming beneath me, hard and forcefully, I gripped his shoulders and shivered into my own orgasm. Breaths gasping, I bowed my head and groaned. We cried out together. The scent of his skin, hot and salty, filled my senses as he gushed inside me. Hot cum trickled down my thigh as he pulled out with an exhale. Arms dropping to his sides and head falling onto the chaise, he was elated.

I shifted. The vibrator tumbled to the floor with a *clunk*. Curling up my legs, I settled onto his lap and we shared the blissful tremors of after orgasm.

Six

Snuggled between soft white sheets, buried beneath the light but warm white goose down comforter, and face smushed against my pillow, I sensed the brightness of morning beaming through the window, but wisely, kept my eyelids shut.

I spread a palm over the bed beside me, but my fingers didn't venture over warm male muscle or even the surprise of a lax penis draped across his powerful thigh. Not in bed? I didn't hear the shower running. But I did hear some clatter out in the kitchen.

Jean-Louis had worked up an appetite last night. The man had sexual skills. In spades. I should probably drag myself out of bed and make him breakfast but...alas, I am not a breakfast-maker. I love eggs, bacon, muffins, all that morning jazz. But I love it most when someone else makes it for me. Like in a restaurant. Crumpets or rye toast and a piece of fresh fruit over granola were all I usually bothered to make on my own.

I turned onto my back, stretching out my legs beneath the sheet and curling my toes. Bed lingering was a skill I had proudly mastered. Yes, so it was a work day. I generally didn't start the official work stuff until around ten. One of the advantages of being my own boss and setting my hours. Don't hate me because I'm a layabed.

"*Bonjour, mon abeille.*"

Savory scents suddenly wafted into my nostrils. I pulled the sheet down and opened my eyes. A gorgeous Frenchman wearing my yellow silk robe with the black bee embroidered over the chest held a plate of what smelled like eggs and toast. He beamed.

And I fell hard.

"Seriously?" I pushed up to sit against the pillow, pulling the sheet with me to cover my breasts. (I don't know, something about eating bare-chested felt weird.) "Who *are* you?"

"I am Jean-Louis," he announced proudly.

"No shit, you are Jean-Louis. And he is some kind of perfect man who cooks like a chef and fucks like a dream."

"You have not yet tasted my eggs. I did what I could with the little food you have in your fridge."

"Hey, I've looked in your fridge. It's emptier than mine."

"*Touché*. It is easier to take out when one eats alone. Here's to many more meals to share and a full fridge."

I accepted the plate, which boasted the fluffiest scrambled eggs I'd ever seen. They looked like yellow clouds, sprinkled with some green flakes. I mentally searched my fridge inventory but hadn't a clue what the green could be. Didn't matter. The first taste made me wonder what the hell I'd been eating all my life. Certainly hadn't been eggs. Not like these eggs.

"*Ça va*?" he asked after I'd shoveled in a few more bites.

I nodded, but wasn't going to waste breath on talking. Egg clouds. Mercy. The toast even tasted better for reasons that were beyond explanation. Same toaster. Same apple jelly. Just...well, this breakfast had been made for me. With love.

Aww...

Corny? Yep. But tasty? Oh, baby.

Jean-Louis leaned in and kissed my forehead. "Much as I would love to linger in bed with you, I've a nine a.m. class. That gives me half an hour to shower and get my notes together. Perhaps we can share lunch break?"

"Sounds like a plan. Maybe I should cook for you?"

His smirk didn't hide his estimate of my ability to fulfill that fantasy suggestion. "I did see a bag of salad in the fridge," he said. "That'll do. See you at noon?"

"Yes," I said around another bite. "Thank you."

He shed the robe, and the sight of his tight ass paused me from eating. I followed his muscular structure up the landscape of his back to the flex of his shoulder blades as he pulled on the dress shirt. Shirt first. I liked that. And his cock was at half-mast, which bobbed under the length of the shirt hem.

Who cared about clouds of eggs?

"Eggs must be eaten quickly or they will cool," he said with a wink over his shoulder. "My pants are out in the living room. *A bientôt*, Hollie."

That meant: see you soon. I forked in another cloud as he strolled out of the room. A few minutes later my front door opened and closed. Only four hours until I could see him again for a lunch break. I supposed I should try to fit some work in there as well.

This relationship was going to dig into my work time. Which sounded not at all bad. But I did need to support myself.

I finished the last egg cloud and crunched the perfectly toasted bread, then swung my legs over the side of the bed. If I could get lost in work, the time would fly.

ÅÅÅ

That afternoon Hollie left after we'd washed the plates in the sink. The bag of salad she'd brought over had served a sufficient lunch. I'd spritzed some lemon juice, olive oil, and cracked pepper on it for a touch of flavor. And when I'd felt the desire to make love to her—because her giggle set off some kind of Pavlovian sex bell in my brain—I'd eyed the clock. Ten minutes until my IT class resumed. I was on a tight schedule this week, teaching an online class from nine to six daily. So I'd kissed her and promised to see her after work.

She'd said something about working a while then taking the afternoon to put together the bookshelves she'd ordered from Amazon. I hadn't too much hope for her mechanical skills, but she did tend to surprise me.

During an afternoon break, I brewed coffee, strong—what I craved was an espresso—and checked my schedule for fencing classes. I had one student this month, which came in on Thursday evenings. He was my age and he was doing it more for the exercise following a car accident, to strengthen his thigh and calf muscles, and he was proving a quick learn.

When six o'clock flashed on my laptop, I assigned my students reading for the night, and bid them *au revoir* until tomorrow.

I stood and stretched my arms over my head, then did a few fencing lunges that pulled at my leg muscles, as well as my back. Sitting before the computer all day worked hell on my body. I did try to stand often, but when doing so, I tended to pace and walk out of view of the webcam.

I should step out for a jog. I changed into some running pants and shoes and checked out the window. Dark already, and looking chilly. I pulled a sweatshirt over the T-shirt then headed out, intent on running around Les Invalides. The military museum boasted great running aisles and green parks.

An hour later I headed home, paralleling the Seine, and by the time I knocked on Hollie's door my heart rate had slowed and I was feeling the stretch from the run. Nothing was better than a good workout.

Except sex.

The door opened. A hand reached out and grabbed me by my shoulders. Hollie's green eyes were wide and...desperate?

"Help me," she pleaded.

The emergency was in Hollie's bedroom. She wasn't bleeding or gasping for breath. Instead, she tugged me to the center of the room where boards and screws lay strewn on the hardwood floor. I quickly assessed that should directions be followed correctly, perhaps a bookshelf would result from the scattered ephemera.

"You are having a time of it," I said to her.

"I've been working on this all afternoon."

"Really?" I bent and picked up the instructions sheet written in English. Only eight points to the assembly. It couldn't be that difficult.

"I'm lousy with a screwdriver," Hollie admitted. "I had to actually run out to buy that one. And I bought the wrong one, the one with a cross shape on the end, so I had to return for a straight one."

Chuckling, I knelt before the boards and tugged off the sweatshirt. I could have this assembled in no time, but I was hungry.

Brandishing the screwdriver, I offered, "I will rescue you."

Hollie wrapped her arms about my neck and kissed me. Her hair smelled like vanilla and the brush of her breasts against my back lured me to turn and kiss under her chin then down her neck.

"All I ask in reward," I said, "is you feed me."

"I'll need to run out for groceries."

"Why don't you run down to the bistro around the corner?" I dug in my pocket and pulled out the leather wallet. From inside I plucked two twenty euro bills and handed them to her.

"Oh, I can't take that." She shooed the money at me.

Americans. They had this thing about accepting help that annoyed we French.

"Hollie." I grabbed her hand and slapped the money into her palm. "Bring me food."

"But I really can't take your—"

"Kiss me," I demanded.

Startled by my tone, she blinked and then did as I'd commanded. Mm, she tasted like tea and her hair tickled down my cheek.

"Now, you stuff that money in your purse and go out and forage for your lover, *oui*?"

"*Oui*." But, caught in a dazed grin of pleasure, she didn't move.

"*Allez vou*!"

She shook out of the daze and nodded. "Right. I must feed my big, strong man. I'm off!"

I chuckled as she headed out, leaving me behind to flex my biceps. Oh yes, I was her big, strong man. And even if she'd said it playfully, I took it to heart. I couldn't remember the last time a woman had complimented me. Was that the reason I had so quickly fallen for Hollie? Did she feed some sort of need for reassurance that brewed within my soul?

Hell, where had those thoughts come from? I was here to save the day for my pretty girlfriend. And she adored me.

All was well.

AAA

A week later, I had organized the bookshelves. I kept fiction in the bedroom, and the six shelves were only a quarter filled. I'd have no problem filling them up before the end of next year. Out in the living room I'd organized the non-fiction according to the Dewey Decimal System because, yeah, I'm a geek like that. Didn't matter that I only had the History, Natural Science, Mythology and Travel categories at the moment. Four shelves were filled with travel guides (mostly Paris), historical costumes, and gorgeous Dorling Kindersley guides to bugs and beetles.

Jean-Louis had been impressed with my collection of French history, and he'd browsed and then borrowed a volume written by Oliver Bernier about Paris in the 18th century.

Sharing books with my lover was some kind of all right. (As a reader, you understand.) But how often does it happen in real life that you pair up with someone who was equally as interested in words? I'd found a man who shared my love for books, and with whom I could discuss my latest read over coffee at breakfast, or as we strolled along the Seine feeding sunflower seeds to the pigeons.

Life had become idyllic. I couldn't argue it, and I wouldn't.

And as if to spread frosting to life's delicious cake, it was snowing big, gentle, fluffy flakes outside my window. Sure, it would probably melt because it was still too warm to last, but that didn't mean I wasn't excited for the afternoon walk Jean-Louis had called to invite me on earlier. He'd said he would stop in and choose my clothing, so I should stay in my robe until he arrived. I wasn't about to question that mysterious invite. In fact, I reveled in the subtle domination he exerted at times.

I tugged the thin yellow silk robe tight because the tiny apartment was drafty in the wintertime, and I'd yet to invest in a space heater to place beside the bed. The apartment was cool because the windows were so big. But I wouldn't trade those floor-to-ceilings for more warmth any day.

Life may have been drastically different for me if not for those windows.

Strolling into the bathroom, I brushed my teeth for the second time today. I'd eaten a garlicky vinaigrette on my lunch salad. My hair looked...passable. In the growing-out phase, it was finally dipping below my shoulders and actually had a wave to it thanks to the thickness. Chestnut brown, and not a gray strand yet.

I crossed myself in thanks for that because my female relatives generally went completely gray by age forty. My mother had boldly resisted dying her gorgeous platinum locks, and had looked like one of those older models with the flowy, long silver hair.

Please don't let those Scandinavian roots take hold in my scalp, I whispered to whatever color gods would listen. I made a mental note to say a prayer for color longevity next time I was in Nôtre Dame. Yes, I have my moments of vanity.

Inside the medicine cabinet, my fingers waggled before a few tiny vials of essential oil perfumes. I rarely wore them because my vanilla bath salts generally did the trick. Today I decided to go for a change and selected the clove-spiced-chocolate scent called Vixen. A tap of fragrance to my neck, and there, between my breasts.

A rap at the door rushed me around to answer it. I fell into Jean-Louis's kiss but quickly pulled away as my hands slid over the rough gray wool coat he wore. Nickel buttons dotted the lapels and queued down the front in a military style.

"This is...different."

"My winter coat. It is chilly today."

"It's thirty degrees."

"Like I said, *brrrrrr*." He made show of shivering and closed the door behind him.

I wanted to laugh. I shouldn't laugh. As a hearty Midwestern girl, I didn't start to shiver until the mercury dropped below zero. Heck, I wore sandals until the snow fell, and I can't remember when I last wore a winter cap (Because you know, it's all about protecting the coif; frozen ears bedamned).

Paris rarely neared the single digits, and it was early, I admit, for such low temps before Christmas. But he did look handsome in the long coat that skimmed his thighs. Black leather gloves and a gray- and blue-striped scarf at his neck finished the look.

"You're like some kind of GQ model, you know that?"

"You are the only woman I want to stare at my pictures then."

The texture of the leather gloves gliding up and over my breasts hardened my nipples and I pressed myself against the rough weave of the coat and tilted my head to catch the kiss he delivered to my neck. His nose was still cool and it tickled my skin.

"Mm, you smell different. Spiced chocolates?"

"You like it?"

A long, sucking kiss below my jaw answered that one nicely. He peeled away the robe and I let it fall away, slinking down my legs to the floor, leaving me naked and he dressed for the Snowpocalypse.

Clinging to the front of his wool coat, I tilted my head as his kisses drew a hot trail down my clavicle and to a nipple, where he sucked it hard. My entire body curled up against his, as if it wanted to become a part of him. Could I? Could I crawl up under the coat and melt into him? Infuse myself into his being?

He lifted me, his mouth still at my breast, and carried me into the bedroom. When I landed on the bed, his gloved hands pushed down my wrists and pinned them to the down comforter near my shoulders. I felt small and bare beneath this fully dressed man. It was a sexy kind of vulnerability that arched my back. I cooed teasingly, and lured him to tend the other nipple.

I hummed deep in my throat, and my legs wrapped about his hips, encumbered by the coat. Thrusting up my hips, I rubbed my bare mons against the rough wool. Ridiculously wet, and squirming against the restraints he maintained at my wrists, I gasped, "Yes, please. Fuck me, Jean-Louis."

"I thought we were going for a walk?"

"Just a quickie? Don't take off your coat. I want you like this."

"Well, I have plans..." His tongue lashed my nipple and I cooed in reaction.

"Plans?" Oh, God, let me get off. It wouldn't take long. My pussy hummed and the harder I rubbed against him, the closer orgasm loomed. "Wait. Don't tell me your plans. Just..."

Another deep, lingering suck at my nipple pulled my back off the bed as I sought his intense ministrations. I gyrated my hips up against him and had succeeded in moving aside the coat. Beneath, the tailored trousers rubbed my clit, which was thick and swollen, wet with need.

"Come," he whispered at my ear.

And that simple word, issued on a hush, and followed with a lash of tongue over my nipple, set me off.

"I am," I murmured as the dizzying crash of success burst like a mini explosion in my groin. It wasn't one of those earth-shattering, shouting kind of orgasms, but rather, an exquisite, finely-honed spark of pure pleasure. "Oh, yes."

I wriggled beneath him and he dropped my wrists so I was able to reach up and pull him down, and not quite force, but certainly push his head lower. He tongued my clit, and that was all it took for a second burst to buck my hips.

Panting, I gripped his hair and pulled up his head. He winked. "Is good?"

"Is good."

ÅÅÅ

I have never selected the clothing with which I wished my lover to adorn herself. Hollie had...not a lot of clothing on hangers. The majority was strewn over the easy chair in her bedroom and on the floor. But she seemed to know what was where in each of the piles. I did appreciate that she'd hung the lace dress I'd purchased for her.

"This one," I said, dangling a red wrap dress that appeared thigh length (easy to lift up) and light and loose. "And you've a long winter coat?"

She fluttered about the bedroom, her cheeks still flushed from the orgasm I'd given her on the bed. Like a butterfly flitting into the red dress and then pulling her wings closed to cinch before her waist, she smiled and retrieved a knee-length coat from the rack. Perfect.

I stood beside her after she'd pulled on the coat. The wool coat I wore was the same length, but it was a little big for me, which was also perfect. I'd wrapped a blue scarf about the lapels, and Hollie pulled it off and threaded it around her neck. I liked it better there. And I adored it when she pushed the fabric to her nose to smell it.

"I love wearing you on me," she said. "Where are we going?"

"For a walk on *la rive droite*. You up for a surprise?"

She nodded eagerly. I leaned in to kiss her eyelid because those bright blue eyes flashed up at me like a puppy ready for play. I had some play in mind for her that she might protest, so I intended to keep the plan under wraps until she guessed it.

It had snowed last night, and some of the sidewalks had been shoveled, while others I gripped Hollie's hand and we walked on the street to avoid slipping. Once we reached the Eiffel Tower everything was cleared. I picked up in the middle of a Fallout Boy tune and Hollie hummed along with me, casting me a knowing glance as we crossed a street hand in hand.

"I adore you," she said.

"Why? Because we like the same songs?"

"Yes. And because you're so good to me." She tugged the scarf up around her neck.

"You cold?"

She snuggled up closer. "Nope. Got my big, strong Frenchman to keep me warm. Oh! Look at the Tuileries!"

The royal gardens lie across the bridge, and the espaliered trees, bare of summer leaves, glittered with hoar frost.

"It's like a faery land." Hollie rushed ahead, and I lingered, content to set *mon abeille* free.

If she knew my plans, she might grow anxious. We'd once mentioned our secret fantasy places for where we'd like to have sex. At the time, I had sensed she would be reluctant to play out my fantasy. As was I reluctant to have sex in the snow with her. I didn't think my cock could withstand the cold. Then again, if I owned a cottage in the countryside in which to indulge the winter sex foray, then why not give it a go? I am generally up for anything.

Thinking of which, I must check in with my lawyer regarding the divorce situation. I needed those papers signed. Now. I intended to start shopping around for some land, perhaps with a chateau already on it, but couldn't do that until all ties to the wife had been severed. With a machete.

Why was she making this so difficult?

Because she could. And because I was learning (too late) that she was a greedy bitch.

I didn't think Hollie would ever act as my wife was now. But what man could completely know a woman? I had fun with Hollie. We had great sex. I enjoyed being with her and talking for hours. But it had also begun that way with my wife.

I realized I was clutching my coat right over my heart. What the hell? It hurt to go through this business of tearing apart what I'd once thought was going to be forever. I think... Yes, I know, my wife had broken me. Ripped out my heart and slashed it with her bright red nails.

It did help to have Hollie's brightness in my life to counter that heartache. Hollie made me smile again. But if I thought about it too much, I might decide it was wrong. Was it fair to Hollie? Was she my rebound woman? Could I *have* a rebound woman while still legally married? Did she consider herself the other woman? She was an affair, to be sure.

I wanted more. At this moment in time, when the woman I loved was pointing out the sparkling snow-dusted trees to me, trying to get my attention by jumping and waving her hands, I wanted all of her.

Yes, I did love her because she was a little crazy. Not psycho crazy, more like sexyfuncrazy. And that made my heart relax, and I was able to breathe into this affair.

"Were you lost?" she asked as I approached and wrapped an arm about her waist. She kissed my cheek. A cool morsel. "You didn't see me."

"I was thinking."

"Good, bad, or ugly thoughts?"

I shrugged. "Eh."

"Don't give me that Frenchman's excuse."

"Frenchman's excuse?"

"Yeah. It's that 'eh' you do. You and your ilk are masters at it. Tell me what you were thinking about?"

I clasped her hand and directed her toward the Louvre, the former royal palace that paralleled the vast gardens. "I was thinking how this divorce is dragging on and I wish it was over."

"Oh."

I'd known she didn't want to hear that. But it wasn't as though I could always shelter her from my messy situation. It felt oddly deceptive to not tell her about it. And I didn't like deception. Lies and mistruths burned like the devil's pitchfork in my soul.

"After the divorce, I want to start looking for land about an hour out of Paris," I said.

"Really? To move to permanently?"

"Maybe. If I can find a chateau, perhaps. But it could serve as a weekend home or summer retreat."

"Sounds decadent."

"Earlier, I was thinking about your fantasy of having sex in the snow. If I owned a chateau...well then."

"Sexy snow angels! My halo would be huge. Oh, and your angel would have a penis dangling between its legs."

"I should hope so."

In a burst of laughter, Hollie tugged me onward. We took the concrete stairs up from the garden to street level and crossed in the middle of the street because there was surprisingly little traffic. The museum was slower in the afternoon; that is why I'd specifically chosen this time.

"We're going into the Louvre?" Hollie asked. "And you're talking about sex fantasies. Oh. No."

She stopped walking and her shoulders visibly dropped. I clutched her hand reassuringly and kissed the back of it.

Her eyes sought mine. "Are we going to...?"

I tried a sweet shrug with a smile. She bit the corner of her lip. Nervous? Or scared to death?

Had I gone about this particular surprise the wrong way?

Seven

We entered the much-needed warmth of the museum beneath the glass pyramid in the main courtyard called the Cour Napoléon. The pyramid was completed in 1989, and hadn't been a huge hit with the Parisians for its juxtaposition of the ultra-modern within the historic architecture. I thought it was gorgeous, and in the summertime, the clouds reflecting on the sun-infused glass created a fantasy facade.

I wasn't surprised the museum was dead, only a few dozen patrons milling about when normally there were lines. But I couldn't focus on our luck.

Jean-Louis had brought me here to have sex. In front of the Mona Lisa. Because that was his fantasy. And I do recall agreeing to accompany him on said quest to achieve that particular fantasy only because, at the time, I'd thought it would never happen.

Now here I stood, clutching his hand so I wouldn't go down. Because really? Sex in the Louvre? With people milling about? And guards in practically every room watching the people?

"Hollie?" he whispered at my ear. "Are you okay?"

He'd asked the same of me that first night we'd met in person at the All Saints Day party. "I..."

I was going to be sick.

No! I would not let nerves ruin this...this adventure. Right? This could be an adventure. The vixen within me was jumping for joy at such a prospect. Covert sex with a gorgeous Frenchman in the most famous museum in the world? Go, super crazy live-for-the-moment me!

Soon enough, the introvert in me would join in and get on board.

Maybe?

"Let's wander," Jean-Louis suggested. He tugged his coat open and led the way.

I didn't say a thing. He'd flashed his museum card and paid for me since I hadn't thought to bring along my purse, in which, I did have a museum card. I simply smiled and allowed him to take the lead. I didn't want to ruin this for him. It would be fun. Daring. Sexy!

Oh, mercy. I clutched each end of his scarf, snuggled about my neck, and focused on the delicious sable scent of him wafting from the fabric.

"We don't have to do it," he said as we strolled the wide marble hallways. His heels clicked, and my boot heels tread a muted thud in bass harmony to his. "It was something I thought would be fun. That's why I wore the long coat."

Oh. My. God. And that's why he'd selected my clothes. The wrap dress and the long coat. I realized now he'd picked things that would be easy to access—no panties!—and yet, would also—hopefully—conceal.

Such a sneaky Frenchman.

He tugged me near a wall and clasped my hands and kissed the cool knuckles. Yes, I was still cold. I wasn't sure I'd ever warm up because my blood had stopped pumping out of fear.

His kiss was like a Godiva truffle sitting in the middle of a Target-brand chocolate box. Unexpected. Such a treat. Something I'd never share with anyone. Melty and warm, and I wanted more, more and more.

I leaned against him, and he tilted his hips forward so I could feel his hard-on beneath the thin trousers. Oh my God, I actually wanted to do this. To feel him inside me while standing here, in a public place. I could do it right here. Turn around and lean back against him while he slipped up my dress and slid inside me. To any who passed by, we'd look like a couple embracing, standing off to the side after a long day walking the museum.

But his fantasy was to do it with the Mona Lisa watching. In a small, brightly-lit room that afforded no safe walls with which to lean against to hide our stolen liaison. And I knew there was always at least one guard in the room, if not more.

"I want you," I whispered. My introvert cringed. *What the hell!*

"I always want you. I won't force you to do anything, Hollie. You know you are safe with me."

I nodded. He was a good man. And that's why I wanted to do this for him. And it wasn't as though the thrill of danger and getting caught didn't appeal. A tiny part of me was already hiking up my skirt for him. It was my vixen. I did adore her.

Ok, so I'd let her out to play.

"Let's go see what the Mona Lisa is up to." I pulled him down the hallway in the direction where I knew the famous painting hung.

I am not an overtly sexually-adventurous woman. Yeah, so I had sex in windows with complete strangers (just the one stranger; and we were dating now). And yes, I'd done the cyber sex thing, as well. Again, only with Jean-Louis. So maybe this was a natural step toward fortifying that relationship and keeping it fresh?

Did we need fresh? We'd only been together a few months. Hell, we shouldn't go stale for many more months, am I right? I confess, I wasn't sure regarding the shelf life of relationship freshness. I'd been a serial one-month dater since I'd moved to Paris.

And did I need to have public sex to please my man? I didn't want to be one of those women who felt if they didn't do a certain thing then they would lose their man's interest. I wanted to do things for him because it made me feel good to, in turn, make him feel good.

We entered the room that featured the painting, the sight of which always initially startled me. The "Mona Lisa" by Leonardo da Vinci was so famous, and I saw it often in books, magazines, TV shows, even movies. It's larger than life. Except, it's not, really. It's a small painting. Her dimensions are less than two feet by three feet. Much smaller than one would expect for an icon.

And the thing that always struck me as funny was that it's exhibited in a room along with the largest painting in the Louvre. It threw a person's perspective into overdrive to turn and look upon "The Wedding at Cana" by Paolo Veronese.

I clasped my lover's hand to prevent him from venturing into the small crowd of about two dozen people who lingered before the famous Italian chick who had teased art lovers for centuries in wonder over her relationship with da Vinci. A guard was posted to her left, and his eyes scanned the crowd. He motioned to a woman who held up her cell phone, determined to snap a pic. She dropped her hand, but I suspected she would wait for the guard's inattention and then quickly claim proof that she had seen the famed portrait.

Turning around, and clasping Jean-Louis's hand, I strolled closer to the massive painting on the wall opposite the Mona Lisa. No one noticed this painting until after their encounter with the Mona Lisa, and most simply raced out, their goal achieved, on to McDonalds for celebratory cheeseburgers and cokes.

"I've always wondered how he painted that," I said. The massive image featured a wedding feast in Cana with Jesus as a guest of honor. It was stretched over a canvas measuring twenty-two by thirty-two feet. "On a ladder? With the canvas on the ground and him crawling all over it? Or did he have an inordinately long paintbrush?"

"I love it when you think too much, Hollie."

His hand slid along my thigh and I felt my coat inch up. The man was so going for it. And I stiffened, craning my gaze over my shoulder. The guard before the Mona Lisa was answering a question posited by one of the patrons. An elder couple walked before me, brushing my elbow. I sucked in a breath.

No, lingered at the back of my tongue. But the word felt wrong. I trusted Jean-Louis. Heartbeats thundered as his fingers grazed my bare ass. I sensed his wool coat fell over my thigh and forward, concealing his actions. I hoped it did, anyway.

"Stop me," he whispered. "If you must."

I shook my head, but couldn't find voice. Anxiety wiggled my fingers, so I clasped them to my chest then tilted my head to catch his kiss against my ear. Did we look like a couple embracing? Oh, mercy, I felt his erection land on my ass. Hot and solid and—oh, baby.

He groaned and one of his hands spread across my stomach. I scooched my feet apart more, and subtly tilted my hips to spread my thighs.

I made eye contact with the guard. He knew. He had to know. He glanced to the right. Maybe he didn't know.

I slapped down one hand, catching Jean-Louis's arm. But at that moment I felt his cock enter me. *OhmyGod*. We were doing this. And I was bent forward slightly, as if I wanted to get it on. But oh...that feeling of him entering me, having to push a little to fit his bulging head inside me and then the glide of him seeking the darkness that filled us with such exquisite sensation.

Everyone was watching us. All cameras were pointed at the lewd couple by the doorway. *Flash, flash, flash!*

No. I wouldn't let my imagination ruin this one.

Oh, fuck me, he was so hot. A moan tickled at the back of my throat, so I bit my lip. A shimmy of pleasure sparkled under my skin. You know, the inexplicable tingle of giddiness that could only be described as sexsparkle.

I righted, and felt his cock slip from me.

The guard tilted his head, his eyes finding mine. I managed a smile, and then turned my head to whisper to Jean-Louis. Nothing going on here, just a conversation while my lover embraced me—and pushed his oh-so-wanting penis inside me. I felt it again glide in easily because I was wet. Really? I didn't know how that was possible with the nerves, but this time he made it in and pumped once. Twice.

"The guard sees us," I hissed.

"Perhaps. Fuck, you are so hot."

Behind Jean-Louis, someone bumped into him and apologized. "*Excuse moi.*"

I gaped, stunned that this was happening. At the same time, how awesome was this? I was having public sex! It felt—well, rushed. And not so intimate. Kind of nerve-wracking.

And then I discovered a moment of utter connection. As if we were alone in the vast universe. Attendants at the Cana wedding who had decided to rejoice in the celebration by enjoying one of their own making. The guard's eyes had shifted to someone holding a camera high to take a shot of the Mona Lisa.

La Joconde was watching us with that irrepressibly mysterious grin.

Jean-Louis gasped near my ear. "*Merci, mon abeille.*" And then I felt the hot gush as he came inside me. Seriously. The man came with but two pumps. Exhibitionism must be his thing.

He slipped from me and I felt him adjusting his pants and zipping behind me, well concealed by his coat. I tugged down my coat and then pressed my thighs together. Ah shit.

Jean-Louis grabbed my hand and we hastily headed out, but I had to sort of crabwalk, trying to keep my thighs together. "Wait!"

"We must hurry out," he said. "The deed is done."

"Yes, but..."

"What is the problem, Hollie?"

I pushed him toward the wall and he covered me in an embrace, finding my gaze and looking as if I might have actually committed a crime.

"You are dripping down my thigh," I whispered as I kissed the corner of his mouth. "I need something to wipe it off or the walk home won't be pleasant. And it could prove embarrassing. I can't believe you actually came."

"It was thrilling. It was not so for you, I could sense that."

"No," I rushed out. "I kind of liked it. It freaked me out, but I'm glad you got off. Ohh...it's almost to my knee."

He tugged the blue scarf from around my neck then snuck it up under my skirt. I hugged him, looking to the side. If the passing patrons knew what we'd just done.

What we had just done!

Okay, I was marking today a success, even if, as I'd said, it had freaked the hell out of me.

With a few swipes, Jean-Louis cleaned my thigh. He rolled up the scarf and stuffed it in his pocket.

"Don't forget that there," I said.

"Not something I want the dry cleaners to find. I'll do laundry later. You good now?"

I nodded and kissed his mouth. I kissed him long and deep. I wasn't shaking anymore. I was flushed with exhilaration and a strange kind of accomplishment. And knowing I had helped him to achieve a fantasy he'd desired, notched up all those feelings double-time.

"I adore you," I said into his mouth as the kiss ended. "Even when you surprise me with the scary stuff."

"You find my penis scary?"

"Not at all. But your penis in the Louvre is...unexpectedly anxiety producing."

"I'll grant you that. I suppose we'll have to find a snowbank and have sex on the way home?"

"Let's shelve that one for a more private venue."

"Works for me." He kissed me once. Twice. And I hugged up against his body heat. "I love you, Hollie."

And I almost answered with the same sentiment, but...didn't.

Eight

We picked up produce and fish on the way to Hollie's apartment. I was in the mood for pan-seared salmon. She didn't have any cooking sherry in her poorly stocked cupboards, but I figured the moscato might give it a sweet kick. I directed her to make a salad with the spinach, walnuts and feta, and promised to teach her an easy vinaigrette in a few minutes.

I tended to slip into chef mode when in the kitchen. It was the counterbalance to the analytical side that oftentimes ruled my brain. I couldn't get away from work, and studied the latest IT trends even when lying in bed with a book in hand. I always had a new computer manual loaded onto the ereader for traveling, and uh...bathroom reading.

Don't judge me because I do guy things.

A pair of hands slid around my torso and Hollie hugged me from behind. "That smells delicious," she said.

"Two more minutes on the flip side and *voila*! You have the salad ready?"

"As requested. Uh..." She twirled to lean against the counter and face me. "Just so you know, I am on the pill."

I winked and prodded the salmon with a two-pronged fork. "I assumed as much. But thank you for telling me. I should have asked sooner. I am usually more responsible."

"You've enough to worry about lately. It occurred to me, as you were dripping down my leg in the Louvre, that I was safe. We are safe. Until we don't want to be."

I tilted my head at that comment. But I didn't want to address it. Because, yes, I did have enough to worry me lately. To consider unprotected sex wasn't on my radar.

"Let me set out some plates," she said.

I managed to grab one of her hands as she pulled away, and tugged her back to kiss her on the nose. "Thanks for going along with the fantasy this afternoon. You could have told me no, and I would have been fine with that."

"I could have. But I think I secretly wanted it more than you. I was so freaked, but also, I made eye contact with the guard when you were inside me."

"And?"

"I think he knew. And I *liked* that he knew." She pressed her palms together before her mouth and gazed up at me. "How weird is that?"

"Vixen." I kissed her eyebrow. "Go." And the other eyebrow. "Set the table. And later, I'll make sure you get your just reward for participating in the adventure."

"I like the sound of that."

Plates clattered as she set the table, and I didn't hear my mobile ringing in the winter coat I'd tossed across the chaise until Hollie pointed it out. I rushed for the phone. It was a weekday, and I was always on call for work-related stuff. Being the boss made that unavoidable.

I shouldn't have answered that call.

AAA

Jean-Louis's voice softened as he spoke, and I paused as the salad bowl clinked onto the tabletop. On the stovetop, the fish sizzled. My mouth watered. And I did want to learn how to make the vinaigrette. But I was compelled to tilt my head to catch the one-sided conversation not fifteen feet away from me.

His tone hardened and he swore in French. Out of the corner of my eye I could see him pace the length between the chaise and the front door. He looked up, and our eyes met. He gestured with a sweepingly dismissive hand. Don't mind me, the gesture seemed to say.

But I couldn't *not* mind him. The man grew angrier with every word he spoke. And now he'd switched to using all French. When the door opened and he stepped out into the hallway, I decided he'd wanted the privacy.

Yeah, so I was a snoop. But it hadn't sounded like something from work. To get him that angry? On the other hand, I knew nothing about his work. And certainly there were situations in the workplace that could push anyone to swear.

I swung into the kitchen and turned the burner down so the salmon wouldn't overcook. It was probably done. I had no clue. The only time I'd attempted to make fish had been helping my mother fry up walleyes after a family fishing trip. And I had been nine, so guess how much I'd actually done?

I crept around the fridge and glided my fingers over the silverware on the table as I strolled into the living room. Through the large floor-to-ceiling windows to my right, I suddenly noticed something on the street below.

"What's he—?"

Jean-Louis was crossing the street, phone to his ear, and one fist beating the air before him. He paused before his building, still shaking that fist. The concierge opened the door.

"Seriously? What has gotten him so upset?"

To have walked out on our dinner like that?

He entered the building, and I furrowed my brows like a good little disappointed girlfriend. Hmm...

Hands to my hips, I wandered into the kitchen. Okay, so there might have been a touch of a stomp to my steps. That was the rudest he'd ever been to me. I'm sure it wasn't his fault. Whoever was on the other side of his phone conversation was the real villain.

Did I want to know who it was?

I clasped my arms across my chest, hugging myself. Parts of me were curious, but another, deeper, more knowing part was fearful. Could it be her? The wife? The God-damn-it-when-would-she-sign-the sucking-divorce-papers-and-let-him-be-free wife?

I pushed the frying pan to the back burner and turned off the heat. The salmon smelled crazy good. He'd sprinkled rosemary and pepper in the mix and, mmm... My stomach growled.

A darkness inside me curved my mouth down and I clutched a fist against my chest. Had he cooked for *her* like this?

Of course, he must have. The man had once loved her. Enough to marry her. I'd quickly come to learn that one of Jean-Louis's ways of showing love was through cooking. He may have created this very meal for her.

I didn't want to eat it now. And not because he'd had a life before meeting me and had treated women as well as he did me. I should appreciate that fact about him. When in a relationship he gave his all. What woman didn't want that from a man?

Was he going to return?

I stepped over to the window and peered across the street. It was never easy to see into his living room area. Just too far off, and the night darkened everything. Sometimes when his TV was on, I could see that bright little light. No light on in his bedroom, either.

I sighed. "Disastrous end to a perfect day."

Every relationship had its disappointments. I shouldn't take it so hard. I should stop thinking about this because I'd have us on the brink of a breakup the more my brain stirred about with the imagined possibilities.

I sat at the table and eyed the salad. Without the vinaigrette, I didn't want to eat it.

"Oh, stop pouting and grow up," I muttered. Whatever had prompted him to leave without a word was important to him. So in turn, I should honor that. "Right."

My flail into a tantrum was officially over. I dished some salad onto my plate, and then commandeered the parmesan-pepper dressing from the fridge which Jean-Louis had poo-pooed as 'full of added sugar'. I managed to eat a few bites of the salmon because it was ridiculous to waste good, hot food. And oh, it was melt-in-my-mouth delicious.

When my cell phone rang, I dashed for it. Jean-Louis apologized for his abrupt departure.

"I am so sorry," he said again. "My lawyer called with information about..."

About the divorce proceedings.

"The thing is, she is going out of town for the holidays and says she won't have time to review the changes until after she returns."

She, being the wife neither of us wished to name. My heart dropped to my gut and landed in a soggy, sugary bed of spinach.

"The holidays are weeks away," he continued angrily. "She is doing this to piss me off. And it worked. I am no longer in the mood to eat. I have a student coming over soon anyway."

"You can come over after that," I said. "I'll warm your supper up for—"

"Hollie, no! I said I am in no mood. Do you understand?"

His admonishing tone gave me a shiver. "Yes. Sorry."

I'd never felt smaller. Like a child who had been chastised for accidentally breaking the good china.

"I will see you tomorrow." The connection clicked off. Just like that. No goodbye, *au revoir*, or even an, I love you. I actually stared at the glossy surface of the phone for a few seconds, thinking maybe it had been accidentally cut off and his name would flash back on the screen with a re-call.

Alas.

Tossing the cell phone to the chaise, I wrapped my arms across my chest and hugged my biceps. Bowing my head, I felt a hot tear touch my skin. It wasn't so much his anger that hurt me, but that he'd directed his irritation at me when it had nothing to do with me.

That was rational thinking.

The irrational part of me remembered the chocolate truffles we'd bought for dessert. I headed for the fridge, intending to show no mercy to anything sweet.

AAA

I clicked off my mobile and tossed it onto the leather sofa. It bounced off a computer manual and clattered onto the floor. Really? If the call hadn't been misery enough, now I may have destroyed the mobile.

I couldn't force myself to investigate. Instead, I swung around and grabbed a practice foil from the hook on the wall. I slashed it through the air before me, executing a brisk riposte on an invisible opponent. The sound of the blade cutting the air was satisfying, especially when accompanied by a guttural growl and a hissing curse.

The bitch was going on holiday and she didn't have time to read through the changes I had made to the divorce documents. Changes made to please her. She would look at them when she returned in the New Year.

The damned holidays were yet weeks away! She was playing with me. And her lawyer was allowing it. And my lawyer—

"*Merde*!"

I slammed the foil against the back of the sofa. It didn't cut, the aluminum blade was not honed and the tip was covered with a plastic cap to prevent injury. I wished I had a practice dummy. I'd rip off the plastic cap and stab that bastard again, and again, and...

"Fuck it." I tossed the foil to the floor and it clattered up against the wall.

Running fingers through my hair, I gripped and pulled at my temples. A glance out the window spied the darkened windows of the building across the street. I'd left Hollie without saying goodbye, without eating. And I'd been rude to her on the phone.

But if I'd spoken to her any longer I would have sworn and probably called my ex-wife a bitch out loud. Hollie did not deserve my anger directed toward her. It was best I showered and prepared for the fencing class. I wasn't going to climb out of this twist of anger any time soon.

My wife was making everything so difficult.

I hated calling her wife, or even thinking the label. Bitch was a crude term that only emerged with my anger. I felt guilty for using it. But that guilt felt good, and it provided catharsis when I needed to vent vocally.

The mobile rang, and I dashed to it, glad to find the glass screen was not cracked from the fall. It was a text message from my student. He was cancelling because of a family emergency.

Just as well. I pushed the *off* button and connected the mobile to the recharge dock in the kitchen. I'd make it up to Hollie tomorrow. And hope she didn't hold it against me like a certain woman was expert at doing.

"Bitch," I muttered yet again. Couldn't help it.

I marched down the hallway, ripping off my shirt and tossing it to the floor. I hit the shower with a yell, a cathartic release of voice. And I punctuated that sound with a pound of my fists against the slick tile wall. Bowing my head under the shower stream, I closed my eyes and shook my head.

I had never thought to become a part of my own cautionary tale.

Nine

At noon, I Skyped Hollie but she was brisk with me. She'd taken a last-minute shift at the map shop and wouldn't be home until late because after work she planned to meet a girlfriend at Angelina.

I was disappointed I wouldn't see her today, but maybe I deserved the shut out after last night. That whole woman scorned thing was working a number in my life right now. But I didn't suspect Hollie's engagement was anything but normal life, not premeditated to avoid me.

Maybe?

I hurried through the afternoon class and got my students set up with reading homework for tomorrow, and then dismissed them an hour early. There were five in the online class, two from Ireland, and three from here in France. They worked for various companies. None was qualified to actually teach virtual machines after this course. I did keep my eye open for possible employees during the classes.

After work, I set out to pick up a single man's dinner. At the wine shop, I selected a particularly dry Zin. I'd worry about finding the right food to match with it as I walked. I strolled the Quai de Conti in the 6th arrondissement, parallel to the Seine and paused before an elite home decor shop that sold furniture from centuries past, and imported knickknacks to take home and set in a corner where they would collect dust.

The featured piece of furniture in the window caught my eye. It was gray velvet and tufted, the color similar to the chaise in Hollie's living room. And it was huge and round.

"She would love that."

She certainly hadn't the room for it at her place.

"But I do."

I strolled inside and purchased the piece. And since the driver was in, they would deliver it today. I couldn't wait to see Hollie's reaction.

ꓥꓥꓥ

The crowd at Angelina made the line stretch down the sidewalk, and our wait near twenty minutes. Even though the weather was chilly Melanie and I didn't mind. We were bundled with scarves and gloves, and standing close to the building we didn't catch the blustery December wind.

"Where are you spending Christmas?" I asked as we neared the door, eager to finally breach the threshold and stand inside. Though I guesstimated we still had another five minute wait once inside. "Let me guess. Last year it was Greece. The year before, some sandy beach in Morocco. So this year I'm thinking skiing in the Alps?"

"*Cherie*, I hate skiing. I don't like the danger, you know," Melanie said with a flit of her hand that said 'yes, I am a snob and pretty, so suck it' but without any snideness. She was a tall, gorgeous redhead who could attract a man from across the ocean with but a flutter of lash. And she collected lovers the way I collected books. "Burkhardt and I are traveling to Dubai. He promises to buy me whatever catches my eye."

"Which could be diamonds, furs, watches, or a sportscar."

"All of the above!"

We laughed and the doorman signaled that we should enter the building. Melanie swept off her leopard print silk scarf with élan and unbuttoned her coat; shaking her hair over a shoulder with a practiced tilt of head only a model could manage.

"What about you, Hollie? Will you still be sleeping in your sexy Frenchman's bed by Christmas?"

"I hope so," I said without thinking.

Her raised eyebrow only made me jealous of how perfectly tweezed it was, and that I would never manage such a gorgeous arch.

"I know what you're thinking," I felt the need to say. "We've been involved since September. Why such a long relationship?"

"Exactly, my dear. You don't want him to think you actually want this thing to get...cozy." She mocked a shiver.

The line moved up quickly, and the hostess gestured we follow her through the elegant but crowded dining room toward the back where we were seated at the wall before an old gilt mirror that reflected Melanie's perfect hair and my wind-blown tangle. I avoided preening and shuffled off my coat before sitting. I already knew what I was ordering, and it wasn't going to be savory or healthy by any means, even if it was suppertime.

One should never waste a trip to Angelina by ordering off the dinner menu.

The waiter handed us menus and told us he'd return. Melanie thanked him in perfect French.

Which reminded me. Jean-Louis had asked me to take a French class. I suppose I should look into that. Next year. I mean, I didn't want to push it. Learning a new language was quite the endeavor. I had to work up to it slowly, be really sure I was in for the experience. And that I wanted to do it for me, not just for him.

Because cozy sounded good to me.

I leaned across the small table and asked Melanie, "What if I'm up for cozy?"

"Oh, *cherie*, no."

"Why not? He's adorable. He loves me. I think I could love him."

"Love doesn't have to last forever. In fact, a few weeks are just right. You can love him like crazy and fuck him as crazily. But you have many years ahead of you, Hollie. And he is married."

She stated it as a finality, and should I be so stupid as to ignore that pertinent detail then woe be unto me.

"You told me the wife is stringing him along with the divorce?"

"Yes." I sighed. "You know, I initially felt like I was the other woman, but the more I think about it, I'm beginning to feel that she is the other woman."

"Interesting."

But she wasn't all that interested. I could tell that from her dismissive tone and her insistent need to make eye contact with the waiter.

He responded quickly, and Melanie touched my wrist before I could order. "I'll do it, she said. Then she proceeded to order us hot chocolates (to-die-for; trust me) and macarons for me (she knew me well) and a fruit tart for her (her excuse to eating healthy because there was fruit nestled in the custard and sugary glaze).

"Hollie, I think you are in danger," Melanie said after the waiter had flitted away. "Are you emotionally involved with this man?"

"Yes."

Simple as that. It had been over two months. Hard not to see the man almost daily—even if some times were only through a window or via a computer screen—without becoming emotionally involved.

"I see." She rapped her glossy red fingernails on the edge of the white linen tablecloth. "Then I wish you well," she said airily. "He is a handsome man. Educated. Successful. I just hope he doesn't break your heart."

"Heartbreak is a two-person enterprise," I suggested. "I don't believe it can ever completely be one person's fault. I am willingly investing my time in him. I have to expect he will do the same. And should his heart change about me then I'll face that when it happens. Not like I haven't been dumped before. And I have dumped a few guys in my lifetime, as well."

"Don't call it dumping, *cherie*. It is merely moving onward. Packing up one's necessities and leaving the heavy baggage behind. One must always walk swiftly away from the past. And flip it the bird when doing so." Her wink relaxed my apprehensions. "So does that mean you and your Frenchman have Christmas plans?"

I wiggled on my seat to think about it. The holiday was only a few weeks away.

"We haven't discussed anything yet. His mother is a world traveler. His father lives in Marseille. I'm not sure if he spends holidays with his family. I'll probably send my dad a card. You know we're not close."

"Family is tedious," Melanie stated. "But be thankful you still have some. And don't ever let the ties between you and your father grow too thin."

"I won't."

I knew Melanie and her parents were estranged because of money. They were rich and they wouldn't give any to their daughter because they wanted her to move home to New York and start a family while Melanie was content to travel the world and collect oodles of lovers. Stupid reason to deny a child financial support. But Melanie didn't need it. She could take care of herself nicely (thank you, sugar daddies).

Now that I thought of it, what would I get Jean-Louis for Christmas? I'd never been big on holidays and exchanging gifts. Okay, that's not entirely true. I loved getting presents. It was the buying presents for others that drove me batty. I was thankful most people liked getting gift cards. Made gift giving less stressful.

And in that moment the perfect gift did come to mind. Oh! I'd have to make a trip to Shakespeare and Company, the famous ex-pat-founded bookstore that sat across the Seine from Nôtre Dame. If my gift idea were to be found, that store might have it.

The treats arrived and I poured a serving of hot chocolate into my white porcelain cup emblazoned with the Angelina logo. It was thicker than my grandma's gravy. And oh, it was delicious topped with the Chantilly cream served on the side in porcelain demi-cups. I bit into a macaron and took a moment to praise the heavens for chocolate.

"Uh, huh," Melanie said from across the table. She held her own thankful vigil. "Here's to chocolate. And love," she offered, putting forth her cup to clank against mine.

Surprised at the toast, I matched hers and offered, "And to hot sex."

"Hallelujah. But not with the assistance of those silly blue pills."

"Blue pills?" I paused mid-bite of another macaron. "You mean to get it up?"

Melanie nodded. "My last lover was a bit older. We were in Berlin a few weeks ago. He took good care of himself and had a great physique, but when we were between the sheets and I was primed and ready..." She leaned forward over the table, lowering her voice, "He excused himself to take a pill. Said he needed it!"

"Wow. Way to kill the moment."

"Right? As if I wasn't enough for him. So he returns to bed with a big grin on his face and says it'll take a bit to get him hard. Meanwhile, I've come down and want to roll over and go to sleep."

"Men. They think sex isn't sex unless they get off. They can't imagine having sex and letting the woman have pleasure. No hard-on? No fun."

"Exactly! And do you know that thing stayed hard for over two hours? Hollie, I can only fake it for so long. Needless to say, I haven't seen him since."

I rolled my eyes. I couldn't imagine being in such a situation. Buzzkill, for sure. "I'm so glad Jean-Louis has evolved."

"Really? He doesn't need to come every time?" Melanie asked with great doubt in her tone. She ladled another cloud of Chantilly cream into her hot chocolate.

"Nope. In fact, sometimes it's all about me."

"Well then, I will not continue to berate you for your tediously lengthy relationship, *cherie*. Sounds like he's a keeper after all. But if he ever brings out the blue pills..." She sighed and tilted back a healthy swallow.

"I'll tell him Melanie would like to have a word or two with him."

"Yes, do that, please. We must stop the insanity, one man at a time."

The two of us laughed over that one, and didn't care that the tables around us were staring. Had they heard our risqué conversation?

If so, I could only hope the old man seated across the table from a younger lover would take our words to heart.

I hadn't seen Jean-Louis yesterday and I missed his sexy smile. As well as his iron-hard abs that undulated like well-oiled machinery as he pumped above me. And his rigid cock. And his throaty groan when he came. And the sparkle in his eyes when he glanced over his shoulder at me while cooking. And the sable rum scent that lived in his pores. And...

Yep, I was over being miffed at him for his abrupt departure during what should have been a romantic dinner for two. The poor man. That wife of his was putting him through hell. And I wanted to know all the details.

Then I didn't want to know anything. Because to know would make me a party to the conflict. And as much as I wanted to know what sort of woman he had fallen in love with and married, I also didn't think it was right to be included in what should strictly be a matter between the couple.

I could tell myself that, but did I buy into it?

Hell no.

I did want the juicy details. And I was thankful for another shift today at the map shop. It kept me from dashing across the street to my lover's loft and drilling him. I didn't even know the wife's name. I didn't want to know it.

Jean-Louis and I had kept our names secret for a month before revealing all. Names were so powerful. And I think if I knew *her* name, it would become an earworm in my brain. She'd haunt me. I didn't need that kind of headache.

Before landing at work, I ventured a block further to Shakespeare and Company and—score! They had exactly what I had hoped to find. The day could not get better. I had found the perfect Christmas gift for my lover. And now I could set that worry aside and concentrate on work.

Hours later, snowflakes fell heavily outside the map shop window. I'd only helped one customer since arriving at noon for my shift. Richard, the shop owner, had sounded rattled, and said he'd be in later, around six, to take over for me. I'd said I could handle a full shift until eight or even ten if the tourist crowd was heavy, but he'd insisted.

Days like today could be maddening if the shop didn't get a few customers every hour. Tourists bustled about on the snowy sidewalks. Photographers captured their opus works of the nearby Nôtre Dame festooned with a white draping of snow, and the *bateaux mouches* even glided up and down the Seine in this weather.

I suppose if you're crazy enough to vacation in Paris in the wintertime, you'd want to do it all, even the hop-on/hop-off bus tours that stopped up the street from the shop. Tourists could get on the bus and hop off at a popular landmark, then get on another bus when they were finished, and do a circuit of the city.

I spied a crazy couple, bundled in winter coats, knit hats, scarves and mittens, sitting on the open top of a bus.

"Must be from Iowa," I muttered, and smiled at my own joke.

Yeah, we Iowans were known to jump in freezing lakes clad in only our swimming suits for the heck of it. We held turkey bowling tournaments on shiny ice rinks. We even ran marathons during blizzards. Because we're cool like that.

I was thankful Paris didn't see as much snowfall as Iowa. And living in the city, I could take the métro anywhere without having to walk out in the elements too far. Life was grand.

Toss in a handsome Frenchman who adored me? I must be living the high life. And please, don't shoot me down. I intended to float on this cloud as long as possible. Even if Melanie poo-pooed the long term relationship. At least my man didn't need a little blue pill to get it up.

Heh.

The afternoon crept by. I had dusted every framed map on the walls, all the stacked upright map files, and even Richard's desk in the back room. The pink eviction letter still sat in his in-box. He'd not said anything to me about it, but when I did the math, I figured he needed to vacate the store before Christmas. Happy Holidays! Not.

I would ask him about it when he showed later. I needed to know that he was going to be okay, that he had finances, a means to survive. He was a good man. I had overlooked the odd pass he'd made at me a few weeks ago. He'd remarked about my tight sweater and sexy shoes, and had stared at my breasts an inordinately long time. I'd marked it off as a bad day. Or maybe he was taking the blue pills, too?

Laughing, I shook my head, and sat down behind the cash register, catching my chin in a palm. The snow had stopped. Street workers shoveled the sidewalk and chattered around the cigarettes hanging out the corners of their mouths.

I laid my head down on my forearm and...dozed.

The shove to my arm woke me like a pitiful movie heroine, hair smushed against my cheek and muttering, "What?"

"Do you often sleep while working, Hollie?"

Richard. Shit. It was never cool to allow the boss to catch you snoozing.

"This is actually the first time it's ever—"

"An explanation isn't necessary," he said in sharp tones that heightened his British accent. "It'll make what I have to say all the easier. No patrons today?"

"A few."

I pulled the sweat-sticky hair from my cheek and tugged down my blouse. Whew! I must have fallen into some REM. I actually felt a little disoriented.

"I don't sleep on the job, Richard. In fact, I got a lot done—"

"I'm going to have to let you go, Hollie."

Arm extended to display the excellent dusting I'd done today, it hung there, caught in the odd moment as I rewound those words through my head.

"What?"

"You're sacked, Hollie. Sorry. Have to do it. Can't have my employees sleeping on the job."

"But I never sleep. Trust me, it was so slow and I was watching them shovel outside, and... You aren't seriously going to fire me because of this?"

He strode into the back room, and I shuffled around the cash register after him. "Richard? Come on, it's almost Christmas. I promise it will never happen—"

He put up a palm, stopping me. I stepped back at the rude dismissal. I'd never seen him act so confrontational. But beyond that, he was just being unkind.

"Is something wrong?" I tried. My eyes veered toward the pink eviction notice. "If you need to talk about it."

"Hollie, please." Richard's shoulders sank, his back to me. When he exhaled heavily, I could feel his pain as a dark cloud entering my heart. He turned, head bowed, and splayed out his hands. "It's not because of you sleeping. It's because..." The man winced.

The tension that tightened his jaw and reddened his face made him look older than his forty-some years.

"It's because you have to close the shop?" I asked.

"Close the— What? Hollie, what are you—? Oh."

"I opened the eviction notice. I'm sorry. I do sometimes open your mail."

He shook his head and gestured curtly with a slice of hand. "I'm handling that. I've had to cut back to two employees. I should be able to manage."

"Oh." And out of the half dozen employees I hadn't made the cut.

My shoulders dropped. As did my heart. Rationally, I knew this wasn't about me. The man had to do what he had to do to survive. Emotionally, I wanted to cry. I'd never been fired before. I'm the exemplary employee who always goes above and beyond. I look forward to employee reviews, knowing I'll get a raise. And the customer *is* always right.

"I tried to get you to leave a few weeks ago," he muttered, unable to make eye contact with me. "When I—er, made the pass at you."

"You—"

Wow. Now that had been sneaky and low. And stupid. I could have filed sexual harassment charges against him. Well, not really. It had been an accidental flirtation, or so I'd thought at the time.

"You could have been honest with me," I said.

"I didn't know what to do. I was reacting. And I thought if you didn't feel comfortable at work with me, you'd leave. It was a stupid attempt. Please don't make this any harder than it already is, Hollie. Can you leave now? I'll send your last paycheck through the post."

That was abrupt. It was only four. I had agreed to work until six.

What was I thinking? I'd been fired. I didn't need to stick around and make the man feel any worse than he already must.

"I'll get my things."

I shuffled around Richard and walked numbly into the back room. I wanted to grab my stuff and flee. But the weather forced me to bundle up in my coat, mittens, and finally wrap a scarf around my neck. I took off my heels and exchanged them for the boots. The Shakespeare and Company bag I crushed against my chest, clinging to it as if a life preserver.

Richard stood behind the cash register, head down, as I passed by. No thanks for the years of work and great service?

What was I thinking? He was in a bad place right now. I should leave as quickly as possible.

I paused at the door, and turned to him. "Have you heard anything about the map?"

The man twisted his head uncomfortably and nodded. "It's not authentic. Wrong year. Da Vinci wasn't using the knotwork device when that map had been fashioned."

"Oh."

He had been so hopeful for the map he'd found in an old Scottish castle. If it had been genuine, he could have sold it and had oodles of cash to keep this store thriving. I had been the one to encourage him to submit it for authentication after realizing the knotwork design on the map key was that of Leonardo da Vinci. Or so it had seemed.

A vicious wave of justice rippled through me. Served the man right for firing me.

"Sorry," I muttered, both for the wicked thought and for the tough times that had befallen him. I pushed the door open and stepped into the brisk air.

By the time I got off the Metro in the 7th, the tears would not relent. I blinked at them as I marched down the sidewalk toward my building. I shoved the bookstore bag into my purse and zipped it up, thinking how the day had gone downhill quickly after the high of such a find.

Stupid Richard. I didn't need that job. I liked having the opportunity to get out of my apartment every once in a while and to talk with people. Besides, I had the bible job for the fantasy writer that would give my income a boost.

Stupid Da Vinci map. Why couldn't it have been real?

He'd made a pass at me in hopes that I would quit? That was the most inane, idiotic...

Suddenly I was glugging tears. I pushed a mittened hand over one eye. I stood at the corner across the street from my building. When I looked over a shoulder Jean-Louis's building concierge winked at me.

I rushed through the door, nodding to the concierge, but keeping my head twisted so he couldn't see my tears. On the second (third) floor, I stood before Jean-Louis's door. I had the digital code. I could enter it and walk right in.

I tilted my forehead against the door. Tears splattered the wood door.

Ten

I caught Hollie against my chest. She'd been crying, and still was. She was so quiet, but I felt the soft heaves in her chest against mine. I stroked her hair and tilted my head against hers.

"Tell me," I said as I closed the door behind her.

When next I saw her, I'd intended to surprise her with what sat over by the window, but I couldn't think of that now. Something had upset her. Was it because we hadn't spoken for days? If anyone deserved an on-the-knees apology it was Hollie. She had no reason for tears. But if I had pushed her to this I would never forgive myself.

"Richard...f-f-fired me," she gasped out.

Whew! I wasn't in the doghouse. And yet... "*Mon abeille*, I am so sorry."

She clung to me, hugging me. It felt natural to rub her back, providing a nurturing touch that wasn't at all natural to me, but rather surprised me of what I was capable. Hugging and offering a reassuring shoulder to lean on? Not my style. Sure, the closeness and sharing came easily enough when we were making love. That's what two people did when they had sex. But to simply hold someone when they were in pain?

"He actually said," she whispered and then shuddered, "that's the reason he made the pass at me."

"A pass?"

"Oh, I never told you. Weeks ago Richard made a weirdly awkward pass at me. Leered at my boobs. He said he was hoping I'd want to quit then. That it would make it easier for him so he wouldn't have to eventually fire me. Isn't that awful?"

"And that didn't work so he sacked you. How?"

"Just told me I was finished. His shop is in trouble. I understand. He can't afford to pay me, but—wait." Standing on tiptoes, she peered over my shoulder. "Why do you have a fuck-me-sized ottoman in your living room?"

I smirked at her sudden swing to curiosity. "I was going to surprise you—sort of an early Christmas present—but hadn't expected to greet you at the door with you in tears."

"Oh, Jean-Louis." She hugged against me, and—*merde*—my erection strained against my pants. Impossible to keep down at times, especially when Hollie was so close. She noticed, and giggled. "I'm sorry. I guess the unexpectedness of being fired freaked me. Like I said, I understand. Richard can't afford to pay his part-time employees. I've never been fired before. Makes me..." Her sigh blew against my throat. "Do you mind if I use your bathroom? I want to splash some water on my face. I shouldn't have come straight here until I'd worked through this a bit."

I kissed her forehead and hugged her tightly. "I'm glad you came to me when you were feeling low. Means a lot to me. Go splash some water on those tender tears. Maybe take a shower and you will feel better? I'll pour some wine."

"Make it a double," she said as she walked down the hallway.

He sat on the ottoman, the setting sunlight falling across the side of his face and shading his gray dress shirt to charcoal. His profile was pure Gascon, those hearty, boastful men of adventure and French heritage. Prominent browline, and fierce nose that was straight as a blade. Hair that did as it pleased, (and it always pleased me). A firm, decisive jaw. Strong, it said. And yet, it was also kind and comforting.

Good thing I had decided to come up here instead of going home to muddle over getting fired. I may have dug out the chocolate and Michael Bublé. And no one wanted to see me in that kind of funk.

I tilted a swig from the wine goblet sitting on the kitchen counter. Cool and fruity. Num.

I felt better now. I could put this behind me. Because really, if Richard wished to save his shop, he had no choice but to do what he had. And I'd had no choice but to have a mini-breakdown. Without doing so, I may have sunk into said funk for days. It had been good to get it out in an explosion of tears. And a shower.

Yes, I'd climbed into the shower for a quickie. After, I'd tugged on a plaid cotton robe I found in Jean-Louis's closet and belted it loosely. I smelled like sable rum now, and no one could feel sad when they smelled like their lover.

I wandered to the ottoman and Jean-Louis patted the tufted cushion before him and drew up his legs to sit cross-legged. "Sit here," he said.

A wicked smile curled my lips.

"I don't want to fuck you," he offered.

My smile dropped.

"Let's be quiet together. *Oui*?"

Quiet did sound appealing.

I sat before him, back facing his chest, pulling up my legs to sit cross-legged. Outside, thick snowflakes danced in the gray sky. If I could own a solarium that was completely glassed in, I would put a big bed in the middle and spend my winter days snuggled beneath the goose down comforter and flannel sheets gazing at the gorgeous world.

"You feel better after a shower?"

I nodded. "So much better. Thanks for being my safe place to fall."

Jean-Louis leaned in, his nose brushing my hair, and whispered, "Can I touch your skin?"

"Please," came out as a form of amen that I wanted some higher power to acknowledge as I felt my lover's presence in every breath.

Ever so slowly, the robe slipped down my shoulders, then loosened and fell as if water to puddle at my elbows. I closed my eyes. I didn't want sight to interfere with this experience.

The gentlest touch swished aside my hair and relegated the wet strands over one shoulder. My bare breasts tightened, the nipples hardening as the sweep of cool hair tickled my skin. But it was the next touch that undid me.

One finger landed on my shoulder and softly glided its horizontal measure. Barely touching, but firm enough so that my skin reacted to his skin. Not quite magnetic, more a tease of contact that shivered down my spine and tilted my head forward.

His fingers journeyed down my arm, slowly, seeking. Learning. At the curve of my elbow, his touch glanced inside the silken soft inner crease and lingered there. Skin heated skin. I sighed. Parts of me were rapidly warming. This quiet touching was such a turn-on. And he hadn't spoken a single word.

I didn't want him to speak. I only wanted to feel.

And smell. The tint of his aftershave alchemized in the air and I felt as if he surrounded me as his finger glided onward. There at my wrist, he paused. Perhaps testing my pulse beat? It was fast, because it matched my anticipatory heartbeats.

And when his finger glided across the bracelet lines that demarcated my wrist from my hand and over the meaty base to land my palm, it felt as though he touched me everywhere. There, at the base of my spine where it tingled. And there, at my ankle where I imagined I'd been kissed by a snowflake. And yes, there, at the lower curve of my ass where my thighs met glutes.

He spread his hand over mine, not clasping, just drawing in my aura. Reading me. I suddenly wanted to ask him what it said on that page of my palm, but instead kept my eyes closed and my senses focused to his command.

Curving his fingers about my hand, he cupped my fingers inward and then drew them upward to hold my arm outstretched. I thought we could fly together. Drift through the snowflakes outside and never land, always safe within each other's arms.

Now he drew my arm up and toward my body, bringing my hand down toward my shoulder where I felt his breath hush against the thumb. He sniffed my skin, and I shuddered. And then he placed my hand on my thigh and with his other hand performed an exploratory glide along my opposite shoulder.

As his finger traced my skin, I realized I absently stroked my thigh, mimicking his barely-there touch. I wanted to touch him. And then I did not. I tilted back the untended shoulder. My nipples were tight because the air before me was cool, facing the snowfall. And behind me, and moving all through me, was Jean-Louis.

Once at my wrist, he again bent my arm and brought my hand up to sniff and then planted the softest kiss there at the crease where thumb meets forefinger. A dash of his tongue teased the arc of skin. I knew from certain historical research that spot was called the purlicue. The place between the thumb and finger. So sensitive. Deliciously devastating to have it licked.

Now I did moan, the agony of my restraint tainting the air with sound. I thought my desperation might move his touch faster, make it more focused, perhaps between my legs or to caress a breast, but he did not answer that unspoken desire.

Instead, both sets of his fingertips touched my shoulders and then slowly journeyed down my back, moving slightly to the left and right, drawing wings for the flight I most desired. He mapped out all portions of me, learning this, the largest and most sensitive organ on my body—skin.

Such a touch felt to me as if he were encountering the female form for the first time, tracing the shape of my structure, marking it in his thoughts. Drawing a mental map with such detail to rival the exquisite artifacts sold in the map shop.

And as the touch glided downward, achingly slow as he marked each vertebra I learned him. He was a patient man, a curious man. A man who respected and adored me.

He loved me.

And I think at this moment I could admit to love. Lost in his touch, I wanted to surrender to everything about him. Every French word I couldn't understand, every movement that caught my eye and made me smile (or yes, horny), every wink and sexy smile that always captured his eyes and made his whole face beam.

Everything about him could be mine. I felt him in my heart.

And there he was, thumbs dipping into those sensual curves that sat above my derriere. Dimples of Venus, they were called. Yes, I was this man's goddess.

The sudden heat of his tongue at the base of my neck tilted my head forward, opening myself, laying bare the canvas on which he wanted to create. He licked down my spine as far as he could, and I felt his hands move around my hips and up my stomach.

I uncrossed my legs. Mercy, but my pussy hummed and I was slick between my thighs. He could own me with a touch to my clit. But I liked the refusal to something so easy, so obvious. Instead, he held me against his chest, the alien presence of the dress shirt in bold contrast to the bareness of this moment.

Take me, I wanted to whisper. And then I did not, because he had taken me. He owned me. He was the master of my skin, and of the shimmering tingles that effervesced high in my mons, cluing me that orgasm was so close. A treat for my patience, my willingness to let him do as he pleased.

And when his hands moved up to caress my breasts, I felt as if he held something valuable, and he tendered his touch as if for a princess who mustn't be broken, yet held firmly, protectively.

Urgent breaths lifted my breasts up in his grasp. And with an exhale, I wondered if a finger would trace my nipple. I waited for that delicious contact, and then—his hands were gone.

"Come for me," whispered at my ear.

My body relaxed, commanded by his voice. And surrender rushed up to spill from between my legs as the orgasm shivered through my being and shook my shoulders against his chest.

I panted. Once. Again. A smile broke on my lips but the usual giggle didn't rise. I let my head fall against his shoulder. Eyes still closed, I could see him in my heart, bold and bright.

"I love you," I whispered.

Eleven

Weeks later...

I had won the argument for a medium-sized Christmas tree after I reassured Jean-Louis that I would be responsible for cleaning up the fallen needles daily. I didn't expect the tree to dry out in the short time we would have it up. Christmas landed in two days. We'd brought in the tree last night, and I usually got rid of that sucker right after New Years. Of course, we'd put it up in his apartment. Mine was too small even for this slender pine.

Mmm...it smelled great, and made me only a little homesick for Iowa. (I'd worked my fifteenth winter at a Christmas tree farm.) I spent the afternoon running lights through the branches while Jean-Louis had taught a class online in his bedroom. I'd suggested a quickie during his lunch break, and it had been fast and festive. So much so, that the man had ended up with tinsel hanging off his erection at one point during the liaison.

I'd snapped a picture of Monsieur Eiffel all decked out for the holiday (with his permission) and while I wanted to put that as my screen saver on my phone, I knew that my less-than-exacting technical skills could likely send the Christmas Cock to my client list by mistake. So I transferred it to a For My Eyes Only file.

Dinner smelled delicious. After emerging from the bedroom around five, Jean-Louis whipped up a veggie lasagna with lots of zucchini and ricotta and had put it in the oven.

"How about this?" he called from the sofa where he had selected some music and streamed it through the wireless speakers positioned throughout the loft.

I opened a box of fragile glass ornaments and bobbed my head to The Beastie Boys' version of a Christmas song. "I like it!"

By the time he'd joined me to look over the half dozen boxes of shiny new ornaments I'd chosen from the *supermarché* this morning, the song segued to Joan Jett's "Crimson and Clover".

"I love this one," I crooned, and picked up a few bars in my reasonably decent singing voice. "*Over and over...*"

Jean-Louis took the ornament box from my hand and set it aside, then pulled me close. He swayed me into a slow dance. Outside the window, heavy snowflakes drifted down. The faint December sun was setting. My man held me close, his chest humming as he sang to the music. My heart felt light.

Heads bowed together, our noses touched, but our lips did not. We both smiled. Our breaths mingled. The anticipation of a kiss was sweeter than eggnog, yet it was nice to nuzzle. To enjoy the closeness that didn't require anything more than our hands clasped and our hearts synchronizing in rhythm to the music.

I nuzzled my nose against his neck and kissed his skin. Sable and bay rum filled my senses. "Don't get me anything for Christmas," I said while Joan Jett serenaded us.

"Don't tell me what to do," he said lightly, and turned me to sway toward the center of the room behind the sofa. "I'll give you the moon if I want to."

"Then no one would be able to see at night, and there would be great calamity world round. Crashes. Blackouts. Disasters."

"Yes, but I would be able to see you by the light of your moon."

"Fine. Then I'll buy you a rocketship so you can come visit me."

"You see? We will have one another this Christmas, sitting on the moon, holding hands."

Romance, meet Monsieur Sexy. He's all mine, girls.

"But seriously." I couldn't drop it. The music switched to something jazzy. "I don't want a gift. Promise?" What I'd gotten was nothing, really. And I hadn't indicated I couldn't get him a gift.

He shrugged, and grabbed my hands. A sexy hip shimmy drew my eyes to his agile form. "Do you cha-cha?"

"Nope. But you must." He stepped forward, and I followed his lead by stepping backward. The man's hips shifted to the beat. Like a pro. "Seriously? Have you taken dance classes?"

"No, Margot used to dance competitively."

"Margot? Is she a former girlfriend?"

He shimmied and shook his head. "My mother. I've always used her first name. Same with my grand-mere, Beatrice. My eleventh summer I was Margot's fill-in practice partner while my dad, Pierre, was off having yet another affair."

"Oh."

That was a sobering explanation. But he didn't elaborate, so I tried to follow his moves. I couldn't keep time musically, no matter how well I thought I could. Blame it on my adamant refusal in grade school to learn to play an instrument or join choir.

"Song change!" I announced as the music switched to a jingle-bell tune. It was catchy and demanded I bounce on the balls of my feet. I pumped the air with my fists. "Mashed potato!"

"Ah, I know that one." We matched each other with our actually-kinda-good renditions of the dance. But who can screw up the mashed potato? "Excellent! Now, how about the waltz?"

My lover swept out my arms and stepped to the side. His chin lifted and for a second I thought I'd fallen into one of my more recurrent fantasies of dancing with the sexy Ukranian dance pro on Dancing With The Stars. (I'm waiting for you Maksim. Call me.)

"*Un, deux, trois,*" Jean-Louis directed as we moved around the vast practice area and farther from the Christmas tree. Good thing, because if he dipped me, I might take out the decorations with a graceless sweep of hand. "*Très bien, mon abeille.* You are a natural."

"You're just saying that." I pushed him out of my grasp and assumed a haughty rock-slut pose, one arm extended over my head. "Let's do eighties headbanging. Now that I can handle."

I stretched up both arms, flashing the devil's horns signal with my fingers and pumped my head.

"I love the 80s hard stuff!"

Jean-Louis swung up an air guitar and strummed a few chords. Head banging, he whipped back his non-existent long hair and landed on his knees, stretching back his shoulders as he plucked out a burning riff on his Rickenbacker.

"You know, long-haired rockers make me cream my panties," I said. I shimmied over to him and straddled his legs, shaking my bootie to—okay, so Frank Sinatra was crooning about chestnuts right now, but we were in another world. "So do guitar players." I drew my hands over his hair, pretending it was long as I drew it out. "Will you take me backstage and fuck me?"

"Wait for my guitar solo first. *Oui*?" He winked.

Pompous rock star. I fake screamed like a crazy fan girl.

Amidst the silliness, the door buzzer rang. Weird, only because it was a Friday evening and we knew Jean-Louis had no fencing students scheduled until after the holidays.

"You expecting someone?" I asked my guitar hero, who was in the middle of his solo.

"No." He stood and handed me his instrument. "Hold this."

I accepted the air guitar like a true fan and clutched it to my chest while Jean-Louis answered the door. Turning, I skipped and bobbed my head. I'd missed the 80s completely, but that didn't mean I hadn't tried to resurrect it in the early 2000s for lack of any interesting music on the radio. Oh, to have been the age I am now when the rockers wore their hair long and their spandex tight enough to reveal every contour of what lie beneath.

I heard the door close and spun around with a dramatic strum of an air chord. Jean-Louis didn't notice my antics. Head bowed, he stood reading a yellow card. His face tightened. His brow furrowed. His hand hung at his side, and his whole demeanor suddenly exuded quiet.

"Jean-Louis?" I dropped the guitar and actually stepped over it. "What is it? What's wrong?"

Gliding a hand over his bicep, I felt him flinch beneath my touch. Words barely whispered from his throat, "*Mon pere est morte.*"

I didn't even have to think to interpret that muttered sentence. He'd said his father was dead.

Pushing away from me, he walked to the sofa and sat. The card flicked in his grip.

I rushed to sit beside him, but didn't do more than touch his knee. Tension wavered off him, and I didn't want to make a wrong move. I'd received news of my mother's death six years ago. I can still remember that sudden hit. The world changed. Instantly. And yet, it had not. And I had been left struggling amidst a mire.

"Can you talk to me?" I persisted, sensing he was being sucked away from me with every breath I took. Even though we sat next to one another he grew remarkably distant. "Do you want to?"

Finally, he handed me the yellow card. I took it and glanced over the words. All in French. But I was pretty deft at making out most words. This is what I pieced together:

To whom it may concern: We regret to inform you of Monsieur Pierre l'Etoile's passing yesterday afternoon at four p.m. A massive coronary stopped his heart. He has requested no funeral services. A will is scheduled be read December 28th at the offices of Montreaux & Gische in Marseilles. You are requested to attend. Condolences.

To whom it may concern? I gasped at the utter cold delivery of his father's death. He'd had a heart attack. Poor man. Jean-Louis was in his mid-thirties. His father couldn't be older than fifties or a young sixty.

My breath hushed out in a sigh.

"My father," he said on a raspy tone.

I nodded. Ran my fingers along his arm. When he didn't open his fingers for a clasp I rested mine on his wrist. Unsure what to do. I wasn't the most compassionate person, but I could relate to how he was feeling. That mire that I knew so well. It was a muffling, loud, and yet, wickedly silent place to stumble into.

Moments ago we had been dancing and having a great time. I glanced to the Christmas tree where beneath sat boxes of glittering ornaments. This was the worst Christmas present a man could get.

"Do you want to talk about this?"

He pushed up from the sofa, unsettling the telegram so I had to grab it before it slipped to the floor. I set it aside on the coffee table, next to the laptop and a thick computer manual. He strolled down the hallway toward his bedroom.

He didn't want to talk. Of course, he needed time to digest the news. The cruel method of delivery stabbed at my heart.

Pierre l'Etoile.

Etoile meant star in French. My lover's last name meant star. This was the first time I had learned his surname. Can you believe it? While it should have fascinated me, gave me a giddy feeling to have the knowledge; instead I could only wrap my arms across my chest, grasping high at my shoulders, and bury my face against a forearm.

He must feel so alone right now. He'd lost his father. I didn't know much about his family. His mother was a world traveler and Jean-Louis saw her once a year, if that. But they had a good rapport and emailed each other often. Yet he called her Margot. Weird. His father, on the other hand, I knew nothing about. I recall Jean-Louis saying he and his father were not close. And he had just dropped the comment about his father's affairs.

I wanted to know everything. To feel as if his family was familiar to me. But now was not the time to have that conversation. I just wanted to wrap him in my arms and be there for him.

I glanced down the hallway. No sound from the bedroom. The door was open. Men didn't cry. They should. But they rarely did. He needed to cry over this.

Well, that was my thinking. I didn't know what was best for him. It was selfish of me to think tears would help. Wiping away my own tear, I stood and tiptoed down the hallway. Couldn't let him see that I was so easily affected by sad news. I had to be the strong one.

Once at the bedroom door, I didn't hesitate crossing the threshold. He stood before the window, looking out. The view framed my bedroom window across the street. The thick, nickel-sized snowflakes falling through the sky were too fantastical for such a somber mood. I assumed he wasn't seeing anything, his vision unfocused on everything before him. But he must be feeling so much.

"I'm here for you." I approached slowly. "Tell me to leave if you need me to. But otherwise—"

He turned and tugged me into his arms and bowed his head against mine. His body subtly shivered, wracked with grief. I hugged him tightly, and we stood there before the window for a long time. We didn't speak. It wasn't necessary. Bodies consoled. Skin offered comfort. And when finally he did speak, his voice was strained, as if he'd talked for days and his vocal chords had but a few tones remaining.

"We weren't close," he said, still clutching me to his hard, shivering body. "We had differences. I didn't know the name of his third wife." He sniffed back tears. "That I received a telegram announcing his death was no surprise."

I rubbed my palm up and down his back.

Suddenly he pulled away but held me by the arms. His gaze met mine so intensely I blinked. "I should go to Marseille."

"Of course, for the reading of the will. Were you his only son?"

"Yes. Though I can't be sure if he had other children with his other wives. If I go, it'll change our plans for Christmas."

"We didn't have any plans, lover." I smoothed a hand along his cheek. "And this is more important. I'll go along with you. If that's okay?"

"I'd like that." He hugged me and I felt as though he were comforting me. And maybe he was.

"I love you, Hollie. I'm blessed to have you in my life."

No, I was the one blessed to have found such a kind and lovely man.

Twelve

The day after Christmas I boarded the train with Hollie, destination Marseilles. What was our Christmas like? Subdued. I made us *coq au vin* and we drank two bottles of wine then made slow love in the moonlight that spilled through my bedroom window.

No presents. Much as I'd love to shower Hollie with diamonds, I had managed to grab a bit of the moon for her. Sprawled upon my bed, her skin had glowed in the moonlight. It is a memory I will never lose. *Mon abeille et le luna.*

Besides, I can give her a gift anytime.

And I neither want nor need any material object from Hollie. Holding her in my arms on Christmas eve and waking to her smile the following morning was more than any man deserved.

I admit I've been at odds about Pierre's death since receiving the cold, heartless telegram. Shouldn't I be heartsick and sobbing? I couldn't find that place in my heart. Though I sensed it would open up when I least wanted it too. I trusted sharing my pain with Hollie, but it was still difficult to see her giving me the big, sad eyes. I did not want her to have to comfort me. That was what the man was supposed to do for the woman.

Maybe. Grief was new to me. Hollie had experienced it with her mother, so I sensed she was anticipating my fall into a funk. Yet again, I wasn't feeling it.

I wanted to focus on getting to the will reading, and then return to Paris and get on with my life. I didn't expect Pierre to leave me a thing from his multi-million-valued estate. We'd had a falling out six years ago. Right around the time Hollie's mother had died. Hmm...

Anyway, I'd chosen to go the route of entrepreneur in the vast and unknown world of online business and computer software. My father, a University of Paris alum, who held a degree in art history (I'd never paid attention to his exact study; yes, one strike against me) had been appalled I'd not wanted to follow in his esteemed footsteps. He insisted I accept his money to cover university courses. My refusal had brought the worst out of him. I'd never in my lifetime heard my father curse. He'd said fuck that day. Not a common oath for a seasoned Frenchman to use. The word had resounded with disappointment and resentment over his independent son's staunch refusal to conform. To be like his old man. He'd ordered me out of his office that afternoon.

I hadn't returned since. Nor had I called him. I had emailed him when I'd put up VSquire's business shingle. No reply. When I'd made my first million I'd thought to email him, but had decided against it. I wasn't much for bragging, and it would have only been a desperate attempt to win Pierre's attention. I didn't need his attention. I'd been doing fine on my own.

I believe we all love in our own manner. Some need to constantly shout it out and perform displays of affection. Others can know love and yet not need the other person's shit in their lives to bring them down.

The l'Etoile family has never been close. (Did you get that from my use of my parents' *prenoms*?) We've never gone on yearly vacations, nor has Margot stayed home to bake cookies and treats for me. I'd been closer to the nanny in my younger years, and when I'd hit puberty, my teen years had been spent alone in the afternoons studying, or with a few select friends gazing at the girls at the local coffee shop, or hitting the trails on our mountain bikes.

I have grown accustomed to taking care of myself.

Probably why hooking up with my wife had felt right. Though she'd traveled extensively, it had felt natural not to have her in the home and always by my side. I hadn't needed reassurance that she loved me with frequent platitudes.

I'm not sure I can recall a time when Pierre had said that he loved me.

Didn't matter now. He was gone. And my life went on.

This thing with Hollie was opposite of everything I had been conditioned to accept as real and family. And you know what? As new and curious as it was to me, I embraced it. I loved that Hollie was always at my place and that she hugged me often. It felt natural to hug her back, when I can only remember one time my entire life that Margot hugged me.

Don't shake your head in pity for me. It is all that I know. I don't feel as if I've missed some emotional bond requisite to a healthy relationship with my parents. And I consider myself lucky that my childhood was not abusive, and in fact, rather privileged.

Yet I am learning a different way now, and eagerly following the path down which Hollie leads me. She is the moonlight to brighten my darkness.

And now, as I squeezed her hand and she smiled with her eyes closed because she'd been trying to fall asleep for the first four-hour leg of our journey, I was thankful for windows. And silence. And for this woman's daring venture into my heart.

Enough of the sappy thoughts. I wished I hadn't been holding Hollie's hand while she nodded off because now I didn't want to extricate it. I'd wake her. Yet, I needed to check my email.

I worked my mobile from the front pocket of my trousers with my left hand, and attempted to scroll through the menus. It took a while, but eventually I'd gone through the dozen emails and scheduled practice sessions for my students for the next few months.

The train was due to stop in Lyon to pick up more passengers, then it forged straight on to Marseille. We'd arrive in the city at six p.m.. I'd arranged a car to take us to the hotel. I managed to snag the luxury suite, which was a coup during the holidays. It would serve as a belated Christmas gift for Hollie.

I wished this trip had been during summer. I would have liked to take her to the nude beaches to see her reaction. Would my vixen have bared her breasts with as much confidence as the locals? I'm not sure. Not sure I'd want her to. But seeing how she adapted to new situations fascinated me. When we'd had sex at the Louvre, she had been nervous as hell, but had quickly adapted, and had found it exciting and, dare I say it, fun.

I think that is what I loved most about her. She wasn't afraid of much, not even my dark moods.

I would like to see her in a tiny bikini, her skin bared to the sun, her breasts firm and high. They jiggled only a little when she walked. And her long torso emphasized her narrow waist and sexy hips. Sprawled on a beach towel with sunglasses on and a book in hand would suit her.

Tucking away the mobile, I rested my hand on my lap because...*oui*, I was getting a hard-on imagining Hollie lying on the beach naked. Sun warming her skin. I closed my eyes...

First, to get her naked. I'd have to go about it casually, perhaps accidentally dust some sand on her thigh, where the bikini bottom pulled away from her skin as she moved her leg. The sand would sprinkle over her pussy and she'd wiggle at the irritation.

Lying beside her, propped on my elbows, I'd tilt my head against her leg to inspect. A glimpse of her labia teased my libido. An inhale detected soft vanilla, sand, and coconut. We needed to take care of the situation, and fast.

She'd look around from behind her dark glasses, eyeing the nearby sunbathers, most of them completely nude, some with breasts bared, others lying chest down to reveal browned bottoms. She'd worry at her lower lip, and I would sense her anxiety.

I'd lick my lips and dash out my tongue near the bikini bottom. Mmm...she smelled so good. That coconut sun lotion made me want to lick her. So I did.

Her thigh muscle tensed and a gasp of pleasure made me smile. My hard-on pulsed against the beach towel. Of course, I was completely bare, my white ass burnished by the ocean breeze.

The beach was no place for sex, and the sunbathers would look down on any who viewed them overtly or engaged in sensual play. So it was difficult for me not to crawl on top of Hollie and start making out with her, rubbing my cock between her thighs.

She shimmied down the bikini bottom and worked it off with her toes. Then she untied the top and her breasts sprang up, a pair of rosy-tipped sun worshippers.

She commented on how the warmth of the sun felt so good on her pale Iowa skin. The deep maroon aureoles tightened into buds that demanded suckling. I was turgid and realized I rocked my hips against the towel, dragging my cock against the terrycloth. Christ, that felt good.

She asked if I was horny. Of course not, I replied. Here? *Pas ridicule*!

Was that an arch of brow behind those dark sunglasses?

Hollie lifted her book and resumed reading. And I drew in the scent of coconuts and sex. With one more pump of my erection against the towel...

My spine stiffened and I sat up abruptly from my lazy drift into fantasy. The train rocked. I glanced around. No eyes on me. Hollie continued to snooze.

And I discreetly adjusted my erect cock.

AAA

I hadn't accompanied Jean-Louis into the will reading. Hadn't been invited. And had I, I would have refused. This was a private moment for him. He'd tell me about it later. And if he did not, I would have to accept that. Though, I knew he would tell all. In his own time.

It was festival time in Marseille and the city center had been festooned and decorated to look like a quaint Christmas village, replete with straw manger featuring the baby Jesus, and everywhere *le Pere Noel* climbed chimneys. There was no snow, and it was actually quite warm. In the fifties.

I'd tugged my winter coat open and kept my scarf wrapped about my neck, but gloves weren't necessary. Besides, I was wiping away tears, and it was easier to do with my bare fingers than a leather glove.

Another teardrop slid down my nose and I sniffed at it. With all this time to myself, I'd gone from lamenting Jean-Louis's loss to wondering when he would break down and allow in the grief. And then, thinking about grief and its relentless attack, I'd drifted to that evening when I'd gotten the phone call about my mother.

She had been killed in a car accident. Struck by a drunk driver who had two previous drunk driving convictions on his record. The impact had sheared off the front of my mother's Audi and had literally tugged her body out with it. She'd been killed instantly, or so I'd been told. The officer who had told me that had followed with the odd notion that I should be thankful for that.

I don't know how any part of a person's death can be a cause for thanks. It doesn't feel right to make even a small part of such loss a positive.

I had cried for months. Perhaps even years. Hell, I still cry when thinking of my mother. As I was now. If only I had been able to give her one more hug. If only we had gone to the movie that night instead of rescheduling for the next weekend because we hadn't wanted to stand in line on opening weekend and fight the crowds. If only I had been more comfortable with telling her I love her. All the time. Not once in a while.

If only.

There would always be if onlys. I knew rationally that death came to us all, in ways and manners for which we could never be prepared. It would never be perfect. It would always make us wish *if only*.

I covered my face with my hands as a few glugging sobs escaped. There weren't many tourists walking near the bench across from the courthouse where I sat. But when someone gently touched my shoulder I almost shrugged them away and the words *fuck off* tickled my tongue.

Until he spoke, "*Mon abeille*?"

Ah, shit. He'd caught me crying. And not even about him.

I dragged the side of my hand across my eyes, trying to squeegee off the tears. "How did it go?"

"All is well. But you are crying. What is wrong, Hollie? Are you sad?"

I nodded. Sniffed the mutinous tears that insisted on showing him how weak I could be, and—such a girl! Girls cried at everything. Men were so stoic. He'd not broken down and cried yet. And thinking that made me cry even more. I wanted to see him break down. There was something so wrong about that. Wasn't there?

Sitting beside me, Jean-Louis hugged me, his leather glove wrapping about one of my shoulders. He smelled warm and like tobacco. Someone in the room must have been smoking a cigar. He may have taken a puff from it if proffered. I liked the oaky scent.

"I shouldn't be doing this," I said softly. "I'm sorry, but I was thinking about you. And then I started to think about my mom. She died. I told you that. I miss her. But now is not about me. I should be comforting you. Oh. Sorry. I just..."

He held me so perfectly. Not too hard, not too lightly. As if he were some kind of stoic rock that had been designed to bear my pain. Reassured, I tilted into him, sniffling against his chest. Hot tears rolled down my cheeks and dropped onto his coat. He didn't say anything. I didn't want him to say anything.

My mother would have loved this man. I suddenly needed her to know Jean-Louis. I wanted her to be there at my wedding someday. I wanted her to spoil my children and sneak them treats when I wasn't looking. I wanted to tell her I loved her.

"I want her back," I whispered.

Enfolded within his strength, I must have cried for another five minutes before my tears finally ceased. Jean-Louis stood with me, and we walked silently back to the hotel. He went immediately into the bathroom. I heard him run the water in the sink. Probably washing the day away. Then he took a shower, but following his ten-minute stint the water ran into the tub as if he were filling it.

When he appeared with a towel wrapped about his moist hips, he said he'd run me a bath. But as I stood to head into the bathroom, he caught me in his embrace.

Sky-gray eyes danced with mine. This trip had begun with a dance. A silly dance beside the Christmas tree that had ended terribly with a cold telegram. I didn't know what to say now. What was there to say? We'd shared our pain. Or I had shown him mine.

"Thank you for coming to Marseille with me," he said. "You make it easier to pause."

"To pause?"

"Tears came to me in the shower." He looked aside. His nostrils flared. His jaw tightened. Then as quickly, he focused on me. "I will miss him."

Compelled to wrap my arms about him, I gave him the hug that I wanted to give my mother. My arms wrapped about him forever and endlessly and into tomorrow. Our bodies knew one another and sighed in relief. We said I love you without words. I heard him sniff. I sensed a slight pull away from me, his pectoral muscles tensing against my chest. But he didn't let me go.

"Give it time," I managed to say, though I wasn't sure if I was also comforting myself.

His body moved as he shook his head. "I will order in while you take a bath, *oui*?"

"Sounds good. Are we headed to Paris tomorrow?"

"No, I'd like to spend another day here, looking around, doing the tourist thing, if you don't mind."

"I would love that. I think we could use some fun."

"We can." He kissed my forehead. "I'll rap on the door when the food arrives."

Thirteen

Hollie lingered in the tub after I informed her room service had arrived. The wine was chilled and dry. The salad wilted. But the lamb showed promise. The view from our sixth floor room looked out over the blue-green Mediterranean Sea. I'd never gone sailing. It wasn't something that interested me. Slight fear of deep water. (Don't tell anyone.)

Though certainly there were some excellent bike trails around here. And knowing that Hollie was a fan of Alexandre Dumas gave me an idea that we should visit the Chateau d'If out in the Bay of Marseille. It had been the setting for *The Count of Monte Cristo* and I was pretty sure they gave tours of the fortress.

The bathroom door opened and Hollie exited in a cloud of lavender steam. It wasn't my favorite scent (soap provided by the hotel) but on Hollie it smelled glamorous.

"Do you like biking?" I asked.

She tugged the sash of the terrycloth robe and accepted the wine goblet. "Why do I sense your version of biking is far different than the pleasant summer roll through the park I envision?"

She smiled behind a sip, and that was all I needed for my shoulders to relax. While I poured myself another goblet, she sorted about in her suitcase for something.

The day had been long and trying. I'd not been disappointed to learn Pierre had left everything to his thirty-year-old third wife of eight months. She was also six months pregnant. Future half brother for me. *Salut!* (Er, no.) Pierre owned property by the sea and stocks and bonds. I'm quite sure there was nothing in his possessions I'd miss. And I was pleased that the unborn child's mother would be taken care of in the wake of his father's death.

The widow had worn a hat with a black veil over her blonde hair. And her low-cut black suit had exposed some serious cleavage. I wonder if Pierre had paid for that pair? I hadn't attempted to speak with her. It had felt weird. Not right, or even necessary.

So now, to put this all behind me. The focus of Hollie would help me with that.

"What about Chateau d'If?" I offered.

"Oh, that's right!" She strolled over with a wrapped package in hand. "It's close, isn't it?"

"Five miles out? Want to check it out tomorrow?"

"Yes!"

"I was hoping you'd say that. What is that? It is not a Christmas present, is it? You had rules."

"Those rule did not indicate I couldn't get you something." She handed me the heavy object, which I guessed might be a book from the size and shape. "It's something I wanted you to have. I didn't give it to you on Christmas Eve because it was so lovely simply being the two of us that night, quiet and making love. But now, well, it feels like you need something to pick you up."

I sat on the chair beside the table and tore away the gold mylar wrapping. I did enjoy presents, so I wouldn't argue the gift. And when I saw what it was, I gasped. Running my fingers over the fading gold lettering on the maroon spine, I could but gasp again.

"*The Three Musketeers*," Hollie provided eagerly. "This edition was published in 1898. It's filled with gorgeous illustrations."

The copy was exquisite. A shield with crossed swords on the front bore the title in more fading gold ink. I had not seen an old version of the book in such good condition. It was over a hundred years old! And indeed, the illustrations were gorgeous. It was printed in English, but that mattered little. I paused on an illustrated page that featured Cardinal Richelieu kneeling before the imperious Milady de Winter.

"Hollie," I whispered. My heart swelled and tears wobbled in my eyes. It had been rare to receive a meaningful gift from my parents. Necessities such as school supplies and shirts had been the norm.

"Do you like it?"

I grasped her and pulled her into hug. Words were impossible. This moment was perfect. She knew me well. I would cherish this book endlessly. It felt more valuable to me than any figure in my bank account. This woman knew my heart.

"Can we read it together?" she asked.

I nodded and sniffed back silly tears. She'd made me cry, damn it. But the emotional display felt okay. "We will read it together. Thank you, *mon abeille*. It means much to me."

"You mean much to me, Jean-Louis. Now, let's eat. I'm starving! Lamb? I haven't ever tried it," she said, sitting down and starting right in.

I wrapped the book back in the mylar paper and set it in my open suitcase. I didn't want to get food on it. Wiping away another tear, I sat before the table. Wow. Talk about a surprise attack of emotion.

"This is good," Hollie said. "Not as good as what you might make, but I'm hungry."

"As am I." Whew! I could handle this. Wasn't going to think about any other reason to let the tears come. Hollie was cheery and so pretty. I would use her as distraction from the insistent tug within my heart.

We ate quickly, chatting about the things we'd seen in town that we might check out tomorrow. Small talk. It felt odd, and yet I was comfortable with it. I didn't sense that Hollie was going to dive at me with questions about Pierre. Did I miss him? Was I sad?

Of course I did and was. But right now even if I had wanted to wither into grief, I couldn't. I actually felt the same. And if I thought about that too much, that way lie madness.

It was the gift that had brought up the emotion, that was all.

"It would please me to bring you into town tomorrow and buy you some pretty things," I said. "You've only ever allowed me to buy you the dress. Maybe some shoes?"

"I do love insensible shoes. Are you in a shopping mood?"

"I believe so."

"If it makes you happy. But here I thought you'd take me to a nude beach."

"Your tits would freeze." She laughed, and I joined her. "But if you are determined?"

"No, I think the weather helped me dodge a bullet because I sense you would take pleasure in watching me navigate a nude beach. You do like to watch me struggle with my comfort zone."

I'd never thought of it like that before, but she was right. "I like to watch you no matter the situation."

"Voyeur."

"Exhibitionist."

"Only for you. I would never flash a complete stranger."

"You did once. Through our bedroom windows." I winked at her while sipping the wine. "It pleased me."

"I like to please you, Jean-Louis l'Etoile. You know, that's the first time I learned your surname. When I read the telegram."

"Huh." It hadn't occurred to me that we'd not done the official introductions. I offered her my hand across the table. "Monsieur Jean-Louis l'Etoile, ever ready to please you, Mademoiselle."

She slid her hand into mine. "Hollie Peterson. And I am more than ready to please you, Monsieur."

Twisting on her chair, she slipped off and onto her knees, and crawled around to kneel before me. Gliding her hand up from my bare feet, along my calves (I was wearing a towel) and up along my thighs, she leaned in and asked, "Tell me how to please you, Monsieur l'Etoile?"

Mmm... There were so many answers to that loaded question. I glanced to the book lying on top of my things in the suitcase. Need I ask more? The most interested party perked up at attention in my lap. I did like Hollie on her knees before me.

And then, I did not.

"For starters, get off your knees."

"But...?"

"*S'il vous plâit*," I insisted.

She stood and leaned forward, putting her lips close to mine but not quite touching. She had seduction in mind. And while I couldn't argue a preference for contact, I wanted something different from her right now. I gently pushed her back so she hovered over me expectantly.

"It pleases me," I said, "when you know what you want, and do not balk to take it. Whether it be sex or the truth in a conversation. The thing that pleases me most about you, Hollie..."

I stood and took her hands in mine. "Is your strength. You know who you are. You don't make excuses for that. Promise to never make excuses to me?"

She nodded. Those bright blue eyes dazzled.

"And promise to always ask me for what you want, need, or desire?"

She nodded again.

"Don't ever feel as if you can't talk to me. Because what pleases me is this connection we share. I can be quiet with you and feel safe. And I can be silly with you and know you are not judging me. And...I can be sad with you and know that you understand me."

"I do. Jean-Louis, I do understand you. You are my sexy Frenchman, who is stoic and proud, yet also kind and soft. You feel, just as I do. And you ache and hurt. Thank you for being open with me."

"I'm probably not so open as I should be."

Her grin warmed my soul. "You're learning."

I kissed her then because there was nothing else to be done but to communicate with our bodies. To enter one another and share those unspoken things that might never come to voice, but could be interpreted through skin, scent, and heartbeats.

Pushing Hollie's robe from her shoulders to drop onto the floor, I led her to the bed and climbed onto the plush temperpedic island frosted with fluffy duvet and crisp cotton sheets. We nestled within the cloud, our bodies spooning together as if the magnetic attraction between our electrons demanded it. Her thigh nudged my erection but I was content to simply lay with her in my arms, wandering into the teasing pleasure that rubbing my cock against her skin would produce, but then not needing that kind of satisfaction from her right now.

It was her heartbeats against mine that focused me and lured my head against her chest to listen. To close my eyes and embrace the life beside me, and to know I was safe.

And loved.

I woke to the nipple-tightening sensation of a man's tongue venturing up the inside of my thigh. I had a flash of Jean-Louis and I falling into bed together naked last night, but then not having sex. Holding one another, we'd fallen asleep. I don't think I'd stirred once during the night.

But now, with the sun teasing my closed eyelids, and an expert tongue landing on my clitoris, I was thankful for the arousal. I spread my legs and my lover hummed his approval.

Mm, yes, right there. I arched my back, and pressed my fingers into his thick, curly hair. The heat and wetness slicking my clit brought me to instant horny. I bent a knee, drawing my legs wide, hoping he'd dive in completely and never surface.

What a way to wake up.

"Drink me," I murmured, sleep husking my voice. Biting my lip, I moaned and tilted my hips upward, silently insisting he go deep.

He concentrated on my clit, dancing his tongue down each side of it where the firm pressure radiated tendrils of effervescence within my pussy. A thumb pressed the head of it, rubbing it softly, then a testing squeeze as if to keep it from slipping away. That is what did it. That exacting pressure lured the coils of orgasm to focus there at the power point. Was it the place of my superpowers?

The thought of it made me giggle prematurely, and my lover glanced up to see what was the deal.

"Don't stop," I gasped.

And with but a lash of his tongue down the seam of my labia, and yet another firm press to my clitoris, he launched the orgasm and I blasted off into the stratosphere. Head thrusting back into the pillow, I cried out to the morning, a cock announcing the day.

And thinking that word made me reach down and grasp for his steely cock. But he lay between my legs, his tongue still working the landscape of my pussy, as I bucked and spilled wet upon him. I couldn't reach the goal.

"*Bon matin*," he murmured and nuzzled his mouth over my shivering labia. "I love you."

Bags in hand, we headed down the hallway toward the elevator, Hollie in the lead. She passed the lift and went straight for the stairway door.

"Why do you never take *un ascenseur*?" I asked. "Are you claustrophobic?"

"We've discussed this." She held the door for me, and I stepped through. "I have a fear of getting stuck in a tiny Parisian elevator and being trapped like a corpse in a coffin."

"I don't think the corpse minds the small space," I offered.

"Bad analogy. I don't want to risk it. And maybe it's to do with cramped spaces. Can you tell me you trust the elevators of Paris?"

"Most of them. I have been stuck once, but it was only three hours, and the woman stranded with me was very pleasant."

"Really?" She paused at the lobby door and I stepped right up to her, pressing my chest against hers. "Was she pretty?"

"I'm sure fifty years earlier she attracted the men in hoards. She was eighty. Not my type, either. A redhead. She shared with me adventures of her son's journeys through Africa. It was an interesting three hours."

My hands occupied with two heavy bags, I leaned in to kiss her. I wanted another taste of her. And another. And another.

This morning, I'd bought her two pairs of Jimmy Choos because she had squealed with such delight over the purple velvet pair that I knew the red patent leather ones were a necessity. And the visit to Chateau d'If had been awesome, mixing fiction and history and our shared love for Dumas. We'd skipped breakfast (though I had dined on pussy; *exquis*) and planned to eat a late lunch on the train.

"I'd like to get stuck in an elevator with you," I said. "It would be okay for you if I was with you, *oui*?"

"Let's hope we never find out."

I followed her out through the lobby to the car I'd called for earlier. "You can't avoid them all your life."

Hollie paused before getting into the back of the limo. "Watch me."

Her wink was too cute to be dangerous, and I followed her inside the car and pushed her down on the seat to kiss her silly. She protested with whimpers about the driver. "He knows where to go," I reassured. And we didn't come up for air until the driver cleared his throat and repeated for the third time that we'd arrived at our destination.

After a light meal on the train, I begged off from chattering with my enthusiastic partner by closing my eyes and telling her to give me half an hour to relax. She stuffed earbuds into her ears, and the song she dialed her iPod to was some heavy rocker tune from the 80s. I did love her eclectic music taste. It matched mine.

I was thankful for the quiet, the gentle rocking of the train on the tracks as we zoomed north toward Paris. The man seated across the aisle from us and facing our direction had gray hair past his ears and wild eyebrows. Trim, and dressed in a light-colored suit, he resembled Pierre.

At such a startling thought, I closed my eyes.

I hadn't seen Pierre l'Etoile in over five years. But the last time we'd spoken he'd worn a beige linen suit and had always pushed his hair over his ears, a quirk of his.

My jaw tensed and I could feel the strain at the corners of my eyes. I tilted my head toward the window and feigned sleep, while I surreptitiously wiped a tear from my cheek.

Damned old bastard was finally making me feel something toward him. Should I have accepted the money? Gone to university? I wouldn't have been happy. But it would have made him happy.

Fuck.

I felt Hollie leave her seat and when I knew she had gone, perhaps to the lavatory, I sniffed and used a shirt cuff to dry my eyes.

Idiot Frenchman, sobbing on the train. Get it together, Jean-Louis. The old man was gone. And I had done the right thing. I'd followed my passion.

You know you did not. You followed the money.

I was passionate about VSquire. But yes, the cooking would always be a part of my soul.

I didn't believe in regrets. But this felt like something deeper, something I might never completely dive into—and didn't want to take that plunge. So I'd shove it aside. I had to. It was the only way I'd make it home without blubbering on my girlfriend's shoulder before a trainload of passengers.

He hadn't been sleeping. But I sensed Jean-Louis wanted a few minutes to himself, so I got up to wander about the train. I stopped in the bathroom. It was bigger than an airplane bathroom, which relieved me only a little because—okay, maybe I was claustrophobic. I quickly washed my hands and splashed my face with water. That refreshed me.

The dining car paneled in dark wood boasting red-velvet seat cushions featured a bar. I bought a crisp moscato and sat in one of the window seats for twenty minutes, watching the snowy countryside zoom by. The postcard view featured a jagged horizon of snow-crusted trees that glistened under the afternoon sunlight. Made me only a little homesick for Iowa. France didn't get nearly as much snow as we did in the States. And I did not miss having to shovel heavy, wet, heart-attack snow, and plodding through slush and ruining my shoes.

You see, I had been destined for Paris long before I'd moved there. I hadn't the patience for snowboots when heels and cute suede flats looked much nicer, even in the winter. Nor, as I'd grown older, had I appreciated the winter activities like snowmobiling or skiing or sledding. I was a city girl to the core.

You most certainly can take the country out of the girl.

Tonight was actually New Years Eve. I wondered if Jean-Louis might like to go to a club. Really do the New Year up with a bang. I wasn't much of a bar hopper, but maybe a quiet place and a couple flutes of champagne would be all right? We'd be in Paris by early evening. It might be the thing to lift my lover's spirits.

Either that, or he'd insist he wanted to stay home. Which, I should expect. He had lost his father. Everyone grieved so differently. I know I wouldn't have wanted to go out partying a week after my mother's death. Perhaps it would be best not to bring up the idea of partying.

I wrinkled my mouth in thought. I'd play it by ear. If all else failed, maybe we could start reading the book together. He'd loved the gift. I'm so glad I'd thought to look for it for him.

I passed the bathroom on the way to our car, and call it the effects from the wine, but a sexy idea zinged into my thoughts. Jean-Louis smiled as I returned to my seat, and I leaned in to kiss him. "Come with me," I said.

"You find the bar?" he asked.

"I did. I should have brought you some wine, but I didn't."

"Then where are we headed?"

I pushed open the bathroom door and tugged him inside, reaching around him in a hug to lock the door behind him.

"Pants down," I said. "This is going to be a quickie because it is so cramped."

He nuzzled his nose into my hair and nipped at my ear. "Sort of like an elevator, eh?"

I hadn't considered the resemblance to my most feared nemesis. And now that he said it...

"*Oui*. You will master your fears now and I will help." His trousers unzipped and his pants dropped at my heels.

"I don't want to master anything right now," I protested. "I just want a fast fuck."

He dove to my jaw and nuzzled a biting kiss there. "As you wish."

I was wearing a skirt with tights, so I realized this wasn't going to be easy. Not if I wanted to keep my shoes on and the tights. Which I did.

"Think we can manage this?" I pulled down his boxer briefs and wrapped a firm clasp about his at-attention cock. "I don't want to get undressed."

His hand slid under my skirt and tugged at the tights. "I am talented in putting you in the right position, *mon abeille*."

I squeezed his hardness firmly. "I want—no, I *need* this. Inside me. Pumping fast."

I shimmied my hips to assist as he pulled down my tights and his fingers glided over my pussy. I was wet because the spur-of-the-moment adventure excited me in ways I'd never thought possible. Standing in a small, snug box that smelled like air freshener? So not romantic. Mastering a fear? Forget about it.

The rocking motion of the train banged Jean-Louis's shoulders back and forth between the walls. If I thought about it too much I'd demand escape. Right now. Before the tiny box got stuck between floors—

His finger entered me and I sucked in my lower lip, tilting back my head. Who cared about cramped little boxes? We were not between floors. All that mattered was Jean-Louis's hot skin against mine and that his finger stroked inside me, glancing the sweet spot.

I worked his cock up and down within my circled fingers, eliciting a hiss from him. "More," I said.

He obeyed, pushing two fingers inside me, his knuckles kneading my thigh with focused pressure. I wanted to pull off my sweater and let him bite my breasts, gently, hungrily, but I didn't want to risk the time. This was the only lavatory for two cars. Quickness was key.

Jutting my hips forward, I guided his penis between my legs and he moaned appreciatively as my thighs hugged him. He pumped between my legs using the friction to amp up his pleasure and juice his rod. The train joggled and he pressed both hands out to the walls to stop from plunging into me and taking us down.

I caught his erection with my thighs and this time didn't let go until he'd entered me, just the head of him, because that was all we could manage in this awkward position. But that small connection felt so good. The two of us joining, when all around us the world remained unaware, going about their way, doing their random things.

And we were fucking. Furiously. Grabbing a stolen moment of excitement and pleasure. Using it to disguise the underlying grief. And forging it into a persuasive means to forgetfulness.

"You're so hot," he said, clasping me across the back and lifting me onto my toes so he could glide in deeper.

With my thighs pressed together and him driving into me, his every movement tugged at my clit and a sudden, surprising jolt of orgasm shot through my belly and mons. I gasped against his neck and kissed him hard, there beneath his chin. Body shuddering against his, I squeezed my inner muscles and Jean-Louis's body jerked against mine as he came. Clutching me tightly, so I wouldn't fall away, his body pulsed a few times as he road the pleasure wave.

He pulled out and reached around me for a Kleenex from the dispenser then slipped it over the cum on my thighs.

"To a wondrous New Year," he said, and kissed me deeply before we heard the knock on the door.

ÅÅÅ

The woman who had been waiting outside the bathroom returned down the aisle and shot me a long hard glare as she passed. Yes, yes, so we'd been fucking in the loo. Get over it you old bat. Ha!

I clasped Jean-Louis's hand and he cast me an effervescent smile.

I kissed his hand and said, "I love you."

"That makes me a lucky man."

"You think?"

He nodded.

"Do you want to go out and do up the town tonight to celebrate the New Year?"

"I would love that."

"Really? You don't think it's too soon after...?"

"Not at all. We both need to get out of our heads, *oui*? We'll start at the Crazy Horse, then there is a club in the 9th I would take you to."

"The Crazy Horse? Isn't that a sex club?"

"They feature the follies."

"So, half naked women but no naked men? How does this figure in to my kind of entertainment?"

"If I can find a naked man for you will that make you happy?"

I slid a hand over his lap and squeezed his cock, which grew noticeably firmer. "I already have one."

"We don't have to do the sex show. If it would make you uncomfortable? I would like to see you watching it, though."

"Be a voyeur at my side?"

"Of a sort."

"It is your MO."

He smirked and winked at me. "I don't think it's the kind of show one watches to get off. It is art."

"And dozens of bare breasts for your viewing pleasure." I kissed him. "I'm up for it, as long as we can hit a dance club afterward. I want to fill my brain with loud music and get a little tipsy. Not too much, though. I am a teetotaler."

"I'm not much of a drinker myself. I will make sure you do not get drunk, Hollie. We will begin the new year with a bang, *oui*?"

"Only if the bang means you putting me up against the wall when we get home."

"That's exactly what I meant."

Fourteen

I watched Hollie's reaction to the mostly-nude dancers on the stage. We had only been able to get seats in the back, but that provided for a better view of the entire show. Which was disappointing. The Crazy Horse had become too touristy since I had last been here. I heard English whispers bantered in the audience, and many other languages as well. The seedy atmosphere smelled like stale sex and popcorn.

No self-respecting Frenchman would have taken his date here. I had failed New Years Eve.

Hollie clasped my hand and leaned in close. Her vanilla scent softened my regret. When she kissed my jaw and dashed her tongue along the stubble I probably should have shaved, I tilted my head against hers and we swooned together through the rest of the show.

"Not as risqué as I'd expected," she announced as we filed out of the club and I vacillated on whether or not to hire a taxi or to take the Métro to a club.

"I am sorry," I said. "That wasn't even titillating. They were selling nipple pasties in the gift shop. Remind me never to take you to any place that has a gift shop."

I mocked a horrific shudder then hailed a cab. I wasn't about to let my girl struggle in the Métro in those sexy bow-tied high heels.

Seated in the back of the cab, I hugged her close and slid my hand inside her dress. Sexy, bold blue. Toward the end of the show, I'd discovered it was one of those dresses that wraps and ties at her waist. She had worn the same for our liaison before Mona Lisa. I had but to slide my hand inside and over her breast. And Hollie snuggling closer to me from the cold? The evening just got better.

"The only strip show I want to watch," I whispered at her ear, "is the one from my window."

"I wish I could see better into your living room window."

"Why is that?" I wondered as I toggled her nipple lazily.

"Then I could watch you teaching fencing," she said. The cab soared through the city. A constellation of red taillights streaked by. "I'm so curious about it. I want to see my musketeer in action."

"Perhaps you could attend a practice session one time."

She squirmed when I gave her nipple a squeeze. "I don't know. Would that be weird for your student? But maybe you could give me a lesson?"

I hadn't thought of that. It sounded like fun. And I knew it would end in a sexy tumble on the ottoman. "Deal. That club!" I pulled my hand from Hollie's dress and rapped the window. "*Arret*!"

The cabbie pulled over and I tossed a twenty-euro bill up front, thanked him, and escorted Hollie to the front doors. It was a classy place that only let in those they deemed trendy or stylish, or rich. We were nodded in immediately. I suppose the Zegna suit had done the trick, but I liked to think it was the gorgeous woman on my arm whose sexy gams had drawn the eyes of the bouncer downward.

The dark decor was a study in variegated shades of blue. Blue neon everywhere. Blue lights up under the bars. Blue dance floor. Even the waitresses wore shiny blue skirts that were so short a man could spy a peek of ass curve when they bent over the tables. Nice.

I slid a hand over Hollie's toned ass—her blue dress matched the decor—and nuzzled a kiss against her neck. "What's your drink?"

"Let's do champagne."

"I'll grab us a couple. You want to find a table?"

"I think I'm going to dance. I love this song!"

And she slipped away toward the dance floor, leaving me to marvel at her ever-changing facade. The fun, spontaneous vixen turned and winked and waved at me. And earlier today I'd held the sex-starved slut against the bathroom wall on the train. And yet, yesterday we'd held hands and I'd consoled her over her mother's death.

"*Monsieur, voulez-vous danser*?"

I turned to gaze into a gorgeous set of green eyes surrounded by lush black lashes. My eyes dropped to the unavoidable breasts that plunged up from a tight black leather corset. Glossy red lips curled into a teasing smile. Mercy.

"Champagne," I uttered, dumbly nodding toward the bar. Though I felt compelled to add, "*Très jolie, mademoiselle*." I winked in approval and then pushed through the crowd toward the bar. I would never stop admiring the female form. And tits? Loved them. But my heart belonged to Hollie.

I laid down my black credit card on the flashing blue neon bar. Let the celebrating begin.

Though certainly I did recall Hollie telling me not to let her drink too much. I was a two-drink kind of guy. I didn't like the man I became after drinks number four, five, and six. Such excessive drinking should be reserved only for after biking stints with the guys while sitting around a bonfire.

Four goblets of champagne later—for each of us—I decided buying a bottle was more reasonable. Hollie stood in my embrace as we danced to a slower tune, the dance floor flashing azure beneath our feet, and the crowd brushing and pushing against us. Music bounced off the walls and jittered in my eardrums. Some teeny-bopper singer who wore his pants down around his thighs and was famous for puking on stage. The song was annoying.

But Hollie and I were in our own world. Nothing else mattered.

"You bought a bottle?" Hollie saw the waiter deliver the bottle to the table we'd staked out near the dance floor. "You are such a...a lover boy."

She was drunk. I neared inebriation, but I could hold my alcohol better than she could. She had slipped into a melancholy, which I'd decided wouldn't do for an end of the year send-off.

I led her to the table and instead of pouring another goblet, I tilted back a swallow straight from the bottle, then lifted it to toast the crowd, "*Salut*!"

"Let me have some more of that joy juice," Hollie slurred. "Mmm..."

"We must do resolutions," I suddenly decided.

Hollie's head tilted against my shoulder and she sought my crotch with her hand. One squeeze was all it took to make me hard. You bet I could get it up on a bender.

"I resolve..." she muttered, "to get you off tonight. And tomorrow night. And forever after that."

"I will do the same!" I announced loudly with another raise of the champagne bottle to toast the crowd.

The music had grown louder and it thumped in my brain as if a relentless Poe-inspired torture. My heartbeat matched the techno pulse, and the muggy air seemed to hold me upright even as my shoulders swayed forward and back. An unavoidable grin lifted my cheeks.

Very well, I was feeling the alcohol, too.

"We should fuck." Hollie gripped my jaw and laughed when our gazes wobbled. "Maybe not. I think I'm feeling sick."

Ah hell. Fresh air was in order.

"You were not going to let me get drunk," she admonished. "Bad Frenchman. *Très* naughty."

"You had two drinks."

"Two? It was more like..." She held up three fingers, eyes crossed, and she readjusted to add her other hand with—I wasn't sure how many fingers that was. "Fingers?" A silly grin curled her lips. "I like it when you put your fingers in me, lover boy."

"I can do that right now. Move closer. Open your legs for me, woman."

"Wait. Where's the lady's room?"

"You want to fuck here in the bar? *Oui*!"

I tugged her out of the booth, but the hand I grabbed wasn't moving. Hollie jerked me to the edge of the dance floor before I could spy the bathroom. I wobbled, but did a double step skip, landing with a jump and a splay of arms before my lover.

"Just me," Hollie stated with an admonishing jab of her finger to my chest. "I need to puke."

Eloquence had gotten lost in that last goblet of champagne. I pushed her toward the dance floor. "That way."

I didn't puke. But man, I'd needed an escape from the claustrophobic crowd. And that music! I was so over funky pop tunes overlaid with bass-heavy rap riffs. I'd meandered, zigzagging like a pinball between dancing couples, to the ladies' room. Only, the bathroom had been clouded with cigarette smoke, and I'm sure there had been a couple fucking in the far stall. Hell, it could have been a threesome for the number of shoes I'd counted beneath the metal divider.

Jean-Louis had been waiting outside the bathroom door to whisk me outside and head for home. Good call.

The Métro car was packed. And my head was spinning right round, baby, right round. Like a record, baby... Yikes! The nightclub's techno beat still clanged about in my head and hips. I didn't think I was standing still. It's hard to tell when the people all around me were bobbling as if dancing in a club. I clung to the steel pole as if to let go would send me hurtling into outer space where my head would implode from the loss of atmospheric pressure.

Actually, that might feel good right about now. An implosion would relieve the dizzy spinning up in this crazy drunk chick's cranium.

I felt Jean-Louis's hand slide up my thigh and under my skirt. I hoped it was his hand. If the hand in question belonged to someone else...

Oh, mercy, I did not feel good. Check, please?

I shifted my hip backward, banging the man behind me, whom I hoped was my guy. He smelled like my guy, only with a distinct tinge of whiskey. We hadn't drank whiskey. That I know of.

Ugg. Thinking about whiskey stirred my gut in an unpleasant roil.

"Not now," I muttered. The hand glided between my legs from behind. "Jean-Louis!"

He pressed his body against mine, resting his chin on my shoulder. Just focusing long enough to make eye contact with him hurt my brain, or maybe I was too sensitive and not in the mood.

"I must touch you," he pouted. "I cannot stop."

"Not with everyone so close," I whispered, sure I was screaming.

In fact, the guy immediately before me, clinging to another steel pole, eyed me lasciviously. I shook my hips in an attempt to dissuade Jean-Louis's intent pursuits. He only leaned in tighter, nuzzling his mouth against my neck. His fingers tweaked at my pussy.

"You are so beautiful," he singsonged in a drunken melody so out of tune with my spinning head. "Let's do it now."

"No!"

The car rolled to a halt, and the doors opened. I tore away from the handsy man and wobbled out onto the landing. The chilled air brewed an awful mix of urine and body odor, and I gagged to keep down my stomach. When I turned, I landed in Jean-Louis's arms. I pushed him away and staggered toward the exit stairway. "Not now!"

If the man wanted to get some, he'd have to wait until we returned to the privacy of my apartment. What was it with him and his odd fetish for public sex?

"You jilt me!" he called in drunken English that was only sad now. But no more sad than the two of us, so wasted we could barely walk a straight line. "My lover she is fickle!"

He followed me up the stairs as younger couples dodged around us chattering and having a good time. The kind of dancing and drinking we'd just imbibed should only be allowed for the under twenty set. I was getting old.

Frigid air blasted me in the face and sent a welcome shiver from my neck out my sleeves and down to my toes. It momentarily erased the need to toss my cookies. I inhaled and turned left. My apartment was five blocks away. A virtual trek across the desert, vast barren landscapes, and the Arctic tundra all rolled into one.

I could do this.

The world swirled and I wobbled. A step plunged my Louboutins into slush and the cold water oozed under my arches. Something hard crashed up against my side. The something smelled like whiskey. Groping hands embraced me and tweaked my nipple. Jean-Louis pulled me in for a kiss.

I didn't want this. I couldn't do romance now. And I most certainly did not want to have sex when my only goal was to hang my head over the toilet.

"Why not?" he called as I staggered onward. "Just right here. I am wearing my long coat!"

Again I was captured, crushed against a limestone wall laced with winter-dried vines. His hands deftly slipped up under my skirt, and my thighs, which were too weak to care about pleasure, quivered.

"Jean-Louis, you are being a monster." I shoved him away and he stumbled backward.

The man couldn't be as wasted as I, but his steps angled and he caught his back against a street pole. If I ever drank champagne again, would somebody please murder me to put me out of my misery?

I stuck out my tongue at him. He gestured at me dismissively and gave me that thrust of his nose that indicated I was being a poor sport, then walked on ahead, calling back that I was a poor lover. Or maybe he said *mean* lover. I was in no condition to interpret his French right now.

The asshole wanted to get it on? Fuck this. I'd show him how mean I could be.

Pulling open my coat, I struggled with the wrap sash that secured the dress across my stomach. Meanwhile, icy snow melted into my shoes and soaked my feet. I shouldn't have worn the Louboutins. Why hadn't I gone with the boots? I slipped on some wet snow and flailed wildly. The bastard didn't even turn around to notice I had almost gone down in a graceless sprawl.

A group of men strolled past me, and when they were clear, I tugged down the coat and let it drop. The dress clung because the jersey was like that. I struggled with the tie across my waist. My fingers weren't doing what I needed them to do.

Bed. I needed bed.

After I puked.

But foremost? I needed the Frenchman to be kind to this drunken sot whose head spun so wildly I wanted to wrap myself about the nearest tree trunk and cling until the storm had passed.

Peeling open the dress, I called out to him, "You want this, Monsieur Eiffel?"

Jean-Louis swung around. "What are you doing?"

The chill air tightened my bare nipples. I immediately regretted my hasty decision to show him who was boss. Who was I kidding? I felt the bile rise in my throat. Hoots and a whistle from behind me riddled a sharp heat up the back of my spine.

Jean-Louis rushed toward me. Yet from behind, I felt a hand clutch my arm.

"I will take what you are offering," said a male voice that was not the Frenchman I knew and loved.

The stranger jerked me around. I staggered and landed my palms against his chest. My bare breast brushed his coat sleeve. Pushing to get away, I felt hot tears spill down my cheeks.

"Unhand her!"

"You don't want her? She says I can have her!"

I managed to kick the man's shin. He laughed, as did his cohorts, who gathered close by. I couldn't see beyond the man's leering gaze, which was fixed to my chest. I hadn't worn a bra or panties beneath the dress tonight. Only thigh-high stockings.

Grabbed from behind, I was torn out of the stranger's grip and flung to the side. Jean-Louis's fist soared past my face as I stumbled toward the ground and the heap that I saw was my coat. I heard the crunch of fist connecting with nose. The men watching all groaned suddenly, then cheered.

"*Elle est tout a fait fou*," Jean-Louis growled at the pack. "*Allez*! Leave her be. *Foutre*!"

I knew what those words meant. No, I didn't. Maybe? God, I was cold. And pissed off.

"I am so tired of your French!" I shouted to the world, because I wanted everyone to hear me. "I will never learn it. I don't want to. What kind of stupid language makes you learn if a word is a male or female before you can speak it? It's stupid! Fucking stupid!"

Clutched from behind and pulled upright, I felt the warmth of my coat hug against my back. Jean-Louis struggled to pull the sleeve up my arm. All I wanted to do was push him away. Staggering, I slipped and fell completely into his sure grasp. And so I relented, desiring warmth more than distance.

"You called me crazy in the head," I protested as he tugged me down the sidewalk. "See! I do know French! *Canard*!" The coat flapped open. He stopped and tugged it closed then pulled the ties tightly. "I am not crazy!"

"You are crazy drunk!"

"So are you. Let me go!"

I struggled to release myself from his firm grasp, but couldn't win. Performing a sort of run-walk alongside his swift pace, we quickly gained our neighborhood. By the time we reached my building's front door, I couldn't move another inch. Cold, tired, and feeling as if my next step would result in a technicolor yawn, I shivered.

Jean-Louis swept me into his arms. The concierge was not on duty. Probably out partying. I hoped he was a kinder drunk than my lover was. For his wife's sake.

I don't remember the flight up three stairs or Jean-Louis searching for the apartment key in my coat pocket. The next time my eyelids fluttered open I was falling onto my bed, back first, arms splayed. My coat was still on, but my dress—oddly—hung wide open.

When had I torn open my dress? My shoes were still on my feet. The bows drooped and one bow was pulled free, the end of the black velvet ribbon crushed and soggy. They would drip wet all over the bed...

Who cared? The pillow felt like a warm cloud and so I turned my face into the cozy refuge.

"I am sorry, *mon abeille*," whispered against my ear. Whiskey, sable, and spice filled my immediate sensory range. "I am a cad. I will go home and see you tomorrow."

As he stood, I managed to grip some part of shirt or sleeve. "No. Don't leave me. Please. Stay with me."

"Very well. Over...there."

He stumbled across a pile of clothing and landed on the big easy chair by the window. I'd once sat naked in that chair and jilled off for his pleasure as he'd watched from his bedroom window across the street.

And now....

And now. What had we done?

Fifteen

I woke with a start. My body slid down in the chair. Back muscles spasmed painfully. I caught myself by gripping the chair arms before landing on the floor. *Merde*, I was in pain. And it wasn't my head. I could sleep off any drunk. But I usually did it prone and in bed.

Why I'd chosen to sleep in the chair last night was beyond me. I'd pay for it the rest of the day. Carefully, I stood and eased my spine this way and that to work at the tightened and kinked muscles stretching across my back. I wanted to twist my head side to side but my neck protested.

When had I become a decrepit old man?

I eyed the bed. Dirt spotted the end of the white comforter, and the sheets were mangled as if they had lost a fight. Hollie wasn't in bed.

I checked my watch. Eleven a.m.

"Fuck." I needed eggs, toast, and lots of orange juice. And a double espresso.

Wandering into the living room that was too bright by far for a chill January morning, I found Hollie sitting on the velvet chaise, barefoot, the yellow robe wrapped loosely about her body, her head bowed over the glass of fizzy water on the coffee table before her.

Last night returned to me in a horribly clear flashback. We had drunk far too much and the dancing to mix it all up inside hadn't helped. Sometime after the last bottle of champagne I had decided that a couple shots of whiskey would hit the spot. Idiot. I had manhandled Hollie on the Métro. I rarely got so wasted I treated a woman with such disregard. My drunk asshole self had risen up.

Yes, I had one of those. Didn't we all?

But that I had continued to prod at her and had been the one to press her to such an action as to strip on the sidewalk killed me. A stranger had grabbed her. Could have raped her. Because I had been an asshole.

I studied my bruised knuckles. Even half out of my gourd I'd delivered a powerful punch to the assailant. He'd gone down, and his friends had wisely carried him away, with apologies. The evening should have never gotten so out-of-hand.

Now I rushed to Hollie and knelt before her legs. I wanted to prostrate myself and lay there for eternity to atone for my cruelty. I laid my head on her knees and reached up to clasp around her hips.

"I'm so sorry," I said.

Her fingers worked in my hair. The touch was too gentle, too comforting.

"I was an animal. So cruel. Please forgive me?"

"We were both wasted," she whispered, as if to speak any louder would split open her skull.

I could relate.

"It's over, Jean-Louis."

What? No. That was too final...

"Let's put last night in our past," she said. "We both did things we regret."

"But if it hadn't been for my actions you would have never—"

When I looked up she pressed a finger to my lips. Normally I would have licked that finger and sucked it into my mouth. Oh, my aching back. Ah, my idiot self.

"Thank you for staying with me last night," she said softly. She tapped my bruised knuckles. "And thank you for the rescue."

I would have never the need to rescue her if I hadn't— Fine. I couldn't change what happened last night. Indeed, we had done things worthy of regret.

"My head is still spinning," she offered. "You want some ginger ale?"

I shook my head. "I don't have a hangover."

"Bastard."

I managed a chuckle. "Sorry. If it makes you feel any better, I may never get this kink out of my back after sleeping on the chair."

"I feel minimally better." She sighed and again stroked my hair, sending good shivers over my scalp. "Let's never drink so much again."

"I can agree to that."

The phone in my front pants pocket jingled. I ignored it as I leaned in to kiss Hollie's cheek. She smelled like vanilla and booze. "Want me to run you a hot bath?"

Again the phone jingled.

"Sounds like what the doctor ordered. But I can do it."

"I will do it for you," I offered. "You sit and relax."

"Answer your phone first."

I sat back on my haunches and checked the phone. It had rang through and a text message showed. From my wife. She was returning in a few weeks and would bring the divorce papers to me. Signed.

"Important?" Hollie asked.

"Uh, yes. My wife," I provided. "She'll be signing the papers soon."

"Soon." Hollie chuckled and shook her head. "I've heard that one before. You know, maybe this thing has run its course." She stood and stepped around me. Strolling to the window, she then turned to eye me through a messy spill of chestnut hair. "You and I? We've had a great time, but..."

"But?" I muttered to myself. What was she saying? This wasn't going to be a kiss-off. It couldn't be. "It was one mistake," I said, standing and following her into the kitchen. "A big mistake, yes, but we were not in our heads last night."

"You said you wouldn't let me get drunk." She set the glass in the sink and strode toward the bedroom.

I raced around to meet her before the bed and gripped her by the shoulders. Fuck, my back hurt like a mother. She pushed my chest and struggled out of the desperate grasp.

"Hollie? You are hung over. I will let you be alone and return later when you are feeling better."

"I think we need a break from one another," she said.

The words hung in the air like stale laundry on the line.

"No." In my mind I had screamed that softly-spoken word. "I think you are out of your head still. It's not over. It can't be over. I love you."

"I thought I loved you."

She tugged the robe opening tightly across her chest, her eyes wandering away from mine. My heartbeats stopped. I couldn't breathe. Such words were not coming from her mouth.

After a sigh she said, "Everything happens for a reason."

My jaw dropped open. Words escaped me.

"I don't know, Jean-Louis. Don't make this so difficult. I mean, come on. You have a wife."

"That didn't stop you from jumping into this relationship. From fucking me. From letting me fuck you!"

I fisted a hand and shook my head. That was no way to derail her sudden need to jump ship. If I was smart, I'd leave and do as I'd said. Return later when we had recovered from our ridiculous drunken binge.

But I couldn't walk out on her. She meant more to me than a sudden surrender in hopes to appease.

"Leave," she muttered.

"No." I crossed my arms. "This is you and your silly ideas about romance. Didn't you tell me you and your friend only date men for a month then dump them? I am not so disposable!"

Wincing, she rubbed a finger along her brow. Her gaze fell to the floor beside of the bed. "My shoes are destroyed," she said with disbelief.

"I will buy you a new pair. I will buy you twenty pairs!"

"That's not the point! Jean-Louis, I stripped in the middle of Paris last night and was manhandled by a stranger."

I pulled her into an embrace and thought that if only I could hold her long and firmly enough I could make it all go away. Reverse last night, and instead make it an evening we'd decided to spend at home, making love to celebrate the new year.

I didn't want to begin the year with a fight. Or worse, a breakup.

"Jean-Louis, just go," she whispered. Her arms strained against my chest. That she wanted to push me away stabbed at my heart. It was a rebuff I could not afford after losing Pierre. "Please."

I let her escape from my self-imposed desperation. She wandered into the bathroom and slammed the door. I felt that rejection tear through my heart. As I'd felt it once before when I'd learned my wife had been unfaithful, had never really loved me.

My throat dried. I tried to swallow, to make sense of this argument. The shoes. Her plead for me to leave. The whiskey. Why had

I drank whiskey? And why had I been such a bastard to her on the Métro?

Give her time. It will be better later.

I hoped for that. But as I left Hollie's apartment and wandered down the stairs I had the worst feeling this could be the last time I stood in this building. And perhaps I'd have to keep my bedroom curtains drawn from now on.

ÅÅÅ

I cried so much while soaking in the bathtub I wondered if the tub water would overflow with my tears and spill onto the bathroom floor. I sat there, a disgruntled mermaid, until the water grew cold and I began to shiver. I hadn't washed my face, I realized, when I stood before the mirror and saw the black shadows under my eyes from last night's smudged eyeliner.

What a mess. Why had I gotten so drunk? And had I just broke up with my fabulous French lover?

"Fuck."

I shook my head at the crazy lady in the mirror and wandered out to the bedroom. Landing on the bed face first, I lay there through the afternoon, drowsing and not caring that my stomach rumbled for food.

At one point I peered over the edge of my pity boat and spied the damaged Louboutins.

"Double fuck."

Sixteen

I don't know what the hell had happened with Hollie yesterday morning. I'd given her the space she'd asked for all day. Had resisted calling her in the evening. Had even resisted standing before my bedroom window to wait for her to appear like the goddess behind glass that she was.

We had not broken up. No, it had been the hangover talking.

That was my hope.

In the bedroom I picked up the copy of *The Three Musketeers* from my dresser and pressed the cover to my nose. Smelled old. But the faintest hint of vanilla had been imbued within the cover fibers. Or was I imagining Hollie's scent?

I needed to smell her, to feel her, to kiss her and hold her tightly.

Setting the book aside, I pulled out my mobile, sat on the end of the bed, and dialed Hollie's number. Glancing out the window, I could see clearly into her bedroom, but she wasn't in there. Until I saw her run out from the bathroom and toward the kitchen.

The phone picked up. "Oh. Jean-Louis."

Really? That's how she answered the phone after the argument we'd had? A lackluster *oh*?

Was this the right thing to do? Should I have waited for her to call me? What the hell was I doing? Why were my hands clammy? Would I ever get a relationship right?

"It was a mistake," I started, but then realized I wasn't sure what to say. How to smooth over her fears that the relationship had gone sour over one bad night? "Hollie?"

Her breath hushed over the phone line. "Can you give me some space?"

Ah, fuck me. Space? What was that about? *Merde*, I'd screwed this up. What an idiot. This relationship was real to me, so valuable. Yet, did I know what a real relationship even looked like?

"Hollie, you can't be serious. One minute we are in love and the next you are pushing me away?"

"Jean-Louis, please, give me this. I think I need a few days. I love you. I really do. I know that I do. I'm just..."

Her pause killed me. One breath, then another. I wanted those breaths on my mouth, at my throat, against my chest. She was right across the street. We shouldn't be doing this over the phone.

"I'll give you a call in a few days."

The connection clicked off and I must have sat there for long minutes staring at the display, at Hollie's tiny avatar, her happy smile and bright blue eyes. I had done nothing—nothing—to deserve this treatment.

Had I?

Fine. I was an asshole. A *canard*, as she had called me. Yet I had apologized. What more did she want from me?

"Christ." I almost flung the mobile to the floor, but it suddenly rang and I recognized the caller. I had two fencing students today. "*Oui*?"

He would be late, but I told him to take his time. That would give me a chance to work out my frustrations by doing some pre-workout pushups. What I needed was a punching bag.

But first. I searched the directory on my mobile for a flower shop.

AAA

I met Melanie for lunch at the Regina Hotel. Not Angelina. (I know.) But the line to get in was thirty minutes long, and it was snowing out, so when Melanie suggested the hotel but two blocks down the Rue de Rivoli I didn't balk. No matter that it would cost me a fortune to nibble on *hors d'oeuvres*. I needed the culinary retreat.

As usual, Melanie ordered for us. It was easier. Me with my English and so few French words, and the waiter darting me the sorry looks? Nah. I could allow Melanie to play the man's role every time and it didn't bother either of us.

Which reminded me that I had yet to take Jean-Louis's suggestion to begin a French language course. Did that mean I wasn't devoted to the relationship?

Don't go there.

I was not going to overthink things today.

"You sounded panicked," Melanie said after we'd received a salad, which was approximately two lettuce leaves, one slice of carrot and a blop of something yellow that I wasn't sure I wanted to test. "It was a good thing I have a two-day layover before dashing off to Madrid. All is not well with you and Monsieur Sexy?"

"We had a fight and I told him I needed space."

"Ooh."

Yep, that had been a telling oh. The short oh was one of those condescending 'I told you so' ohs that Melanie used freely, and which annoyed me. The long, extended oh was a merciful 'I can relate' sort of oh that she employed less often but with more gusto.

But this ooh had said: Oh. Uh-huh. Tell me all about it, *cherie*.

So I told her about our disastrous New Year's Eve fight and me getting groped by a strange man. Which was my fault for stripping in the first place.

"No, no, no," Melanie interrupted. "Jean-Louis should have protected you."

"He was wasted, too. And he was walking in front of me, so he didn't see how stupid I was acting. And when he did notice he punched the guy out. He had bruises on his knuckles that I noticed when I was telling him to leave me alone."

"Good for you. Any man who lets a date go so far as that one did is not deserving of you."

"Yeah, but, Melanie..." A sigh spilled out my repressed emotions. And I felt a hot burn in my core. It was my heart, vying for notice from my brain. So I took notice, and confessed, "I love him."

"You are saying that word because it is expected of you. *I love him*," she mocked. "Oh, sure you do. Because that is what girlfriends say. They think it is what men want to hear. But it is just a word when used in that context. Real love is different."

I clamped my mouth shut before I blurted out something like, "Like you would know, Miss Mile High Club and Change 'Em Every Two Weeks?" Instead, I dipped the carrot medallion in the yellow stuff and crunched. "Whoa!"

The yellow blop tasted like wasabi on steroids. It seared my tongue. "Oh, fuck."

Melanie pushed the water goblet toward me and glanced around. Yes, we were in a fancy restaurant, so why the hell had they sneak attacked me with the hot stuff, knowing full well I'd need a fire hose to put this burn out?

"Lettuce," Melanie coached. "It will stop the burn. You are only supposed to dip not scoop, *cherie*. That stuff will put down a strong man."

"You're telling me," I gasped as I furiously munched the icy-crisp lettuce. Seemed to do the trick. Not really. I gulped more water.

"So you are on the market again?" Melanie provided cheerily as she tried her best to ignore my antics. "I know a man—he is French—who will take you to a fancy show and treat you to an exquisite meal and expect only a kiss at the door. He is a real gentleman."

"Melanie, no." One more swallow of water. That helped. Somewhat. "I meant it when I said I love Jean-Louis."

"Right. You love him so much you've told him to stay away from you."

Stating the obvious was not going to win her any points today. "Tell me about your love life," I tried, to deflect her accusing stare. "Show me your latest bauble."

"Oh!" Her eyes lit up and she leaned forward, tucking a gorgeous swath of red hair behind her ear.

I can't believe I hadn't seen those diamond stunners flashing at me even through the thick hair. "Wow. Those are bigger than the blueberries I had on my toast this morning."

"From Guy on Christmas Eve."

"Ah. Ghee," I said, saying the name, but imagining it in my head as it was pronounced. Always reminded me of clarified butter. Who named their son after lard? French or not, that was a name that always made me laugh.

"Yes, yes," she said waving off my curling smile. "You laugh all you like. I can cash in these sparklers for a cool ten thousand if need be."

"They are gorgeous, Melanie. Don't sell them. If you ever tire of them, you can loan them to me."

"Your lover doesn't give you fancy gifts?"

"Okay, now you're being a snot."

She conceded with a shrug and we laughed it off. Lunch arrived, and I was thankful the plate was absent any yellow fire sauce. Digging into the creamy risotto, we chattered for another hour before doing the double cheek kiss and promising to see each other in the spring. Melanie's work schedule would keep her away from Paris that long.

"I'll miss you!" I called as she hailed a cab and skirted off to her fabulous life.

Standing across the street from the gilded Joan of Arc statue, I shivered against the cold and tucked the blue and gray wool scarf tight about my neck (yes, I'd stolen it from Jean-Louis, *after* he had washed it). Did she really have such a fabulous life? Certainly the world travel must be interesting. And being an extrovert, Melanie's socializing and partying were a perfect fit for her.

But she returned home every night to an empty apartment. Sure, she had lovers, men who told her she was beautiful and who gave her pretty things. But I suspected that she must be empty when standing alone in her kitchen, wondering what she would cook for one. Had to be. Maybe a little?

I didn't want her to be unhappy, and perhaps she wasn't. But I wished her a great romance some day, when the time was right. Every woman deserved a man who loved her, no matter what. Even those women who told their lovers to leave them alone.

Feeling lonesome for my Frenchman, I stepped across the street and veered left for the closest Métro station. It was too cold to walk the half hour home.

I arrived before my building as a floral delivery truck pulled up. The concierge opened the door for me, and when I had made it to the stairway he called after me.

"For you, Mademoiselle!"

I turned to find a massive bouquet of red roses looming nearer. The man behind the blossoms muttered something in French.

"He will bring them up for you, Mademoiselle," the concierge explained because he knew my mastery of the language was nil.

Now would have been an excellent time to take the elevator. Poor guy had to wind up three flights of a tight staircase. I tipped him a five-euro bill because that was all I had in my purse, and, after I'd cleared off the books, he set the bouquet on the living room table.

I counted. Four dozen. Wow. And they were half opened and the blossoms were each as big as my fist. The red velvet petals plushed against my fingertips. A heady perfume rose from them. I felt like Dorothy in the poppy field as I breathed them in.

On the tiny red card was written: *Vous me manquez.* I didn't have to look up a translation. It meant: *You are missing from me.*

Ah fuck, the Frenchman wins again.

"I miss you, too."

Kneeling, I leaned in and wrapped my arms about the bouquet because I'd never seen so many roses at once and I wanted to feel them, take in the volume and scent. He certainly knew the way to my heart. Heck, he'd already found his way there, this was merely a stop to jam under the door to keep it open.

I should probably call him, but with a glance across the street I could see the action going on in his loft. Sword play. I wished the view was better. I only caught glimpses of a man in white vest and a sword slashing the air.

I had been serious about him teaching me to fence. It would be a great way to spend more time with him. Study his physique in motion. Was naked fencing a thing? His email address was *nakedfencer*, after all.

I sat on the chaise and put up my feet on the table, my toe twitching at one of the rose petals.

We had both been wrong.

He'd been an asshole, but the booze certainly had something to do with that. And I had acted ridiculously. Again, I was going to blame it on the booze. We weren't normally like that. And I genuinely believed such an incident wouldn't again occur.

So I could forgive him. But first...I had to forgive myself.

"Next time we go to a club," I vowed, "just one goblet of wine for me."

AAA

After a shower, I wandered into the bedroom naked and spied him standing there in his boxer briefs, a notebook pressed to the window. How long had he been standing there? I hadn't noticed him when I'd gone into the bathroom twenty minutes earlier.

The page read: Call me?

I picked up the phone and waved it at him, then dialed his number. As soon as he answered, I rushed out, "I was selfish. I wanted time to think about things. And I've thought about it."

"And?"

"And, I've never been in such an intense relationship before. I think I actually freaked out. Got nervous that maybe I'd destroyed something so good. I don't want to lose you, Jean-Louis. I love you. I miss you. But I don't ever want to get drunk at a club with you again."

"Agreed. All that champagne was a bad decision. Don't even ask me about the whiskey."

"We can drink together. And I like getting a buzz, but let's do it at home next time, okay?"

"Agreed. But I am sorry, too."

"You are forgiven. Let's put it in the past." I walked up to the window and pressed my palm to it. "Want to do the window thing tonight?"

"Why not? Though I wish I could touch you right now."

"Yeah, you're right. Windows are for beginners. Give me five minutes. I'll be right over. Do not change."

"I'll leave the door open for you. I'll be waiting in here." He winked at me and I blew him a kiss. He caught the kiss and pressed it over his heart. "Love you, *mon abeille*."

So I hadn't stayed in the bedroom. I'd gone to the kitchen to get a glass of water when Hollie walked in. She dropped her coat on the floor revealing she wore nothing beneath.

Catching her wrists with my hands, I kissed each one then glided my tongue along the soft inner skin of her elbow and up her neck, finally landing on her mouth. She sighed into me. I indulged in her warmth, her sweetness, and the visceral relief at having her back in my arms.

Her fingers found my cock, hard and ready under my boxers, and she shoved them down so I could kick them off. Both naked, I turned her around and pushed her against the back of the sofa. Grasping her across the stomach, I spread her legs and without asking, hilted myself inside her.

The pressure of her insides squeezing about me, and the heat of her combined with the incessant need to get off, to piston myself inside her was incredible. I pumped at her furiously. Gripping the back of her neck gently yet firmly, I took from her. Yes, taking, no giving. I needed to get off. To stake my claim. To fucking nail this woman to the sofa.

"Yes," she hissed. "Harder." A tilt of her hips opened her to me and allowed me in deeper.

I swore. Fifty colors of bliss washed before my eyes. And one perfect orgasm stiffened my muscles and I shot into her, filling her. Owning her. Making her mine once again.

I wrapped my hands about her, clasped her breasts and pulled her up against my panting body. Sighing over her shoulder, riding the orgasmic aftershocks that jerked my cock against her derriere, I laughed. And it felt wondrous. And I knew how she felt after every orgasm that made her laugh.

"I love you," I whispered.

"I love you more," she replied.

Seventeen

So, we're good, me and Monsieur Sexy. Every relationship has its stumbles, right?

The past few weeks had been bliss. I worked days. Jean-Louis worked days. (He had another upcoming business trip, but that wasn't until spring. I had him for another two months all to myself). We shared meals together, at whoever's place we managed to land. We slept together at that same place. Most of the time we had sex. Some nights we snuggled and chatted about our dreams and aspirations. Then we fell asleep listening to each other breathe. Very cool.

And those roses he'd sent me as a makeup ploy? They just dropped dead a few weeks ago. Those puppies lasted over two weeks. Amazing. I scooped up a few dried petals I hadn't noticed from under the coffee table and tossed them in the garbage. Tied up the full garbage bag, slipped my feet into a pair of flats, and headed down to the lobby. Dropping the garbage in the closet designated for the building's waste, I then skipped outside and across the street. Without a coat. It was mid-February, but it was amazingly warm in France. In the fifties. I loved it.

High-fiving Jean-Louis's building concierge, I then raced up the three flights of stairs. I knocked on his door, but then I punched the digital code and entered. He was expecting me. And—

"*En guarde*!"

Pinned against the wall by a blade to my neck, I almost shrieked, but then I giggled.

"You are not supposed to giggle when threatened by a musketeer," he insisted, maintaining a stern demeanor. Stepping back and swinging an arm toward the wall he grabbed another weapon. "Here!"

He tossed me a fencing foil and I tapped the side of his blade with mine, setting him back. I delivered a riposte to his lunge and backed him across the room toward the sofa. After a week of daily lessons I'd picked up a few moves. Generally we used masks and vests, but I sensed he would never hurt me. Though I did worry about him losing an eyeball from my misplaced blade.

"Surrender?" he challenged, blade tip to my heart.

"A musketeer never surrenders," I defied, with a lift of brow.

"I am the musketeer."

"No, I believe you are the evil Cardinal's guard. Take that!"

I dashed away his blade and swung to deliver a deadly slash across his thigh. The blades were not sharp along the length and the tips did have the red plastic button on them. And yet...

Jean-Louis yelped and grasped his thigh, falling to his knees. He was a good faker. But never in bed. Nor was I. A woman who faked orgasms was asking for a lifetime of disappointment.

What was I doing? Right. Defeating the enemy.

I nudged my opponent's shoulder with the toe of my shoe and he collapsed onto the floor, rapier clattering across the hardwood and imaginary blood spilling in a crimson pool beside his leg.

"I win!" I announced, and strolled toward the rack on the wall to replace the fencing foil.

Suddenly from behind, I was grabbed about the neck. My palms slapped the wall. Jean-Louis's erection nuzzled against my ass through the clingy brown leggings I wore.

"You are too cocky," he said. "Definitely musketeer material. But you must never leave the enemy bleeding. Always pierce him through the heart and watch him die."

Yikes. That was macabre. Bloodthirsty, even.

"I still win," I whispered, and jutted out my ass to rub against his cock. "You know why?"

"Why?" Now his hands cupped my breasts.

"Because having been defeated by the finer swordsman, as part of your punishment you have now agreed to be my willing slave. Over there." I nodded toward the ottoman before the window. "Sit down. Wait for me."

Jean-Louis collected his rapier, returned it to the hook on the wall then strolled over to the ottoman and sat, falling backward, arms spread. He wore comfy jersey pants, and from my vantage the sun shone across his lap, highlighting the thickness in his lap beneath the fabric.

I traced my upper lip with my tongue. Instead of going to him, I strolled to the sofa and knelt on it, propping my elbows on the back. I faced him. "I want to watch you care for your sword," I cooed. "Make it nice and hard for me."

He sat up, answering me with a wink.

"And then make it drip for me."

His hand eased over the bulge in his lap. "I can do that."

He tugged down the pants—no boxer briefs beneath—and his penis sprang up, hungrily seeking attention. He slid down the pants and kicked them aside.

"Shirt, too," I directed. I wasn't about to be deprived the scenery of those ripped abs.

The tee shirt flopped onto his pants and he gripped the main stick. A musketeer took great care with his sword. It was as if a third arm to him. Always there and at the ready. Monsieur Eiffel was ever ready.

His penis straightened with a gentle glide of his curled fingers up the shaft. Each up and down direction tugged the foreskin over the crown, and then down to reveal the head that grew deeper in color as his erection engorged with blood.

Eyes closed and head tilted back, he leaned against one palm, while falling into a sort of meditation of sensual experience. We'd watched one another get off for weeks at the beginning of our relationship. And when we'd graduated to cyber sex that, too, had been one-sided sex. Since then, we'd spent so much time mingling limbs and tasting skin and touching legs, breasts, asses, and hair, that it felt new again to watch this singular practice.

My nipples hardened and I rested my breasts upon the back of the leather sofa. Fingers playing over my tee-shirt, I lightly grazed a hardened peak. "Mmm..." I said out loud. "That ottoman sees a lot of action."

He smirked and said, "You have an ottoman fetish."

So I did. Sounded weird. But seriously? Sprawled across a large round piece of soft velvet furniture in the middle of a room, stranded with my attentive lover, was my kind of fetish.

Jean-Louis hissed and squeezed his cock. His hand now rapidly milked his shaft, coaxing it toward lift-off. His gaze met mine. A quirk of brow. His wink devastated. He liked it when I watched him. I—ouch!

I'd bitten my lip and my cry had paused Jean-Louis in his intent motions. "What?"

I tasted blood. All I could do was laugh and shake my head. "Don't stop. You're almost there."

"Come help me." He patted the ottoman. "What is it you always say? Pretty please?"

He didn't need to ask twice. Pulling my shirt off as I approached displayed the sheer black bra beneath. My nipples were dark peaks. I dropped to my knees before him and glided my hands alongside his thighs on the velvet. He spread his legs, inviting me in closer.

"You want a kiss?" I asked, looking up sweetly into his sky-gray eyes. They were a subtle blue. The color of the sky after the rain. "Or just a lick?"

"Both," he said. His cock, the head red and engorged, bobbed before me. Teasing me. Tempting me. "*S'il vous plâit.*"

Pressing my lips to the head of him seared his heat against my mouth. He was hot and smooth, a wicked tool that we could both use to our own means. I gripped his shaft; the veins bulged against my palm. My thumb rested along the thick underside vein, and it squished when I put gentle pressure on it. So full.

Dashing out my tongue I licked the tip of him. He swore softly and lay back, stretching out his arms. His fingers touched each side of the round cushion. Gliding a palm up his belly and across the soft dark hair that curled about his cock, I took my time licking down to the root where I detoured and painted thick strokes over his testicles. The tender jewels hugged up tightly against his body. He was so ready.

I wanted him inside me.

Shuffling out of my leggings, I almost stumbled, but caught myself above him. He smiled that knowing Frenchman's grin. *I have you entranced*, it said. *You are weak around me.*

Oh, yes, I was.

Mounting him, I directed his cock between my folds, slicking the head until it glided effortlessly up and down, over my clit. Right where it counted most. I rubbed the power spot with his heated rod, using it as if it were a vibrator. But the real thing was so much better than steel or silicon and a power button. Pressing hard to him I worked up and down in small, deliriously delicious movements, then with a shift of my hips to redirect him to my slit, I plunged down upon him, taking him in deeply.

He hissed again. The man was on fire and that heat radiated within me. Every part of me tightened. All my muscles, my skin, my jaw, my pussy grew tense.

And with but a few determined thrusts from him, he coaxed away the tension and I released, as simply as that, and came in a shuddering, shouting, laughing victory.

ÅÅÅ

Snuggled on the sofa under a blanket, Hollie and I watched a movie that streamed from the laptop. *La Femme Nikita* was one of our shared favorites. An oldie but a goodie, I loved the heroine's growth from hardened criminal to self-assured yet even harder assassin.

The scene where she leaves her boyfriend was playing now and Hollie nuzzled her head against my chest and looked up to me. "This can work," she said.

"This what?"

"Us. I mean, for a long time. I love you, Jean-Louis. More than I ever thought I could love someone."

I kissed her. Sometimes hearing it felt so good. Like a reassurance I hadn't known I'd needed, but did. "A long time sounds good to me."

Did that mean we were destined for marriage? Possibly. But I didn't bring it up. It wouldn't be fair with my wife still lingering on the sidelines. My lawyer reported she was back in town after an extended stay in Greece. With a lover? Most likely with a number of lovers. I suspected that was one woman who could never mutter 'This will work for a long time'.

"I called my realtor yesterday," I said, touching the remote to turn down the sound on the laptop. "As soon as the divorce goes through I want to start looking for a place in the country."

"That would be some kind of dream. A chateau in the French countryside."

"Then I will get a dog, and maybe a cat."

"I'd visit you if you owned a cat. I'm holding out judgment on the dog."

"Visit me? Hollie, if I find land, I want you to live with me. In a chateau that has vines crawling up and down the outer walls. Like, happily ever after."

She lifted her head to gaze into my eyes. A wrinkle impressed along her temple from lying on my chest. She was cute. So pretty. And possessed of a gorgeous soul. And I felt as if, no matter what we went through, she was the one meant for me.

"Happily ever after sounds perfect," she decided, and laid her head back on my chest. "Tomorrow is Valentine's day."

"I know. I have a surprise for you."

"Goodie. I considered making you dinner, but that wouldn't be a satisfying present. I have my own surprise for you. Should we make it a date?"

"*Oui*. It's a Friday, so I'm taking the afternoon off from work. You can do the same?"

"Deal. I'll come over around four, after I've finished my work."

I hugged her. We fell asleep on the sofa as the movie credits rolled, then I startled awake and carried her into the bedroom and laid her on the bed. I loved the way she moved as if a cat, stretching her body along mine, pressing her breasts against my ribs, and tucking her head between my arm and chest. *Mon abeille.*

Happily ever after?

I honestly believed we could have it.

Eighteen

Today is a day a majority of people abhor. The hearts and kisses day. The 'if you don't get chocolates or flowers you suck' day. Been there. But, you know, it's not like the masses understand we are actually celebrating a Roman saint. And if he was a saint, would he condone all the sex and hookups we engaged in in his name?

I think this was the first Valentine's Day I'd been in a great relationship that actually made me want to do something a little crazy. Like wrap a winter coat over my naked body (artfully decorated with glitter) and head out to surprise my lover.

I did say a *little* crazy. Wasn't like I was striding through a public venue with the intent of flashing my lover. Been there. Don't want to think about that one. Ever again. I was just dashing across the street and keeping this adventure between the two of us.

My Louboutins protested the wet tarmac as I strolled across the street. But seriously, they had been through worse. After the New Years Eve fiasco I'd decided to wear these puppies to shreds. I had to get my thousand euros worth out of them, didn't I?

What little snow Paris had gotten was melting thanks to the nearly fifty-degree temp today. I smiled at the building concierge and entered behind a tall woman who wore an elegant gray wool top and skirt set. After admiring the swing of her blonde hair, my eyes fell to her shoes. Sleek steel heels and a black patent leather pointed toe. Killer.

I wished I could wear gray. Gray was such a classy color. Kudos to her for making it look uber-stylish. Ah, Parisian women. They possessed *je n'est ce quoi* in spades.

And then I did something out of character. Or rather, long overdue.

Having gotten over my elevator fears thanks to my fast fuck with Jean-Louis in the train lavatory, I followed her into the tiny box because—what was that entrancing scent? Mm... Must be a spendy perfume. Chanel No. Seduce Everyone In Your Vicinity. Score another point for the Parisian chick.

"That perfume is lovely," I offered as the door closed. My muscles didn't even clench in terror. She'd get off at the next floor so I could handle a little elbow-to-elbow in the contained space. "What is it?"

"Lanvin, darling."

Her thick accent was not French. It was throaty and coarse. German?

The elevator glided past the second floor. "Oh. You should have pressed the button for the first floor," I provided. "The next floor is residential only."

Her thick-lashed summation of me suddenly made me feel like I wasn't wearing the coat. And this chick was not impressed by the glitter. Did I have some sparkle showing at my neck? I should have taken the stairs. See what happens when I tried to be adventurous?

The doors glided open and out she stepped, striding with purpose toward Jean-Louis's door.

You know that expression: I have a sinking feeling? Yeah, it's really like that. My heart plopped on top of my stomach and I think my lungs even dropped an inch or two as I struggled to breathe calmly. But each inhale drew in her pricey perfume and I was on the verge of passing out from Lanvin overdose.

The woman paused before Jean-Louis's door and actually sneered at me. "Who are you?"

"I'm Hollie. I live across the street," I stupidly provided.

"You are here to see Monsieur l'Etoile?"

"Yes." How I adored his last name. My own French star. "Are you sure you have the right floor?"

"American," she stated with so much disgust I was inclined to believe it myself. "Jean-Louis knows *you*?"

I nodded. And as fast as a lightning strike, my brain computed the situation, and I suddenly knew who she was. My ankle gave out and I actually wobbled before catching myself against the wall with a palm.

"Stupid Americans. You cannot stand in your expensive shoes? Ha!" She reached for the door buzzer, but paused. Black eyeliner emphasized her evil glare. "You should leave."

How I found the courage to stand upright on my overly high and slightly tattered Louboutins, I don't know. But I did. And I pushed before her and tapped the digital code into the lock. "No, maybe you should leave," I said, and called out Jean-Louis's name as I entered the apartment.

The German followed on my heels, though I sensed she paused in the doorway. A glance found her with hands to hips, glossy red lips parted seductively. Really? She was going to try that shit with me standing right here?

Jean-Louis strolled down the hallway from the bedroom in jeans and nothing else. Sunlight flashed on his abs, and emphasized the Adonis arches that lured my eye toward the crotch bulge that always satisfied me. He smiled—and then stretched his gaze over my shoulder.

"Greta?" fell out of his mouth like a piece of bad sushi.

The wife. She had to be. Who else could it be? I knew he didn't have another lover.

Just the wife.

"Who is this American slut, Jean-Louis?" The German bitch crossed the room and stalked right up to the man who looked as if the carpet had been tugged out from under his bare feet. "Are you having an affair on me?"

"On you?" He chuckled. Stroked his jaw with a swipe of his fingers. His abs flexed as he stabbed the air with a finger. "Greta, we are separated. I can fuck whomever I choose. A condition you took to heart but months after you said I do!"

I clutched the back of the leather sofa. This was going to be war. And I wanted a front row seat.

No, I didn't. This was private. It was between Jean-Louis and his gorgeous soon-to-be-ex wife. She looked like a freakin' model. I couldn't figure his taste in women. Stand me next to her and no man would notice I had eyes, let alone a perfectly nice rack.

"I should come back later—"

"No!" Greta said, fisting a punch through the air as she turned to me.

"Yes, you should," Jean-Louis said. He swung around to grab my hand and led me toward the door. "I am sorry about this, Hollie. I didn't know she was coming."

"Does your wife need an invitation to stop by and visit her husband?" the German growled. She thrust up her fists and blurted out an oath that I hoped was German and not some demonic invocation that would send me to Hell.

"I don't want to be in the way," I said.

But.

But for some reason, Jean-Louis tugging me toward the door felt oh-so-wrong. I was the woman who loved him. Who cared for him. Who made him happy. Why should I be the one to leave? "But maybe you should introduce me to your, uh...*her* first?"

"Hollie, really? She will only scream and yell at you. It is what she does."

"I do not!" The wife clicked across the room and put herself right up in our space. "Yes, Jean-Louis, introduce us."

"Greta, you have no right."

"No right to what?" She thrust out her hand toward me. "I am Greta l'Etoile. You are Hollie the American slut?"

My fingers clenched and if I'd been slightly less nice, I would have swung a slap at her model-thin cheek. But I was nice. It's what we Midwesterners were so proud of. Niceness, and, apparently, stupidity.

"You see?" Jean-Louis wrapped a hand about my arm, his intent in pushing me toward the door. "You don't know Hollie, Greta. Be decent."

"Really? I'd guess the last thing she subscribes to is decency. Got anything on under that ugly wool coat, slut?"

Now I did lunge. Jean-Louis caught me by both arms. My fingers were fisted, swinging blindly before me. Why was I defending myself from this low piece of je n'est ce trash? She was intolerable. And plain mean.

I wouldn't sink to her level. I couldn't.

"I'm sorry." Releasing my fists, I flexed my fingers at my sides. I turned and hugged Jean-Louis, knowing it must drive Greta mad to see her husband, whom she hadn't respected enough to stay out of other mens' beds, holding another woman.

Albeit, a woman who wasn't nearly as glamorous and sexy as his wife.

No, I wouldn't go there. I would not compare myself to...that.

"Give me a call when she's gone," I said and then kissed him on the mouth.

He pulled from the kiss as quickly as it happened. I couldn't be sure it was because he hadn't wanted the kiss or he simply wanted to show his wife some respect. Not that she deserved any.

Fuck St. Valentine. This is what I got for wanting some flirtatious fun on a day that celebrated the old man's death? Thanks, Karma. Been awhile. Fine time to show up.

Jean-Louis held the door open. Walking through it was the worst walk of shame. Ever. In all recorded walks of shame. This one was it. Because I was leaving my lover alone with his wife after she had called me a slut more times than was necessary.

The door closed without so much as him calling goodbye to me. Not even an *adieu*. No, I didn't want *adieu*. That was a final sendoff, 'go with God', as in, see you in the next life.

Adieu, Greta.

Greta. Now that I knew her name I would never get it out of my brain. It stuck up there like a cockleburr. Greta. Greta. Aggh!

Shaking, I wandered to the elevator and stood before it. To think, I'd popped my elevator cherry with *the wife*. That was wrong on too many levels.

Behind me I heard shouting on the other side of Jean-Louis's door. The man was giving as good as he was getting. It was a side to him I'd never seen. Anger so vile it raised his voice and had made him brush me off as if crumbs to be swept under the carpet.

He'd sent me away.

My finger hovered before the elevator button. I shook my head, and scrambled off toward the stairs. Two steps down and I stumbled, catching myself on the railing and allowing my body to descend until I sat on the bottom step of the second floor landing.

The shouts were muffled, but they were still going at it.

"I could have loved you!"

I cringed at her shout. Really? *Could have?* Meaning, she probably had not been in love when they'd married? Greta, you are a first-class bitch.

"You don't know how to love one man at a time!"

One point for Jean-Louis.

"And you do?"

What had she expected? They'd been separated for a year. She had been screwing around on him since the third month of their marriage, which had only lasted a year before they'd separated. And she was surprised to learn that Jean-Louis had moved on with someone else?

I recalled the strange feeling I'd gotten when we'd been Skyping one another after our relationship had progressed from window sex. I'd felt as though he were reluctant to meet, to bring it to the next level. And I'd been angry with him, even while I'd known if anyone were going to back out on the relationship it would be me with my one-month-to-detonation dating rules.

That was when he'd confessed he was married. But only after I'd run into the building manager and the old man had let the big secret slip by assuming I was Jean-Louis's wife.

When I had spied Jean-Louis in the window the first time and we had flirted through glass, I had been exactly what he had needed. A woman interested in him, someone who had obviously boosted his tattered ego, yet also someone at a distance. He hadn't been ready for the face-to-face.

For skin.

And I could completely understand now after having stood in Greta's universe for five minutes. She was a storm, and I believed when angered, she could level everything and anything in her path.

I glanced up the stairs. It would be foolish to return to the scene of the crime. And I wouldn't help Jean-Louis at all by popping in my head and giving his wife fuel to rage even more.

Reluctantly, I walked down and out the front door, crossing the street with a shiver as a breeze tickled up and under my coat. So much for the glittery surprise. How had she known I was naked under the coat? Was I flashing?

It must have been a good guess. Bitch. Yeah, I was going to call that one as I saw it.

Poor Jean-Louis.

It was nine in the evening. I wandered into the bedroom, skin still putting off steam from the hot shower. The light by the bed was on, but it was dim. I wondered if they were still having it out across the street?

Some Valentine's Day this had been. If I saw a red rose or a box of chocolates it would only remind me of Greta's greasy red lips. Bleck.

Motion in Jean-Louis's bedroom caught my eye. Across the street, he rushed to the bedside table and grabbed a notebook, scribbling something on the paper. Pressing it to the window, I then read his note, "Can I come over?"

I nodded and gestured that he could. I hadn't locked the door yet, so he could get in on his own. Crawling into bed, I pulled my knees up to my chest, the robe parting, and settled against the pillows.

What would he have to tell me?

It would be ridiculous for him to report anything but that the wicked German bitch had handed him the signed divorce papers. Had my being there thrown her off course? Had she reconsidered after seeing that her husband was happy and had found someone new? I'd never forgive myself if that were the case.

Ah! There I go again. Thinking too much. My thinks always went a thought too far.

Sighing, I leaned against the headboard and listened as the front door clicked open. Jean-Louis shuffled off his shoes then turned the lock in the door. He padded into the room, and I patted the bed beside me. The way the low lamp lighted the room, his broad frame cast shadows on the walls. He sat facing me and I noticed his eyes.

"You've been crying," I said.

He bowed his head. The slightest nod of agreement. When he looked up I pressed my lips together to prevent my own tears from falling. I hated seeing the defeat in his eyes.

"It hurts me," he said quietly, "that I couldn't make it work."

"Did you want to?"

"Of course, from the start. I didn't marry her on a whim."

Right. This man was honorable. Trusting. Truthful. Who didn't get married thinking it would be anything but happily ever after?

"Come here."

Lying down, he nuzzled his head against my stomach, tucking his hands against my thigh. I stroked his hair. Had she ever held him so gently?

"She said she hates me," he said. His exhale shuddered his shoulders against my hip. "I don't know what I did. I only ever loved her."

Now tears pooled at the corners of my eyes. He was a man lost in a world that didn't care. A world that rushed and moved and raced, and when it finished with something, tossed it aside for something new. He had chosen the wrong woman with whom to share his heart. And I could feel the wrenching ache that must have cracked his heart in two.

There was nothing I could say that would seal up that crack. Only time would heal him completely. And I was willing to hold him for as long as it took for that healing.

I wrapped my arms around him and bent to kiss his head. Nuzzling my nose in his soft hair, my tears spilled into the strands.

"It's over," he whispered. "She left the signed papers."

Not another word was spoken. I held him as he softly sobbed. He clutched at me. His tears wet my skin.

Together we would face the future.

Nineteen

A month later...

I never cried when I was a child. Margot would always chastise me and tell me to act like a big boy. Boys did not cry. So crying in Hollie's arms on that night after Greta had left had opened me to her. Splayed me out, vulnerable and small.

And she had held me through the night.

I think about it every so often. Her gentle acceptance, her quiet charm. Her exquisite ability to calm me when I most wanted to push her away and close myself off from the world.

Hollie is the soul I was meant to meet but got sidetracked on the way to that meeting. Perhaps I'd needed Greta's infidelity to redirect my path. Now that Hollie and I were together, I believed nothing could ever part us.

The shower curtain swished aside and there stood my naked *abeille*. I grasped her dry hand and pulled her inside, losing grasp as quickly for my hands were slick with soap. We almost toppled but I caught us by slapping a hand to the tiled wall behind the shower spigot where it was still dry. Her hand coiled about my cock and began to lazily slick up and down.

"The movie starts in an hour," she said.

I'd suggested we take in the latest flick starring Romain Duris, her favorite actor, and she'd jumped at the chance. Didn't matter that there would be no subtitles. I assumed she would get the gist of the plot, if not enjoy mooning over the actor.

"I am jealous," I said as she squeezed my cock tighter, which lured me down to kiss her on the neck. "You are in love with another Frenchman."

"Maybe he's my freebie?"

"Your what?"

"You haven't heard about the freebie?"

"Apparently not. Mm, yes. Just like that." I clasped my hand about hers and directed her motions slower and longer, stretching the foreskin up and down the head of my cock with each thrust.

"A freebie is that one person we are allowed to have sex with, even though we are committed and in love with one another. The key is that the freebie fuck must be a celebrity that you've zero chance in hell of ever meeting, let alone, falling into bed with."

"Ah, I understand. I will give you Duris as your freebie. Though, should he see you in those heels and that sexy black lace dress, I will become worried."

"You think I could turn his head?"

"Most definitely." I kissed her jaw, and groaned against her lower lip as the imminent orgasm crept up my cock in a fiery blaze that prepared for liftoff. "Do I get a freebie?"

"Of course. Who is she?"

I considered the many celebrities that could turn my eye. None of them held a candle to Hollie. Because what we saw on the screen was merely an act, a facade. The actor beneath the character was a regular person who was generally made to look more attractive with makeup and lots of surgery.

But, if she insisted...

"Monica Belluci," I offered.

"Ooo, Vincent Cassel's wife. You know he would be number two on my freebie list."

"You have a whole list?"

She increased the speed of her motions, hand slicking up and down, and I uttered a non-word of restrained pleasure.

"We could play swingers," she suggested. "You and Monica and me and Vincent."

"Deal," I offered. Because Hollie was all I ever wanted and needed and— "Fuck yes."

I came at her direction, spurting onto her belly, which the water washed down her mons and curled into the soap tendrils. I tugged her to me, and we slipped again, but this time I was able to gently lower us down to sit in the tub and I bent to sup between my lover's legs.

⅄⅄⅄

I had handed in the bible to my fantasy author client two weeks ago, and today I received an email congratulating me on a job well done. Also, he offered me a permanent position to organize the bible for all books in the series to come.

I replied with a quick yes and thanks. The extra paycheck would cover my lost income from the map shop. And to celebrate, I'd take the afternoon off. Sort of. While I had no plans to work, I did have plans to run down to the US Embassy and renew my Visa for another three years. It felt right for now. If I renewed for a permanent Visa then I'd have to consider French citizenship, and no matter how in love I was with Jean-Louis, I don't know that I'd ever become an ex-pat. Maybe? I'd have to do more research into it.

I was over Iowa, for sure. I had a couple long-distance girlfriends whom I emailed a few times a year, but no friends I had to rush back to see in the States. Paris was my home now.

But really? If I could take a moment to get all smarmy and feel-good, home wasn't a place on the map. I'd discovered home was standing in Jean-Louis l'Etoile's arms. And falling into his kisses. And lingering against his skin after we'd made love.

How's that for feel-good?

I also remembered I'd promised Jean-Louis I'd pick up something for dessert tonight. The man spoiled me by cooking most nights. But tonight he had online classes until six, and had said dinner would be nothing special. So to decorate the table, dessert was necessary.

The client I'd wined and dined before Christmas had decided to invest. To celebrate, I'd called my realtor and bought champagne. Over the dense flourless fudge cake Hollie had defrosted for dessert I told her my good news.

Clapping gaily she stood and landed on my lap with an effusive kiss and hug. "*Felicitations*," she said. "Well deserved."

"Tomorrow is Sunday. I want to take you for a drive in the country."

"A celebratory drive? Sounds like fun. And it's supposed to be in the seventies the rest of the week. I must dig out my sundress and sandals."

"You like the country life, Hollie?"

She shrugged. "I've never actually lived in the country. I was a suburban kid. But I do have fond memories of my parents dropping me off at the grandparents for my annual two-week stay. It wasn't until my teens that I finally figured out mom and dad never actually did go on the vacation they said they were taking, and instead went home and had lots of sex. I loved working in Grandma's garden. But that said, I am a city girl to the core."

"I can envision you standing barefoot in the grass with a cat in arm and your skirts blowing in the breeze."

"It's a dream, isn't it?"

"Dreams exist to come true some day."

"Hmm, what about you? Got any Green Acres fantasies for yourself?"

"A nice quiet summer home, so I could work in the city and take the summer off to spend in the country. Maybe have a few vines to grow my own wine."

"You know how to do that?"

"I don't know how to grow anything, let alone grape vines, but I am willing to learn." A kiss tasted the chocolate cake on her breath. "Hollie, with my income and the money I have stashed in savings and investments, I wouldn't ever have to work another day and could live quite well."

"Really? I knew you were well off, but that's nicely well off."

"It is. But I don't think I could ever stop working. I love what I do. And like you, I am a city boy. But to have the freedom to walk outside and stroll through the vineyard and throw a stick for the dog?" I sighed.

"You will get that dog someday."

"I hope so. I will do the dishes tonight because you brought the dessert, *d'accord*?"

"Really? Because you made the risotto. And it was fabulous."

I gave her that Frenchman's dismissive shrug of shoulder. Very well, so maybe we Frenchmen did possess a common gesture that defined our heritage. Ha! "I like to cook for you. It relaxes me after a long day before the computer."

"You know what relaxes me?"

I waggled a brow and glanced over to the velvet ottoman.

"Let's do the dishes together," she suggested. "Then we can get to the sex faster."

AAA

The drive south of Paris was less than an hour once we'd crossed the ring road. After we'd passed through a small village replete with a clock tower and home bakery, the last fifteen minutes of the drive were spent on a treacherous gravel road that wound through tall grasses and lavender fields.

"Those are grape vines." Jean-Louis pointed out the bare-branched black silhouettes of craggy tree-like soldiers lined in militant rows every so often. "They are just getting their leaves. I'm not sure when the grapes come to the vine, but I know harvest is late, in October or even November."

"Isn't that called winter wine when the harvest is so late?"

"I think so. You know about wine?"

"No more than what I've read on the labels, but I'm willing to learn."

He clasped my hand. "I'd like to learn with you. Could you be a vintner's wife?"

"Really? When did the wife thing come into play?"

Jean-Louis drove the car up a long drive and parked before a chateau that was fronted by gorgeous willow trees that hung over a stone courtyard. An old iron table and two chairs sat near a fieldstone wall that looked out over a field that boasted more of the blackened grape vines.

"It comes into play right now," he said.

My lover turned off the ignition, got out of the car, and swung around the hood to my side, where he opened the door and squatted before me. He tucked his hand in a pocket and when he pulled out a ring I let out a peep.

Really. It had been a freakin' peep. Like I'd opened my mouth but words didn't form and only a high-pitched sound popped out.

"Hollie, I love you."

Tears welled in my eyes as he spoke. The French accent, something I'd always wanted in a man, sang like music in my heart. And his eyes, so genuine and true, held mine captive.

"I adore you, and admire you," he continued. "I would be honored if you would be my wife."

I opened my mouth, but he put up a palm to stay my reply.

"I want you to know I've been thinking about this for weeks. I know this is fast after the divorce. I don't want you to think you are the rebound wife. I had to look that term up, and I hate it. You are not that person to me, Hollie. You make me happy, you make me feel safe, you make me feel more love than I have ever known. You make me so happy to live in this moment, and to have the opportunity to share it with you. So don't let some silly ring sway your answer. You can think about it for awhile."

I grabbed him by the face and kissed him hard, leaning out of the car and against his body until we fell backward onto the grass bordering the drive. He started to laugh but I wasn't having it. I deepened the kiss and sought the core of him. That place within him where I fit perfectly. Because I was there. He'd welcomed me in. And I never wanted to leave.

"Yes," I said. "Yes, yes, and yes."

"You don't want to think about it?"

I shook my head. "You are the man for me. I love you. I want to make wine with you, and chase the dog with you. And I want to pick vegetables from the garden and make meals with you. I want to have your baby!" I said with a determination that surprised and excited me. "Can we do that? Can we have a baby?"

"*Oui*, I would like that. Right now?"

"Uh." I looked about. The realtor had given Jean-Louis the lockbox combination and told us to take our time this afternoon. We were alone. Baby-making was in the cards. "Maybe?"

"You are getting ahead of me." He sat up and I tumbled onto his lap, leaning against his shoulder as he pulled up my hand and slid the ring onto my finger. It fit like a dream. "Let me digest your yes first, *oui*?"

"Deal."

I studied the ring. It wasn't a diamond, but rather an opal that caught the sunlight and dazzled brilliant azure and emerald embedded within a milky background. Surrounding the oval center stone was a crown of amethyst. I'd never seen anything like it. It looked as if it had been made for a princess.

"I was browsing the diamonds," Jean-Louis offered, "when that one caught my eye. The salesman said 'oh, *non, Monsieur*, that is not an engagement ring'. But it reminded me of your heart. Bright and colorful and with so much depth."

"It's beautiful. I love it."

And I kissed him again, tumbling us onto the grass, which smelled sweeter than I'd ever thought grass could smell.

In fact, the air out here was delicious and intoxicating and I wanted to inhale big gulps, but I wondered if I'd grow dizzy with the heady delight. Maybe it was the proposal. Maybe it was the ring.

For sure it was the sexy Frenchman.

The cottage was more of a chateau, a two-story brick and limestone building that had been built early in the nineteenth century, and had been impeccably cared for by one family through the generations.

My realtor reported the family had moved further south, toward Nice, and wanted to unload this property, all fifty acres of land, along with vines, a wine cellar, and gardening shed. And the price was right. Not outrageously high, nor so cheap I had to wonder what was wrong that I couldn't see.

While Hollie inspected the cupboards and turned on the faucet to taste the water, I wandered up the curving stone staircase that landed at the door to a large bathroom. A free-standing copper bathtub would get good use by Hollie, I felt sure.

She'd said yes! I had hoped she would. Had certainly thought she would. But then, who knew? A yes meant staying here in France with me. That's a big step to take for an American. She probably hadn't given that much thought yet. I should go reword the question and include the part where marrying me meant living in France permanently.

No. I mustn't risk her changing her mind. She could. I'd have to accept that— Aggh! I had become an over thinker such as Hollie. This was not good for my soul.

I'm not sure what I would have done had her answer been a no. After the rejection of divorce, my heart was a fragile thing. Was I jumping into another marriage too quickly? Perhaps that was the reason for my sudden leap into overthinking?

I did have a tendency to fall in love fast. It was the nature of my heart. I was always in it to win it. And this time around, I had confidence the woman was not going to be so cruel with my heart. When Hollie said she loved me, I believed her. And every time I heard her say as much, I could almost feel my broken heart close up and heal, grow stronger.

Kind of wishy-washy sounding for a guy? It was my truth.

Hollie skipped up the stairs and brushed past me, jumping into the bathtub. "This is so cool! Do you think it's real copper?"

"I believe so. This bathroom is big enough to dance in."

"Or put an ottoman right there." She pointed to the corner of the room that would, indeed, look great with the big gray ottoman in it. "Let's put it there and then make a baby on it."

She looked up at me, her knees pulled to her chest and arms wrapped about her legs. Girlish glee sparkled in her eyes. Brighter than the opal ring. And I could envision her dreams of the two of us making love on the ottoman, here, in our home.

"I think that can be arranged," I said, and winked.

She gave me a thumbs up, and then reclined in the tub.

I strolled out to check the next rooms. A large master bedroom at the end of the hallway was walled with a huge bay window. It looked out over the vineyard and the little green gardening shed.

"There's an old man walking up the driveway." I passed the bathroom where Hollie lay daydreaming in the tub. "I'm going to run out and say *bonjour*."

He wasn't that old. Perhaps in his sixties? He introduced himself as Hugues Planchett and told me he had tended the vines for the family for two decades. If I was interested in buying the property he hoped to continue, at no charge, of course. He requested but a few bottles of wine for his labors.

I liked the guy instantly, and wished I had a bottle of wine to break open to celebrate with him. I explained that my brand-new fiancé was inside going through closets and cupboards, but that I had my fingers crossed she would want to stay.

Hugues shook my hand and tipped his hat and headed down the gravel road. And I turned at the sound of someone rapping on a window.

She stood in the bedroom window above, waving down at me. Her eyes followed Hugues' retreat for a few seconds and then—she lifted her skirts and flashed me her pussy.

"Oh yes?"

Hugues was well out of view so...

I unzipped and out sprang my cock, already hard and ready for action. I stroked it for the woman in the window, and a comforting bliss fell over me. This was how we had begun. Separated by glass and without a word we had communicated our desires with one another.

Hollie pulled off her sundress and turned to wiggle her derriere at me. Mm... I pumped my cock harder, imagining my tongue gliding down her ass and between her legs to sink deep inside her wet heat.

Just thinking about my tongue slicking over her clit loosened the tension in my muscles and then, as quickly, tightened everything, including tugging my balls up against my scrotum.

Hollie's palm pressed to the window and both breasts formed pale circles against the glass.

And I laughed as I came.

Yes, this was my future. Our future. Here we would live happily ever after.

The End

Wait a second.

Don't close this book yet.

Michele Renae, here. I can't end this story. I love Jean-Louis and Hollie too much. I had such a great time writing their story. And do you know, I had only ever planned it to be the first part, WINDOW? But mid-way through that short story I realized I wanted to write more about the couple. To learn them. And I learned a lot about them in the course of putting letters on the page, forming words about their liaisons, following their whims across the computer screen.

I hate turning the last page of a book. It's done. Over!

Because the inevitable question is: What happened to them later? A year or two after their happily ever after? Are they still together? Did they fight and break up? Did that monster ottoman actually fit into the bathroom? What about that baby? And the dog?

I want to know more!

So if you'll indulge this writer, allow me to add one more chapter. A look beyond. Something to reassure me that the path I set for these two is the right one and that they are doing fine.

The Next Chapter

Two years later...

The hot August sun beat on my scalp and I itched between the hair strands I'd pulled up in a loose bun. My hair had grown long over the years, and I loved to tug it into a sexy ponytail, or, as with a hot sunny day, coil it up, stab a wooden hair pick into it, and not have to worry about fashion.

I slapped at a mosquito. They were rare here in the vineyard paralleling the chateau. Yep, I just used both those words—vineyard and chateau—in a sentence as if they were my own. And they are!

Jean-Louis and I have lived in the chateau since about a month after first looking at it two years ago. I have been in heaven since. The air is clean and fresh out here. The vast night sky sparkles with stars. We make love in the big bedroom on the king-size bed set in an old iron frame with the stars watching over us.

And we also make love on the ottoman. Which looks awesome in the bathroom! Seriously, there is something about an ottoman. I don't know what it is, but I have another one on order from a furniture shop in a nearby village. I plan to put it in the porch room that connects to the kitchen and which looks out over the front courtyard. A delicious nook for reading and lazing in the afternoon sun.

And that thing about us spending the summers out in the country and the rest of the time in Paris? Total bupkiss. We love this place so much we spend eighty percent of our time here. Jean-Louis did keep his loft in Paris because we couldn't conceive of not having a place to stay in the city. And he travels for work about a month out of the year. But you know what? I guess you *can* take the girl out of the city.

And I've learned to love dogs after the tiny Tibetan mastiff Jean-Louis brought home a year ago turned into a waist-high, two hundred pound bear that still acts like a puppy.

Josephine tolerates the beast. Poor kitty. Oh, he's tough enough to give the dog a swat. And that was not a pronoun mistake. Josephine is a boy. I made a mistake in checking his plumbing when naming him/her. Ah well. Jean-Louis calls him Joe. That helped improve *le chat's* image problems.

I eased a hand across my back and waddled down a dirt row between grape vines. Hugues, the neighbor down the road, was our gardener and he tended the vines, but was in the process of teaching me what he knows. Jean-Louis would love to learn about the vines, but he's been uber-busy this past year, on the phone when he is not online. He's in the process of transferring most of the teaching work to a new set of employees and he intends to remain the acting CEO of VSquire. That will free him up from teaching and traveling, and require he merely work online from home.

"Smell," Hugues said from the other side of a narrow vine. A sun-weathered hand thrust through the green foliage to present a cluster of new grapes coated with gray fuzz.

Er... I knew looking at that nasty gray stuff the grapes had something wrong with them. But ever curious, I leaned in and inhaled the musty scent.

"*Pas bon*," I said.

Of course, everything I said to the man was in French. Yep, I've picked up the language. Had to. Jean-Louis, when he was busy, tended to speak French and forget I am American. I loved that about him. I think he possesses a sort of osmosis vibe that sends the language directly to my brain. That's my story and I'm sticking to it.

"*C'est de la pourriture noble*," Hugues explained. "It is noble rot. I will have to spray this batch or it will spread."

"Sounds not good."

"It is workable, Madame Ollie." The French weren't big on pronouncing the H at the beginning of names and words so when Hugues said it, my name always sounded like Ollie. "We should take a break. I brought lemonade in the cooler."

"Oh, that sounds delicious—"

The sudden male shout from up by the stone courtyard startled me. I don't know why it should. Jean-Louis had been on the phone for an hour, and it wasn't a pleasant call, from what I'd gauged by the frequent swear words and insistent pounding of his fist against the wooden table that rattled the tin oil lamp.

A gruff dog bark sounded from down the aisle and Acteon hurtled toward me in his usual *I'm coming to the rescue* style. He fancied himself one of those Saint Bernards with the rescue cask about his neck, yet when he arrived at the rescuee, the beast forgot to land softly, and generally pushed the victim over and landed on them with vigorously happy puppy licks.

I dodged through the vines and Hugues grabbed my arm, aiding my escape. He knew what would happen if I didn't clear the runway.

"Go to Papa!" I encouraged the dog. "Go give him a big hug!"

Acteon maintained his course down the aisle and bounded up toward the courtyard where I couldn't see Jean-Louis, but I did hear the collision. A male ouff! and a doggy bark of happiness. Jean-Louis laughed, and I relaxed as I patted Hugues on the arm.

"Always does the trick," Hugues offered.

"That dog is the perfect foil when Jean-Louis is wound too tightly. Oh." I gripped my stomach. Something...was moving.

The phone had flung out of my grip when Acteon collided with my body. I hadn't seen him coming, so he'd taken me down from behind. Knowing it was easier to surrender to the puppy love and just go down than to fight it by trying to fend off the beast, I did that. Falling to my knees, and then rolling to my side and back, I accepted the weighty mass of fur and slobber.

The business on the phone could wait. We'd been throwing back and forth the same stupid ideas we'd been muddling over for weeks. I needed to step away from the situation. View it from a more relaxed perspective. Perhaps, as my colleague suggested, step outside of the box.

I could do that.

Reaching into my pants pocket I grabbed the puppy treat I always carried with me (Hollie kept a jar by the door so I need never leave the house without one) and held it high.

Acteon scrambled off me and sat alert, his dark doggy eyes fixed on the prize.

"You want this?"

Acteon barked eagerly.

I tossed it down the hill into the lush grass that Hollie insisted I not mow too short because she liked to pad barefoot through the softness. Acteon bounded off and I—heard a female scream.

Dashing to the stone balustrade that overlooked the gardens below, I searched the rows of verdant vines and spied a flash of pink skirts.

Hugues called out before I could spy the old man's salt and pepper hair, "Ollie is broken!"

"Broken?" Frozen there, my heartbeats thundering, my system tried to determine if this was a fight or flight situation. Had she fallen? Broken what? Where was she? My brain suddenly switched from business to life. "Broken. Hollie?"

I ran toward the edge of the courtyard where my wife wobbled up with the help of Hugues gripping her at the elbow. The front of her long pink skirt was wet and she gave me a wobbly smile. "It's time."

"Time for..." And even as my heart burst and I didn't think my smile could get any larger, the reactive part of me switched over to all systems go. "Time for the baby! *Oui*! What to do? Ah!"

I hugged Hollie quickly but carefully and then led her to the center of the fieldstone courtyard before the house. "Stay right there. Breathe!"

She quirked a smile at me.

I dashed into the chateau and grabbed the suitcase that had been sitting by the door for a month. Hollie had packed it with nightclothes, makeup, and baby clothes for her stay in the hospital. Grabbing the car keys from the hook by the wall, I swung outside and flung open the car door. Tossing in the suitcase, and sliding behind the wheel, I fired up the engine.

That idiot cat was sitting on the hood. "*Allez vous en*, Joe!"

I shooed at it vigorously. The cat gave me the standard superior smug cat face. I beat on the windshield and hissed at the insolent. It dove off the hood. And I shifted into drive. Rolling down the gravel drive, I adjusted the radio, and checked my hip to ensure my mobile was with me.

Checking the rearview mirror, I—

"*Merde*!"

Slamming on the brakes, I shifted into reverse and returned to park before the chateau. I flew out of the vehicle and over to my waiting wife.

"Really?" she said, as I led her to the car.

"It was your responsibility to get in the car. We practiced this."

"Uh-huh. I would laugh to see the nurses at the hospital if you had showed up without me."

I helped my wife bend to get into the passenger side, but she paused. Her fingers clutching the door window turned white.

"Hollie? Is it painful? Will you make it to hospital?"

She nodded vigorously. "They meant it when they said this was going to hurt. Yeah, I think I'm good to go now. Just...take the bumps carefully, will you?"

Closing the door behind her, I dashed around and this time before I put the car into drive I turned to check that my passenger was with me. There she sat, abundant, her cheeks rosy and eyes bright.

"I love you," I said to my pretty wife who sported a grape leaf tucked in the strands of her brown hair. "You're going to have my baby."

"I am," she said. Her sun-toasted skin beamed. This country life was good to both of us. "My water broke, and I'm sitting on your new Audi seat."

"I'll buy a new seat."

"I don't think you can do that."

"I'll buy a new car."

"I love you. And remember, anything I say during labor should not be used against me at a later date."

"I'll remember." I leaned over to kiss her. She tasted sweet like grapes and summer. "Half hour drive to the hospital. Buckle up, *mon abeille*. We're going to become a family."

ÅÅÅ

When we arrived at the hospital Hollie was moaning and in intense pain. A nurse arrived carside to help her into a wheelchair. Hollie gripped my hand and managed a weak smile. Sweat coated her brow. She'd stopped joking with me ten minutes into the drive.

I could not bear to see her in pain. And the drive to find a parking space had been the longest five minutes of my life. The sun had set, and there were no parking lot lights. I fumbled with my keys when I got out of the car, then dashed toward the hospital. Stopped. Turned, and raced back to the car to grab Hollie's bag.

Whew! This having a baby thing was hard work.

Now, two hours later, Hollie had been given permission to push the baby out. She clutched my hand like a prizefighter and put all her effort into the task. Labor. Yes, that was the perfectly excruciating word for it.

I felt helpless standing there beside her, offering mere words of encouragement. If I could take the pain and do the work for her I would have. Humbled by her strength, I pressed my forehead against hers. I inhaled the sweet scent of sweat and vanilla and could feel the effort her body expended with her work.

"The head is out!" the doctor announced.

"Go look," Hollie gasped.

Not wanting to let go of her hand, but being of a curious nature, I moved down and behind the doctor where the nurses had said I was allowed to stand. There it was! A tiny head.

Actually, that was a large head to be coming out of my wife's vagina. How the hell did a woman's body—? I shouldn't think about it too much. That was Hollie's forte, thinking too much.

With another grunt and focused effort from my wife, suddenly the baby's entire body slipped into this world. The doctor held the child firmly and then...

And then the strange thing happened.

"Fluid in the lungs," the doctor reported to the nurse standing beside her. "Prepare the incubator."

"What is it?" I asked, wanting to reach in and hold my child. "Is there something wrong?"

"Monsieur l'Etoile, you have a daughter," the doctor said, still holding the baby away from me. Was the child oddly colored? Did her skin look violet?

"*Mon fille*? I have a daughter?"

"*Felicitations*."

An alarm buzzer suddenly sounded. Everyone in the room moved swiftly and without regard for me. Two nurses dove for Hollie, and I realized she was lying still. Her eyes were not open.

"What is wrong?"

The doctor moved around me, carrying my daughter. The cord had been cut. I hadn't been allowed to cut the cord. What was happening? My heart thudded. I couldn't find words. Why was my baby so oddly colored?

"Something is wrong?" My feet stumbled backward. The wall caught my shoulders and spine.

"Everything will be fine, Monsieur l'Etoile. The baby has swallowed fluids into her lungs." The doctor placed the tiny being inside a brightly lit plastic-enclosed bed, and a nurse began to massage her tiny body. "Just need to give her a brisk massage. You should sit down, Monsieur."

I wasn't processing well. Massaging my baby? That sounded acceptable. But why hadn't they put her in my arms? And Hollie. Why wasn't my wife awake and alert? What had happened to her?

I stepped toward the bed, but a nurse caught me in a surprisingly firm grasp. "You need to stand aside right now. She's going to be fine. Let us take care of her. She's had blood loss."

"Blood loss," slipped from my mouth. My heart dropped. My knees wobbled.

I gripped for something solid. It was the nurse's arm. "I must hold her," I said. "She needs me."

"Then sit here in this chair. You can hold her hand while we work."

"Yes." Blindly, I was directly toward the chair. I don't remember sitting.

But I'll never forget clutching my wife's hand as if to pull her up from the depths.

ÅÅÅ

The scent of peppermint brought me to life. Well, not as if I was dead. I'd been resting because...whew! I'd just given birth. To a baby.

Who was...well, I hadn't met him or her yet. I didn't know if it was a boy or girl. How much time had passed? Why had I passed out?

Is this thing on? What does a girl have to do to get a little applause after pushing a baby out from between her legs?

Shifting on the hospital bed, I felt the comforting warmth of a hand in mine, and so I squeezed. Jean-Louis, whose head had been lying on the bed beside my shoulder, looked up at me and smiled. How much did I adore those sky-gray eyes?

"You are awake. How do you feel?"

I shrugged, then did an inner assessment on my body. I felt lighter, and achy, and...relieved. "I feel like I pushed a watermelon through my vagina. What happened? Why was I sleeping?"

"You passed out. There was some blood loss, but not so much it worried the doctor. She said to let you rest, and I was inclined to do so. You worked hard, *maman*. We have a daughter."

"Really? A girl?"

He nodded, and leaned in to kiss me. I couldn't worry about morning breath because his kiss was the perfect reward for my hard work. My husband's mouth against mine. And he felt warm and so right. He anchored me to this realm.

We'd made a baby. (I suspect, on the ottoman.) A little baby girl.

"Where is she?"

"The nurse took her out to weigh and do all the measurements. She was...purple when she was born."

"What?" What kind of crazy had invaded my husband while I had been out? "How long have I been snoozing?"

"About an hour. The doctor said our daughter swallowed fluid into her lungs, so I watched the nurses massage her for a while. About five minutes and the color slowly blossomed on her skin. She is fine, Hollie. Ah, here she is."

The door opened and in walked a nurse carrying a baby swaddled in a pastel yellow blanket. Jean-Louis stood and kissed the infant's head, then looked to me with the proudest new father smile. "I got to hold her earlier, but not for long. I ran down to the gift shop for some gum while I was waiting. And I bought her something."

I shifted on the bed to sit up against the pillows and didn't mind whatever it was that roiled inside my gut. Hell, my body had been through the wringer. There was bound to be shrapnel, of which, I'd ask the nurses questions later.

Right now, I wanted to hold that precious bundle. Jean-Louis took our daughter from the nurse. He bounced lightly, as if by rote. He cooed at our baby. A teardrop splat onto my nose, followed by so many others.

"What is wrong, Hollie?"

"Nothing," I said, though the tears streamed quickly. "I'm so happy. You're a daddy. And you look so good at it."

"Eh." The Frenchman's concession to agreement without agreeing too much. God, I loved him. "Here is our daughter, *mon abeille*."

He sat on the bedside and handed me the baby. And I laughed at sight of the bright yellow and black striped hat on her head. It had two black antennas bobbling up from the top. "A little bee!" He must have bought the hat in the gift shop.

Did I mention how much I loved the man?

Beneath the hat a perfect round face with closed eyes and a teeny nose and pursed lips slept. She was perfect. Had I made this? Jean-Louis had helped, too. Wow. We'd made a baby.

My husband kissed the baby's nose and she wrinkled in response, her entire body wiggling and then settling. She knew he was her daddy. Oh, but I couldn't wait to watch him spoil her and love her and stand protectively beside her as she learned to ride a bike, soar high on the swing, and even go on her first date.

"What's her name?" I whispered, feeling exhaustion waver through my body.

"I'm not sure. She is a bee, that is for sure."

"Bea," I said. "Short for Beatrice. Didn't you say that was your mother's name?"

"My grand-mere's name. It's pretty. You are *mon abeille*, and she is *mon petit* Bea. I like it. Do you?"

I nodded and hugged our daughter against my breast. "I love you. Both of you."

"We are a family. Thank you, Hollie. For loving me."

"Take us home," I said on a sigh, and then drifted into sleep.

The End (for real)

Yep, that's it. That's the end, or probably a new beginning for Jean-Louis and Holly. And Bea! I hope you enjoyed reading about them. And I thank you for reading Paris Secrets.

Please visit my website: MicheleRenae.com

For some pictures that inspired this series, check out my Pinterest page at: pinterest.com/MicheleRenaeX

Follow me on Twitter at: @MicheleRenaeX

Did you know that Michele Renae is a pseudonym used by Michele Hauf to write erotic romance? If you're interested in darkly sexy paranormal romance, check out Michele Hauf's world of Beautiful Creatures at:

MicheleHauf.com
@MicheleHauf
facebook.com/Michele-Hauf-Author
pinterest.com/toastfaery

Made in the USA
Columbia, SC
02 April 2021

35329843R00241